THIS IS A KISSING BOOK

A STAND ALONE GRUMPY SUNSHINE, HOCKEY, WORKPLACE, ADVENTURE ROMANTIC COMEDY

ELLIE HALL

Paperback ISBN: 979-8-9955916-0-3

ABOUT THIS BOOK

I hate my boss. Never mind that he has major Clark Kent energy.

We're not going to have a wild fling where we throw caution to the wind in a storage closet, then fall fast and hard on a sultry night while at a fancy resort during a business trip. I abide by all HR rules in the workplace, mostly.

I despise Linc and he abhors me. That's the way it is and how it will always be.

End of story.

Except we have to interact every day because I'm now his personal research assistant as he tries to woo some obscure investor for the company. Probably lost a bet or something and got stuck with me. I don't know much other than I've been reviewing scanned files, searching for handwritten letters.

It's confusing.

So are the fluttery feelings when we stay late together after having a breakthrough. When I catch his gaze lingering on my legs—last I checked, they're nothing special

—he's probably calculating the quickest way to push me out a window.

I'm the cheer to his blah. The cream to his black coffee. The tick to his tock. That's to say there's a sudden urgency as he drags me on a side quest, *National Treasure* style, and we're crawling through ruins like Indiana Jones and Marion Ravenwood.

See? The guy hates me.

But then we almost die and before I realize it, his lips are on mine. And I like it. Apparently, he does too because it happens on repeat. The kiss, that is.

When I find out what he's really looking for, I realize that I may have had him all wrong and start to wonder just how thin the line is between love and hate.

This enemies-to-lovers, workplace, mistaken identity, hockey-lite, adventure romcom by USA Today bestselling author Ellie Hall will give you all the feels, laughs, and heart eye emojis wrapped up in a sweet, closed-door, open-hearts kissing book.

Tropes include:

- Grumpy sunshine
- Hate to love
- Workplace
- Mistaken/hidden identity
- Hockey-lite
- Adventure romcom
- Forced proximity

READER NOTE

Dear Reader,

I want to tell you how this book came to be, because it starts with a penny. My grandmother used to say, "Find a penny, pick it up, and all the day you'll have good luck."

Every time I see a penny on the ground, I think of her. Every time I pick up a penny, I think of Abraham Lincoln, which brings me to ... my daughter being right.

One day, she came home from school and announced, "Mom, did you know that everyone thinks about Abraham Lincoln at least once a day?"

I don't know where she heard it. I'm not sure it's true. But I couldn't stop thinking about it.

Because it's pretty much true for ME.

Those pennies, I tell ya.

The Gettysburg Address alone is proof that the sixteenth president of the United States had a way with words. His was the kind of writing that makes a person put down whatever they're doing and feel the heft of history. (When I read it, my eyes mist over with tears. Every. Single. Time.) So naturally, moved by emotion, my romance-obsessed brain asked an important question. What did Abraham Lincoln write when he wasn't saving the Union?

What if Abraham Lincoln, one of the most eloquent men in American history, wrote love letters to Mary Todd? Private ones. The kind not meant for history books or museum displays. Just a husband, writing to his wife, from the heart.

That idea would not leave me alone. Once Jules and Linc showed up and started arguing in my head, I had to tell their story. (They were very loud about it, for the record.)

However, I want to be upfront about a few things. I love history, but I'm a novelist, not a historian. Any discrepancies, liberties, and creative leaps in these pages are entirely mine and entirely inspirational. This is fiction, and I had a wonderful time playing in that sandbox. Please enjoy this book in that spirit.

You'll also notice a little hockey in here because if you've read any of my other recent books, I'm not usually in a sandbox so much as an ice rink.

One more thing, if you're a longtime reader of mine, you know I usually write in series, so I'm stretching into the land of standalones here. But don't worry, you'll find a few familiar Easter eggs tucked throughout these pages as a little love note to those of you who've read my other stories—and if you haven't yet, there is a great big sweet and swoony world to explore.

Okay, actually, this is the last thing. I hope you enjoy the kissing. There's a lot of it.

With love (and a lucky penny),

Ellie

1

JULES

MY LIFE IS CURRENTLY on a tangent. This isn't where I expected to be. Yet here I am.

Seated at my desk, I pop a Lindt chocolate truffle (the one with the crinkly wrapper) into my mouth just as the phone rings—because of course it does. The chocolate shell cracks between my teeth as I fumble for the receiver and I answer with my mouth still half-full.

"Cowections Pwocessin—" I swallow, nearly choking. "Meridian Holdings Collections Processing Department, this is Juliana. How may I help you?"

The line is quiet and then a deep, rough-around-the-edges voice says, "Is this Frank Andresen's office?" It's the kind of baritone that shouldn't be street legal on a Friday afternoon when I'm already dreaming about the weekend.

I clear my throat, still tasting hazelnut. "Not even close. But you sound desperate, so I'll help you, anyway."

"Desperate?" Amusement warms his tone like a beach bonfire. "That obvious?"

"You have that 'I've been transferred three times and might commit violence' quality to your voice."

He laughs, and the sound is warm caramel dripping down my spine—completely inappropriate for a professional phone call.

He says, "Three times, actually. But who's counting?"

I twirl the phone cord around my finger, then catch myself. What am I, thirteen, on my first phone call with a boy? For all I know, this guy could be my boss's age, married, or a troll. "Well, you've reached Collections Processing on the thirty-third floor. Frank Andresen's office is seven floors up and literally above my pay grade."

"Sounds about right," he mutters.

I can't tell if he's annoyed or amused. Maybe both. "What do you need? Maybe I can point you in the right direction before you hit transfer number four."

Another pause, longer this time. Maybe he hung up? I pout and am about to do the same, but pop another chocolate into my mouth. This week has been long.

He huffs a heavy breath. "I'm trying to reach him about a personal matter."

"Ah. The 'it's personal' call. Always a pleasure."

"You sound like you're familiar with those," he says, picking up on my sarcasm.

"You have no idea. My boss is—" I stop myself. "Never mind. Not your problem."

"No, go ahead. Now, I'm curious."

I shouldn't. I *really* shouldn't. But the way he's talking to me like I'm a person instead of a robot on a phone line makes me throw caution to the wind.

"My boss has been particularly," I search for a word that won't get me fired if this call is recorded for quality assurance, "efficient lately."

"Efficient?" He sounds like he's smiling. "That's diplomatic."

"I'm a very diplomatic person."

"Somehow I doubt that."

I help myself to another chocolate when his comment boomerangs. "Excuse me?"

"What are you eating? I heard the wrapper. Sounds like something crunchy."

My cheeks flush hot like I've been caught. "I got in early today and have been staring at a screen for hours. I'm all out of coffee, so I switched to chocolate."

"What kind?"

"Does it matter?"

"Absolutely. Chocolate preference says a lot about a person." His voice turns even more intimate.

I'm acutely aware that I'm alone in the office. Wendy and Carmen are already at our staggered lunch breaks. Feeling like I could blow away on the wind, I unwrap another one, deliberately letting the foil crinkle near the phone. "Oh, really. Do you have a degree in candy psychology?"

His laugh is rich and genuine. "Maybe I do. Let me guess, you're eating one of those round Lindt chocolate truffles."

I nearly drop the phone. "How did you—?"

"The wrapper has a very specific sound. Also, they're pretty good."

"Pretty good?" I'm grinning now. "How about outstandingly delicious?"

"Nah. I stand by my claim."

"What about Reese's Peanut Butter Cups?"

"Basic."

"But delicious. Snickers?"

"Too much going on. It's like they can't decide who they want to be. Plus, the peanuts crowd out the other flavors."

I giggle. "You have very strong opinions about candy."

"I have very strong opinions about most things. But I'm willing to hear your defense of the Lindt chocolate truffle." His voice drops into yet a lower register.

My stomach flips. Then, remembering where I am, I sit up straighter, ready to debate. "First of all—"

We talk about chocolate, and I insist the Lindt hazelnut truffles are the best flavor (he playfully disagrees). Next thing I know, I'm telling him about the time my brothers started an underground candy market at school, trading lunch money for their trick-or-treat stash.

"Did you aid and abet?" He sounds impressed.

At a whisper, I confess something that not even my mother knows, "I stole from them."

"That's either genius or the start of a criminal career."

"Both?"

We laugh and I'm twirling a piece of my hair now.

"I like the way you think." The words wrap around me like sunshine.

I tingle inside and the space between our words crackles, is charged. Like the air before a summer storm.

I glance at the clock. I've been talking to a stranger for fifteen minutes and completely forgot about the provenance reports waiting on my desk, my outfit for tonight's outing, and everything except the voice on the other end of this line.

"This has been charming," I say to break the spell. "You never told me your name."

The line clicks. Someone cuts in—sharp, impatient, and unmistakably my boss. "This is Frank Andresen."

My stomach drops. Frank Andresen. The CEO. My boss. The man whose name alone makes grown professionals straighten their ties and check their reports twice.

I start to apologize, to explain, but the phone transfer must've belatedly gone through. The line clicks again before I can speak. It goes silent.

Still holding the phone, my heart hammers against my ribs. The office feels too quiet, too empty. Did Frank Andresen just hear me laughing about Halloween candy? Did he hear me call his—relative, colleague, friend—charming? Can you hear my internal panic on the top floor of the building?

More importantly, who was I talking to?

I hate my boss is not a thought I should be having, but he interrupted the closest I've had to a flirty moment in forever.

Why is this my life?

My job in the Collections Processing Department of Meridian Holdings isn't the worst. However, I didn't expect to be working in an entry-level position as a cataloging assistant, doing the drudge work of digitizing documents, basic data entry, organizing files, pulling materials for senior researchers, and performing preliminary research inquiries.

Then again, logistically, legally, technically, I'm not supposed to be here.

Don't get me wrong, seeing facsimiles of old texts and pieces of art the public hasn't laid eyes on in hundreds of years feels like Christmas morning for a history nerd like me, but it's not quite where I saw myself as an enterprising college student. Then again, I never quite made it to graduation day. For all intents and purposes, Meridian Holdings believes I graduated from the prestigious Sierra Institute with a major in art history and a minor in museum studies.

While the office girlies, Wendy and Carmen, enjoy BLTs from the Tasty Trolley, complete with complimentary butterscotch pudding cups on Fridays, I pull out my tomato and mayo sandwich from my soft-sided lunch box. If only I could afford the B in a BLT.

My father had some rough dealings, and his debt was passed on to me. I've always been just behind the eight ball —scrambling to catch up. A day late. A dollar short. Or in this case, 26,000—ironically, my age minus a few zeroes.

I'd rather his legacy didn't include his counterfeiting expertise, but when you inherit both daddy issues and really good forgery tools, I couldn't very well not take the lemons I was given and make lemonade, er, a fake document.

We'll overlook that I may have committed a felony. I'm more than capable of doing this job, so it's not like I took it from someone more qualified. Nor am I a nepo baby. More like a repo baby, since my father's vehicle was repossessed the week I got to his house.

I just hope the world I've carefully curated never collides with the reality of my past. Though I wouldn't mind meeting the guy who was accidentally patched into my phone extension.

2

JULES

WENDY RETURNS from lunch with Jeannie in tow for her daily "tea time." She gossips about our boss, Chief Executive Officer Frank Andresen, and how he's grooming his son to become the VP, never mind that he probably isn't qualified. I can imagine the system collapse when a guy who has no idea how to run a business like this drives it into the ground.

I said I hate Frank Andresen, but I never said he wasn't exceptional at elevating Meridian Holdings into a multimedia empire—ownership and management of prestigious art auction houses, rare book publishers, museum consulting firms, and digital art platforms.

It's a hybrid of the Smithsonian's research power with Disney's marketing reach. Give the devil his due. Frank Andresen runs a tight operation.

Maxine Drecken, his acting COO, is no different—cut from the same corporate mold—execs who treat their employees like bots.

I return to my computer and work on transcribing the slanted script dated June 1726—this very month, but hundreds of years ago. These are the names and records of real lives, real people inked in time. How could I not be fascinated?

Carmen gets back from lunch with what should be a butterscotch-pudding smile. Instead, she looks frantic. Talking a mile a minute, she says, "Did you see the interdepartmental memo that just came through?"

Wendy's head telescopes out from behind her computer screen like an ostrich. "Just got it. We have a mandatory meeting with Executive Operations for a special announcement."

Carmen wipes perspiration from above her upper lip. "You know what this meeting means. Restructuring."

Abruptly, the temperature in the room seems to change.

Wendy joins in the panic. "Code for layoffs."

"I didn't hear about a merger." My pulse accelerates.

They're both pale from the kind of nervousness that suggests I'm not the only one who needs to keep this job. We could close off from each other. Send discreet emails to connections in the company to ensure we remain employed. Instead, the office girlies and I gather in a circle. Carmen, our matriarch, leads us in a quiet prayer.

Before she concludes, Wendy adds, "And if we're going to get bad news, please include catering from Flour Hour, the bakery and sweet shop that opened two blocks over. If I'm getting the axe, I need a cinnamon roll to stem the pain."

We chuckle, but really, this isn't a laughing matter. For the last year, these women and I have become a well-oiled machine. We can't claim that we keep the business afloat, far from it, but we do our jobs without any wheels coming off. Not only that, but we've been through real life together —the birth of Wendy's son. Carmen's husband having shoulder surgery. We've gone to Cubs games and cried together when the final episode of "The Sweetheart Report" aired. I cannot believe Jenessa chose Colin!

We spend the next hour speculating about the meeting. Did someone finally get caught stealing the vanilla bean coffee pods? Carmen is convinced we're being sent on a mandatory team-building adventure retreat, which sounds like my personal nightmare—I'm a homebody.

To Frank Andresen, everything is urgent. The way I see it is that art and documents have endured for hundreds of years. Some for thousands. What's the rush? We'll get everything cataloged, insured, and properly accounted for. No need to strike fear into us employees that if we don't get things done *yesterday*, the world will end.

From across the room, Wendy gasps. "Juliana, remember, you applied internally for the job of research associate. Maybe the position opened up and you're getting it."

Doubtful, but I flash an appreciative smile. Moving up in Meridian is an impossibly slow climb—apparently, Frank's hurry has its limits. Plus, I don't really want anyone making inquiries into my educational background or work history. *Shh.*

As the afternoon creeps by and the clock clicks down to the meeting time, our nervousness turns into grasping at optimism. What'll follow is scared silence, but we're not quite there yet.

"If you could have any job, what would it be?" Wendy asks.

Carmen's nostrils flare. "I'd be the axeman. I've always wanted to tell Hershel in the Mailroom, 'You're fired!'"

"Because he asked if you're single?"

"I'm sixty!"

"And a foxy lady." Wendy shimmies her shoulders.

It's true. Carmen is gorgeous and has the classic good looks of a star of the silver screen. As a rule, I don't follow modern celebrity stuff. Mom raised me with the belief that if it didn't happen while Elvis and Marilyn Monroe were alive, it's not relevant. She says those were the days of true glamor. The kind I aspire to, never mind that most days I feel like a raccoon—a nighttime bandit with dark crescents under my eyes from taking on too much work. People think I'm a pushover, but really, I just want to learn every aspect of this business and prove myself. (And maybe, deep down, if my fake diploma is discovered, I'll be granted clemency since I've made myself indispensable.)

Whereas Carmen is classic elegance and Wendy is modern trends, I'm somewhere in the middle, usually adding a little splash of flair to my humdrum work attire—sparkly heart earrings today.

"What about you, Wendy?" I ask.

"I'd be a stay-at-home mom."

"Solid dream job," I say without irony.

My mother was a Las Vegas showgirl when—surprise!—I came along. She'd have preferred not to work two jobs so she could spend more time with me.

"Your turn, Juliana," Carmen says.

"My dream job at the moment is research archivist. I love the stories old documents, manuscripts, photographs, and artwork tell." I gave up on that a few weeks ago when HR didn't so much as acknowledge my submission.

"You're such a romantic." Wendy smiles.

We continue to play the "Disract each other from the pending meeting" game.

"Any big weekend plans?" Carmen waggles her eyebrows at me since I'm the only single one of our bunch.

"Going out with Oly tonight." My best friend insists on

being my flirting sherpa, guiding me through the wilds of the dating world.

"I thought she was recently married," Wendy says.

I nod. "Nate is out of town this weekend."

Looking forward to getting dressed up and gabbing like old times with my bestie over a platter of appetizers, then singing karaoke is the only thing that's keeping my mind from doom-obsessing about the upcoming meeting.

After we close out our tasks for the day, we march to the assembly room downstairs. A heavy sense of foreboding accompanies my every step. I wonder if this is a *before* moment and whatever comes *after* will change the trajectory of my life forever.

Wendy looks like she might cry when she doesn't see the sideboard populated with pastry boxes from Flour Hour. Carmen, stone-faced, is prepared for war.

In short order, the meeting is as corporate as they come, but swift.

There aren't any layoffs. Phew.

Meridian did not buy the Louvre. Wendy is disappointed.

Nor did they accuse anyone of stealing those little instant coffee pods—Carmen suspects Hershel and has him locked in her crosshairs.

What happened is that Andresen announced the appointment of new managers to oversee the expanding digital archive project, to coordinate between our physical and virtual collections and to oversee cross-departmental integration.

I tune out the corporate jargon. New managers, same grind. At least I still have a job.

The relief has me sailing buoyantly home rather than sulking on the bus, followed by the train, while sidestepping what looks like—but does not smell like—mustard on the platform.

No sooner am I through the door of my Logan Square studio than my phone rings.

Oly makes an exaggerated *Ooh* sound that can only mean one thing. She's canceling. I'm a sinking ship. The shore is far away. Goodbye, cruel world.

"I'm so sorry. Nate's trip was scrapped because he was laid off."

Sympathy quickly replaces disappointment. I'd tell her about my day and the near layoff scare, but she has to console her husband, so we're off the phone in record time.

I don't mind being alone, but sometimes silence can almost be louder than a summer concert in the park.

Guess it'll be me, a girl dinner, and a rerun of "The Sweetheart Report." Before I put on my quitting-for-the-day clothes, I check the Meridian Holdings employee app to make sure I didn't miss anything important—like I was actually let go and can go commiserate with my best friend and her husband.

I want to keep my job, but Friday nights at home, when I've been anticipating fun plans all week, can be their own kind of reality check sandwich.

The little red dot indicating I have a Meridian app message glows. I read the email from HR detailing that I've been transferred to the thirty-ninth floor with the title "Special Projects Assistant."

This must be a mistake. I reread the message while the neighbors with whom I share a wall argue as usual. Screechy and Grumbly bicker about replacing the toilet paper roll.

If only they had real problems.

Like the error HR made.

To my neighbors, I holler, "Guys, the solution is simple. Rock, paper, scissors."

Screechy and Grumbly are quiet for a moment as if contemplating my advice.

I follow up with, "But only paper wins." It doesn't follow any logic, but neither do their arguments.

I don't want to be single forever, but if that's what being in a relationship is like, they can keep it and their TP. However, I do want romance. The love song kind ... or even a love letter.

Not likely.

I check my employee profile in the app. Sure enough, my job title has been changed. I'm now a Special Projects Assistant. It sounds innocuous enough, but the thirty-ninth floor is the shark tank. Way up there is where the executives lurk—the Franks and Maxines of the world.

The message doesn't give specifics, only that I have to report to L. Sullivan. He's probably another stiff in a suit who thinks the words *please* and *thank you* are optional. I have a feeling I'm going to hate him, too.

3

LINC

A SHIVER BRUSHES across my skin, and it's not because I'm gliding off the ice after my teammates and I endured the Ottawa Outlaws coach's debrief practice after the finals—we only made it two rounds. It's basically an opportunity to lace up one final time at the end of the season without the pressure of a big game.

Butcher, one of the top defensemen in the league, claps me on the shoulder as we walk down the hall toward the locker room. "Nice assist, Linc."

From behind, Bīriņš calls in broken English, "But let's see you polish up that saucer pass. I want to see it on a gold platter."

"You mean a silver platter," I counter.

Having caught up with me, I get a pair of finger guns. "Ah, I see. The Stanley Cup is silver."

"Yep. And I'll work on that if you remember that the puck doesn't belong in our goal," I tease.

When we enter our home arena locker room, everything is the same as when we left—a roll of tape on the bench under my locker stall. Bīriņš's shirt is on the floor. There is the usual mess that the assistant coach scolds us about. The shower farthest on the left drips. The light in the bathroom area is slightly brighter than in the main section. The AC pushes against the slight humidity from the sweat of over a dozen grown men returning from exerting themselves.

Yet, the air is different.

I can't put my finger on it, other than that I've felt a similar feeling twice before.

One was when I graduated from high school. Yearbooks were being passed around. People were saying their good-byes. Some of the girls were crying. Mrs. Benes hugged everyone. The guys were acting chill, as if it were a regular Thursday.

The other time was when I left college. But like missing the passing of a baton, that same nostalgic feeling of change was there and then slipped through my fingers as the rush of all that was coming toward me after being tagged for the NHL barreled my way at top speed.

There wasn't time to reflect.

Though I feel that slight shift, a stirring, unease. The best way I can describe it is like a torch has been lit while, at the same time, a candle goes out. It's strange because I'm not an overly reflective kind of guy.

I just do my thing on the ice, have a good time, and pretend my father's disappointment that I'm not frothing to follow in his footsteps doesn't exist.

Nope. Hockey is my life.

"Summer plans?" our captain barks from the center of the room, where he stands atop the tile rendition of our team logo. I've never heard Holden Goudreau speak in complete sentences at a normal volume.

"The river," Bīriņš shouts, miming basking in the sun on his boat.

Stevens, who also plays defense, smiles widely, likely thinking about his wife and three kids. "Family time, bros."

Butcher says, "Getting ready for next season."

A few of the guys tease him for being a suck up. He's not. The man is built for the ice, a veritable machine on skates. That could be said about all of us to varying degrees.

Turning to me, Pete Johannessen, left on the front line, says, "And our wittle bittle *Linc-y* poo will be at his summer internship."

I bristle at the nickname and roll my eyes, not wanting to think about what awaits me in Chicago for the next few months.

"My father and I had an agreement, and it's time for me to uphold my end of things."

"Must be hard being a nepo baby," Butcher says, but there's no edge to it.

They know I earned my way onto this team fair and square. However, the employees occupying the upper floors in the gleaming building on Wacker Drive likely would have a few comments to make if I ever took over my father's position.

Which is not happening. There are legitimately qualified people who deserve to be the CEO of Meridian Holdings. Yet, Dad is grooming me. Or attempting to.

I'll be sticking to hockey, thank you very much.

But as I pack up my gear bag one last time before going home for a few months, a peculiar feeling that things won't be the same when I return here next season chills me. Or maybe it's just that I'll be changed.

WHEN I LAND IN CHICAGO, a sleek black car waits. I expect instructions from my father's assistant to pop up on my phone when I power it back on, but instead, it's from the old man himself with two directives. Shave and meet him at the office early tomorrow.

I grunt. That's not exactly a typical Frank Andresen move, but the dreaded time has come for me to make good on our agreement. This means he's taking it seriously.

The Outlaw in me wants to keep the beard that I let grow each season, but I'll play by his rules. For now. He'll remind me it's what my mother would've wanted.

When I get to my place on Lake Shore, overlooking Lake Michigan, I glance at my reflection in the floor-to-ceiling windows. Admittedly, I look like a disheveled caveman, not top-shelf corporate material.

Because that definitely isn't who I want to be.

I pause in front of the family photo on the mahogany open shelving. Mom was smiling. We all were. In her soft, yet all-seeing eyes, I can almost hear her remind me to be a good sport and play along.

I will. For now.

I'm about to text my father to see if he wants to grab a steak when I remember he's out of town until tomorrow's meeting—the start of what's sure to be a summer as pleasant as a sunburn.

Looks like I'll be dining solo, which I don't mind after the ordeal with my ex. Most women I've met are after my paycheck or don't understand the commitment I've made to my sport—it turns out that getting into a serious relationship is for dummies. At least, that's what I tell myself.

The next morning, I begrudgingly shave, slap on some cologne, and put on a charcoal gray suit. We wear them to games, but the way I'm dragging is the opposite of my usual excitement and anticipation, the hum in my veins before hitting the ice.

Sliding on my glasses, it's time for me to go incognito.

The driver delivers me to the glass tower with panoramic views of the Chicago River and Lake Michigan. Dad considers this the apex. For me, that would be a packed arena, battling for the puck, and scoring the winning goal.

Who am I fooling? I wouldn't mind having my name on the Stanley Cup either.

Everything about Frank Andresen is like a dignified masterpiece—a pricey one, too. I want my legacy to be, "He crushed it on the ice."

As I get out of the car, recalling the many times Mom and I would visit my father at work, I hesitate. Deep down, there is something I want more than the top NHL trophy or for my name to go down in hockey history.

My fingers find the penny I keep in my pocket.

The story goes that on my parents' first date, my mother spotted a coin on the sidewalk, stopped, and picked it up. Happened to be from that very year. She considered it lucky. It could also be that she was a descendant of the man printed on the piece of US currency.

She always kept it with her. I have it now. Never leave home—or play a game—without it.

Dad scoffed, wondering what she needed with a penny when he'd made a mint. But I heard him calling her his lucky penny when they thought they were alone. So I guess the guy has a soft side somewhere under his gruff, Captain-Serious demeanor—one only she ever saw.

Standing on the sidewalk well before operating hours, I flip the penny. Heads, I'll go inside. Tails, I'll keep walking.

The copper coin catches the morning sunlight like a little wink as it flips in the air. The moment seems to slow down. A shiver cools my skin much like it did yesterday at the Outlaws' practice facility.

However, before I catch the coin, I suddenly know what I'm going to do.

As far as my father is concerned, I'll march in the corporate charade parade. But I'm going to use every connection, database, and resource to honor my mother's memory and find the letters she always believed existed.

I'll get answers. I'll make a different sort of history.

Then I'll win the Stanley Cup.

4

LINC

DROPPING the coin safely into my pocket, the sun shines blindingly off the glass of the nearest door. I don't want to make a spectacle by using the main entrance. Bīriņš wasn't wrong about me being a nepo baby. Not that I've ever taken advantage of my father's billions.

Then again, the car and place I have on Lake Shore are thanks to him. Though if I had my way, I'd stay in Ottawa or join Bīriņš on the river—his sister married an American, and she and some of his relatives live here too.

My hand closes over the handle of the side entrance door, but it doesn't draw open. It could be locked, but through the glare of the sun on the glass, someone with long hair is on the other side. Again, I try to pull, but at the same time, she must be pushing.

In upscale buildings like this, there aren't "push/pull" stickers to help those who don't know how hinges operate. However, I've used this entrance numerous times and am certain the door opens outward.

Again, we're both pulling—me inward, her outward—

creating a ridiculous tug-of-war with a glass door between us.

Squinting my eyes through the reflective surface, I catch a vague impression of movement. Blonde hair catches the morning light. She seems confused about what's happening. And I'm already irritable because I have to be here.

"Lady, it's not like I'm trying to prevent you from exiting," I mutter.

She must realize what's happening and steps back. With an exaggerated flourish, she gestures toward the door to indicate that I go first.

When I pull it open, she steps forward when I do. We do an awkward shuffle, both of us deking in the same direction.

My father is here at dawn, and it's only shortly after. The sooner I get our meeting over with, the quicker I can implement my plan. Not that I quite have that worked out. This foolish delay is throwing me off.

I expect her to say something snide like, *Whatever happened to ladies first?* Instead, with an amused smile, she asks, "Shall we dance?"

I stare at her blankly. My mind is already forty floors up in the corner office where my father is waiting, probably checking his watch and cataloging my failures. I don't have time for cute strangers and their sidewalk comedy routines.

She huffs and her expression shifts from playful to annoyed. She mutters, "Sheesh. What's with the major zero-fun given vibes? It's Monday!"

I indicate that she goes. I should say something. Instead, I just stand there like an idiot, caught off guard because that shiver slides over me again. I'm certain it doesn't have anything to do with the cool early morning air or the climate control of the building.

"Tough crowd." Her full lips form a slim line as she breezes past me.

As she hurries by, I get a brief look at her. Blonde hair with hints of strawberry and light freckles scattered across her nose like flecks of gold.

Then she's clicking away on heels that I'd much prefer to see moving in the opposite direction—toward me. She's cute. Pretty. Hot. Gorgeous. Giving my head a shake, I toss the thought into the penalty box.

Eyes on the goal, Linc.

As I enter the building, the lingering scent of cherry blossoms and almonds leaves me with the distinct impression that I missed an important opportunity. Dancing in the doorway with a pretty woman?

Head in the game, dude.

As I board the elevator for the top floor of the Meridian building, I straighten my tie and prepare to meet Frank Andresen.

His secretary is already here, which means the woman who invited me to dance downstairs doesn't work for him. Or if she does, it's in another department. Not sure why that should matter.

Get in the zone, bro.

Meeting my father at this hour is not for the faint of heart or the distracted. He hasn't built a billion-dollar company in the art world by being unfocused. While some people daydream, he accomplishes. While others plan to address *later*, he executed yesterday.

If I didn't know better, I'd swear the man devours his competition for breakfast instead of steak and eggs.

From his position of command behind a massive, polished antique desk—one I imagine he wishes were the Resolute Desk, complete with the moniker "master and commander"—my father watches me enter his office as if he already sensed I was in the building.

Everything in the space is oversized and imposing, from the executive chair that could swallow a normal person to the conference table that stretches along one of the two walls of floor-to-ceiling windows like a landing strip.

Even the silence has weight, broken only by the barely audible hum of climate control keeping everything at the exact temperature required for preserving priceless art, along with the ticking of a grandfather clock that kept time in the White House until 1861. It was one of my father's many gifts to my mother when they were courting. Ironic that it's in here.

He glances at it and then at me again. "Abraham."

"Dad."

He starts to get up, but I quickly cross the room and extend my hand. "No need for formalities. In fact, you can call me Linc."

I've lost count, but I've told him this no less than ten thousand times. At least.

"Abraham is your given name. Abraham Lincoln Andresen."

"Even Mom called me Linc." It's not that I'm ashamed of it, but literally every male on my mother's side was named after our late, great ancestor.

"Your mother indulged you—" He hesitates, which is unusual. Actually, the man has never faltered a day in his life. He glances at the clock. "She loved you."

Love? That's a word I've never heard him speak. I expect him to pull off a mask, action movie style, or turn to ash like a vampire. Deadlines, productivity, and profit margins are all part of his vocabulary, but love?

Definitely not.

Not that I'm looking for him to express anything of the sort, but it's unexpected, and I'm still slightly off-kilter from the door encounter with the woman downstairs. Time to rewind. Actually, to the woman with the sweet voice, my call got lost in the Meridian phone tree before Frank Andresen interrupted the other day.

As if noticing my wandering thoughts, my father pulls me back to his purpose. He spends the next thirty minutes outlining my role—to learn what running a corporation means, the benchmarks I'll need to meet, the departments I'll oversee, why sentiment has no place in leadership, and how this is my final chance to prove I'm worthy of inheriting his empire.

We settle the identity question with something of an "undercover boss" solution, but not because he's having me spy on anyone. At least I don't think so. I'll use my mother's maiden name. The father-son connection stays private, as does my NHL career—optics for the first case. His indifference for the second.

"Why not promote Maxine Drecken?" I ask, referring to the acting chief operating officer.

A shadow crosses his expression. "Son, I'm thinking about your future."

So why does the woman with blonde hair from the doorway downstairs float into my mind?

5

JULES

UNPOPULAR OPINION: I like Mondays. It's a fresh start to the week. Anything could happen, even small miracles. So after a weekend of being held in suspense—certain HR made a mistake about the new role—when the Meridian Holdings app notifications pinged at zero dark thirty, indicating I had a personal message, I thought it was a correction.

I also secretly hoped Andresen felt bad about keeping us late on Friday and was giving us the morning to sleep in.

No such luck.

I'm on the thirty-third floor with Wendy and Carmen, packing up my desk while they pepper me with questions. "I read the notification word for word. Checked, then double-checked that it was intended for me. Marcel messaged me personally to confirm I'm moving departments."

Wendy tips her head from side to side. "It is unlikely that another Juliana Lindley works for the company."

I give her a wide-eyed *Ya think?* look, then regret it

because this is a "we all lose" rather than a "win-win" situation. The office girlies and I had a good thing going here.

"I thought the meeting on Friday was just about the new management system," Carmen says, scrolling through the app, presumably to make sure she didn't miss any notifications.

"Never mind staying late, Marcel told me that Andresen and the new exec, Mr. Sullivan, wanted me here early and then—" I start.

"Your new boss?"

I nod, exasperated. "He's a no-show."

Carmen hisses, "The pair of snakes!"

Wendy bounces on her toes. "Maybe that means you're staying here."

"I wish. One of the women who works on the exec floor said he was in a meeting and told me to come down here to pack my stuff. It's definite."

I puff my cheeks. Thanks to the pointless early arrival, I missed my usual Monday morning coffee shop stop and the precious quiet before the week's corporate bloodsport commenced. When I finally snuck out for caffeine and oxygen, a power-walking stiff in a suit nearly mowed me down trying to get in the building.

I tuck my candy bowl into a file box when my phone chimes—another Meridian notification.

Carmen and Wendy pop up like prairie dogs.

My hope dies fast—the notification is from L. Sullivan, informing me in the smuggest possible terms to return to the office "at my earliest convenience" and to "make timeliness a priority going forward." I want to stick my tongue out at my device.

"That was him. I have to go," I say, hefting my box.

Carmen hugs me. Wendy, knowing the dangers I face,

slides some Dove chocolate in the box for extra reinforcement.

Remember when I said I hate my boss? Still true, maybe more so because I also preemptively hate my new boss. That's double hate. Hate squared. Hate on top of hate. Hate in duplicate.

Wendy, Carmen, and I have always had a long leash—junior employees who deliver avoid micromanagement. But with this new structure, I doubt Sullivan will extend the same courtesy. I can already feel him breathing down my neck.

This reminds me of how, when I was new to driving, when a more experienced driver was in the car with me, I'd get nervous and inevitably—and accidentally—honk the horn or stop short when pulling into a parking spot. Same as when someone watches me type. When left alone, spellcheck is hardly necessary. When someone is watching over my shoulder, it's like I'm suddenly using my toes instead of my fingers to make the words appear on the screen.

Taking a breath as deep as the Mariana Trench, I exit the elevator.

The space the girlies and I shared in the Collections Processing Department was almost cozy—three desks in a triangle, modern wall sconces, a little personality, a touch of charm. Up here, it's marble and mahogany ego. Polish and power plays. From the upholstered leather chairs to the hand-woven rug, even the silence feels expensive. In the reception area, two desks flank a runway that leads to the main office, where I imagine Mr. Sullivan sits in a wingback chair while stroking a Persian cat.

He'll probably demand that I feed him green M&Ms or

whatever it is that goblin men consume instead of grapes like a Roman emperor.

However, a framed lithograph that looks remarkably like the Gettysburg Address draws my attention. I pad closer, but a clatter comes from the main office, and I whip around. Two women freeze in place.

When they see me, the taller one says. "Oh, I thought it was him."

"I'm Juliana Lindley. The new—"

The shorter one with a broad face narrows her eyes. "Yes, we know who you are."

"It's nice to meet you," I say, drawing on my manners and expecting them to introduce themselves.

"We're preparing things for Mr. Sullivan." The way the taller one says his name makes me wonder if *L. Sullivan* should have more gravity in my mental contacts list. So far, it hasn't rung any bells.

The shorter woman points to one of the desks in the entry area of the office. The placard says *Misha Perkins*. The other reads *Veronica Meller*. Presumably, these belong to each of them, and they're not keen to make room for me.

Misha orders, "Take that stack of files to Ms. Drecken's new suite."

Veronica, the taller one, adds, "Matt, the executives' gopher, is probably in the hall. Just give them to him. He'll know what to do."

Turning on my heels, I shake off the command and the lack of so much as a "please" and do as told, hoping to be fast in case Mr. Sullivan returns. Surely, he'll think I misread his directive to come to the office at my earliest convenience to mean at my leisure.

After such a cool first impression, that won't fly around

here. I also pray I don't forget how to be courteous and morph into a snobby secretary.

I haven't spent much time on the executive floors and feel like I'm going to get in trouble because I don't have a hall pass.

The corridors are wide and eerily empty—neither Matt nor the other assistants rush around with file carts or armloads of paperwork. I entertain myself by imagining actual gophers scurrying around with tiny briefcases, and I'm still grinning when my phone pings. Sullivan again, probably.

I glance down at the screen and nearly crash into a wall ... of chest. Suit, tie, solid build—must be the assistant I'm looking for. Flustered, I don't look up. "Sorry, I'm—"

Panicking about getting fired and suspicious that Veronica and Misha are sabotaging me. I shove the files into Maybe Matt's hands, U-turn, and call over my shoulder, "Please bring those to Ms. Drecken."

The elevator takes forever to arrive and a figure drops in to wait beside me. It's barely after nine a.m., and my internal tailspin dives deeper when I realize he's wearing the same gray suit as Maybe Matt. Same large stature, too. Come to think of it, similar build and posture as Doorway Dance Guy from earlier.

The chances are slim to nothing. I got this. I imagine myself like Rocky Balboa facing off with those seventy-two limestone steps in Philadelphia—that was my father's favorite movie. I'll rise to the top, even if I have to take the slow elevator.

Eyes glued to the lacy, golden veins on the night sky marble floor, I don't dare look up at the masculine figure beside me.

The elevator must be taking the scenic route.

The man beside me jiggles his watch and checks the time. Then he draws an executive badge from his suit jacket and swipes it across a panel on the wall.

Clearing my throat, I still don't look up and mumble, "Is that to hurry it along?"

"We'll find out." His voice is low, quarried from the deepest mines in the earth.

"I didn't know that was a thing. This gives me a new goal to reach executive status." My laughter sounds muffled like underwater gunfire.

"Good luck with that."

Alrighty, then. Possibly Matt is as dry as toast. No doughnuts for him next Monday!

The elevator dings and we both step inside. In the small space, his words and low timbre echo in my head. If he'd said anything else—recited poetry in Italian, for instance—I'd have considered his voice alluring, the kind I'd like to hear read an audiobook about true love. Instead, it was dismissive, almost smug.

Still not shifting my gaze, I sense he holds something—the files, no doubt. This can only mean one of two things. The man was indeed Gopher Matt and Misha was mistaken about the location of Ms. Drecken's new office. Or I mistook an executive for the executive aide and he's going to report me to HR.

Suddenly claustrophobic, heat rises to my cheeks and cold sweat makes me wish I had the budget to buy silk or linen rather than synthetic blends. My shirt's fabric clings to me in a way that will soon necessitate an extra application of antiperspirant.

The illuminated number buttons are like old English script I need to decode. My breathing sounds like I'm slurping the bottom of a smoothie through a straw. My stomach decides to rebel and makes a weird squelching sound.

If Probably Not Matt is aware of this, he doesn't reveal it, standing there stiffly in his expensive suit—from what I can see, it fits him well. The faint gust of cologne that wafts my way would be enticing in any other setting.

He gets out on the same floor as me, but by some act of mercy, we walk in opposite directions. Of course, my shoes squeak.

Squeak, squeak, squeak goes the little mouse as she scurries away from the big bad cat.

I don't dare look back.

6

JULES

VERONICA AND MISHA are a pair of vultures awaiting fresh kill in the main office.

In a barely audible hush, one of them says, "He walks like a jungle cat."

"A wild cat." That's Veronica.

"King of the Jungle."

That would make *this* the jungle. Makes sense that I feel very much like prey when I hear a voice say, "I asked you two to bring these files to Ms. Drecken's office."

When in a high-stress situation, the three survival instincts are fight, flight, or freeze. I do the latter because I hear the low tone of the man's voice before I see him. I know who it is.

And I'm in trouble.

Also worth noting, there's another entrance to his office.

Not-Gopher-Matt is my new boss, and I just mistook him for errand staff.

I consider crawling under the nearest desk or making a run for it, but both options will result in my dismissal. I need this job, so I take my chances and remain on my feet.

Misha scuttles by me and, with her nose in the air like a snooty socialite, she doesn't so much as peer my way.

Veronica looks me up and down like I'm in frumpy, off-duty attire. "Mr. Sullivan will see you now. I'm confident you'll dazzle him."

Smoothing my shirt, I draw a deep breath. My father, for all his flaws, was never intimidated by anyone—not even when it probably would've been in his best interest. He knew some sordid folks. Mom sure did dazzle on the Vegas stage. I'm made of half fearlessness and half dazzling. I can do this. Without hesitating or giving my new boss another reason to loathe me, I enter the cold, minimalist office.

I instantly recognize the gray suit, solid stature, and height—the impressive watch around his wrist, half hidden by the custom-tailored jacket cuff, and the large, masculine hands that no longer hold Ms. Drecken's files.

I'm out in the open. It's too late to bolt. His gaze pins me in place, burning with what feels like icy fire.

When I finally look up, meeting a pair of dark blue eyes framed by glasses on a broad, rugged face composed of hard angles, bearing no amusement, my inhale snags.

It's the same guy from the doorway early this morning. The one who wouldn't dance with me. Who refused to laugh.

L. Sullivan. My new boss.

He looks me up and down with bold disdain. As if I'm beneath him. As if I'm bitter chocolate and he prefers vanilla—safe, predictable, and sweet. Like I'm abstract art and he only understands a classical canvas.

"Hello, sir," I meep.

The way he examines me makes me feel like a used car, ruining any chance of us being chums.

"Julia? I understand you're my new special project assistant."

Like a seabird that swallowed a fish, I clear my throat. "It's Juliana, and yes, sir, that's my understanding."

"I expect you to manage your time efficiently."

I nod, feeling chastised. Had it not been for the aforementioned women, I would've been at my desk as originally ordered.

"Would you like me to bring those files to Ms. Drecken?" When he doesn't answer right away, I add, "My apologies about the mistake earlier."

"No, that was a task for Veronica or Misha."

I'm about to explain that they passed it off to me, but it seems he already gathered that. Giving a small nod of acknowledgment, I wait for Smug-y McGruffins to bark orders. I'm familiar with the cold, calculating type of man who thrives on order, efficiency, and perfection—and L. Sullivan is the epitome of the uptight and ruthless businessman.

His eyes graze over me. He blinks once, twice, three times from behind his Clark Kent glasses. If this were any other circumstance, I'd consider him exceptionally handsome. A perfect specimen of a wild cat in human form. The little shooting stars in my belly agree.

But this is a very tall concrete jungle and it's a long way down to solid ground.

From behind us, like we're between scenes at a theater, a couple of members of the building's maintenance staff change out Veronica and Misha's desks for an L-shaped unit with storage in a sleek, modern style.

In the moments I have my back turned, Mr. Sullivan disappears into his office, leaving me unsure of what to do next. I spend the next ten minutes arranging the items from downstairs on the slick surface of my new workspace. After that, I smooth my skirt. I take a seat and log in to the computer, hoping my credentials are the same. Sure enough, I'm inside the Meridian Holdings interface and expect to find some tasks in my inbox.

Nope. Apparently, my new boss just wants me to keep this swivel chair warm.

I twiddle my thumbs.

My leg jitters.

I take a few deep breaths.

Sneaking a truffle ball, I let the sea salt and caramel milk chocolate melt on my tongue.

I wonder if it would be acceptable for me to set out my bowl of seasonal sweets—I went to the specialty candy store near my apartment and picked up summer-themed novelty gummies. I picture Mr. Sullivan sweeping them off my desk in one broad stroke, sending the sunshine and beach ball candies to the floor like sticky confetti. The office girlies and anyone who visited our department appreciated them.

Through the frosted glass entry to his office, I make out a dark silhouette—broad shoulders that are rigid with an authority that comes from working in the upper levels of the world. I imagine him as a man turned to stone by Medusa, whose harsh reality morphed him into a monster. I bet he doesn't let himself eat so much as a hard candy. Not even a mint. His breath probably smells like sewer water. His mouth all puckered and cracked with dry rot.

I wrinkle my nose. Why am I thinking about his lips? Ew.

When L. Sullivan isn't occupying his dragon lair, he's likely working out in a gym until his knuckles bleed and his calluses are so thick, he's lost all sensation in his palms.

The man is undoubtedly beastly.

My interoffice email pings. I find a provenance gap report request—Wendy says these are my specialty. I won't argue with that. While I am fully capable of basic data entry, I lock in and track down the discrepancies before lunch.

My stomach has been making the squelching noise on and off all morning. How long do leftovers last? I originally made the tuna fish salad last Thursday. It's Monday, so it's probably okay. If only I could afford something from the Tasty Trolley. I'm glad Sullivan has kept his door shut. Just as I'm about to open my soft-sided lunch box, the intercom crackles.

"Juliette. My office."

As if I forgot where I am and the precarious high wire I'm balanced on, I press the button and correct him. "It's Juliana."

I slap my hand over my mouth and blame low blood sugar. What have I done? If I have to make a run for it, the chocolate stash is coming with me. Priorities, people!

His voice booms through the little device. "Right. Julia. Get in here."

My mother says it's better to throw glitter and confetti at people than harsh words. Everyone knows how hard it is to remove glitter, so if someone is covered in it, they're either a Vegas showgirl like her or got nasty and incurred her sparkly wrath. Unfortunately, I left all of my party supplies at home. This guy would definitely hate coming into contact with anything that sparkles. He'd probably wither up and vaporize on contact.

I look at my tuna sandwich and consider smooshing it into his face, but then I wouldn't have anything to eat for lunch.

Shoes still squeaking, I push through the door. With his

back to me, L. Sullivan stands in front of the floor-to-ceiling windows overlooking the city. He doesn't turn around. Just hovers there like a brooding gargoyle lord surveying his domain, wary of anyone who'd so much as breathe on his rare manuscripts and priceless artifacts.

"I would like you to work on an authentication report for the Eaton Boyd Collection, Julene."

I simmer inside. My name isn't that hard! I need to get a placard like Misha and Veronica had. I'll write J-U-L-I-A-N-A on a piece of construction paper like I'm in kindergarten and tape it to my desk if I have to.

"Juliana," I correct through a tight smile.

"The report, Julie." He doesn't turn around.

A coil inside springs loose. "I submitted it to you fifteen minutes ago. Perhaps if you'd bothered to look past your own reflection in that window, you might have noticed."

My gaze skitters everywhere in the room except for his scowl—sharp jawline, intense eyes cataloging every inch of my every fidget, my every flaw. Dark hair that looks like he's been running his hands through it in frustration. The man is infuriatingly, devastatingly handsome in a cold, untouchable way that throws up a red flag of danger.

"Excuse me?" His eyebrows rise in a gesture that could freeze salt water on a sunny day.

"The Eaton Boyd report." I lift my chin, channeling every ounce of my mother's Vegas showgirl backbone and my father's sometimes foolish dauntlessness. I'm equal parts pluck and spunk! "Sir, it's there, along with the insurance valuations and provenance attestation. All completed while your other assistants were apparently competing for who could take the longest lunch break."

Something flickers in those glacial eyes—surprise, maybe even the faintest hint of amusement before the ice wall slams back into place. "Misha and Veronica assisted with the transition, but they will continue aiding Ms. Drecken. Ultimately, it'll just be you and me in this office." He crosses his arms in front of his chest. "Be that as it may, you need an attitude adjustment, Julana."

I nearly choke on his audacity, but quickly recover and take aim with my glitter guns. "So do your recall skills. My name is Juliana."

The silence stretches between us like a taut cable, crackling with enough tension to detonate the building.

Then a flirty discussion about chocolate filters back. A long conversation that was a great Friday distraction. A familiar voice.

No. This. Can't. Be. Right.

He steps close enough to confirm that the scent of his cologne is going to linger.

"It's you," I whisper.

His eyes glint and his lips curve into something that isn't quite a smile. "We'll see how long you last, Juliet."

Laughter erupts out of me. It's a terrible habit. Purely motivated by anxiety when I receive bad news while in the presence of other people. A way to push off emotions that feel too big to manage.

His expression is granite.

Instead of backing down as he tries to assert dominance, I do the darndest thing. Lifting my chin, I say, "I dare you to try to get rid of me."

His eyes bounce before turning lethal, but I don't waver. I didn't ask for this. Didn't wake up this morning and add "get steamrolled by my new boss" to my dance card.

Does he even remember us meeting in the doorway downstairs?

As bold as my statement was—because really, I'm just a

low-level assistant—my heart is in my throat. And his gaze is on it.

He licks his lips ever so slightly. "You're dismissed."

As I turn to leave, I catch my reflection in his window. My cheeks are flushed, my eyes bright with anger, and my thoughts would land me in HR jail. Behind me, his icy reflection watches my every move.

I'm blazing emotion. He's nothing but frost and sharp edges.

I hate how he made me feel like I was melting under that icy stare. It can't be good that he despises me for no reason.

However, the feeling is mutual.

I hate my new boss, too. Never mind that he's a Clark Kent dupe.

7

LINC

I NOW UNDERSTAND THE EXPRESSION, "golden handcuffs." Staring out of the upper-floor window of this glass aerie at the city below, I'd rather be anywhere than trapped up here in a birdcage. Well, almost anywhere.

As the morning circles back in my mind, I think about the conversation with my father and regret agreeing to this —even if it came with a plan to find something my mother was looking for, to complete her search. I resent his expectations for me when I have a perfectly good career doing something I love.

Then there was the interaction with my new assistant. Juliana. My mind is so scrambled, I can't think about much more than surviving the day. This situation already has me bitter and I'm taking it out on everyone within spitting distance.

I'll take a two-hundred thirty-pound man skating my way with a stick over this any day. But a woman that's probably about five and a half feet tall, with blonde hair streaked with a hint of summer strawberry and light freckles across her nose? I don't stand a chance.

The fact is, I don't want to be here. My original plan was simple: survival of the fittest. Fake it till I make it, suit up and embody the polished and demanding, self-important, condescending executive, and get through this stint without incident—all while completing my mother's search.

But scrubbing my hand down my face now, I know that's not happening. Channeling corporate boss energy, complete with power trips, makes me feel like a complete jerk.

Like my father.

So, Plan B: is to make my assistant's life so miserable she complains to HR and they fire me. Never mind that I'm not technically on the payroll, so who knows if that'll work.

But it's too late to turn back now.

Don't get me wrong, Frank Andresen has his good moments, but I've watched him work enough to know that he didn't build a billion-dollar company by being a softy who outfits his employees' bicycles with training wheels when they should come equipped with the ability to ride a unicycle. There is no staff game room or siesta space in this building.

Once, at a work dinner I went to as a teen, I recall Maxine Drecken, his second in command, likening Meridian's personnel to being nothing more than disposable livestock at a cubicle farm.

Dad didn't disagree, so I took it as assent.

But that's not who I am. I play right wing for the Ottawa Outlaws. We're a brotherhood and the only way to win is if we do it together. Over the years, some players have come along who're in it entirely for personal glory. Of course, we all want to do our best, but if we don't operate as one unit, the whole thing goes off the rails, er, skates, as it were.

So why did I just tear into my new assistant? Simple: I don't want to be here. I belong on the ice, not behind a desk, playing corporate theater. But it's not like I have another option.

She dared me to get rid of her and I don't blame her for not wanting to put up with my ugly mug every day. She probably had a nice office somewhere else in the building—kept an adorable candid photo of her significant other with his arms around her and a bowl of seasonal candies on her desk.

I stagger. Hold on. Yes, she most certainly did. A desk covered in crinkly Lindt chocolate truffle wrappers. It can't be. I glance over my shoulder with a quiet and unsettling certainty that the woman I flirted with on the phone when the call to my father got lost and misdirected is none other than the woman with the sweet-as-chocolate voice.

The intercom buzzes. I noticed Juliana ordinarily has the voice of a contented kitten, but when she talks to me, she sounds like she's fixing for a cat fight. "Mr. Sullivan, a Sir Bīriņš the most highborn, undefeated, handsome, eternal herald of hockey ..."

What is he doing here?

I break out in a sweat as, from the reception area, my teammate's accented voice dictates his ridiculous—and fake—royal name to my assistant and very likely will follow up with a request for her number. The man is like a fly to pretty women. You can't keep him away, yet somehow, despite his bombastic nature, he convinces the sweetest women to date him.

He's going to take the snot out of me for occupying this office. Instead of sending him in, I press the intercom button. "Be right out."

Smoothing my tie, I fling the double office doors open like I'm raiding a medieval castle. Only Bīriņš isn't there.

My assistant stares at me apologetically. Biting her very plump lower lip, she says, "He asked if there was another entry."

I do my best to seem unruffled. Having the guys barge in and blow the cover I'm trying to keep by blabbing about being a nepo baby or NHL player is the last thing I need.

"Where did he go?"

She points a slender finger toward the hall where the side entrance to my office is. Presumably, she told him.

"Thanks a lot, Yulia."

She cocks her head. "Now you're just stretching. Is that even a name?"

I crack my neck because she's right. I could use a stretch. Hit the gym, run off this tension.

Her eyes narrow. "My name is Juliana."

I'll do my best to forget that and the unsettling gray of her eyes. Eyes like my favorite kind of ice, but they're not at all cold.

Best to keep my distance. Feign indifference.

Giving my head a shake, I turn back to the problem at hand which includes but is not limited to tracking down my teammate, finding out why he's here, and getting him to leave as discreetly as possible.

From behind, I hear the telltale creak of a chair.

Turning back to my office, I slam the doors and bear down on Bīriņš. With his hands clasped behind his head, he tilts back and kicks his huge, filthy boots on my desk.

"What are you doing here?" I hiss.

"Rescuing you."

I wipe the dirt off the otherwise pristine surface. "I

don't need rescuing, but you will if you don't take your grubby boots off my desk."

He chuckles and doesn't move, but his gaze skirts the door to the reception area. "In that case, I'm here to save the damsel who you're keeping locked up in this ivory tower."

"She's not locked in? Damsel?" Feeling wrapped around the spokes, I try to get my head on straight. "Bīriņš, you can't be here."

In his ribald and stilted way, he says, "It's officially summer. A beautiful day. My cousins and I are going full throttle on the lake."

"I told you, I have to—" Read reports? Populate spreadsheets? Make my father another million?

"*Icing on the Lake* is gassed up, the cooler is stocked, we're just waiting for you, eighty-three."

Glancing out the window, the sparkling water does look inviting. Through the crack in the door, I glimpse my assistant illuminated by the glow of her computer.

What would she do?

I mean, if I left. Not whether she'd go boating with her friends instead of doing her job. As for that, it's hard to say. She was spunky earlier, firing back at me when she commented on having already submitted the report to me. Then she followed up with a sassy little comment about me staring at my own reflection.

Trust me, that's the last thing I want to do. I much prefer hiding behind my beard.

Cutting into my thoughts, Bīriņš says, "You look like such a dweeb in those glasses."

I angle my gaze at him and then jut my chin toward the window. "Feel like going skydiving?"

His brow furrows, confused for a moment, before he

registers the threat, not that I'd ever throw someone off a building. "Ha ha. Come on. Let's go. You can play hooky this once."

But it's my first day. The clickety clack of my assistant's fingers flying across her keyboard brings to mind her dare to get rid of her. But what if she got rid of me? If I get a bad report, perhaps my father will see that I'm not made for the corporate world and let me go—no severance package necessary.

Smirking, I say, "Actually, yeah. That sounds good."

Bīriņš drops his boots to the floor and launches to standing, letting out a bark of laughter. "I didn't think you'd cave so easily. Let's roll, troll."

I breeze through the main office doors, but when I reach the elevator, my teammate and current partner in crime isn't beside me.

Turning around, the hockey player who could somehow charm ice off the rink is sweet-talking my assistant. She smiles and laughs—maybe nervously. Flirtatiously? I can't tell.

Striding back the way I came, I say, "Bīriņš, shall we?"

He extends his elbow toward my assistant, an invitation for her to loop her arm through.

She steps back slightly. Smart girl. The guy goes through women like I go through skate laces.

"I probably shouldn't—" Her eyes flick toward mine and then away.

"Shouldn't what?" I ask.

"Juliana is coming with," Bīriņš says as if that should've been obvious.

I glower. "What? No. She has work to do."

My assistant crosses her arms in front of her chest. "It looked like you were leaving."

"We are." My teammate winks. "All three of us for a day on the lake. You won't be sorry."

I reply with a sharp look that suggests he'll be sorry if it isn't just the two of us who exit this building.

8

LINC

BĪRIŅŠ IS HAVING one of his "I'm not backing down" kind of days. It's great when we're up against a particularly aggro team. Not so much when I've just barely convinced myself that the plan I hatched to spare myself a summer of corporate bondage is the best course of action.

Planting a large hand on both our shoulders, he guides Juliana and me toward the elevators as if leading us to the dungeon.

Back in college, I trained in jiu-jitsu and could easily put a stop to this, but I don't. The devil on my shoulder suggests I let it play out all the way to the lobby, leaving the CEO with no choice but to terminate my employment.

I don't want to disgrace my father, but it's better to do this "rip off the bandage" style. In the next ten minutes, I intend to prove that I'm *not* an asset to the company, then he can send me on my merry way.

Bīriņš presses the button on the elevator. My thoughts rewind and replay when the cute blonde in the hallway and I nearly collided. She passed off a stack of files, likely mistaking me for someone who knew what to do with them.

She seemed flustered when I flashed my executive badge, using it to hasten the elevator, as I'd seen my father do many times. It's a ridiculous flex, but I couldn't help taking the opportunity to practice my role as Lord Bonehead Boss of Meridian.

With my teammate standing between us in the elevator, this time, I don't catch her cherry blossom and almond scent. Earlier, it brought to mind a rose-colored memory of a trip Mom took me on to Washington, D.C. It was spring and the soft breeze would blow the flower petals from the trees. She called it "rain from heaven." I guess she can confirm that now. We visited numerous libraries on her search for the lost love letters that she claimed were my birthright. After flipping through so many dusty old books, I decided that paper smells faintly of almonds.

One of my favorite memories. Two of my favorite scents.

The elevator dings for the lobby.

After we step onto the shiny marble floor, Bīriņš turns to my assistant. "I bet you look really good sunbathing, Juliana."

I fight the urge to flick his ear. For all I know, this woman could be totally into him and feed off comments like that. Or she could be married. Though no ring.

Her cheeks turn a faint shade of cherry before her lips drop into a flat line. "While I appreciate you using my correct name," she cuts me a glare, "I prefer full-body swimming costumes."

"Like a wetsuit?" I blurt, not sure what to make of her response.

Bīriņš waggles his eyebrows. "I bet that leaves a lot to the imagination."

Her expression pinches with a pout. Presumably, that

wasn't the response she intended. "Um, Mr. Sullivan probably—"

And there it is. I flinch.

"Mr. S—?" Bīriņš doesn't even have my mother's maiden name out of his mouth, likely wondering why Juliana called me that, when she finishes her thought, "has a lot of work for me to do so—"

"Linc," I interject. "Just call me Linc."

Juliana frowns. Seems like she's not keen on skipping class, especially not with me.

I'd like to beam myself out of here as my father materializes, flanked by his assistant and Drecken. He looks at the three of us, undoubtedly recognizing my teammate, and narrows his eyes in my direction, very likely reading this situation accurately. "Don't you have a project you should be working on? This isn't summer vacation."

That's exactly what it is, but even Bīriņš is smart enough not to cross Frank Andresen. My father has the kind of commanding presence that can get the burliest of hockey players to back down.

I would know.

Turning to Juliana, my father says, "Are you the new assistant?"

"Yes, sir. We were just showing this man to the exit—he got lost upstairs—before we head to the reference room." Juliana's smile is convincing ... mesmerizing. Never mind charming the ice off a rink, she could melt it.

Apparently, my father buys it. "Very well. Good day to you all."

Bīriņš starts walking backward, slowly toward the exit, and in a low, conspiratorial tone—as if he'll employ a network of spies if necessary—he says, "This isn't over. I'll be back to break you out of here."

But I'm not sure whether he means Juliana or me.

When we're alone, I bark, "Better get back to work, Julianne."

She narrows her eyes and whispers, "By the way, I'll never share my chocolate with you." Turning on her heel, she gets on the elevator and pounds the closed button before I can board.

I'd rather go to the reference room, anyway. But the question about why she helped me out lingers as I exit onto the lower floor. It's been ages since I've been down here—always with Mom.

The Research and Reference Department occupies an entire level and, on one side, contains climate-controlled glass cases displaying rotating selections from our vast collection that are under examination—ancient manuscripts, first-edition volumes, and authenticated artifacts.

Floor-to-ceiling mahogany shelves occupy the other side, housing thousands of books, while another area contains catalogue raisonnés, auction records dating back centuries, and comprehensive provenance documentation.

The far end of the floor hosts workstations featuring high-resolution digital displays connected to Meridian's global database of artwork ownership information and histories.

White-gloved archivists and authentication specialists work at examination tables equipped with advanced imaging technology, UV lights, and microscopy equipment for analyzing brushstrokes, paper composition, and ink dating.

The room maintains museum-quality environmental conditions with precise temperature, humidity, and lighting systems to protect the invaluable reference materials spanning thousands of years.

Being back here stirs up memories of tagging along with my mother—her showing me the importance of history as she sought to clarify our own. Or, the more I've understood, perhaps solidify her future with my father.

That didn't quite work out as planned.

The buzz of anticipation mixed with the weight of unfinished business fills me as I stalk down one of the aisles with bookshelves on both sides.

There is a reason I entered the building this morning and it is unrelated to visiting the office upstairs.

Mom spent countless hours down here in her final months, chasing threads of our family's history. I can almost see her at one of the tables, white gloves on, carefully turning pages of century-old correspondence.

Dad never came down here with us. I don't want to become the kind of person who lives only for work. When I'm not on the ice, nerding out in these dusty archives wouldn't be so bad.

Unable to shake the pull of the missing letters she searched for, I feel immensely drawn to piecing together the past.

As I venture deeper into the vast collection, like the flip of the shiny penny in my pocket, I gain a new perspective and develop a plan. While spending the summer on the boat with the guys is tempting, if I learn enough about the family business to keep my father satisfied, maybe I can finish what Mom started. Then I can return to what really matters to me. Hockey.

My fingers trail along the leather spines of old books until I find the section on 19th-century America and land on a thick volume about Civil War-era correspondence. I reach for it just as someone on the opposite side of the shelf does the same thing.

"Excuse me, but proper handling requires a permission ticket to access this book, and as I was already authorized—" The voice is muffled by the shelf between us, but I recognize Juliana's sweet purr.

"I know how to handle a book," I say, not letting go. Plus, I'm an executive. Technically, do I need authorization?

She peers through the gap between volumes. A pair of pretty gray eyes widens when they meet mine.

"What are you doing down here, Julieta?" I ask, my tone cocky.

"Cross-referencing something from the Eaton Boyd report."

"Something unsubstantiated?" I accuse when really any questions should be leveled at me, having said the first historical name that came to mind and having no need to receive a report about the Indiana governor's art collection during the nineteenth century. I figured it was best to keep her busy.

She bites her lip. "I was, uh, just wondering if, after Eaton Boyd died, the portrait of his wife stayed in his family or if it went back to the royal collection—she was quite the rebel aristocrat."

"Why'd you want to know that?" I ask, voice flat because she should be upstairs doing assistant-type things—whatever those are.

Pink-cheeked and apologetic, she shrugs. "It was romantic."

I grunt but can't avoid the sincerity and curiosity in her gray gaze.

Then she sasses back, "It's not like you gave me anything else to do."

That changes now. I have a plan and Juliana will be

helping me with it whether she likes it or not. But one thing is non-negotiable. She is my employee, nothing more. This has to remain professional.

My free hand finds the lucky penny in my pocket, the back worn smooth from years of rubbing my thumb over it. Lincoln's profile reminds me why I'm here, buried in dusty archives instead of taking chances on pretty researchers with romantic notions.

"Romance." The word tastes bitter. "People read too much into it. Make up love stories that probably weren't there."

I can almost see my mother wagging her finger at me, wondering why I've resolved to find the lost love letters if I think romance is foolish. Ask any of the women I've dated. I'm not a prime example of relationship material.

Juliana still watches me as if waiting for a smile, to hear a titter like I'm joking. Instead, I pop the bubble of any such notion.

"Romance is just wishful thinking, Buttercup," I mutter.

My grip on the book doesn't loosen. Neither does hers.

This almost feels like another kind of challenge—the opposite of how she dared me to get rid of her.

9

JULES

TOWARD THE END of the week, according to Jeannie's "tea time" reports relayed to me in code via the ever-loyal Wendy and Carmen, it comes to my attention that Veronica and Misha are bitter because they were "demoted."

Apparently, Ms. Drecken's assistants are turning other coworkers against me in whispers and stares because they want to aid the handsome new exec.

It's not like I had a say in the matter. They can park outside his office and receive his steely glare all day for all I care.

My glowy Care Bear heart isn't cut out for this kind of toxic office culture. After my run-in with Sullivan on the reference floor, we've kept a safe distance from each other. The man has a firm grip, a wicked stare, and a smug smile I'd like to kiss off his face—I mean, strangle. You know, if that weren't so violent.

Also, I'm still not sure what happened to the painting in the Eaton Boyd Collection. For now, the mystery remains unsolved because Mr. Party Pooper wanted me to review the Ellicott Collection—a bachelor without a loving bone in his body, according to reports.

That will have to wait because with a stack of Post-its, I create a different vision. Have a new mission. I'm out to prove that not all corporate employees need to be drones and not all executives need to be sons of Satan—Drecken may as well be his bride.

I am going to rise to the top with grace all the way. After all, that's my middle name. Someday, when I run this place, we'll celebrate Mondays with pastries from Flour Hour (that's for you, Wendy!), have a group game night, and wear casual attire on Fridays (come in with your favorite Hawaiian-print dress, Carmen!).

I can see the future as I sit upon a cotton candy throne with not a single member of the Meridian community hating me. In fact, the current top executives will wonder why they were doing things so backward.

However, between now and then, I've mastered the art of sneaking down to the Collections Processing Department when Mr. Sullivan is out for lunch. I'm like a cat whose family moved and keeps returning to its old house, hoping for a saucer of cream. It should be noted that Carmen keeps the good stuff in the break room fridge and doesn't mind when I add a splash. We collectively fear that the non-perishable "creamer" in those tiny cups contains formaldehyde.

My visits to the thirty-third floor have become an oasis in my work day—a brief respite where I can actually breathe without Sullivan's disapproving stare following my every move.

On my way, I leave happy little sticky notes on the desks of all whom I pass.

"Juliana!" Wendy pops up from the supply closet when I announce my arrival.

Carmen bustles over from a filing cabinet. "We were discussing your new boss situation earlier."

I slump into the empty chair at my old desk. At least I haven't been replaced, yet. "Situations have exits. This does not."

"But this is what you wanted." Wendy chirps, far too cheerful for a Thursday afternoon.

I rub my temples where a headache is starting to fester.

I wanted to finish my degree without being saddled with all of my father's debts, then maybe get a real position in acquisitions or authentication. Not become someone's glorified gopher. I've met Matt and have utmost respect for the dorky kid fresh out of college who wears suits that he'll soon fill out if he indulges in the board meeting pastries to quell his sadness.

"The truth is, I should be grateful. A job means security, at least for now. But why does it have to be with *him*?"

"Can we talk about how dreamy he is?" Jeannie appears with a folder, fanning herself dramatically before dropping it off and slipping away. Of course, this snippet will make its rounds through the building, likely morphing into the latest hot gossip.

"Silver fox," Wendy adds with a long sigh.

"I don't see any gray hair," I protest.

"We mean foxy," Wendy clarifies.

"Who are we talking about?" I glance between them, confused.

"Objectively speaking," they chorus.

My eyes widen in question.

Wendy leans forward conspiratorially. "Don't tell me

you don't know. Mr. Sullivan is the head of the company's son."

The words are slow to process, like the geriatric computers in the mailroom.

"We know exactly what he'll look like when he ages. These are the kind of good genes you look for when you get older." Carmen, with her cat-eyes, winks.

My stomach drops. But they must be wrong. The big boss is Frank Andresen. The ogre who occupies the chair adjacent to my new office is Mr. L. Sullivan.

"Jeannie says, and I quote, 'Andresen is scary hot in that intimidating billionaire way,'" Wendy continues, oblivious to my internal meltdown. "'Can you imagine what Linc will look like in twenty years?'"

Frank Andresen has steel-gray hair and piercing blue eyes that seem to see straight through a person and into their soul. He commands every room he enters. The fact that I practically lied to his face last week, while in a hostage situation with Sullivan and his buddy, is an anomaly. Though technically, I intended to visit the Research and Reference Department.

As much as I wanted to go boating with the dangerously attractive Eastern European giant and see if, when water touched Mr. Sullivan's skin, he'd hiss and deflate like a movie monster turning to dust, I didn't want to get fired.

Wendy's eyes cloud over. "I'm having a secondhand crush just watching you two interact."

Mine bulge. "You're what? We're not—we don't—when did you see us interact?" I ask, struggling to get the words out.

"At the quarterly meeting yesterday, in the hallway, outside the east elevator." Carmen nods pointedly.

Wendy counts off on her fingers. "You two have a

certain kind of magnetism. Chemistry. A sizzle. It's undeniable."

But deny it I will. *'Til the death!*

"Admit he's handsome." Wendy smiles sweetly.

Carmen's hand lands on her hip.

I'm not getting out of here before Sullivan is back at his desk upstairs unless I cave.

Clearing my throat, I say, "He's fine."

"Nineties slang F-I-N-E fine?" Carmen asks.

Wendy closes her eyes and nods as if our coworker speaks the truth.

We go back and forth for a few more minutes before I lose the battle as they scale new heights and dredge deep lows by claiming my boss and I are at the budding stage of what'll blossom into an office romance. When I was still working down here, because I was the only single lady, they appointed themselves matchmakers. Last season, they even submitted my name as a contestant for the "Sweetheart Report." They'll never stop unless I relent.

Arms firmly crossed like a barricade in front of my chest, I say, "My boss is objectively attractive in a ruggedly handsome way that's completely at odds with his stodgy executive status. This is not one of those stories that will end with us going from bitter nemeses to madly in love."

"But why not?" Wendy frowns like I claimed her baby is hideous.

"For one, he's my boss. For two, he's horrible. For three, he's not my type."

"Why isn't he your type?" Carmen asks.

As if I'd ever date that beast in a three-piece suit.

"He's terrifying," I say.

"Terrifyingly attractive," Wendy pipes.

"He has a resting brute face. He made Suzie in Licensing and Rights Management cry."

Carmen sighs. "But she's so sweet."

"Exactly." I flip my hand, gesturing to put a fine point on it. "He's not my type because I'm pretty much his maid and I'd prefer a guy who tidies up his own messes."

"Does he make you clean up after him?" Carmen asks, aghast.

I waffle. "Well, no."

"So you're more like a personal assistant. Do you have to fetch his coffee?"

"No, but—"

Wendy whispers, "Does he want you to do other things? We could report him to HR for you."

"No, it's nothing like that." I push back the cuticle on my thumb. "I got my dream job, researcher and archivist, in responsibility only. Not in name. I'm his Special Projects Assistant and get zero respect—"

"You have that look," Wendy interrupts, studying my expression like an art authenticator examining a suspicious Monet.

"I do not. Whatever expression you see on my face is one of loathing. Deep, unadulterated hatred."

They both laugh like I'm Ken from shipping and receiving, who is ready with a new "dad joke" whenever he rolls through.

"The man is minty," I continue, desperate to make my point.

Carmen inhales dreamily. "I bet he smells ah-may-zing."

"Like mint?" Wendy asks.

"Probably more like a rat that just crawled out of a sewer and then stepped in dog—"

"Then what did you mean by minty?" Wendy interrupts again.

I search for the right words. "You know, harsh. Sharp. Like he could cut you down with a single look."

But even as I say it, I remember the way his aftershave lingered in the elevator earlier—clean and crisp.

"Speaking of your minty boss," Carmen says, glancing at her computer screen, "you might want to head back upstairs. He just sent out a company-wide email asking for you."

My stomach lurches. "What kind of email?"

"The kind that says, 'Has anyone seen Julita? I need her in my office immediately.' I assume that's you."

"He still doesn't know your name?" Wendy whispers as if she's about to get in trouble by proxy.

"He certainly knows it, but doesn't hesitate to call me anything other than Juliana. Most recently, he referred to me as Buttercup."

Wendy bounces a little. "Like from Princess Bride? That means he's your Westley."

"You'll fall in love after peril and a grand gesture—a declaration of devotion!" Now Carmen has gone over the top.

"Never." I roll my eyes, but before I can fume, I take my leave.

10

JULES

THE ELEVATOR RIDE to the top floor runs at half speed like a poorly calibrated vinyl record. Where is an executive with his badge when you need one? Oh, right, sending out a company-wide email inquiring about my whereabouts. Why does he *need* me, anyway? My inner romantic reads into the phrasing and I very quickly put it in the time-out chair. Next stop, the naughty step.

Between floors thirty-three and thirty-nine, then down the long hallway, my thoughts jump from him reprimanding me for leaving the office, to gradually worsening scenarios.

Maybe someone saw me take those fancy gel highlighters from the supply closet recently. It wasn't stealing, exactly, more like gathering supplies for when I'm working from home. Sometimes my colleagues ask for my help with their projects. It's not my fault, which often results in longer hours, some of them at home.

Perhaps Sullivan discovered I don't actually have my degree.

I knock on his office door, thankful my shoes aren't squeaky today.

"Come in, Julian." Mr. Sullivan stands behind his desk, rolling up his shirt sleeve as if preparing for a fight ... or to tease me with his toned forearms that could've been chiseled from marble by a master craftsman.

"You wanted to see me, Mr. Sullivan?" Concurrently, I ask my cheeks to remain their normal shade because ... forearms.

"Call me Linc," he says without looking up.

That explains L. Sullivan, but not what the office girlies downstairs were saying about him supposedly being Mr. Andresen's son. They must've been mistaken.

Mustering boldness, I say, "Then you call me by my name. Juliana."

"Okay, Julana." He works on the other shirt sleeve now, folding the fabric neatly.

My eyes glaze over, then I give my head a shake to come out of this stupor. I speak slowly and with emphasis when I say, "It's Jul*i*ana."

Jewel-EEE-ah-na! It's not hard unless you're a dumb butt.

He finally looks up, and I catch the ghost of a smirk playing at the corners of his mouth. "My apologies, Miss Lindley."

The way he says my last name with confidence suggests he does indeed know my correct first name. His voice is like a whisper to awaken the butterflies sleeping in my stomach.

"I have a new project for you," he continues, tapping the papers on his desk and showcasing firm muscles against tan skin.

"What about the Gettysburg painting authentication?" I ask, referring to another task he saddled me with.

"We'll be doing both."

Of course, he'd double my workload. I bite back my initial response and settle for, "Lucky me."

His lips twitch. "I need you to research its provenance." And then he starts to mansplain the concept.

"I know what provenance is," I interrupt, then immediately regret it when his eyebrows rise.

"Do you?"

"The ownership history of a piece. Documentation proving its authenticity and legal ownership through time."

"Good." His tone is patronizing enough to make my teeth clench. "Then you'll understand the importance of being thorough."

Rifling through the papers, he mentions wooing an obscure investor, a postmaster named Eli Ligget from Indiana, and tracking down handwritten letters that may or may not exist. It's confusing, scattered, and seems like he and another exec made a bet, and whoever lost had to take on the project. Though I vaguely recognize the name from my Eaton Boyd research.

"Any questions?" he asks when he's finished.

"Only about eighteen hundred," I mutter, starting with why he looks so good in those glasses and ending with whether he's always this impossible or if it's just a special gift he reserves for me. Instead, I go with, "When do you need this completed?"

"By the end of the week."

"This Friday?"

"Is that a problem?"

"That's tomorrow."

"Oh. Right," he says as if he's been boating with his buddy and lost track of time. I happen to know he hasn't been on the water since he broods at his desk all day or staring down at the sheet of glassy liquid below the building.

"By the end of the month, then."

"That's in two weeks."

Shall I lady-splain that these types of projects take time? Lots of time, especially if I'm the only one working on it.

"Would you like help?" I can't read his sarcasm meter.

"Not from you," I blurt like a ball rolling downhill.

A shadow crosses his features. "You know what? You're a real peach, Yulia."

My lip juts out as I try to decide whether I should be offended or lean into the sass and his repeated misuse of my name.

Glitter, Juliana. Use the glitter!

But I don't. I possibly do something worse. "If that's the case," my voice drops, "then bite me."

The words are like typewriter keys striking paper, leaving behind ink that cannot be deleted by the simple pressing of the *backspace* button. My heart stops, restarts, then tries to pound its way out of my chest.

Those are fighting words, and we both know it.

Instead of backing down or apologizing, I square my shoulders and meet his gaze dead-on.

And wouldn't you know it, the guy's lips quirk, and he says, "Bite you? Gladly."

The silence that follows is so charged I'm surprised the smoke alarm doesn't go off, telling us to evacuate the building.

Instead, I skedaddle to my desk. It's only when I'm seated that I realize I'm trembling and the full weight of what just happened hits me. I just told my boss—possibly the son of the Meridian CEO—to bite me. In a tone that could generously be described as flirtatious and accurately be labeled as career suicide.

What have I done?

I'm convinced I'll be fired before the end of the day. I refresh the company app. Keep my email inbox updated. But I'm still employed when I ride the Blue Line to my studio apartment.

My phone buzzes with a text from my mom just as I'm fishing my keys out of my bag. After greetings that include a vague "work is fine" recap, she asks if I'll be able to make it to her and Brad the Dad's anniversary dinner in September.

I'm about to respond when Screechy and Grumbly—the couple next door—start their nightly argument through our paper-thin walls. Tonight's topic appears to be a criticism of how to best dispense toothpaste—from the bottom of the tube, obviously. One of them presses from the middle, sending the bulk of the paste in the wrong direction.

I consider telling Mom about Linc Sullivan, the disaster that is my professional life, and the fact that I may have just flirted my way out of employment. Instead, I go with a promise to try to make it home for the anniversary party.

After we end the call, I'm settling in with leftover pizza and my streaming queue when my phone buzzes with a notification from the company app. My blood freezes when I see the sender: L. Sullivan.

This is it. I'm unemployed. I read the message.

> L. Sullivan: Need you to review the Fairfax Collection files tonight. Send. notes. Meeting with a client first thing Monday morning.

Frozen, I try to ignore the text bubble as my pizza grows cold in my lap. The Fairfax Collection is in a different department. A Friday night work request sent via the company app is verboten.

This is either a power trip of epic proportions or he's testing to see how far he can push me before I break. Maybe he wants me to quit. Perhaps he's a sucker for finding his stapler jiggling in a dome of gelatin.

I'm not above petty pranks.

The man brings out the worst in me. The sarcastic, rebellious side that got me in trouble throughout high school and college. The part of me that my mother gently referred to as "spirited" and my professors called "challenging."

I type and delete at least four responses, ranging from acquiescence to suggestions about where he can file his request. Finally, I just get to work.

AFTER WORKING all day Saturday and after church the following day, I meet Oly for our standing monthly brunch at Toast, a hipster joint that takes the concept of avocado toast and elevates it to an art form.

I order the "Renaissance" (multigrain bread with ricotta, honey, and fresh berries). Oly goes with her usual "Minimalist" (butter and sea salt, because she claims it lets her taste the bread's true essence).

"You look tired," she says as we sip our jumbo lattes—you could swim in the mugs they have here.

"Good morning to you, too." She's not wrong. I hope the caffeine is fast-acting.

Oly has been my best friend since college, back when we used to spend entire weekends sharing clothes and staying up until what she called the wee hours, analyzing every interaction we'd had with whatever guy had caught our attention that week. Things are different now that she's married. I'm happy for her, but I miss our marathon debrief sessions.

After we get our food, I pop a raspberry into my mouth.

She says, "Talk to me."

I tell her about the job change, about Linc and his impossible demands, and the way he makes me feel like I'm constantly on the verge of saying something I'll regret—or outright running my mouth. I conclude with the weekend work request, er, demand.

Her nostrils flare, righteously angry on my behalf. "The absolute nerve of some people."

"Right? And the worst part is, he's ..." I struggle for the right words.

She inclines her head. "Attractive?"

She knows me so well. "Insufferably so."

She sing-songs. "You're in trouble."

"I despise him and he abhors me. That's the way it is and how it will always be."

"Uh-huh." She doesn't sound convinced.

"I may have also taken something from the office," I add quietly.

"Juliana Lindley!"

"It was just gel highlighters ... and some Post-its. Turns out I put them to good use."

Oly gives me the look—the same one when I'd suggest skipping class to go to the Art Institute or when I'd spend my meal plan money on books instead of food.

It's not like I forged my diploma or anything. Oh, wait. I did do that. However, no one can know that tiny detail if I am going to avoid having to move back in with Mom and Brad the Dad.

ON MONDAY MORNING, I drag myself into the office like I'm at the prison gates, starting a life sentence. Linc is already at his desk when I arrive, looking annoyingly fresh and put-together in a way that suggests he actually gets eight hours of sleep instead of lying awake wondering if his research assistant is a fraud.

"The Fairfax files, Julissa?" he asks without preamble.

I grumble and then hand over the folder, trying not to notice how his fingers brush mine during the exchange or the way his aftershave makes me want to lean close ... and yeah, like the little weirdo that I am, press my nose to his neck and inhale.

The office girlies are right about one thing. Linc is handsome in an effortless way that has probably gotten him out of trouble for his entire life. Dark hair and deep blue eyes behind a pair of glasses that make him look distinguished. I imagine that he's picture-perfect right out of the shower. Not that I would ever think about that.

Only problem, and it's gigantic—along with his ego—it turns out his personality is awful.

Thankfully, he's gone most of the day, but returns just before it's time to clock out. He says, "The Fairfax files were thorough."

I pause at the door, hand gripping the frame. My back to him. "Is that a compliment or is there a *but* coming?"

His gaze drifts up and down my body. Or he's worried about the finish on the wood framing as my nails dig into it.

Warmth rises up my neck and wraps around my cheeks

like a hug from behind, but that can't be right. There's no way this man is appreciating my assets. Though I am wearing my favorite skirt.

Peeking over my shoulder, his gaze lingers on my legs—last I checked, they're nothing special. He's probably calculating the quickest way to push me out a window.

11

LINC

COACH CAN PUT me through a series of ten-pass chaos drills, and I won't so much as raise an objection. I leave nothing but sweat on the ice.

But put me behind a desk all day, and I want to take a nap. I admit, I've dozed off more than once in the last couple of weeks since taking on the title Executive Curatorial Officer. It's a junior position even though it's part of the executive department, meaning it's pending until my father decides I'm not COO or CEO material, like he hopes.

In addition to the search for the letters, his team sends assignments to me on the inter-office app. Because I have no interest, I pass them off to Juliana.

Yes, it's inconsiderate and unprofessional.

No, I'm not entirely clueless about the operations around here.

But being in this building instead of taking a summer break after a grueling hockey season makes my brain feel like it was soaked in gasoline and lit on fire. Dramatic, I know. However, I have zero interest in filling my father's shoes—they're the kind that only go in one direction.

Away.

Plus, my assistant is competent and seems to enjoy art history, and if I'm entirely honest, I enjoy her even—especially when—she's self-righteous and sassy.

Why do I keep having these thoughts?

I'm probably more useful at home. Where I have a couch. Can put on the ceiling fan. Wear athletic shorts, no shoes, and close my eyes.

I exit my office into the reception area, where Juliana studies something on her computer screen. Her long, shiny hair cascades over her shoulders. She tilts her head as if considering a chess move and then bites her lip before clicking her mouse to move the cursor.

Deceptively innocent. I swallow thickly.

As if sensing me watching like a creep, she snaps those sugar eyes of hers my way. I've noticed her watching me ... also like a creep. She thinks I'm attractive even if she claims to despise me. Takes one to know one.

Gaze straying to me as if she's deciding between two painfully boring options, she returns to her work.

Voice sleepier than it should be, I say, "I've decided there are two kinds of people in this world. People who take naps and those who consume vast amounts of coffee in order to get through the day."

Her eyes flit to the thermos on her desk and then at me as if I just confessed that I'm an alien from outer space. "Is that a problem?"

If it wasn't clear, she's the latter. I'm the former—a napper.

I want to tell her it's not an indictment of her character. I was just making an observation. Talking to her the same way I would to anyone when I realize that I let my Mr. Executive mask slip. Since setting foot in this building, I've played the role of hard-nosed administrative manager and now I've revealed my human side.

My lips quirk with a smile.

Her expression darkens. "Well, Mr. Sullivan, thank you for illuminating me with your theories."

We got off on the wrong foot. I admit that. I'm afraid it's too late to change course. At least with the way she's staring daggers at me. Hockey stick in hand, I'd double down. Here, I'm on thin ice.

Her cute kitten looks make me want to soften, to scratch her belly. But I know better. She has claws hidden under those painted nails.

"Don't let me distract you. Have those reports done by the end of the day, Hoolia."

"Going to find somewhere more comfortable to nap?" she mutters, apparently having abandoned her attempt to correct me when I use the wrong version of her name. "And for the fifty-seventh time, it's Juliana." She makes a note on a Post-it, gets up, and sticks it on my chest.

My hand traps hers before she can pull it away.

She stifles a gasp as she looks up and peels her hand away while I remove the note.

It says *Juliana.*

It's like she's marking me.

She glares at me with fire in her eyes.

Or not.

With a snort, I head toward the elevator. As I ride down, having left my assistant with the run of the office, I imagine her propping her feet up on my desk like Bīriņš did when he made an unannounced visit. Actually, she'll probably booby-trap it. I'll have to check for whoopee cushions and thumbtacks in the morning.

It's probably not good for us to be together in the same small space. We're like fire and ice.

After almost twenty minutes in midday traffic, by the time I get back to my condo and loosen my tie, I realize Juliana has occupied my mind the entire time.

My jaw aches from clenching it because after I talk to her, I feel like I've just chowed down on a dump truck full of gravel painted to look like a bowl of ice cream.

She somehow brings out the worst in me and I kind of hate myself for it. My muscles tingle with restless energy. So much for a nap. I change into running clothes to burn off whatever it is she does to me.

FOR THE REST of the week, I remain in the office all day like a good little worker drone. On Friday, the summer sun gleams off the tower, promising heat as I park underground.

Just outside the office door on the thirty-ninth floor, an older woman with a floral shirt stops me in the hall. Peering up at me through thick glasses, she says, "Linc? I thought that was you. My, you've grown up."

Unfortunately, I don't recognize her, but I assume she's been here since I was a kid and would tag along with Mom.

I offer a standard reply. "Like a plant, if you give kids water, they tend to grow."

With a sweet smile, she says, "You've turned into a fine young man. Your mother would be so proud."

That twists the little acorn of grief inside that I fear will never go away. "Did you know her?"

The woman's grin shifts into one of apology on my behalf. "I'm Nancy Dowds. Your mother and I met in junior college. She was still Mary Sullivan back then. We were both broke, so we'd share lunch. Kept us trim." She pats her ample belly and smiles. "Times have changed."

This woman's identity still isn't ringing a bell, but my mother made best friends every time she went to the grocery store, so it's no surprise that she'd know long-term Meridian employees. However, we're not advertising that I'm the chief executive officer's son, so I hope she doesn't call it out.

The door to the office is cracked open and more than likely, Juliana is already at her desk. I sniff the air and detect her telltale cherry blossom and almond scent. Then again, it somehow fills the office even when she's not here.

Nancy goes on to tell me about the time Mom brought everyone little chocolate acorn treats. She bounces as if she can still taste them.

I'd help make the little peanut butter cookie balls, shape them like an acorn, dip them in chocolate, then add another chocolate "cap," and roll them in chopped peanuts, topped with a little pretzel stick stem.

"Acorns were her thing," I mumble.

Nancy shakes her head with regret. "It goes without saying, but I'm sorry for your loss. You were so young. She was, too. It's a shame."

"Thank you, ma'am. That means a lot." And I mean it sincerely. I gobble up whatever stories about my mother I can, like cookie crumbs.

She gazes upward slightly and adds, "And your father was never the same."

She's got that right, but it's time for this conversation to be over.

Instead, she launches into another tale about how, when I'd visit the office with my mom, I'd wear a little suit to match my dad. "I bet he's proud to have you here, preparing to take over the Meridian empire."

And that's the nail in the coffin.

Ending the conversation as gracefully as I can, I say, "I'm not too sure about that. But thanks for remembering my mother. I hope you have a good day and a great weekend."

Placing a pudgy hand on my arm, she gives it a tap and then totters down the hall.

Taking a lungful of air, I smooth my tie and enter the office, complete with a coffee for my assistant because I'm ... trying not to be a total jerk and make up for what she thought was an insult last week. It's just not in me to be so mean. At least, off the ice.

12

LINC

AS I ENTER THE OFFICE, instead of welcoming me with a "good morning,"—not that I ever greet Juliana that way—Juliana says, "So it was true. You're Andresen's son."

I hold out the paper coffee cup.

Her lips drop with a frown. "This isn't Medieval times. I'm not your cupbearer. Nowhere in my job description does it say I have to test your coffee to make sure it's not poisoned. Believe it or not, there are people in this world who love me and don't want me dead."

I blink a few times, mouth agape. The comment was delivered so dryly, I can't tell if she's joking. "It's coffee for you."

Her head bobs slightly. "Oh. Well, thank you."

She reluctantly takes it and curls her fingers in such a way that they don't come into contact with mine. Peering up at me, she asks, "Did you tamper with it?"

"What? Why would I?"

"You're under oath, sir."

A ghost of a smile floats onto my lips. "No, Goolia. I did not."

She flashes me a playful, sassy look. "If I die, the blood is on your hands."

"For the record, someone who'd do something like that probably wouldn't admit it."

She pouts as if hating that I'm right. Eyes narrowed with suspicion, she sniffs the coffee, which is more cream than anything caffeinated—how I noticed she likes it.

"You trained me to be wary," she says.

I know the feeling. I suppose it was only a matter of time before people found out I'm the son of the company president. Dad wants to keep it quiet and certainly doesn't want to advertise that I'm a jock, either—his words—rather than the reality that I'm a professional athlete.

I turn to go into my office, then pause. Lips tight, I answer her question, "About being an Andresen, it's an unadvertised fact. Let's keep it that way."

"That explains a lot." Her eyes flash.

Nancy's reminders of my mother softened me, but now it's like Juliana just aimed a ray gun my way, lighting up our ongoing, slow-burning bickering. "What's that supposed to mean?"

"You're competitive about everything and obviously not at all happy to have a veritable summer internship."

"My father is hard to say no to." Especially when he insists this is what Mom would've wanted for me. But Juliana doesn't need to know that.

She juts her chin toward the door and the hall where I'd been chatting with Nancy. "You're charming when you want to be."

So she did overhear.

"But I get the sense you'd rather be on the boat with your buddy."

"You're not wrong."

"So is this tough love? You've been on one long party barge bender and now your father wants you to take life seriously?"

I almost burst into laughter. Party-barge-bender? Far from it. My life has consisted of years of early morning practice, dryland training, and intense games. Disciplined diet. Managing every minute of my day. Then again, Bīriņš does have a Viking Motor Yacht, set up for fishing and wakeboarding. It's large, as he likes to point out, but it's not a barge.

Juliana must think I'm a rich kid screwup. I cannot hide the smirk on my face because nothing is further from the truth. Unlike some guys, hockey skills didn't immediately come to me. I wasn't born with a stick in my hand and skates on my feet, but I loved the feeling of playing—and winning—so much that I worked my butt off to make it onto a college team. Then the NHL was purely something I earned after essentially throwing away any semblance of a social life and turning my focus entirely to the ice, the puck, and the purpose of getting it into the goal.

"A spoiled billionaire brat. I bet you'd like that to be true," I say.

She shrugs and shakes her head slightly as if not sure how to respond ... for once. I've observed Juliana enough to know she's not a genuinely mean or rude person. Quite the opposite, actually, but there is something about the two of us in the same space that sets the room on fire while the other fans the flames.

Squaring my shoulders, I ask, "What's your impression of me?"

She tilts her head, studying me like I'm a painting with a questionable attribution. "Do you want the diplomatic version or the honest one?"

I can't help chuckling lightly. "Try me."

"You're a trust fund man-boy who thinks value is something you can buy and sell." Her voice is matter-of-fact, no malice. Just brutal honesty. "You probably have an MBA purchased with a generous endowment and three different pairs of boat shoes."

I can't help but laugh. "Four, actually." I don't, but the way her eyes flare makes me want to hear more.

"Of course you do." But there's the hint of a smile tugging at her lips. "You see dollar signs where I see stories. You're here because Daddy made you, not because you care about preserving history."

"And yet you helped me out with said daddy in the lobby when Bīriņš wanted to take us boating." I lean against her desk. "Why?"

And why do I like her raw honesty—even if slightly off base—to all the "pick me" puckering up from most of the women I meet.

The smile disappears. "Because even a privileged chucklechump deserves basic human decency."

I bark a laugh. "Chucklechump?"

"You asked for honest."

"Chucklechump?" I repeat. "That's a new one."

"*Chuckle* because you approach everything in life like it's amusing and *chump* because I was trying to think of a word that wouldn't get me sent to HR. In my defense, you asked me to be honest. If you are going to apply disciplinary measures, that's my defense."

I brush my thumb over my bottom lip only so I don't burst into laughter. "No detention for you today, Miss Lindley."

I'd had her full attention and she quickly looks away as if ready to get back to work, but this is just getting interesting. I study her face, looking for cracks in that pretty facade. "So what would it take to change your mind about me?"

She arches an eyebrow. "So you're saying that I'm wrong?"

I shrug nonchalantly because why would I care what she thinks of me? Why do I?

Lifting her chin, she says, "Show me you care about something other than profit margins and naps."

"Sounds like a dare."

"Do you choose to accept this mission?"

It cannot be helped, I laugh again. How can she be so funny and insolent at the same time?

"Your turn. What's your impression of me?" The words seem to tumble out before she can catch them as her face immediately shifts—eyes widening slightly before she presses her lips together, like she's trying to swallow the question back down. Instead, she takes a sip of coffee. Her cheeks flush pink and she suddenly finds something fascinating about the papers on her desk, shuffling them unnecessarily.

Rocking back on my heels, I fold my arms in front of my chest, trying to think as my father would. He'd say Juliana is idealistic and impractical—someone who prioritizes the story behind the art over factual details and makes decisions based on emotion rather than business sense.

"I mean—" She clears her throat, smile wavering in a way that suggests damage control. "Not that it matters what you think, obviously."

But the vulnerability leaked through for just a split second, and we both know I caught it.

"You really want to know?" I ask, softer now.

She lifts her chin and pulls up the drawbridge—I

imagine there are crocodiles in the moat surrounding her castle. "Forget I asked."

"Too late." I drop my hands down on her desk and lean forward, capturing her gray eyes. But the harsh, corporate exec script falls away. Instead, the truth escapes. "You're passionate about things on your heart. Whip-smart in a way that makes me feel like I'm constantly playing catch-up. And you have an ability to see beauty in old paintings that makes me wonder what else I've been missing."

She goes still.

"But you also drive me absolutely insane because you act like I'm some kind of corporate villain." To be fair, that's the role I've been playing.

"Not a villain exactly." She speaks quietly, still not meeting my eyes. "More like ..."

"What?"

Finally, she looks up. "Exactly what I expect from the thirty-ninth floor." The disappointment in her voice hits harder than any insult could have. "Oh, and I helped you out in the lobby because my father left me with a pile of debt rather than a successful empire. Maybe try caring a little. You have no idea how much you've been blessed."

My breath skids and my throat tightens because she must carry around an acorn of grief, too. "I'm sorry for your loss."

She nods somberly. "Yours too."

"It was a long time ago." I look away because even after all this time, I still miss my mom.

"What was her name?" Juliana's tone is gentle instead of the sharp, adversarial one used in our back-and-forth banter.

My defensive posture melts and I smile like I would at a friend.

And just like that, something shifts between us.

13

JULES

MY BOSS HAS a faraway look in his eyes. When he doesn't answer my question, I repeat it. Someone once told me that people die twice. The first, when they pass from this earth, and the second is when their name is finally lost to history. I have no intention of being immortalized in any way, but I think it's important to remember our dead. If we don't, we could get too close to forgetting that we're still alive.

"What was your mother's name?"

For the first time since L. Sullivan entered my life, he looks more human. Almost vulnerable.

"My mom's name was Marie," he says finally. "Marie Sullivan Andresen."

"Ah. That's where the Sullivan comes from." I wonder if it was to honor her, if it's his middle name, he's playing "undercover boss," or if he really doesn't want to be associated with his father.

That hardly tracks because a guy like him would want to shout that he's an Andresen from the rooftops for clout, to leverage the name and the connection at every opportunity. Right?

Linc tells me a bit about his mom, including how she taught him that a mighty oak tree was once a tiny acorn.

Thinking about my own mom, my voice is tender when I say, "She seemed like a special lady."

His eyebrows lift with surprise.

I add, "I'm not being sarcastic."

"She was. She loved books, romance stories especially. Used to say they reminded her that love is worth the risk."

"She was right."

He blows an exhale through his lips as if disagreeing. "She was crazy about art—in museums and nature. Whether it was a long line for a new exhibition or the first blossoms of the season, she said it was proof that beautiful things are worth waiting for."

"Once again, I agree. Wise woman."

This is not the cocky consultant I've been sparring with all these weeks. It's like someone just switched out the painting I was studying for a completely different piece—same frame, entirely new picture.

He continues, "She was a woman of great faith. Not the preachy kind, but the lived-out kind. She helped me believe things would work out, even when they looked impossible."

"I would've loved to have been able to meet her." And I cannot imagine a woman like that married to the dreaded Andresen. Then again, grief changes people.

Linc pauses. "She would have liked you, actually. She had a thing for people who spoke their minds."

I lean forward slightly. "Even when their 'minds' are telling you that you're wrong about everything?"

"Especially then." He almost smiles. I bet it would transform his entire, stony face.

"Is that so?"

"She used to say the most dangerous person in any room was the one who agreed with everyone."

I nod, inspired by that insight and feeling oddly honored by the comparison to someone who clearly meant the world to Linc. For a moment, the guy I've told myself I hate disappears. We're just two people talking about someone special.

He sits halfway on my desk. Before, I would've thought he parked himself here to prove me wrong, but now I wonder if he intends to continue this conversation. After seeing these two different sides of Linc, I'm not sure. Then again, I've been anything but my usual cheerful self around him.

"You give off only child energy. Am I right?" I ask.

His expression falters just slightly. "My mom had the kind of cancer that kept her from having more kids."

My heart breaks. "I'm sorry, I didn't—"

"It's fine." He waves me off as if allergic to pity.

Returning to familiar ground, I tease, "Maybe that's a good thing. The world probably only needs one of you."

Behind Linc's glasses, his eyes crescent with mirth. "I imagine you're the little sister type. Am I right?"

I huff but fight a smile as I cock my head. "Are you saying I'm a brat?" The man has clearly never met my family.

"I'm saying you have 'youngest sibling energy.' You know—charming, says and does whatever she wants, gets away with everything, and probably had everyone wrapped around her cute little finger."

Cute, huh? My lips ripple with a smile. "Actually, I'm the oldest."

His eyebrows climb slightly toward his hairline. "I stand corrected."

"In addition to working nights at The Lucky Nugget Casino as a showgirl, returning home in time to get me off to school. She'd also pull the day shift at a nearby diner. Then Brad the Dad swept her off her feet, they got married, and had triplets. Life changed significantly after that. Although those snot-nosed goobers were annoying, we had a family. The boys are four years younger than me, so they're twenty-three now."

"Triplets? Three babies at once?" he asks as if only just now grasping the concept of multiples.

"Bryce, Brian, and Brody. The 'bros.'" I roll my eyes, but there's affection there too. Can't help it—they're annoying, but they're family. "They work in sports now. One wants to be a coach, another's in sports marketing, and the third thinks he's going to be the next big sports broadcaster."

He shifts slightly as if uncomfortable. "Let me guess—they forbid you from dating anyone. Would try to embarrass you in front of the boys you brought home. Would be obnoxious any time—"

My stomach flips. The comment makes me feel like I was walking down a set of stairs and missed the bottom step.

"It wasn't like that." What I mean to say is that I didn't bring boys home. "They're protective in theory, jokester jocks in practice. Think of them as overgrown, hyper puppies who never nap." I give him a pointed look. "Unlike some people I know."

"Hey, I don't nap—"

"You literally have a pillow stashed in the drawer of the shelving unit in your office."

He starts to defend himself because it's not true, but then says, "Have you been poking through my things?"

"No, I'm just observant." Affronted by the accusation, I straighten my posture.

Without advance notice, an application, or so much as a choice, I was promoted to exec assistant. Fishy. So, of course, temptation dangled like a carrot on a stick. I gave in and snooped around L. Sullivan's office. It could not be helped. Disappointingly, I didn't even find anything interesting—not even a pillow. I made that up.

Linc pushes to standing and stretches. I watch, half expecting his shirt to lift and expose his trim waist, a tease of toned abs. Just assuming. The guy is one big muscle under his suit, given the way the fabric hugs him. But his shirt remains firmly tucked in. However, making a half turn toward his office, he cradles his head in his hands like he does during naptime. I only know this because once, he left the door cracked open.

Linc's eyes graze over me as if he's counting every freckle on my nose, every tremor on my lips, every twitch in my fingers. I'm suddenly warm all over as two little pink flags rise on my cheeks.

He smiles.

I blink.

It's gone. Must've been my imagination.

Flustered, I swiftly move on. "The bros are still obnoxious, yet somewhat lovable. They're adults now, but when they were kids, it was exhausting."

"I can just picture you as a mini-mommy, micromanaging them."

"Someone needed to facilitate order. But Brad the Dad makes my mom happy, and when they met, she no longer had to work two jobs. So I put up with the chaos, broken furniture, and frogs on my pillow. Family's family, right?"

"And your dad?" he asks.

My walls slam back up. I'm quiet for a long moment, debating how much truth I want to share with this man who somehow keeps catching me off guard. Why am I even considering telling him this? To show him I'm human? Maybe hoping he could act that way toward me more often? I can't reveal too much, otherwise I could raise suspicion about my degree.

Or maybe that's just my guilty conscience.

Clearing my throat, I say, "He struggled with gambling throughout my childhood. It ultimately drove my mom away—that's what brought her to Vegas." My fingers find the edge of my desk, needing something solid to hold on to. "Later, he had a serious accident that left him needing daily care."

"And you stepped in," Linc finishes for me. "Family's family."

I nod. Despite how it felt like my father abandoned us and the pain he'd caused, I couldn't do the same to him.

It's like our family photo albums sit on the desk between us, raw, honest, unedited. Mostly. I can't believe I just told Lincoln Sullivan—Mr. Privileged Executive himself—about the messiest parts of my life.

"I'm sorry—" His expression softens as his massive, hulking figure fills the doorway, backlit by sunlight. He could be someone's Superman.

It's a sight so stunning I almost need to shield my eyes.

But that's not my reality. In the real world, it's like I just took off the fig leaves and feel exposed. I stand abruptly, needing to move, to distance myself from this conversation that went too deep too fast. "We should probably get back to work."

"Right. The Fairfax files." He nods in my direction and then breezes into his office, leaving me with his clean, minty scent and a case of distraction that carries through until lunch.

Later, on my way back from the lobby, I crowd toward the elevator as everyone hastens to be behind their desks by one o'clock and not a minute later. The last one was crammed tight, so I wait for the next one to ding.

From nearby, I hear a familiar baritone, coming closer. Linc ends a call on his phone before he notices I'm waiting for the elevator. I'm surprised he doesn't flash his exec badge to hurry the thing along.

We both get in first as stragglers load inside, pushing us to the back, shoulder to shoulder. Well, more like shoulder to mid biceps. Until standing this close, I never realized how tall he is. Several inches over six feet.

He smells minty and soapy, likely having hit the gym during his lunch hour. I was hoping to slip out and visit the office girlies on the thirty-third floor, but no such luck, since I had to do my "banking" for the month.

It's a finely-calibrated juggling act of shuffling money around accounts, staggering payments, and hoping the thugs my father crossed receive payment in full and on time.

In the mass of starched shirts and silky blouses, someone is telling a story about the man in the plaza with the talking bird and how he trained it to say, "I quit" whenever someone in a suit walks by.

I think back to my dare, when I challenged Linc to try to get rid of me. The crowd presses us closer together, and when I glance up, I find his gaze locked on me. Is he remembering the same thing?

If so, I really want to keep my job. No need for anyone to get excited.

His lips quirk. I try to offer my best "please keep me" smile. But then neither of us looks away.

The elevator feels smaller suddenly, the air thicker, and not because someone had a hot dog with raw onions for lunch.

My smile falters. His expression shifts—still amused, but something else edges in.

An expert at the staring game thanks to my brothers, I expect Linc to look away first, to break whatever this is, but he doesn't.

I forget to breathe.

Something hot and dangerous crackles between us. There should be caution tape. A warning label at least. My pulse races in a way that's definitely not HR approved.

14

JULES

THE ELEVATOR DINGS, startling me. Turning forward, my nose is within two inches of a man's armpit, forcing me to lift my head again. Linc is still there, looking down at me, close enough that I can see the chips of slate in his blue eyes. His gaze flits from my eyes to my nose to my mouth and back again because there's nowhere else to look. My pulse slows, blipping like a sonar tracker.

As if seeking a target, we remain this way until we're the only two people on the elevator.

We haven't moved as passengers have disembarked.

We don't create space between us when we could step back to our respective corners in the carriage like a boxing ring.

I cave under the pressure, break from the tension. With him looming over me, I tell myself I've miscalculated, and this is my boss reminding me of my place beneath him. It couldn't possibly be anything else. Not when we clearly hate each other. Though no one who's ever hated me looks at me with a burning smolder in his eyes. I fight the urge to unbutton the top button of my blouse and wave my hand like a fan for air circulation.

My voice barely above a whisper, I say, "For your information, just because we had a bonding moment earlier and you demonstrated that you're not a robot under that suit, doesn't change anything."

Wearing a crooked smile, he straightens and faces the doors.

Doubling down, I add, "We're not going to have a wild fling where we throw caution to the wind in a storage closet, then fall fast and hard on a sultry night while at a fancy resort during a business trip."

"You seem to have given this some thought, and there I was, planning our getaway to Cabo."

"Never. We'd be kicked off the island." I steady myself by tuning into my pulse against the mechanical hum of the elevator.

"Shall we test the theory? There's a work conference on the calendar. I bet you'd look great in a muumuu."

I exhale sharply, about to snap at him for taking his friend's sunbathing comment too far—but then the comment clicks. A muumuu? A muumuu! An oversized sack that conceals everything. Of course, that's what he'd think I belong in.

The elevator dings for the thirty-ninth floor. Linc presses the button to hold the doors closed and turns back to me.

"What are you doing?" I demand.

"I just want to know—why not, Julia? Why not us?" His voice drops low, his breath grazing my ear and sending a dangerous ripple through me.

"Because it's against the rules."

Leaning closer, he says, "I bet you've broken rules

before." He arches an eyebrow, suggesting I'm not as innocent as I look.

I keep my best poker face, refusing to reveal he's "warm" if we were playing the hot and cold game. But then it hits me. This man isn't used to women resisting him. Oh, I get it now. He's used to women swooning. Falling at his feet. He's not used to hearing no.

I wouldn't touch him if he were the last man in the building. "If you must know, I think that you're emotionally muted."

"Explain." He leans closer.

"You operate on a low frequency, like a vintage gramophone—everything comes out flat and distorted. Like you're one genuine feeling away from anaphylactic shock."

He glances at the floor and then up at me. "Just because I don't wear oversized sunglasses and put a bunch of weeds on my desk—"

"Wildflowers," I whisper-hiss, tilting my chin up. "They're whimsical."

"They're giving me hay fever."

"Then go home." My smile is sugar-sweet and razor-sharp. "And don't come back."

His answering smile is pure nocturnal predator. "Not. A. Chance. Julieta."

The elevator doors slide open. I don't waver. We don't budge, locked in our stare-down again. "I have three brothers. You have no idea how long I can go," I grit out.

"To the end." He growls.

My heart hammers against my ribs. I lose track of my pulse. It's likely dangerously high. Is that a health risk at this elevation—up here on the thirty-ninth floor?

Flushed and eyes narrowed defiantly, I slowly back out of the elevator. We never came into contact, having maintained at least a sliver of space between us, but it's like I can feel Linc's hands all over my body.

The doors slide shut, sealing him inside since he has a board meeting on the top floor. I remain, staring at my reflection in the polished steel, wondering how my grumpy boss became someone who could knock me completely off balance with just a look. A long smoldering look, but still.

THAT EVENING, I'm trying to focus on the Fairfax files authentication project when Screechy and Grumbly start arguing. Tonight, it's about the thermostat. They may as well be in the room with me.

"Sixty-eight degrees is freezing!" Screechy's voice carries through the walls. "I'm not paying for you to live in an icebox!"

"And I'm not paying to live in a sauna!" Grumbly shoots back. "Some of us don't want to melt into the furniture!"

I sigh and stare up at the ceiling. Time for another diplomatic intervention.

Twenty minutes later, I've negotiated a compromise (seventy-four during the day, sixty-eight at night), mediated a separate dispute about lighting, and troubleshot their Wi-Fi.

I tell myself that even though things with Oly are different now that she's married, I'm, okay. The office girlies are still a few floors down at work and I have the reliable companionship of Screechy and Grumbly.

See? I'm not alone. But maybe, in the depths of the night, I am a bit lonely. Things can look a little stark in the city when I can't even see the stars in the sky.

This is my life. Always fixing other people's problems while my own pile up on my desk.

Speaking of which ... I pull out my phone and open the company app. I need access to the Fairfax archives if I'm going to make any progress on this authentication, but that requires approval from a certain boss with executive privileges. I message him.

Me: I need authorization to access the Fairfax archives for the Fairfax authentication. Can you approve it?

I hit send before I can overthink it and correct my grammar, add punctuation, and use the word *please*. It's almost ten, but Linc is probably still up, getting ready to go to a party or club. He can give me access remotely. Easy peasy.

My phone buzzes almost immediately.

L. Sullivan: Missing me already?

I snort out loud. The man's ego is as big as the building we work in. Like father, like son is a cliché for a reason.

Me: Like a sunburn misses the beach.

Me: Like a printer misses paper jams.

Me: Like an afternoon misses naps.

L. Sullivan: Okay. I get it. Authorization approved. Go home, Jujubee.

Me: Don't tell me what to do, Lincoln Log. Also, I am home.

L. Sullivan: It's Friday night. In that case, go have some fun.

Me: But my big, bad boss wants this completed ASAP.

L. Sullivan: Your big, bad boss wants you to take the night off.

Me: Is that so? I now have that in writing. But how do I know your account wasn't hacked and this isn't a bot?

L. Sullivan: You want verification?

My phone chimes again, and in place of our banter bubbles, a selfie of him comes through. He's just gotten out of the shower—hair still damp and tousled, no shirt visible in the frame, just bare shoulders and that infuriating smirk. My phone suddenly feels too hot in my hands, and I have to set it down on my bed before I drop it.

L. Sullivan: That's your boss reminding you that you're off the clock. Also, here's a friendly reminder to get some sleep. Headed there now myself.

Wait. He's not at a club? A party? Linc going to sleep at a reasonable time on a Friday night does not compute.

Maybe he's right and I should take a break. I've been staring at these documents for hours, and my eyes are starting to cross. Also, I'm thinking nutso thoughts about him ... I have to fortify my defenses!

Me: That's not what I meant about verification and you know it.

L. Sullivan: But it's what you got.

Me: Your ego is showing, Linc.

L. Sullivan: Among other things.

Me: This is highly unprofessional.

L. Sullivan: Good thing it's after hours.

Me: You're insufferable.

L. Sullivan: Yet here you are, still messaging me.

Me: I hate you.

L. Sullivan: No, you don't.

Me: Good night, Abraham.

L. Sullivan: Sweet dreams, Buttercup.

I tell myself the little flutter in my stomach has nothing to do with Linc. It's most likely indigestion from the can of soup I had for dinner, which was a few months past its "best by" date. He probably just got home from a lavish dinner with multiple courses and mistook me for someone he'd flirt with.

ON MONDAY MORNING, I'm already at my desk when Linc arrives, surrounded by mountains of documents. I've been here since seven, caffeinated and focused, following a thread in the Fairfax case that's been nagging at me since Friday night—in addition to the messages with Linc on the company app. Hopefully, it doesn't track how many times I looked at the attachment he sent ... of him.

"Morning, Julipop," he says, setting down a coffee for me.

I glance up, and something in my expression must give me away because his casual demeanor immediately shifts to alert.

"I think I found something," I tell him.

"Related to the Fairfax Files?"

"There are some irregularities in the provenance of several high-value pieces associated with the collection scheduled for auction." I gesture to the papers spread across my desk like a forensic investigation.

He grunts.

"I'm not sure what it means yet, but the documentation doesn't add up."

His expression grows serious. "What sort of irregularities?"

"It seems someone has been very creative with their paperwork."

I look up at him, and for once, there's no antagonism between us. Just concern and the shared realization that there could be something suspicious going on. Something clicks into place. It's subtle but unmistakable—like finding the right frequency on an old radio.

"Show me what you've found," he says, stepping behind me and craning over my shoulder.

As I scroll through the spreadsheet, pointing out the records, dollar amounts, and dates, Linc asks reasonable questions.

Whatever he'd planned to do when he arrived this

morning is put on hold as I reveal the discrepancies in the paper trail. He removes his suit jacket, folds up his sleeves and paces the room, taking in all of this information.

"There is one piece missing from the Fairfax collection. It's called *Echo & Answer*. There is no record of it in the digital archives. Nothing online. No idea of what it looks like. All we know is it was last seen and sold as part of the Douglas Kinnard estate," I say, recapping what we know.

Linc drops his hands on my desk, framing me inside his massive arms. The banded muscles and veins form a tapestry on his forearm as he reads the content on the computer screen over my shoulder. "Are you sure that was the painter's name for that particular piece?"

"That's what it says here."

Forcing back tingles inside, I continue to show him my discoveries.

As I explain the discrepancies in dates and signatures, I catch myself noticing things I shouldn't. The way Linc leans forward when he's concentrating. The subtle scent of his cologne teasing my nose. The contours of his lips when I glance back to see if he's tracking all of this.

There are potentially forged documents in front of me, and I'm thinking about my grumpy boss's forearms.

Focus, Juliana.

Outside, clouds gather for what looks like a summer storm. They're the kind that make me want to curl up inside with tea and a good book while rain pounds against the windows.

But also the kind that makes me grateful I'm not alone.

"This could be bigger than just the Fairfax Collection," I murmur, studying the scan of a signature that's supposedly from 1943 but looks suspiciously fresh.

For better or worse, I'm familiar with these things, given my father's background.

"How much bigger?" The intensity in Linc's voice suggests this matters to him more than just professionally.

Much like in the elevator, when I look up at him, we're barely a breath apart. My inhale catches and my voice is unsteady when I answer. "I don't know yet. But I have a feeling we're about to find out."

Concern pierces his eyes and then they quickly darken. "Actually, it might be better for you to stay in your lane."

"But you requested—"

"An executive summary will do," he says with finality.

My lips bunch together in frustration. I'm just doing the job he asked me to do. Deep research, investigating art history the way a detective would a crime, is where I thrive. He teased me with it and now he's taking it away? I could scream.

An executive summary? I'd like to exec-u-cute him. No, he's not a cute exec. What is wrong with me? I just want to wring his big, muscly neck. Mangle his lips with mine.

Cheese and crackers! I've gone mad.

Giving my head a rough shake, Linc ghosts a smile my way as if he has executive access into my brain with that badge of his.

I have a new thing I hate: the blush that sweeps across my cheeks under his gaze.

15

LINC

THE GYM IS PRACTICALLY empty during lunch—exactly how I like it. No small talk, no autograph requests, just the satisfying burn of weights and the steady rhythm of my breathing.

Not the unsteady kind that happens when I'm around Juliana and not the gasp of shock I tried to hide when she shared the files with me.

I had her look into the Fairfax Collection because that's where my mother's trail went cold. She was convinced there was a painting of Abraham Lincoln that contained hidden symbols, creating a map of sorts that would point toward the location of the lost love letters.

Thinking about this now, I feel foolish. If Juliana knew I'm searching for lost love letters, she'd laugh in my face. Yeah, I'm a gramophone all right. Clunky, dusty, boring. A guy more interested in hockey reps than wild parties. Who would rather track my macros than the latest trends.

No need for me to risk ridicule.

Seeing the discrepancies Juliana discovered, I worry she

stumbled on something sinister, something that other people in the office would rather remain hidden.

No need for her to risk her job. Better for her to drop it and for me to distance myself from her—for a variety of reasons.

After forty-five minutes of pushing iron and all of these thoughts out of my head, I'm ready for my post-workout routine—a cold shower and a protein smoothie from the place across the street.

I'm waiting in line, heart rate still elevated, when I hear a voice that makes my pulse stop.

"Linc-y Linc," the woman squeals.

I turn, and Iva Katz, in all her glamorized glory, struts toward me. Her designer clothes in garish, clashing colors and patterns that demand attention give me an instant headache. Her perfectly applied makeup and plastic smile —the one that once practically had me under a spell—makes me want to turn and run while others in the shop flock toward her.

Being in the proximity of my ex instantly sends a wave of exhaustion and wariness over me. I'm three people away from placing my order and consider ducking out. But I can't get away with going home for a nap and a snack today without Juliana commenting that I'm an overgrown toddler.

I glance over my shoulder as Iva lets out a squeal. I wince as she opens and closes her hand in a wave, then flashes me the one-minute signal, indicating I wait, while she poses for a photo with a fan. Typical.

When she reaches me, she makes a big fuss like I'm the star on center stage when, really, her over-the-top, bombastic behavior and appearance keep the spotlight on her. She wraps herself around me with a hug while I lightly pat her back, pulling away. I hear phone cameras flashing, capturing the moment.

When I break free, keeping my voice neutral, I offer a general greeting, "Hello. How are you?"

"Fabulous, Linc-y baby. I just finished a private tour of a very exclusive art collection." She steps closer, invading my personal space and runs her hand across my chest. "Beautiful pieces, though none as good as this delicious hunk of man. You look good. Have you been working out more?"

The question is like asking a child if they want a colorfully frosted cookie for breakfast when their mother said to eat something sensible. I could bite, accept the compliment, and see where it goes. But I've learned Iva Katz doesn't do anything without an agenda. Plus, cookies for breakfast will only leave me feeling sick.

She reaches for my biceps.

I step back slightly. "Same routine as always."

Her laugh is like a tornado colliding with a hurricane. "I couldn't possibly endure that kind of repetition. *Bore-ring.*" She bops her head. "I've been in three countries for filming this week alone." She walks her first two fingers over my shoulder. "But enough about me. I've missed you, Linc-y. We were good together, weren't we?"

I fight against recoiling. Looking at Iva Katz now, I'm trying to remember what I saw in her. Sure, she's the kind of beautiful that photographs well and opens doors. But standing here, all I can think about is how different she is from a certain woman on the thirty-ninth floor.

Why am I thinking about my assistant ... again?

"We were?" I blurt without thinking about how everything I say or do can and will be manipulated by this woman.

"We could be good again." Her voice drops to a throaty

whisper that used to appeal to my ego. "I know things ended badly, but—"

I interrupt, "I remember you deciding our schedules weren't compatible."

The subtext was that I was *bore-ring,* in her words. I also wasn't helping her climb the social ladder as quickly as she'd hoped with my NHL and billionaire connections.

Boo hoo.

Her mask slips for just a second, revealing something calculating underneath. "That's not fair, Linc-y. I cared about you."

Dead air hangs between us as another fan barges into our semi-private conversation. I mutter, "You cared about what I could do for you."

After another selfie and autograph, she returns with her bright smile. "Guess what? I'm seeing someone new anyway."

Of course, she is and I'm sure he'd really appreciate what she just said to me. My sarcasm dial is turned all the way up.

Without my asking, she supplies, "I'm with Aiken D. You know, the social media star? He's got this amazing channel where he destroys expensive things for entertainment. Cars, musical instruments, sometimes even art pieces." She speaks like she's bragging about dating a doctor who saves children's lives and rescues puppies on the side.

A few of the dudes on my team watch Aiken D, the Demo King's stuff. From what I know, the guy is a trust fund brat who burns through money and relationships with equal enthusiasm. Bīriņš showed me some videos where he destroyed vintage guitars and crashed a Ferrari and a Lamborghini into each other for views. He's exactly the kind of person who gives wealthy twenty-somethings a bad name. The kind of guy Juliana thought I was.

"He sure sounds like a catch," I say dryly.

She leans in conspiratorially and more cameras snap. "He is. And between you and me, he throws the most incredible parties. You should come tonight—rooftop club, very exclusive. Unless you're still being bore-ring and responsible."

She says the last part like I have a character defect, telling me everything I need to know about her priorities and why we didn't work out. Iva sees stability as stagnation, commitment as limitation. She wants someone who'll play her games and feed her need for drama.

I'm not that guy.

I used to think I was heartbroken when we split. Now I realize I was just ... disappointed. In her, but mostly in myself, for not seeing who she really was—someone who wants attention rather than a relationship.

This is why I'm single. Why I focus on hockey. Women like Iva are users and I'm over being garage sale goods.

Even as I think it, an image flashes through my mind—blonde hair streaked with summer strawberry strands, a sharp wit, and eyes that see so much. Juliana isn't like Iva. She doesn't want anything from me as far as I can tell. She challenges me in a way that makes me want to rise to the occasion, not because she wants to tear me down—most of the time. I'll admit that occasionally my ego could use some pruning.

Giving Iva a polite nod, I say, "Thanks for the invite."

Her smile turns brittle. "Your loss. Aiken has some fancy art pieces you might like to see destroyed if you're still bickering with Daddy Warbucks about hockey. His mother is very connected in the art world." She bats her eyelashes. "And the best part, he knows how to have a good time."

"I'm sure he does."

She gives me one last appraising look, like she's calculating whether I'm worth another attempt. Apparently, I'm not, because she shrugs and turns away. "See you around, Linc-y. Try not to be a stranger."

I watch her go and then place my smoothie order, feeling nothing but relief. Whatever hold Iva once had on me is gone, replaced by something else—curiosity about a woman who makes me want to be worthy of her respect.

Back at the office, I can't concentrate. Every time I try to focus on quarterly projections or strategic initiative reports, I catch a hint of cherry blossom and almonds—Juliana's scent—wafting from the reception area.

It's sweet and warm and wholly distracting.

More than once, I find myself peering through the double doors, noticing the way she absently twirls a pen between her fingers when she's thinking, how she gets a little crease between her eyebrows when she's concentrating. Glimpsing a little smile at the corner of her lips when she's ... well, I'm not sure what. Certainly not thinking about me.

And why am I thinking about her so much?

The woman is brilliant. Infuriating at times, but smart and clever and beautiful, too.

At the end of the day, we both pack up, the silence awkward rather than acrimonious. The weather has taken a turn with dark clouds overhead, promising the kind of summer storm that'll keep me landlocked tonight. So much for a sunset boat cruise with the guys.

Jules joins me in the elevator and we both remain quiet.

Could be that the thick, gray blanket outside has a muffling effect.

"Looks like rain," I say dumbly.

"Yeah. Stormy night ahead."

And here we are, talking about the weather. *Not too smooth, Andresen.*

With a little wave, she gets off the elevator at the thirty-third floor as if the heated, intense moment we shared the other day while riding up, never happened.

"Have a good weekend," I call, but the doors close before the words are out.

16

LINC

A HOCKEY FAN gets on the elevator from one of the businesses on a lower level and we take a selfie. I'm thankful Juliana got off early—no need for her to know more about me than she already does.

I hurry through the parking garage and am pulling out when the sky cracks open with heavy rain. While waiting for the light to change, a high-pitched buzzing makes my blood run cold. An insect flies around inside the car, small and dark and definitely stingy. Unless I stop short in traffic, there's nothing I can do.

The thing darts right and left and then repeatedly batters the windshield, desperate but dumb.

On the other side, the wipers slide back and forth, dizzying in the downpour, as the bug, stunned now, flies drunken loops around the interior of my vehicle.

I want to remain in Noah's Ark and the bee wants out.

I slide the rear window down slightly, hoping the fresh air will coax it to freedom, but the downpour must scare it. Now, it hastens to the driver's side window.

Sweat beads at my hairline. Suffice it to say, my bee allergy and enclosed spaces don't mix well.

"Okay, nice little bug. Go on outside," I whisper, as I lower my window, inviting in the torrential downpour and fogging the windows.

The fast, fat drops smear across the windshield as the bee takes an interest in my forehead. I gently swat at it, but don't want to antagonize it. Now in rush hour traffic, I turn the corner a little too fast as if the bee were chasing me. A wave of water rises and sprays ... not only a walk signal pole but ... a woman.

A woman with gray eyes. Blonde hair. And ... a glare.

Oh, this is bad.

It couldn't have been a normal person.

Or someone who enjoys getting splashed by filthy gutter water.

Instead, Juliana stands just outside a crowded bus shelter with no umbrella, completely soaked because of me, as if the rain weren't enough.

The bee does an aerial gymnastics routine as it whirls and loops, frantic. I simultaneously struggle to control the windows, the wiper blades, and the turn signal while wondering what to do regarding the woman I just sprayed with water.

I could keep driving. But as she hollers whatever delicate obscenities she can muster out of that pretty little mouth, our gazes meet.

A flicker of recognition passes across her face, followed by a scowl.

I'm caught.

Without thinking, I stop by the curb and roll down the window. "Get in!"

She stalks over to me, arms gesturing like she regularly

occupies this corner and consults the pigeons about mutual funds. "Why would you—?"

"It was an accident."

"Yeah, right. You're a bully, you know that!"

"Just get in."

"I'm waiting for the bus!"

"You'll drown before it gets here."

"It's fine! I'm fine." But even as she says it, a car speeds past and sends another spray of street water right at her. This time, she jumps back, but her pants and shoes are splattered.

That's it. I throw the car in park and get out, opening an umbrella. By the time I reach her, I'm also soaked, but I hold the umbrella over both of us.

"Let me give you a ride home. It's the least I can do."

Tucked under this little black canopy, I can smell cherry blossoms covered in morning dew. See the plea in her eyes for whatever curse is upon her to be lifted. She studies my face for a long moment as though weighing her options—or contemplating whether she can get away with stealing my car.

"Get in." Clearing my throat, I add, "Please."

I tell myself that if she catches a cold after being out here sopping wet, her absence from work will be on me.

Finally, she sighs. "I'll get your upholstery soaked."

Ignoring her objections, I open the passenger door for her, keeping the umbrella steady.

She slides onto the leather seat and looks up at me. "If I go missing, people will look for me."

I bark a laugh and get behind the wheel. Assured the bee is gone, I seal the windows. Then explain that a stinging insect was inside the vehicle.

She slumps in the seat. "Likely story. You just wanted to see if you could get me with that rooster tail of water."

"Now, why would I do that?"

She shrugs, then, as if uncomfortable with the truth that I'm not the monster she's made me out to be, she adds, "The bee was probably allergic to you."

"I don't think my EpiPen would work on it."

"Well, thank you for offering to give me a ride."

"It's the least I can do."

She's quiet for a beat, then haltingly says, "I'm sorry about the anaphylaxis comment in the elevator."

"No apology necessary."

"Are you always this nice outside the office?" Juliana asks as I wait for a break in traffic.

"Depends on where I am. On who you ask."

"What would your friend ... what's his name? The one who held us hostage to go boating? Bear Claw? Bear Skin? Bear Hug?"

I chuckle. "Bīriņš. Unsolicited advice: stay away from him unless you want your heart broken."

"I didn't know I was in the running as a candidate for anything involving my heart."

I jerk my head in her direction. "You didn't notice the way he looked at you?"

She wipes a drip of water from her hair out of her eyes. "Who said I'm the kind to fall in love?"

"You did," I say, pulling back into traffic.

As if narrating the live-action adaptation of a comic, she says, "By day, he stalks around the office like he has a vendetta against the very floor beneath him. By night, he leaps buildings in a single bound and rescues old ladies from being victims of petty theft ..."

"And apologizes for splashing his assistant with nasty road water."

"If I didn't see the bee fly out of the window when you rolled it down, I'd be convinced you did it on purpose." She sighs.

I grunt. So she did believe me and was just giving me a hard time. But why? "Where am I going?"

She gives me her address in Logan Square, and we settle into uncomfortable silence as if neither one of us can figure out a good segue from the romance, heart, and love conversation. No sooner do I think of a topic that isn't the weather, we're pulling up in front of a converted brick building that would be advertised by realtors as an "artist's loft."

"Thanks for the ride," she says, unbuckling her seatbelt. "I owe you one."

"No, you don't."

She doesn't argue.

I watch her hurry up the front steps, fumbling with her keys in the rain. She doesn't look back, but I sit there for a moment anyway, watching her building like a lurker ... or a doting boyfriend to make sure she gets in safely.

Rubbing my hand down my face, I have to wonder, what is wrong with me?

Late that night, my phone buzzes with a message through the Meridian app. I'm inclined to ignore it since it could be my father, demanding I work on the weekend, but I can't resist the possibility that it could be the assistant who loves to hate me.

> J. Lindley: Regarding that conversation we had this week, we need to talk. ASAP.

I stare at the message, remembering my cowboy move—that selfie I sent her. Probably crossed about fifteen HR lines with that one. I need to keep this professional. But my thoughts are slow to come around to what she refers to. There are a number of things we discussed.

Most likely, it doesn't have anything to do with a romantic getaway to Cabo. Better chances are it has something to do with the discrepancies I told her to stay away from.

I'm only here for the summer and would be better off not getting involved in corporate espionage—or whatever crimes are potentially being committed at Meridian. Anyway, who knows, it could be a genuine fluke. All the same, I reply.

L. Sullivan: What did you find?

Instead of a regular message, I get a selfie of her with her hand on her chin like the "thinking emoji." Not quite quick enough to read between the lines, my phone pings again with a link to an article about recent art forgeries hitting the auction circuit. I read through it quickly, my concern growing with each paragraph. This is bigger than just authentication issues.

My mind races through possibilities and then it lands on one so obnoxious, I can't ignore it. I think we'd be better off having an off-the-clock conversation. Is that what she was suggesting, anyway? Interesting.

I spend the next hour following my hunch, making calls, reaching out to contacts in the art world, and digging into the names mentioned in Juliana's research. What I find isn't about forgeries—it's something else entirely. A wildly unexpected lead on the painting *Echo & Answer* that my mother believed pointed to the lost letters ... and it just so happens I have an invitation to a party hosted by its potential owner.

Maybe. It's a bit of a lark, but what else am I doing tonight other than being bore-ring?

I'm staring at the information on my laptop when I make a decision that's probably foolish. Then again, Juliana is a romantic. She said it herself. Maybe she wouldn't find the search for the lost letters strange.

I grab my keys and head back out into the rain.

Twenty minutes later, I'm standing outside Juliana's building, find her name on the mailbox for 4B, and then when someone exits, I take the opportunity to go upstairs to her unit. The rain has slowed to a drizzle from the earlier downpour as I knock on the door.

When it opens, a cloud of glitter puffs into the air between us. I cough and wave my hand as Juliana's eyes widen. Her hair is damp and in a messy bun. She wears a cozy robe and looks absolutely adorable. And absolutely furious.

"What's with the glitter?" I try to brush it off, but this seems like only something that could be removed with a stiff-bristle brush or a wind tunnel.

"What are you doing here?" she demands. "I thought someone was breaking in. I was in the shower, and—" She stops, looking at me for the first time. "You're not wearing glasses."

"Contacts. Look, I read your message and I know this seems—"

"Sketchy? Yeah, it does." But her anger fades, replaced by curiosity. "Did you take a whimsy and find yourself here?"

"A whatsy?"

She waves her hand. "Never mind. If you know, you know. If you don't, you don't." She wraps her robe tighter around herself. "It's after nine p.m., Linc. What could possibly be so urgent that—?"

"I need you to go somewhere with me. I got a lead."

"What kind of lead?"

I hesitate. I'm not sure how much I'm ready to reveal. "The kind that requires two people."

Her eyebrows pinch together as if conflicted, torn between caution and curiosity.

"Please?" I ask.

A pretty smile blooms on her face. "Well, when you put it that way ..."

Apparently, that's the magic word.

She moves to let me and marches toward an antique armoire and asks, "What should I wear?"

"Something cute," I blurt.

Her head whips around. "Where exactly are we going?"

"Let's just put it this way, I'd rather slog through a swamp filled with alligators."

"No doubt, you'd throw me to them to save yourself."

"Never." And wouldn't you know? I mean it.

17

JULES

THE ROOFTOP CLUB is a modern mixture of glass, polished metal, and wretched excess. It's the kind of event where the bubbly beverages alone cost more than I spend in a year on coffee. And it's the last place I expect to be on a Friday night with my boss.

With all the oddball glitz and glam, it's evident nearly everyone in attendance is trying very hard to look like they're not trying at all. Take, for example, the person wearing purple plastic panel pants, a denim suit jacket, and cowboy boot sandals.

Not my scene, not that I have one. Libraries? Book stores? Art galleries? Coffee shops? Those are my common habitats and I am happy to wear a cardigan and stretch pants.

If I hadn't used my blow dryer to remove the glitter from Linc's face and shirt, he'd fit right in.

He pauses just outside the elevator and takes stock of the space at large. He wears a pair of worn-in jeans and a cotton t-shirt. Underneath that, I can tell he's built of solid engineering. Like God took the blueprints and said, "*Let's make this one massive, towering above the rest. Nothing but the highest quality materials. Fortify him. Reinforced with the strong bedrock of the earth. We take pride in our work and he is no exception!"*

Hesitating because I'm counting my blessings and cursing myself for thinking this way about my boss, he raises his eyebrow sharply as if sensing my candy-eyed weakness or issuing a dare. I can't be sure.

Then his hand lands on the slope of my spine. My pulse rattles like I just drove over a speed bump. A shiver ripples through me like a breeze in the fir trees. I tell myself the gesture is so I don't get lost in the throbbing throng of people drinking and dancing.

I freeze, then look at him briefly over my shoulder, wondering if this is how it starts.

Out of the corner of his eye, he looks me up and down and his mouth twitches.

It's the same hint of a smile as when I answered my door in a robe, only now I'm wearing my one and only little black dress that is more understated than it is elegant. After running my brush through my hair, I quickly blew it dry, letting it loose around my shoulders. Through the crack in my bathroom door, Linc watched me and for a moment, he wore a reverent look on his face that made me think of romantic scenes on balconies, open train windows and hankies, couples rushing toward each other in the airport.

How someone's beloved is both the artist and the masterpiece—beautiful just by being themselves.

Just kidding, I saw the amusement on his lips as if I'd hired a clown to point their makeup gun at me and turn it up to maximum.

No doubt, I'm wide-eyed as we pass two people making out on top of a table.

"Are these your friends?" I murmur, watching a group of scantily clad influencers pose for photos against the city skyline backdrop. It's warm out, but I happen to know where you can get textiles cheaply.

He laughs through his nose. "Friends? Certainly not."

I can't wrap my head around what we're doing here.

As if reading my mind, Linc leans into my ear and whispers, "We have some investigating to do."

I'd like to focus on his proximity and how my hair momentarily got adhered to his stubble like Velcro, but he pulls a penny from his pocket and flips it.

"Lucky penny?" I watch the copper glint like it's winking at me as it tumbles in the air.

"Something like that."

"I once heard a statistic that Americans think about Honest Abe on average once per day."

"I should hope so," he says, then goes still.

His hand slides from my back, which had skillfully guided me through the crowd, to cup my own.

Linc is holding my hand.

His skin is cool, but mine burns like I just touched a hot stovetop. I should know better than to allow this, but it's like our palms are glued together.

I'm so far out of my element that I welcome Linc's presence. That's the story I tell myself, anyway.

"I'm only allowing this so I don't get lost. It's a safety issue," I call, but I don't know if he hears me when a cackling laugh cuts through the music.

His grip tightens.

The actress Iva Katz swans over with a spindly man. He wears a satin baroque suit, has stringy dyed orange hair, and his eyes, lined with black kohl, are bloodshot. She wears designer everything, artfully messy hair, and the kind of smile that's been practiced in front of mirrors.

"Linc-y baby!" Iva exclaims, though her eyes flit from him to our joined hands, to me as though she's trying to solve an advanced calculus problem. "You came after all. And you brought a *friend*?" It's more of a question than a statement.

"This is Juliana," he says, getting my name right for the first time. Ever.

I lengthen my spine and extend my free hand for her to shake. "Nice to meet you."

She doesn't take it. "I'm sure."

"Iva Babe, who do we have here?" asks her Unhinged Circus Person companion.

She looks at me, apparently decides that I'm no one, and says, "This is my ex, Linc-y."

I turn to Linc and, like a political adversary who's about to mount a teasing campaign, mouth, *Linc-y*?

Nostrils flared, as if reading my mind once more, he mutters, "Don't you dare."

The desire to use this silly nickname against him, especially after the corporate power move to intentionally get my name wrong, is almost too tasty to pass up.

Unhinged Circus Person spreads his arms wide like a king, declaring, "I'm Aiken D, but you know that."

I do?

With a spin, he adds, "Welcome to my kingdom of chaos."

He is indeed wearing a velvet mantel with a thick fur ruff.

"Are you royalty?" I curtsy.

Linc laughs but hides it with a cough.

Iva lets out a hollow titter. "In our world, of course. He's the Demo King."

"The King of demolition entertainment." Unhinged Circus Person, aka Aiken, wheezes a laugh.

Iva narrows her eyes in my direction. "So, how do you two know each other? You make such an interesting couple."

Linc and I exchange a quick glance, both starting to speak at the same time.

"We're not—" I begin.

"We are—" he says.

"Friends?" Iva repeats as if hopeful.

I tip my head back with lunatic laughter, matching the vibe of the party. "No, we hate each other."

Linc gives me a lengthy side eye.

Iva and Aiken don't seem to register my comment as he slings an arm around her waist. "We used to be 'just friends' too, didn't we, babe?"

Linc looks at me for a long moment as if measuring something—the barometric pressure of our environment? How these fluctuations might affect weather patterns and predict an incoming storm? Did our conversation in the car make us pals?

He tenses as if he wants to end this conversation. "We should mingle, Jules."

Aiken, the ring master monarch of this side show, interrupts, "Oh, don't leave so soon! I was just about to show everyone my latest acquisition—a boring old painting I picked up at an estate sale. I'm featuring it in my next destruction video, and as a grand finale to our festivities tonight, I'm going to have everyone graffiti the wall it's mounted on."

Linc goes still. "What kind of painting?"

He leans in like he has a secret too juicy to keep private and says, "A Civil War battle scene. We're going to blow it up with a cannon." Aiken laughs again. "Who cares about fusty, dusty history when you can create new art by destroying the old?"

Linc flips the penny again, expression unreadable.

Iva's eyes gleam. "We have connections, don't we, Aikey?"

"Sure do."

"What kinds of—?" Linc starts to ask and then stops himself, likely because he doesn't want to talk to them any longer than necessary.

As if she just entered meh-mode, Iva tugs on Aiken. "This is bore-ring. Let's go. We have important guests to greet."

They drift away, leaving us standing in the middle of the three-ring circus castle. I feel both relieved and deserted. Now what?

Linc surveys the room as if looking for something ... or someone?

Likely not the person wearing a neon gorilla suit and tossing water balloons while on stilts who barges through us, breaking our linked hands.

Rude!

Now separated from Linc as partygoers fill in the space, I turn in a circle looking for the exit to this rooftop. I lament forgetting my parachute at home when a guy with a man-bun and paint-splattered jeans materializes next to me.

Leaning in close, he says. "You are magnetic. I could sense your depth from across the room."

Man Bun smells faintly like Limburger. My gaze flits away, seeking Linc.

He goes on, "Most people are shallow, but you're like a bird of paradise. A toucan, colorful and melodious. I want to see it. Hear it. Be part of it."

A toucan? Not at all interested in his odd overture, I start, "I'm here with—" But I'm not sure what to call Linc after just telling Iva we hate each other.

The guy continues, "I'm a performance artist and I want you to be part of my next piece. It involves body paint." He smolders.

The sea of Avant Garde fashion victims parts just long enough for me to catch sight of Linc, watching Man Bun and me while slowly clenching a fist before uncurling it finger by finger. I give a full, plot-twist stare. Did Linc just pull a Mr. Darcy or does he get carpal tunnel from typing and needs to stretch his hand?

What would it mean if he did the finger flex?

I rush over to him like a distressed damsel. Shouting above the music, I ask, "Okay, so why are we really here? Because my fragile nerves cannot handle much more of that."

Glancing at Stinky Cheese Artist, the sucker has the nerve to smirk.

"And I don't see any evidence of lost manuscripts or priceless pieces of art hidden in the floorboards."

Unless it's the one Aiken was talking about.

Gripping my elbow, Linc ushers me toward a hallway as I watch new money and old money intermingling—confirming my assumptions about the kind of party the son of a billionaire would attend.

The hallway is mercifully, relatively quiet.

"You should've told me to wear my feather-covered bell-bottoms and non-coordinating glow-in-the-dark shirt made out of tissue paper."

"Do you own those?"

"Absolutely not. But really, why are we here?" I demand.

He opens and then closes a door, shielding his eyes as if he saw something that he can never unsee and is desperate for a packet of bleach wipes. "Because this is the kind of thing that requires two people."

I only briefly saw what was behind the door and cannot imagine a world in which Linc would entertain doing that with me, especially after he dated Iva.

Iva Katz, the famous actress, to be clear.

She started as an adorable child star with a cutesy catch phrase, developed into a beautiful young woman featured with the hottest heartthrobs, and then, perhaps gripped firmly in the clutches of fame, decided that playing the Baroness in the saga titled "Mutant Harems of Love Mountain" was a good idea.

But who am I to judge? I'm a self-avowed "The Sweetheart Report" addict.

Even underneath all that makeup, she's undeniably gorgeous.

"We need two people, how? Why?" I ask when we reach the door at the end of the corridor.

"Please be the lookout."

I'm torn, unable to easily say no to his polite use of the word *please*. "That's the third time in our entire relationship—"

He tilts his head in question.

"I meant that's the third time in our hate-tionship that you've said *please*, so, sure. I'll be the lookout. I like polite Linc."

Whether I'll get a polite Mr. Sullivan on Monday is TBD.

Giving me a nod like we're two commandos in enemy territory, he slips through the door. I stand with my back to it, keeping time to the beat of the music and running through scenarios.

If a team of security guards approaches and questions me, I'll plead the Fifth.

Should the neon gorilla on stilts try to stampede, I'll trip him.

If Aiken appears, I'm running. I'll bust through the wall if I have to. I don't care if that foils Linc's plans. Our host is an unhinged circus person whose brain seems to be broken, given what I heard about his viral demo channel.

Only a few women, looking for the bathroom, make their way toward me, and must decide that one person, *me*, doesn't form a substantial line, so the loo must be elsewhere.

It's been almost three minutes and I fear Linc abandoned me when the door opens. He gives his head a shake. "That wasn't it."

"It might be helpful to know what *it* is."

"You're clever, what's the one piece missing from the Fairfax Collection?"

I frown, itemizing the art in my mind, but don't reach an answer before Iva calls out, "Thanks for stopping by, Linc-y. Always a pleasure. Bring your girlfriend again next time."

She wouldn't get an award for that performance, because the way she said *girlfriend* tells me she knows that's not who I am to Linc. Not that I'd want to be.

Ew. Gross.

Not that he'd ever think of me that way. Obviously. Not when he's dated the likes of Iva Katz. But still. There's no need to point it out so passive-aggressively... and with so much panache.

The elevator doors close on her laughter. Descending,

Linc and I stand in separate corners as if we're recalibrating to the baseline of not being blasted with noise pollution that some people call music.

When we reach the ground floor, it takes me a moment to come up with the right words. "That was illuminating."

"Jules—"

That's the second consecutive time he's used that new variation of my name.

"I know I shouldn't let it get to me, but her comment hurts like a paper cut, reminding me of girls in high school." It's immature of me, but I want him to make the raw, tender hurt his problem.

"Ignore her."

"I get it now. This is your world, right? The excess, the wild waste, the people who destroy art for entertainment." I dig deeper, partly because I need him to say I'm wrong.

Pathetic, I know.

"It's not my world," he says firmly. "I don't want anything to do with people like Iva or Aiken."

"But you know them. You dated her." I flip my hand dismissively as if, on second thought, it doesn't matter.

He puffs his cheeks. "Yeah. I did and learned a lot."

"About how to apply guy-liner? Aiken seems like a pro."

"Like eyeliner?" The chucklechump's laughter echoes off the walls of the basement parking garage. "Definitely not that. The only art I'm interested in is the real thing." He pauses and looks at me for a long moment.

Long enough for color to rise to my cheeks.

"The painting in the room was a reproduction and ..." He trails off as his eyes drop to my mouth and then back up as if he's looking at a piece of art.

The same silly, immature part of me who spent lunch

break in the library for all four years of high school and was always passed over by the hot guys wants to believe him. The part of me who felt invisible, who was rejected, wants to trust him.

18

JULES

WE'RE quiet during the drive back to my place. I sense that Linc is thinking, working through a high-level equation where the variables keep shifting. His fingers tap rhythmically against the steering wheel—thumb, index, middle, ring repeat.

When we pull up in front of my building, neither of us moves to get out.

This feels dangerously like junior year all over again—when I got bold. That breathless moment when I realized the boy I'd been arguing with in debate class might actually like me back.

The game we played was pretending we didn't notice when the other person stared too long, acting like accidental touches didn't send electricity up our arms. It was all kinds of awkward, but exhilarating too.

That's not what this is, right?

Monday feels like a lifetime away, and questions are burning in my throat that won't survive the weekend, never mind that we have to keep it clandestine if there is any amount of corruption—at least for now.

"Can I please see your license?" The words tumble out before I can stop them, and I immediately want to crawl into the back seat.

Smooth, Juliana. Real smooth.

He tucks his chin. "And my registration?"

I shake my head. "No, you said this is your father's car. I believe you. Just your license will suffice."

"Do you run a background check on all guys? Let me remind you that you already let me into your apartment. I saw the doilies, needlepoint projects, floral wallpaper, oh, and the Care Bear."

"All guys? First of all, you're my boss. Second of all, I do not own doilies, do needlepoint projects, or have floral wallpaper. Though I wouldn't object. Sounds like my kind of Friday night. However, even if I did, that's not something to criticize."

"I wasn't. But you do have a Care Bear."

I cut him a Care Bear STARE. Which, fine, is adorable and glowy.

He pulls his wallet out of his back pocket. It's leather and surprisingly nondescript. Manly. Though I'm not sure what I was expecting. One made out of holographic material? Gold plating?

He says, "By the way, I'm not officially on the payroll at Meridian."

"How does that work?"

He pinches his license between his first and middle fingers, passing it to me. "Haven't received a check yet."

Of course, he has a good picture, unlike most humans whose driver's license photo is a poor representation of what they look like—ironic since it's used for identification purposes.

I read the stats: Abraham Lincoln Andresen. His

address, eye color: blue, height: six feet four inches—I knew it!—weight a buck ninety-five. I bet his muscles have muscles.

Then my gaze snags on his name. *Abraham Lincoln.* This is either a very good fake ID or there's a story here. One I have to know.

"You want to come up? I have root beer."

"Root beer?"

"Not regular beer. Sorry to disappoint."

"Root beer is my favorite," he says in slow motion.

Then his eyes float over me, coming in and out of shadows from the headlights of passing cars. "Nothing about you could disappoint, Jules."

I suddenly feel quite wobbly inside.

Apparently, he's sticking with "Jules" for the variation of my name. I don't hate it. Maybe I don't even hate him.

He follows me upstairs. I'm keenly aware of how lived-in my single room studio is compared to the office and the extravagance of the party.

In my postage stamp-sized home, to the left of the front door is the kitchen quadrant, designated with a non-slip mat. Along the wall on the right, my sofa and coffee table make up the living room, designated by a jute rug. The bookshelf creates a vague border wall to my bedroom area, designated by a plush faux fur sheepskin that's a delight to step on when it's cold out.

He eyes the Care Bear on my bed, then eyes me, and we stare at each other for a long, meaningful moment.

"Cute," he says at last, breaking the standoff.

I take that to mean he thinks I'm a child. Yay. My thoughts tune to the sarcastic station.

Linc plants himself on one side of my two-person couch —a glorified love seat. I bring him a can of root beer and plop down beside him. It cannot be helped. Our knees brush. The denim of his jeans is like soft grit sandpaper against my bare skin, and neither of us pulls away. Instead, we both take simultaneous sips of root beer as if waiting for the picture show to start.

I have to get a handle on myself. I cannot be tricked. Refuse to let myself be attracted to a guy who hates me. I don't want to become a cautionary tale of heartbreak.

"So," I start, biting the inside corner of my lip. "Abraham Lincoln."

"What about him?"

"The penny flipping, the interest in Civil War paintings, your given name!"

He nods. "He's my great-great-great-great-great-grandfather."

I don't know what answer I expected, but I inhale liquid instead of sipping my root beer. After sputtering a few times, I ask, "Your what?" The words come out as a garbled squeak that would appall my church choir leader.

"On my mother's side. Her family line traces back to the Lincolns."

"You're kidding."

The only likeness between this guy and Honest Abe is the height and those refined cheekbones—they're of the type that many would say could cut glass, but in this case, they could split wood. Whereas Lincoln was all sharp angles and prairie-worn edges, this Abraham Lincoln is handsome in a way that makes my brain forget how to form complete sentences. Full biceps that strain against the hem of his t-shirt and hands that look like they could build something or tear it apart with equal ability.

"Why would I kid about something like that?"

I bump my shoulders up and down. "Clout."

He rolls his eyes as if he's above that. Easy since he's a billionaire's son.

I tilt my head and squint.

"What's that look for?"

"I'm trying to picture you in a stovepipe hat,"

He fights a smile around another sip of root beer. "I have a closet full."

"Giving speeches about preserving the Union ..." I gesture dramatically with my root beer. "Four score and seven years ago—"

He chuckles.

Continuing with the oratory bits and pieces I remember from history class, I'm standing now, one hand pressed to my heart, the other extended like I'm addressing a crowd.

"You're ridiculous." He reels me back toward the couch by my wrist.

No, his touching me and setting my skin ablaze is ridiculous. Feeling flammable, I tuck myself into the corner cushion.

He sets down his root beer and leans forward. "My mother spent years researching our family history. She found documents, traced bloodlines, and was fascinated, but more than that, she was most interested in the love story."

"Between Abraham and Mary Todd?"

"Mom said it was love at first sight. He courted her, but then something happened and they were kept apart before ultimately reuniting. During that time, my mother believed they exchanged love letters. She always wanted to find them." His eyes crinkle with affection and warmth.

It's a rare sight and makes me confident this man would never wear guyliner.

Like a chime indicating I got the right answer on a quiz

show, I realize exactly which piece is missing from the Fairfax Collection. "And the Civil War painting?"

"I believe *Echo & Answer* might contain clues about Lincoln's personal effects. Letters, documents, or something that points to the location of the lost love letters." He runs his hand through his hair. "I know how it sounds. Crazy, right?"

"No. Maybe you want to feel connected to something that mattered to her."

"Yeah." He exhales through his nose.

"And why did it, aside from the obvious that it's a piece of history?"

He's quiet for a long moment, studying my face. "To confirm that true love exists. I know my father loved her in his way. At first, they had a good relationship. But he got swallowed up in work. They never fought or anything, but she kept a journal. It took me a long time to read it—more than the twelve years I'd had with her. But when I finally did ..."

My hand drops on top of Linc's, letting him know I see and feel his sorrow. He thought or hoped his father would be there after his Mom passed away. That he'd step up. Step in. Save her? There are all kinds of heartbreak. Linc is still part lonely puppy under all that raw, cut manliness.

"The content of her journals was mostly upbeat, tracking our day-to-day lives, noting little things as I grew up. It was really sweet."

And tragic.

"She also commented a lot on her relationship with my father. It's almost like, at times, he forgot about her, wrapped up in work. For instance, she kept a little tally of the number of days that passed before he'd simply ask, 'How was your day?'"

My hand presses to my chest. "How sad."

"She always smiled, though, and prayed for him. For us."

I whisper, "She still is."

Breath unsteady, Linc takes a sip of root beer, signaling the conversation is closed.

I say, "So you're really a Lincoln."

"I've read all of his speeches—have the Gettysburg Address and passages from others memorized."

"Wow. So how does a guy related to Abraham Lincoln end up knowing people like Aiken and Iva?" That was not the question I should've asked, but since he was talking about romance and love, it slipped out.

"I dated Iva for about five months. I was her mystery man—she never confirmed publicly who she was seeing because it was better for her image to seem available. I recently ran into her at a smoothie shop for the first time in ages." He leans back against the couch cushion. "As for Aiken, he's her flavor of the week."

I prefer my simple life and the Sweetheart Report to that kind of drama.

He asks, "Do they change your opinion of me?"

"Why would you care about my opinion?"

"What about the Lincoln thing?"

I consider this seriously. "You've given me a lot to think about tonight."

"That's not an answer."

"It's the only one I have right now."

He finishes his root beer and then says, "Back at the party, when Iva and Aiken were talking about us being a couple—"

I nearly choke again and then cover it with laughter. No need to make it any more awkward than it needs to be.

"Ridiculous, right? I mean, you and me? We're very different people. And we're coworkers. Sort of. Not technically, but you know what I mean ..." I trail off.

"Very different." He nods but doesn't quite meet my eyes.

My heart hiccups as I say it. "I would never—don't worry about it. We're on the same page." The last thing I need is for my sort-of boss to think I took that the wrong way. In fact, I pointed out that we hate each other.

Or so I thought.

Linc unfolds himself from the couch, a hulking figure in the small room. "Thanks for coming with me tonight. And for the root beer."

"Thanks for the adventure. Even if it was weird and kind of disturbing."

"Illuminating?" he asks, recalling my comment earlier.

I nod. Very much so. Though not in the way that I initially thought.

19

LINC

JULES and I haven't discussed the rooftop party in the days since, but I've been studying the discrepancies she brought to my attention like they're game film before playoffs ... and analyzing the comment she made at the party.

We hate each other.

We hate each other? That seems extreme. Harsh. Speaking for myself, I don't hate her.

But does she truly despise me? I shift in my seat as if I'm fresh off the ice, stewing in sweaty athletic gear.

If she thinks I hate her, she's mistaken. Admittedly, I came across as pretty aggressive at first. Didn't want to be here. Still don't. I could walk away, but it's easier to fantasize about it when I'm on the thirty-ninth floor than actually staging a walkout, dishonoring my role, disregarding my father's legacy.

I just have to stick it out ... and do my best not to think about my cute assistant.

While I'm here, I'm going to find the lost love letters and I may as well try to do something useful. Turning back to the spreadsheets, the numbers don't lie—if we're right,

Jules uncovered something that could seriously damage Meridian Holdings. But there's still more digging to do because it could be as minor as a staff member forgetting to add a comma, cross a *t*, or dot an *i*.

Or someone could be stealing money.

The question that keeps me up at night isn't *who*, though.

My initial instinct was to protect Jules because everyone knows what happens to whistleblowers, which is probably the real reason why I told her to stay in her lane. The corresponding thought was that my father is involved. If it's true, that's certainly not something to be trifled with. Looking back, my warning could've been delivered more delicately.

When I'm not thinking about that, I'm preoccupied by the *Echo & Answer* painting. It's missing from the Fairfax Collection, but where could it be?

Then there's the nagging thought of whether all of this is connected.

Doubtful, but the letters, though important to my mother, would fetch a high price at auction. As far as I know, Mom was the only one looking for them. But could someone else be too?

I'm hunched over spreadsheets when Jules materializes at my desk, fidgeting with the loose string on her shirt. I've come to know her various laughs—nervous, amused, giddy. Her smiles—obligatory, shy, genuine. That she always adds one unexpected flourish to her otherwise professional outfits—a sparkly pair of earrings here. A pair of patent leather pumps there.

She's like an artist who just can't help but add one more brushstroke to make the masterpiece pop.

But the fidgeting right now suggests she's about to say something completely unexpected.

"I'm the cheer to your blah," she announces, setting down a paper cup of coffee.

I look up. "Hardly."

"The cream to your black coffee."

Delighted by the gesture because I'd been considering sneaking a nap, I take a sip. "There are grounds at the bottom."

"There are not. It was from a fresh pot."

I snicker. Just trying to get a rise out of her, see her blush ... smile, even if it's a harbinger of revenge.

She shifts from foot to foot. For the past few days, she's been doing weird little things, which, after being in her house, are very on brand. The woman is unique, delightfully quirky. A breath of fresh air when she's not acting like she hates the ground I walk on.

Yesterday, I'm certain she was rooting through my desk drawer. Sorry to disappoint, but the only things I keep in here are a notepad, pens, paperclips, a letter opener, a spare phone charger, and a tin of mints. Like an art thief leaving behind a calling card, I found a tiny rubber duck with a bowtie. I noticed she had several on the windowsill in her bathroom.

After my discovery, tit for tat, I went through her desk drawer. I am not one to be outdone. There, I found a small stack of fortune cookie fortunes. All optimistic and each with lucky number eighty-three on the back. Odd. Her desk also houses several types of lip balm, gloss, and lipstick, along with a lot of chocolate. Lots.

I added a fake plastic spider to her stash of paperclips.

Now she's hovering like she wants to tell me something,

but can't figure out how to start. Or she wants to inform me that she's leaving. Or ... I'm not sure what.

Jules keeps me on my toes. This would be a great time to skate a few laps, blow off some steam. Get iced up.

"Is there something you want to tell me?" I ask without looking up from my computer's monitor.

Despite the connection I thought we'd established—I sat on her couch, drank a root beer, told her I'm related to our sixteenth president—we've slipped back into our grumpy boss and cheerful assistant roles.

She pulls a penny from her pocket and starts tossing it, but then fumbles and it spins on my desk before lazily showing heads. The movement draws my attention to her hands, then I drag my gaze up her body. Today, she's wearing a pale yellow blouse with shiny white buttons and a black pencil skirt that fits her like a dream.

I get minor bumblebee vibes and remind myself that I'm allergic to all apiformes.

"Well," she says, still fidgeting.

Now, she's making me nervous, or at least that's what this unusual feeling in my stomach must be.

I draw my penny out of my pocket and flip it. Heads, I go back to work. Tails, I toss her over my shoulder and carry her around the office until whatever it is she wants to tell me spills out of her.

Jules fidgets with a length of her hair, twirling it around her finger. Gripping the coin hard so I don't reach out to feel if it's as soft as it looks, I leave nail marks in my palm.

The power goes out in my brain like during a summer storm. The logical part that categorizes, analyzes, and keeps everything in neat compartments goes offline entirely. All I can process is the way her teeth worry her bottom lip and how badly I want to smooth away that little crease between her eyebrows.

She presses her lips together as if afraid to elaborate.

Then I tell her about the two possible outcomes of my coin toss.

"You wouldn't do that, would you? Surely, it's against HR rules."

I get to my feet and stalk toward her.

She backs up as a slow grin broadens across her face.

I inch closer.

She blurts, "Okay, I told my friends Oly and Nate that my boss is related to Abraham Lincoln and they don't believe me."

I blink, slightly confused, though this is Jules, Queen of Quirk. "Why would you do that?"

"Because before that, I told them I met Iva Katz. Ever since we were kids, Oly has been a huge fan. Let's see, her favorites were 'Secret Liaison,' 'Heart Signals,' 'Arcane Skulls,' and 'Honey Bunny Bon Bon.' Such an eclectic catalog." She smooshes the sentences together.

The cold and familiar feeling of being used forms a brick of ice in my stomach. "Are you—?"

"And Nate thought it was cool that I met Aiken the Demo King. They wanted the whole backstory."

Relief floods through me, followed immediately by curiosity about how her mind works. "Did you mention the painting?"

"Of course not." She looks genuinely offended. "That's our thing, Linc-y baby."

I exhale a breath and want to be annoyed at her for using Iva's nickname for me, but I initially refused to use her proper name. Now, I've landed on "Jules" or Buttercup. I like that too.

Also, might I detect a hint of curiosity? Ridicule? Jealousy? A cocktail of all three? My gaze skates over her, searching for a clue.

She bites her lip. "So, um, they want proof you're real. We could video chat with them, but ..." She trails off, then glancing at the penny in her hand, she adds, "Actually, it was a pickleball bet."

"A what?"

"Pickleball. It's like tennis but smaller." She pinches her fingers together.

"I know what pickleball is. But what's a pickleball bet?"

She waves her hand dismissively. "It's the Fourth of July this weekend and they're having a party. All you'd need to do is show up, play one game, then be gone."

I can't tell if she's serious. With Jules, that's always the question. She's an original, first edition. I've learned to expect the unexpected. On Monday, her lunch was in a hollowed-out coconut because "Mondays in the summer need a splash of tropical pizzazz."

"Do you have any plans Saturday afternoon?" she continues, rushing the words together. "You'd only have to play one game and then you could dip out. No need to stay for fireworks."

I should say no. Bīriņš invited all the guys down to go boating. Plus, I don't know Oly and Nate. I'm not big on social gatherings with strangers and I prefer hockey over pickleball.

But Jules looks at me with a hopeful, slightly desperate expression that's near irresistible.

I rake my hand through my hair and find myself saying, "After the rooftop party, I do owe you."

"So you'll do it?"

I nod.

"Really?" Her body seems to coil as if she's holding something back.

"Yes."

That simple word unleashes this woman and she bounces on her toes before launching herself at me, arms spread wide, before they engulf me. Her hug is all-encompassing warmth. No sooner do my arms close around her than she's gone, abandoning me to the Antarctic. Freezing cold with a pang of longing.

She jolts back. "I'm sorry. I don't—I didn't mean—"

Our gazes tangle together and then a sharp intake of breath—mine or hers, I can't tell—breaks the spell.

My mistake. We're not alone.

Veronica, Drecken's assistant, stands in the doorway, eyebrow arched as if preparing to report us for indecent behavior.

I clear my throat. "I missed my trip to the tailor. She was taking measurements."

Jules narrows her eyes in my direction.

Veronica clicks her tongue. "Sure. Well, Ms. Drecken wants an executive summary of all of the accounts that you've been reviewing."

Jules turns sharply. "Is that typical protocol? In my experience, those are submitted directly to Mr. Andresen."

Veronica narrows her eyes. "Which department did you come from, Miss, um, sorry, I forgot your name? Silly me. You're new here. I can't expect to remember or for you to know a thing about executive protocol."

"Actually, I drafted Mr. Andresen's guidelines for that very thing." Even as Jules says this, she seems to shrink.

"Was that task assigned directly to you? Seems unconventional," I say.

Jules shifts slightly as if the task landed on her desk from someone else who didn't want to do it.

Time to intervene. "I'll see to it that the summaries land on the correct desk."

Veronica sniffs. "I'll let Ms. Drecken know that's your intention."

When the echoing of her high heels disappears down the hall, I ask, "Is that true about the summaries?"

"Unless the CEO changed it. It could be that he passed off the task to the acting COO."

"And who passed it off to you?"

"I'm not a snitch."

Then I was right. However, my father isn't the sort to delegate that kind of thing. Seems slightly suspicious. Not that I should care. But we've been poking around obscure files. Maybe that raised a flag. "Listen, if she or the other assistant asks you for anything else directly, please let me know. Directly."

"Yes, sir."

I pull out my phone and ask for Jules's number.

She stammers about HR rules, but then I lean in and whisper, her loose baby hairs tickling my cheek, "I reviewed the discrepancies. You're on to something."

Her eyes widen with surprise.

"Plus, there's the matter of the pickleball bet."

She texts me the address immediately, as if she's afraid I'll change my mind.

20

LINC

SATURDAY AFTERNOON FINDS me at a community pickleball court in Prospect Heights, a nice suburb for young professionals and weekend warriors. The complex has a generic apartment-living vibe—beige siding, budget landscaping, and functional outdoor light fixtures.

From the parking lot, I immediately spot Jules wearing a blue skort with stars and a red and white striped tank top. I catalog every inch of her as I approach. Those legs. Toned, smooth, and tan. Her hair is off her neck, pulled back in a ponytail. She gestures wildly while talking to a tall woman and a desk-jockey-type, who offsets his time spent sitting with a fitness trainer.

"Linc!" Jules waves me over.

I'm unintentionally walking a tightrope. One slip of the tongue about penalties or playoff schedules and my whole summer as a regular guy crashes down. For once, someone is getting to know me before they know my stats, my salary, or what team I play for. I'm not ready for that conversation to happen over pickleball and burgers.

"These are my friends. Olympia—Oly—and Nate."

Oly gives me an appraising look. "So you're the mysterious boss."

"The Abraham Lincoln descendant," Nate adds with a grin.

Because my competitive spirit cannot be contained, I add, "And pickleball champion. Jules called upon the best."

It doesn't escape my notice that Oly mouths *Jules* as if questioning the nickname I settled on for her. The one that came out when we were at the rooftop party and I felt protective. I temporarily turned into a territorial caveman. Which makes no sense because Jules isn't mine to protect. She'd probably kick me in the shins if she thought for a second I was jealous of the guy with the man bun or irate at how Iva acted.

She folds her hands like she's saying a prayer. "Okay, so here's the thing. It's not exactly a standard pickleball game."

Of course it isn't.

"We need another couple for the Grand Old Flag tournament," Oly explains. "But we play with ... variations."

"Variations?"

Nate produces a jar of actual pickles that look like they came from a farmer's market. "Winner of each point gets to eat one. Loser has to answer a truth-or-dare question."

I look at Jules. "You're kidding."

"It's fun!" she insists. "And silly. But mostly fun."

When we reach our side of the net, I whisper to Jules, "Confession, I've never actually played this game."

Face stricken with horror, she looks like I just warned her that a werewolf prowls behind her. "Um, that's a problem."

"How hard can it be?"

"On a stomach full of pickle juice?"

"We're going to win." I spin my paddle in my hand.

She doesn't look convinced.

Pickleball, it turns out, isn't exactly easy, but I am a professional athlete. The game area is smaller than a tennis court, the paddle is solid, and it's played with a veritable wiffle ball. Jules is terrible and tries to offer a lengthy explanation every time she misses. Oly is competitive and the reigning trophy holder in their community. Nate treats it like comedy hour.

I score a fair number of points, eating my share of pickles and Jules accepts increasingly ridiculous dares. She has to do an impression of Kermit the Frog (adorably accurate), sing the alphabet backwards (she gets stuck at L), and demonstrate her best "trying to be professional at work" face (which makes everyone, including me, crack up because it's a glare cast in my direction).

Unfortunately, I lose our next point and choose truth.

She asks me, "What's the weirdest thing you've ever eaten?"

"Fermented shark in Iceland," I answer.

"Why were you in Iceland?" Nate asks.

"Work trip," I say smoothly.

My other work. The one that involves skates and sticks and gliding smoothly, while I hear the rush of my breath in my helmet and experience the satisfaction of a team working together to win.

Unlike this, but it's not so bad.

The tournament ends with Oly and Nate winning, mostly because I started playing with Jules on my back like a koala—it was one of the dares. She's breathless and glowing a happy grin as we exchange a high five that lingers …

"We're even now. Thanks for coming. You can go," she says abruptly.

I drop her hand, feeling like I was just fired on account of the loss. We'd been having a good time. "Am I being dismissed?"

Her eyes widen. "I meant, assuming you want to leave, you can. I'm sure you have holiday plans. I'm sorry I dragged you into this. I probably owe you now."

Before I can respond, Oly appears. "You should stay for the barbecue. We've got burgers, Nate's famous macaroni salad, and the pool is open if you want to swim. There's a clubhouse with showers, too."

Nate adds, "Plus fireworks later. It's the Fourth of July. We will light up the sky with our patriotism."

Jules looks at me uncertainly. "But you don't have to."

I check my grandfather's watch around my wrist. The smart thing would be to leave. Go home, review more spreadsheets, refortify the distance between Jules and me that's been eroding bit by bit since that night on the rooftop.

"I'll stay," I hear myself say.

Jules's smile is radiant. Because I almost can't endure it, I pick her up, sling her over my shoulder, and march us toward the pool.

"Linc! Put me down!" she squeals, pounding koala fists against my back, but she's laughing.

"Not happening," I say, adjusting my grip as she wriggles.

Instead, I cannonball us both into the pool.

She splashes me and splutters.

When we surface, she looks murderous.

I feign innocence. "What? You were hot."

She goes still as if wondering if she heard correctly.

Yeah, she's hot. Any man would have to be blindfolded not to see that.

She nods as if deciding I didn't mean anything about it

and accepting the third-place trophy. "It is a warm day in July."

I chuckle and splash her. "You know that isn't what I meant."

I catch a secret grin that she squirrels away like she wants to save it for cold weather.

We playfully wrestle before she swims to the deep end. I make chase, grabbing hold of her ankle and pulling her toward me. We pause at the pool's edge, both out of breath.

Sudden awareness shoots through me as my pulse spikes. I'm holding her. Our bodies pressed together, warm and alive.

Voice rough, I take a risk and say, "You're looking at me like that again."

"Like what?"

"With sugar eyes."

Her brow furrows. "Do enlighten me, sir."

Her hair is wet and tousled, her cheeks flushed, and she's looking up at me with those eyes that see through every wall I've built. Eyes that tell me she also thinks I'm hot.

"Like you like what you see," I answer, committing to telling the truth like Honest Abe.

Her breath catches. The only sound is water lapping against the pool tiles and the distant hum of summer insects.

"Sugar eyes, huh?"

"Yup. I've noticed a few times in the office. At the rooftop party. When we were at your house. Today. You look at me a certain way."

She blinks a few times as if caught and deciding whether to double down and grow a Pinocchio nose or come clean.

Instead, she splashes me, chilling us both, which is probably what we need. HR and all.

The barbecue is laid-back and welcoming—the kind of gathering where people talk to each other instead of networking. Oly works in marketing and has strong opinions about everything from the best deep-dish pizza in the city to whether aliens exist. Nate was recently laid off, but tells water cooler stories that have me laughing more than relating, since they all think I'm also a corporate guy.

Jules is different here. Still quirky and prone to saying unexpected things, but there's an ease to her that I don't see at the office. She's not trying to be professional or appropriate. She's just herself.

Hilariously and adorably herself.

We end up sitting by the pool as the sun sets, our feet dangling in the water. She changed into a soft white sundress with little embroidered yellow and red flowers that make her skin look warm and buttery. She adds a sparkly red, white, and blue headband with springs topped with glittery stars.

"This is nice," she says quietly, bonking me with the bobbly stars.

I chuckle. "Yeah, it is."

And it's true. When was the last time I felt so free? So me?

"Can I ask you something?" Jules steadies the stars with her hand.

"Sure."

"Earlier, when I said we were even—did that bother you?"

I consider the question. "Why would it bother me?"

"I don't know. You suddenly had a look on your face like ..." She shrugs. "I don't know how to describe it."

Like I felt rejected? Or maybe I don't want us to be even. I don't want this to be a transaction where favors are exchanged and debts are settled. I don't want the life of a businessman—to turn into my father.

"I had fun today," I say instead.

"Really?" She lights up as if ready to drag me back onto the pickleball court.

"Don't sound so surprised."

Her laughter is bright and unabashed. "At work, you're so serious. All buttoned up. I wasn't sure you knew how to spell fun, no less have it."

Until today, fun consisted of boating and wakeboarding on Lake Michigan with the guys. Jet Ski races and cliff jumping in Hawaii. Paintball and Go-kart bumper car battles. My mother would scold me if she knew about my fun, but risky behavior. But yeah, it's a blast.

Sitting here with Jules, eating burgers and watching kids run around with sparklers is not where I expected to be. It's wholesomely pleasant and delightful. Not my typical fun, but I like it more than anything else I could be doing, whether with the guys or on a yacht, so I stay—talk to Jules's friends, eat a piece of the slightly askew Grand Old Flag blueberry, strawberry, and whipped cream cake she made, and just be with her.

Turns out that fun is spelled J-U-L-E-S.

As the cotton candy sky flattens into gray, then black, she shivers and rubs her upper arms. I give her my sweatshirt. She tries to decline.

"I'm prepared to wrestle you into it so you're not cold."

She lets out a huffy breath, lifts her arms to the sky for the sleeves, and I drop it over her head like I'm dressing her. My mouth goes dry.

Jules bunches up the neckline and inhales.

Hoping it doesn't smell bad, I must be staring in alarm.

She sighs and then notices I'm watching. "Don't say anything about sugar eyes."

I chuckle, diverting my thoughts to the fact that the hoodie looks comically large on her. I'm thankful I had the presence of mind not to bring an Ottawa Outlaws-branded one. Having something real like this, whatever it is and wherever it goes, is too good, too pure to ruin with the added dimension of me being a public figure, a professional athlete, on top of being a billionaire's son.

Stevens teases me about my first-world problems.

But it's all relative, and for once in my life, I'm just me. Linc. The same guy my mother knew and loved. Whatever is building between Jules and me feels closer to real than anything has in a long time.

Later, as the bursts of gold and red and blue burst in the dark sky, Jules gasps at each one like she's seeing fireworks for the first time. She sits close enough that I can smell the summery scent of sunscreen and pool chlorine over the cherry blossoms and almonds.

When they're over, I'm halfway through telling her a random story about how Bīriņš got carried away with the fireworks on the lake one year, resulting in a high-speed aquatic chase, when a boom splits the air. She jumps, laughing, and her shoulder brushes mine.

I forgot about the grand finale and lose the thread.

"Beautiful," she murmurs as red, white, and blue sparkles in the sky.

I don't answer. I'm too busy noticing the faint freckle at the edge of her jaw, the way she presses her lips part slightly.

"What?" she asks, catching me.

"Nothing," I say. Just ... forgot where I was for a second.

The air between us crackles, charged with something that has nothing to do with the pyrotechnics above us. Her breath hitches, and I have the sudden, overwhelming urge to kiss her.

Then a child sprints past us, shrieking with delight and breaks the moment.

Dudes don't get butterflies. They get dragonflies and a fleet of them nearly knocks me off my feet.

21

JULES

FROM PIZZA to the people she lets into her life, Oly doesn't give her stamp of approval easily. She's tougher to win over than a cat being given a bath, so when she pulls me aside after everyone has left and we're cleaning up, I brace myself.

"I like him," she says, which should be good news.

"But?" I ask, knowing it's coming.

"But he's hiding something."

My stomach twists as I wring water out of a dishrag. "What do you mean?"

"Can't put my finger on it. He doesn't quite seem like a billionaire's son summer intern."

I roll my eyes. "If you recall, this whole thing started because I told you about that crazy rooftop party."

"Have you noticed the calluses on his hands? Those aren't desk-job hands."

I have noticed those hands. In fact, he left an imprint on the small of my back. His fingerprints are inked on my skin from when we high-fived and held hands. The desolation when they came apart when I essentially gave him marching orders after the pickleball game.

Dumb, dumb girl.

Nate calls from the other room, where he's sweeping. "Dude couldn't keep his eyes off Juliana!"

"He was making sure my sneakers stayed tied," I insist, but even as I say it, the twisting inside turns into a fluttering.

Oly gives me a look that says she sees right through me. "He called you *Jules*."

"So? He's also called me Julie, Julia, Julianne—" I start counting off the variations on my fingers.

"But he stuck with *Jules*."

She's not wrong. He started calling me Jules and hasn't stopped. No more silly ones like Jujubee, either. Not only that, he stuck with me all night. Made sure I had a steady stream of root beer, a clean towel after swimming, and watched *me* ... not the fireworks.

I tell her about Mr. Man Bun at the rooftop party.

Oly shrieks and the nearby dogs, already on edge from the fireworks, erupt with barking. "He did the Darcy finger flex?"

I nod. "Patent pending."

She grips me by the shoulders, searching my face, and whispers, "Mark my words, he's the one."

My throat bobs on a swallow because while I've always been searching for The One ™, it's another thing entirely to possibly, maybe, potentially know who it is but not be able to connect the dots to "arriving there" with him because of the shifting tectonic plates beneath our feet.

On the way home, I try to convince myself that Linc stuck with me because he didn't know anyone else at the party. After all, I clung to him when we were among the likes of Iva, Aiken, and their friends.

That night, after getting home smelling like bonfire, s'mores, and Linc—still wearing his hoodie, I'm drunk from his fresh minty scent—my phone beeps with a message.

Linc: Had a great time today.

My pulse does an elaborate Zumba routine—I only know what that is because Oly had me take a class with her when she still lived in the city. We also tried barre, Pilates, and sweaty yoga in a room that smelled like egg salad on a hot day. I had to leave after ten minutes.

Me: I did too. Thanks for being a good sport.

Linc: Are you impressed by my pickleball prowess?

Me: Your pickle-eating skills are unmatched.

Linc: So, it's my turn to return the favor.

Me: Please don't tell me you've signed me up for a couples' ballroom dance class. You saw how often my shoes come untied.

Never mind Zumba. My pulse does a cha cha. Why did I write that? Why isn't there an undo button? Suddenly overheating, I tear off Linc's sweatshirt, but his scent lingers.

Hastily, I write back.

Me: I thought we were even.

Linc: The truth or dare variation of the pickleball game upped the ante. I'd like you to join me at a private party on Monday night.

Attend a private party with Linc? My brain immediately spirals into worst-case scenarios and best-case scenarios, which are somehow the same-case scenarios. He can't mean what I think he does.

Me: Is it a luau? I'm only going if there are piña coladas.

Linc: You and the coconuts.

I can practically hear him chuckle. Always at me, ever the little goofball. Not tall and beautiful and elegant like Iva.

Me: I'm coco-nutty!

The moment I hit send, I cringe. When did I go from keeping things professional with Linc to ... this? To being completely, authentically weirdly myself—the girl who makes terrible puns and cops to coconut obsessions?

Linc: I'm afraid it may not be as fun as pickleball. Could give us answers, though.

Me: That sounds mysterious and slightly ominous. Please don't say Aiken will be there.

Linc: It'll be interesting. Promise.

Me: What are the details?

Linc: I'll fill you in tomorrow.

Me: Can I at least have time to read the fine print?

Linc: Not with those sugar eyes.

Me: Sugar eyes? This again. I assure you, I don't understand. Please elaborate.

Me: Never mind. Don't. Whatever it is, I'm not buying or selling.

He doesn't answer.

Me: You can't just drop something like that and ghost.

But apparently, he can, because mine is the last message in our thread.

The next day at work is torture. Linc has meetings until well after lunch, and I only catch glimpses of him in the hallowed halls of Meridian Holdings.

The first time we pass in the corridor, his lips quirk with a smile that makes my skeletal system forget that it has joints. The second time, he actually winks—*winks!*—like we have a secret. The third time, he looks over his shoulder at me as we pass, and I walk into a potted plant.

Thankfully, he didn't see.

I'm not sure what to make of it.

Since the Fourth of July, I've started a rationing program, limiting how much I allow myself to notice about Linc's … everything. Today I'm allowing myself his eyelashes—thick and dark and completely unfair on a man.

Tomorrow, it will be his jawline, masculine and strong—

suggesting whatever he says will be important. Some stubble indicates he grooms but has a full life, so it's grown out a bit before he's had a chance to trim it. From the vantage point behind my desk, I typically have a very flattering angle.

At least, when he's here.

It's become a dangerous game.

When he finally appears at my desk at three-thirty, he smells like soapy mint with a hint of aftershave that now makes me want to ... lick him. No, that's not right. Too extreme. Too ... weird. What am I thinking? But I do want to lean closer and breathe him in. Which would definitely be an HR violation. I tell myself that I'll wash his hoodie tonight and return it to him. I won't find it next to my pillow like I did this morning.

"About tonight," he says, perching on the edge of my desk.

Hyper aware of his proximity, I suffer from the deadly trio of pink cheeks, a fluttering stomach, and a light layer of sweat at the nape of my neck. It's oh-so-attractive.

I swallow thickly. "Tonight?"

He waggles his eyebrows. "The private party. River North. Exclusive showing of a Civil War Collection."

My eyes widen. "Oh. That actually sounds really cool. I thought it was going to be another hipster glamour carnival, only this time in a cave instead of on a rooftop."

He chuckles. "But there is one thing. My father will be there." He winces as if preparing for someone to fix his broken nose. It's not broken, but it may have been once. I'll have to inspect it more carefully. I appoint Wednesday nose day.

"I've met Mr. Andresen." I think of the lobby when we

were with Bear Paw or whatever Linc's boating buddy was named.

"I mean, he wants to meet you, uh, my assistant."

That makes my antenna lift. "Why?"

"Because he's noticed some really good work come out of this office and is convinced that I have nothing to do with it. I mean, probably. When it comes to my father, that's par for the course."

"Does he like golf?"

"Lives for it."

"Anything else I should know?" I recall Linc's comments about his mother's journal and get a very stereotypical blueprint of what life was like in the Andresen household: a demanding father. A doting mother. A son caught in between, who tried to go his own way but repeatedly disappointed the one guy who should've been his biggest support.

He runs a hand through his hair, messing it up in a way that shouldn't be attractive but makes me worry I drooled a little. Friday will be hair day.

"Yeah, actually." He pauses as if weighing something. "My mother believed that the painting we're looking for contained symbols—a visual code like the positioning of a fallen flag, the angle of a cannon, the number of visible stars. She described it like a map for those who knew how to read it."

"Why not just look it up online?"

"It's been missing. Never photographed."

"Ah, which explains our deep dive into the Fairfax Collection."

He nods as if his mind is elsewhere, perhaps on a battlefield of his own, one foot in the past and the other in the present. "I'll pick you up at seven. You looked good in that little black dress, but this will be slightly more formal."

I freeze like a department store mannequin in a window display, modeling the latest in "Corporate Professional-wear" while my brain sprints like a hamster who just took a bath in espresso, running through every word he just spoke.

Mere days ago, we were bickering about quarterly reports, and now I'm mentally cataloging how the light hits his face. Picturing how good Linc would look in black-and-white photography. The sharp lines of his jaw, the way shadows would fall across his cheekbones ... Or maybe sepia, all golden and vintage like those old, romantic Hollywood movie star magazine spreads Mom loves. A girl can dream.

At the end of the day, Misha, one of Maxine Drecken's assistants, summons me, inquiring about reports that are definitely in her job description, not mine. But like the good little worker bee that I am, I bring them to her office, but before I'm able to announce my arrival, I overhear hushed voices hissing.

"Twenty years of loyalty and he's handing everything we've built to a kid who doesn't even want it. The spoiled brat. I've more than earned the official role and I'm not going to let it slip through my fingers without a fight—whether Frank realizes it or not."

A chill breezes over my skin and I hastily drop the files on Misha's desk as she approaches, looking at me as if to ask what I'm doing here.

I point to the material she requested and then scurry away like a scared rabbit. I debate whether to tell Linc about what I overheard between the COO and her assistant.

It feels like ten years have passed before I manage to get home. By seven o'clock, I've changed outfits four times and settled on a navy blue dress that hits just below my knees with eyelet embroidery along the hems. It's professional enough for meeting Linc's father but not so formal that I look like I got lost in my aunt's closet.

I leave my hair down before settling on putting it up and adding a pair of pearl earrings.

That'll have to do because Linc should be here any second. I haven't yet decided on shoes when someone knocks on the door. A tall someone in a suit when I peek through the peephole. I expected to just meet him downstairs.

I open the door and spin in a circle, panicked. He stops my twirling by dropping his hands onto my shoulders. Barefoot, I feel impossibly short, a bit vulnerable. But that may have more to do with the bold smile on his face.

"You look pretty."

"I do?"

I can't read his expression which tells me we're either going to murder each other before the night is through or we're at the start of a side quest that's the beginning of everything.

22

JULES

THE VENUE IS a gallery in River North composed of small rooms with dark wood and dramatic lighting. They must've spent a fortune on placards instructing visitors not to touch or take photographs of the art or artifacts.

It's quite a contrast to the rooftop party. Here, people in expensive clothes mill about with wine glasses in hand and speak in hushed tones about the items on exhibition.

"This is incredible," I whisper as we walk past a display case containing actual Civil War logbooks.

"Stay close," Linc murmurs, his hand finding the small of my back. "Don't want you to get lost in here."

Which, of course, is exactly what happens after we meet several men Carmen would call silver foxes, none of which are Frank Andresen.

One moment I'm following Linc through the crowd, and the next I'm standing alone in front of a display of vintage garments, wondering how I managed to lose a six-foot-plus man in a suit. I wander through several rooms, growing increasingly worried, when two security guards approach me.

"Miss, are you supposed to be here?" one asks, not unkindly but with an authoritative suspicion that makes me instantly feel guilty. Must be genetic.

"I'm with someone ..." I start.

"And who might that be?"

Before I can answer, a voice behind me says, "She's one of my employees and a guest of my son."

I turn to see a man who looks like Linc will in thirty years—same strong jawline, same intelligent eyes, but with silver hair and an air of authority that could command armies.

My mouth goes dry.

"Mr. Andresen," I manage, offering my hand. "Juliana Lindley. It's an honor to formally meet you."

His handshake is firm, his smile warmer than I expected. "The pleasure is mine, Miss Lindley. Abraham has mentioned that your support in the office has been unmatched."

"He did? That doesn't sound like something he'd say."

Mr. Andresen chuckles. "You're right. But I pay attention to what goes on across all floors in my building."

I nod, concerned about what he means by that in light of the discrepancies we've been researching. "He spoke very fondly of his mother, your late wife. She sounds like an amazing woman."

His gaze softens, but he quickly blinks it away. "Thank you. That's very kind of you to say."

We chat for a few more minutes about the exhibits, and I find myself relaxing despite the intimidating circumstances. Frank Andresen is formidable, which I knew, but there is a hidden gentleness underneath that reminds me of Linc.

Two men I told myself I hated. Hatred based on

assumptions, hearsay, and the simple fact that they had authority in my life. Upon reflection, I think I wanted to rebel against having a boss—against the idea that someone had power over me. But now, after getting to know Linc and watching him drop the grumpy boss act (mostly), I realize there will always be a hierarchy. I can't spend my life angry that I'm not at the top. That's counterproductive. I just need to earn my way up—actually earn it, not expect it to be handed to me.

If that's what I want, anyway. Maybe the top isn't all that it's cracked up to be. I'll get back to you on that.

Mr. Andresen says, "I should excuse myself and return to the party. I believe my son is probably frantic looking for you."

After we part ways, I wander through a gallery room, admiring the presentation of the artwork, doubtful we'll find what we're looking for, which we've only ever read descriptions of, never seen.

Linc rounds the corner, slightly breathless and relieved. "There you are."

"Here I am. Almost got kicked out by the security team and I met your father."

He gawks with concern.

"All is well and your dad told me the funniest story about you."

"By funny, do you mean embarrassing?" he asks as we enter another gallery room.

"You betcha," I joke. "It was about the time you got your head stuck between the banister spindles when you were eight and the fire department had to rescue you."

Linc stops walking. His expression turns to one of amusement and he wags his finger. "That didn't happen to me, but is that one of your core memories?"

"Thankfully, my brothers were too young to remember."

"You looked very concerned for a moment, which makes me wonder what's in your personal catalog of humiliation."

He shakes his head, but he's smiling. "You're terrible."

"I'm delightful."

"That too."

I go still and stare at the wall, but not in front of a piece of art. Rather, the thermostat. Is it hot in here? I fan my face because I think we're flirting.

Linc must not know how that little conversation just torched my cheeks as he leads me through several more rooms until we reach a smaller, more intimate viewing area.

"Linc," I breathe, grabbing his arm. "Is that it?"

Hanging on the far wall, softly lit and completely unmistakable, is the painting from the Fairfax Collection. The one that's been missing.

"Would you look at that? I thought it might be here, but it was more like a faint hope. Where have you been hiding?" Linc asks.

I keep watch while Linc breaks the very visible "No photos" rule and discreetly snaps a few pictures of *Echo & Answer*, depicting a battle scene in the Civil War. Abraham Lincoln fills the foreground, backed by rich colors and incredible detail. It's a window into history.

"We need more information. Can you—?" Linc starts.

He goes quiet when a security guard's radio crackles.

We both freeze.

I catch fragments. "... suspicious behavior in the south wing ... requesting backup ..."

My eyes widen. We're going to get thrown out, or worse, I'll get fired since Linc's father is here. I'm prone to instantly spiraling into worst-case scenarios. Must be my guilty conscience. *Thanks, Dad.*

Linc tilts his head toward another exit to the room. "We should—"

We walk briskly toward the opposite end of the gallery, attempting nonchalance despite the fact that we just broke the "no photography" rule. I can hear the guard's footsteps behind us and more radio chatter.

"This way." Linc pulls me down a narrow, dark-paneled corridor lined with smaller exhibits.

We can hear multiple sets of footsteps now and urgent voices. My heart is hammering so hard I'm afraid it's echoing off the gallery walls.

Linc tugs us into the shadows of an alcove with a large Civil War battle scene painting just as the footsteps get closer.

The voices are right around the corner now. "Check that corridor ... two suspects, male and female ..."

His eyes meet mine, and I can see him calculating options. Then his gaze drops to my lips, and his expression shifts. His eyes get heavy.

"Trust me," Linc breathes.

Before I can ask what he means, he cups my face and leans in. His lips hover just above mine—so close I can feel his breath warm against my skin, can count his eyelashes, can see a twinkle in his eyes that reminds me of the glitter bomb.

But who are the bad guys in this scenario? Us for being where we don't belong in the gallery? For being closer than a boss and an assistant should be? For being from different worlds?

And yet, there is no denying the space between us

flashes and crackles with summer storm lightning. After the count of three, the thunder of our heartbeats follows.

His lips part.

My breath catches.

His thumb brushes across my cheek.

I forget about security guards and missing paintings and every rational thought I've ever had.

We're frozen in this moment of *almost*.

It's a breath before the plunge.

My heart is beating so hard I'm sure he can feel it.

His forehead touches mine.

I can practically taste the mint in the air.

One tiny movement forward from either of us and ...

Footsteps pass by us, but I barely register them. All I know is Linc. How his gaze skims mine. The way every nerve ending in my body tingles from his proximity.

The voices fade, but neither of us moves. We stay suspended in this almost-kiss, this moment that feels like standing on the edge of a cliff.

Finally, he pulls back just enough to meet my eyes, leaving me dizzy and wanting.

"What was that?" I whisper, my voice barely audible.

His lips curve into a devastating smile, the one that makes my knees wobbly and unable to function. "That was to leave you wanting more."

I blink at him, still trying to catch my breath. But then reason returns and my brain comes up with an obvious excuse to explain the mental malfunction I just had—there is no world in which Linc Andresen would actually want to kiss me.

Piecing it together, I tap the air with my finger. "Very convincing ... camouflage. Smart to let the guards think we were just two people making out in the alcove. Nothing to see here. Move along, please. Don't tarry. We're consenting adults. But if anyone from Meridian HR asks, we're not boss and employee. Nope. Never saw this guy before. It was a lark, I tell you! A lark!" I cannot make my mouth stop babbling.

"For the record, I never hated you, Jules," he whispers, his voice rough.

"Sure. Right. You betcha." The words come out stilted because my brain is still stuck on how close we just came to crossing a line that we could never uncross.

I scramble, desperate to get my footing because I feel like I'm floating. "Okay, it's fair to say that we've gone from enemies to friends. But no further. That's the plan. Right?"

Even as I say it, I know it's a lie. We've already gone further. That almost-kiss changed everything.

"Are you entertaining that tropical resort work fling scenario?" he teases.

"No, Abraham! Nothing of the sort."

But it has certainly crossed my mind. More than crossed —it has a flight booked and the bags are packed.

That night, I lie awake staring at the ceiling, my thoughts volleying between the almost kiss and the painting we discovered. Every time I close my eyes, I can almost feel Linc's lips on mine, can remember the way his rough hand felt against my cheek.

But when I'm not reliving every second of what could have happened, I'm studying the crude cell phone images we managed to take before the security guards appeared. Something about the painting nags at me, beyond just its unexpected presence.

I swipe through the photos on my phone, zooming in on different sections, trying to identify what's bothering me.

The brushwork, the colors, the signature in the corner ... it's a low-quality blur.

And then it hits me.

I sit up in bed, heart racing with an entirely different kind of excitement.

What if there's another painting?

I grab my laptop, suddenly wide awake and ready to do research. Somewhere in the back of my mind, beyond the mystery and the thrill of discovery, one thought keeps circling back: Linc and I almost kissed.

Sure, it was to throw off the guards. But despite all my protests about staying professional, about being just friends, about it being a convenient decoy, I really, really want to kiss for real.

23

LINC

WHEN I GET to the office, I find a manila envelope on my desk. Stamped across the front is the word *Confidential.*

My pulse kicks up and I wonder if this has anything to do with the discrepancies Jules found. I open the metal tab and then turn it upside down to release the contents, but instead of documents or say, photographs, confetti sprinkles into my hand. Most of them are little shards of colorful paper, but a few shiny metallic pieces read *Happy Birthday.*

Only one person on the planet would do this.

Jules must've taken note that I was turning twenty-nine when she looked at my license.

After I clean it up, I'm back at my desk, wishing I'd spent a little more time paying attention during class while in the business program at college. Who am I kidding? I lived for hockey. Still do. I don't regret placing my focus there, rather than learning how to review quarterly reports.

But it doesn't help that my brain keeps replaying last night frame by frame.

Jules pressed against the gallery wall.

The way her breath caught when I was so close to kissing her.

How she smelled like cherry lip balm and trouble.

I asked her to trust me. She did. Even when everything in her posture suggested that trusting people doesn't come easily to her.

Pretending to kiss was cover. A distraction from the security guards who suspected we were taking unauthorized photographs. They weren't wrong. Instead, it stirred something inside.

"Abraham." My father's voice cuts through my daydream like a referee's whistle. He's standing in my doorway, looking every inch the corporate titan in his charcoal suit. "My office."

I follow him upstairs and down the hall, past the intimidating oil paintings and polished wood. His corner suite overlooks the Chicago River, and he settles behind his massive desk like a king holding court.

Truth be told, I'd rather be one of Frank Andresen's subjects than Aiken the Demo King's, but I digress.

My father steeples his fingers. I make a mental note never to do that. "Interesting evening last night. I had the pleasure of meeting your assistant."

"Jules is excellent at her job." The words come out more defensive than I intend.

His eyebrows lift slightly. "Jules, is it? How ... familiar."

Heat crawls up my neck. "She's professional. Competent. The office runs better with her around."

At least she knows what she's doing, unlike me, who blazed in here thinking I'd play the hard-hitting corporate exec, when in reality, any games I want to be involved in are on the ice.

"I've noticed." He leans back in his leather chair,

studying me with a similar intensity to when he evaluates million-dollar acquisitions. "She seems quite taken with you."

"We work well together."

"Abraham." He uses the Dad tone that has always made me stand up straighter. "We don't mix business with our personal lives. HR exists for a reason."

I open my mouth to protest, to insist there's nothing personal happening, but the lie sticks in my throat. After last night, pretending Jules means nothing to me would be like pretending there aren't stars in the sky.

"Understood," I manage.

He nods, apparently satisfied, but as I'm halfway to the door, he adds, "And Abraham? It won't do well to dig too deep into certain ... historical matters. Some stones are better left unturned."

I freeze. "What do you mean?"

His smile doesn't reach his eyes. "Your mother had many admirable qualities, but her obsession with the past wasn't one of them."

The words hit like a slap shot to the ribs. Mom's journal, her research, and her absolute certainty that the lost Lincoln love letters existed are what keep me here. He always dismissed it all as a romantic fantasy, so much so that our search for them became a secret. But now there's something darker in his tone, something that makes my stomach twist.

He turns back to his computer, dismissing me. "Focus on learning the business, son. Leave the mysteries to the past."

My instinct to stomp out of his office is juvenile, so I square my shoulders and turn to leave like an adult, intending to defy his orders.

Then he calls, "Oh, and Abraham, happy birthday."

I falter, surprised he remembered. "Thanks, and it's Linc."

I walk back to my office on autopilot with my father's warning echoing in my head. Sounded like he already knew exactly what Jules may have discovered. The way he mentioned Mom's research like it was hazardous instead of hopeful.

Not for the first time since I started this internship, I wonder if my father might be hiding more than just business strategies.

The rest of the day drags like overtime in a scoreless game. Jules and I exchange professional pleasantries when we pass in the hallway, but there's a hum of electricity between us now, an awareness that makes me buzz.

Every time she glances up from her desk, every time she strides through the hall, with every breath she takes ... I remember the way she felt in my arms. The way she looks at me with those sugar eyes. No, I'm the one who is left wanting more.

By evening, I'm wound tighter than a goalie before playoffs, so I do the one thing I get right: go to a local rink where an old buddy works, lace up, and skate. I stay and watch a men's league game and then hit the ice again before the Zamboni refreshes it for the final time tonight. Happy birthday to me.

For a few hours, it feels good to be where I belong instead of pretending to be someone I'm not.

It's nearly ten p.m. by the time I get home and out of the shower when my phone buzzes with a text.

Jules: Do you like popcorn?

I scratch my temple like she just asked a riddle. I don't

know a ton about Juliana Lindley, but the woman is clever, quirky, and I'm convinced that her lips are better than birthday cake.

Me: Is this a trick question or are you going to determine my value as a friend based on my answer?

Jules: I'm trying to settle a debate with my neighbors.

Me: Now?

Jules: Every night, they argue from the other side of the wall. I'm the designated judge, but don't take legal advice from me. That's my disclaimer.

I chuckle, surprised, but not by her response.

Me: Yes, I like popcorn, but my teeth are tightly spaced, so I prefer not to eat it because the little kernel things get caught and drive me crazy until I floss.

Jules: Thank goodness you floss. If you didn't, that would mean we couldn't be friends.

I can't tell whether she's serious, but I do have exceptional dental hygiene. Thanks, Mom.

Jules: Okay, so the real question is thus: salted butter or butter and salt?

How is this a question? Do married couples really fight over things like this? Also, she used the word *thus*. That's so Jules. I reply in kind.

Me: The latter, obviously.

Jules: I will inform Screechy and Grumbly of our findings. Also, do you want to meet?

In the month or so that Jules and I have known each other, I've come to be prepared to expect her to say anything. But this catches me off guard. Before thinking, I answer.

Me: Now?

Jules: I know it's late, but I've been researching. Found something you need to see.

Me: Where?

Jules: The 24-hour laundromat near my place. I still have your hoodie. I'll drop you the address. Meet me there?

A laundromat. At midnight. Most women I've dated would suggest meeting at a trendy bar or an exclusive club. Jules wants to meet where people wash their underwear when they should be sleeping.

It's so perfectly Jules.

The place is empty when I arrive, just Jules sitting cross-legged on top of a wide table, laptop balanced on her knees. She's wearing black denim shorts, a tank top, and low-top Converse sneakers. It's a contrast to her work attire and her more formal outfit from the gallery. She's a prism, a jewel and I'm seeing another one of her facets. Her hair is in a messy bun with a pencil stuck through it.

"Fancy meeting you here," I say, sliding onto the laundry folding table next to her.

She grins. "I figured if we're going to discuss potentially illegal activities, we should do it somewhere no one would expect to find an Andresen."

My eyebrows shoot upward. "Illegal activities?"

"I'll get to that." She angles her laptop screen toward me. "First, look at this."

The screen shows a detailed analysis of the painting we saw at the gallery, broken down into sections with notes in bold.

"I've been staring at these photos for hours and I keep coming back to the same conclusion. I don't think there is just one painting."

24

LINC

"WHAT DO you mean you don't think there is just one painting?" I ask Juliana.

She arches an eyebrow. "I think it's part of a diptych."

"A what?"

"It's the name for a piece of art that consists of two panels. Together, they tell a complete story."

"Apparently, one of us did pay attention in college," I mutter.

She shifts and then points to the screen. "Look at the composition. See how Lincoln is positioned off-center? And this shadow here suggests there's something—or someone—just outside the frame."

My pulse quickens. "Like what?"

"Like Mary Todd. Or maybe the painting shows Lincoln before and after a pivotal moment. The Gettysburg Address, perhaps, or ..." She trails off, chewing her bottom lip in a way that makes me want to find out if she's wearing cherry lip balm tonight.

"Or what?"

"Or it could be documenting something more personal. More private or particular, like a post office."

I chuckle because that's classic Jules, being random.

Then her eyes meet mine, eyes as expansive as the sky, and I see the same excitement that hits me when I'm on a breakaway. "Linc, what if your mom was right? What if there really are love letters, and these paintings are a map that leads to them?"

Even though it's a balmy summer night, a shiver runs across my skin. "My mother wrote almost that exact thing in her journal. Only, she didn't speculate about there being a second painting. Hadn't gotten that far, I suppose."

Even the whir of the washing machine fades as the possibility of actually finding those letters grows. "I think you're onto something."

Jules squishes up her face and pinches her fingers together. "There's only one problem. I can't be sure unless I see the original again."

Thinking about my father's comments earlier, I say, "After the, um, security incident, I'm not sure I can get us access."

... and the almost kiss. How can something that didn't happen take up all the air in my lungs, all the oxygen in the room? Sitting so close to her, my body remembers every moment of the almost-kiss.

My gaze drifts to hers. Our eyes lock. Her full lips quiver ever so slightly. My pulse is thunderous. As if sensing one of us is going to do something stupid, she hops up to toss her clothes in the dryer.

When she returns, her expression is mild, a Mona Lisa. "Is it really necessary for us to ask permission?"

Her mysterious smile lingers before what she means hits me.

Lowering my voice, I ask, "Are you suggesting we break into an art gallery?"

"We wouldn't be stealing anything," she says quickly. "Just ... unauthorized viewing."

I hedge.

"Think of it as research."

I should say no. Should remember my father's warning, think about my career, and consider the consequences.

Instead, stomach swooshing, I ask, "When?"

Her eyes twinkle. "Now."

"Now?" I find myself repeating much like the text earlier.

"There's no time like the present! Seize the day, er, night!" She pumps her arm enthusiastically. "Plus, I already scoped out their security system online. They have motion sensors, but the cameras are focused on the doors—"

"You researched their security system?" I hastily lower my voice.

"I may have gone down a rabbit hole." She shrugs, looking adorably pleased with herself.

"Explain."

"While the art on display has value, it's not Picasso or Renoir. More of the special interest sort and on temporary loan. So security is more of the warm-blooded variety than the techy type."

"So you mean there will be security guards?"

"Who spend more time on their phones than watching for suspicious activity during their shifts."

"Still, it sounds sketchy."

"I'll be James Bond."

"You mean a Bond girl."

"Me, a Bond girl? Hardly."

"You have those sugar eyes."

She inclines her head. "What about your slow-burning stare?"

Whatever this is, it stokes the embers inside, starting with the vacant, lonely place I've occupied for so long and spreading like wildfire. I should keep a fire extinguisher at the ready.

She blinks and says, "You have more of a Clark Kent look."

"Are you saying I'm like Superman?"

"If the cape fits ..."

I think of Aiken and his silly cape at the rooftop party and prefer my superheroes without makeup and tights, but I play along. A church bell chimes somewhere in the distance, deep and resonant, interrupting my thoughts.

After the twelfth ring, Jules softly says, "Happy birthday."

"But—" I start, about to comment about the confetti birthday wish, when I put two and two together. It's her birthday and I want nothing more than to give her birthday kisses.

"We're birthday neighbors?" I ask.

Her smile is small, not the kind I'd expect from someone who is so obviously excited about life that she keeps a Care Bear with a cheerful rainbow on its belly on her bed. "That is much preferred to living next door to Screechy and Grumbly."

I chuckle. "Thanks for the confetti. Any big plans to celebrate?"

"It's not a big deal. I don't really do celebrations."

The way she says it, like her birthday is insignificant and just another day, makes something in my chest corkscrew. "Why not?"

She fidgets with the smooth edge of her laptop. "My Dad died a few days before I turned twenty-two and that kind of sucked the fun out of it."

Before I can overthink it, I ask, "If you could have anything for your birthday—anything at all—what would it be?"

She's quiet for a long moment, watching the machines spin. "I've always wanted someone to play me a love song. Like, actually play it. Sit down at a piano or pick up a guitar and play something just for me." She laughs, embarrassed.

A buzzer sounds, indicating the dryer is done. She closes her laptop, hops down, and stuffs the clothing in a mesh bag.

"Can I walk you home?" Not that she has a choice, not at this hour.

"Sure, but the fact that I machine-wash instead of dry-clean my work attire is between you and me. Don't tell Carmen in the Collections Processing Department. It'll spike her blood pressure."

I chuckle and we chat about safe topics—avoiding discussions about burglary and birthdays. When we get to her building, she passes me the hoodie I gave her to wear when she was cold on July Fourth.

"Um, I can't take that right now."

"Why?" She clutches it like a pillow, like she doesn't intend to hand it over.

My lips quirk. "Because I have a birthday song to play for you."

She looks up at me, surprised by the intensity in my voice.

"Hang onto that. You'll need it." Not ready for tonight to end, I hold out my hand, changing direction.

"Where are we going?"

"You'll see."

She slides her soft palm against mine. Our fingers twine together and the contact sends electricity shooting up my arm.

She looks at our hands for a moment before moving. "We're holding hands purely for security purposes, right? I can't have someone try to kidnap me at this hour."

"We wouldn't want that," I say around a laugh.

We walk a few blocks to a small jazz club my buddies and I used to go to in high school—the kind of place that stayed open late and didn't ask too many questions about how many times a patron had traveled around the sun.

The bartender is on his phone as we enter. The place is nearly empty, just a couple in a dark corner nursing drinks and one guy at the bar.

Assuming no one will mind a little entertainment, I sidle up to the piano and take a seat.

Warm lights shine overhead. My hands are suddenly nervous as I settle onto the bench and gesture for Jules to sit beside me.

"I should probably mention I'm not exactly Carnegie Hall material," I say, positioning my fingers over the keys.

"The extent of my musical ability is 'Chopsticks.'"

I chuckle and then start with something simple, warming up and letting my muscle memory take over. It was built during the many years of lessons and my mother's skills as a professional pianist, a soloist in the Chicago Symphony Orchestra and at our church. I tell Jules this as a new melody flows from my fingertips, soft and sweet and entirely for her.

Her jaw lowers slightly as her gaze swings from me to my hands and back again. So things don't get too serious, I change to the birthday song. Despite what she said about not celebrating her birthday, she can't suppress her smile.

"Okay, time for presents," I say, and then change tunes. I begin to sing the first things that come to mind, my voice rough around the edges but carrying the words I've been trying to find since we almost-kissed. Maybe even since we first met.

I sing, "She walks into the office like the summer sun, illuminating everyone. She makes me forget my name, only to remind me to live again."

It's not polished. It's not perfect. But it's real, and it's hers, and when I glance over, she beams.

"Jules with the pencil in her hair, Jules who makes me stop and stare, didn't imagine we'd spend this time, wishing she could be—"

Mine, oh, mine.

It's not quite a rhyme, but it works and I'm afraid it's true.

The last words trail away. The final note fades. Silence stretches between us like a question.

"You wrote that," she whispers. "Just now. For me."

"Now," I say, echoing the question I've asked twice tonight, but as a declarative statement. "Happy birthday, Buttercup."

I play a variation of the song that's popular at kids' birthday parties just to keep things light, so I don't ask another question. Why were the words that came out so natural? The words about making this woman mine?

She's quiet for so long, I start to worry I've completely misread the situation. Then she leans over and kisses me on the cheek. It's soft and sweet.

She rests her head on my shoulder and says, "Will you play it again?"

I do, but I change the lines, making them silly before shifting into a melody of familiar songs.

When my fingers go still again, we get up. I drop a generous tip into the jar on the counter for the bartender, and then we step outside into the balmy night.

25

JULES

MY MOM USED to call me Little Miss Chatterbox when I was a kid because I asked so many questions, shared my thoughts at length, and was fascinated by my detailed dreams that I always just had to share.

I've since learned to keep the oddities of my sleeping brain's imagination to myself. However, I am wide awake on this Chicago summer night and I cannot speak.

Actually, it's almost three a.m.

With the snap of his fingers, er, the placement of them, Linc made my birthday wish come true.

No one has ever written me a song before. No one has ever looked at me the way he is looking at me right now.

"Thank you," I finally manage, my voice embarrassingly thick with emotion.

Alone on the street, we're wandering back the way we came, our joined hands swinging slightly between us. Though this time I'm not sure it's for safety or security purposes.

I jiggle my hand in his and say, "Just doing this so I absorb some of your ivory-tinkling skills."

His laugh is husky. "Haven't heard that expression in a while."

"I'm here to amuse."

Thankfully, the darkness hides my pink cheeks because I don't have any excuses for that other than that I'm touched by Linc's gesture, the words in his song, and what I think the last ones were.

"*... didn't imagine we'd spend this time, wishing she could be—*"

I've gone through the alphabet twice. Countless words rhyme with *time*, but perhaps it was just a close match.

Like *mine*.

"What do you want for your birthday?" I ask as we pause at a crosswalk. "And don't say *nothing*—you can't spontaneously write me a song and then pretend you don't deserve something amazing in return."

"I already got the confetti. Thanks, by the way. I'd expect nothing less from you than having to clean up a mess of colorful paper off my desk."

I laugh. "You're welcome. But seriously. If you could literally have anything for your birthday, what would it be?"

"Are you a genie, prepared to grant me three wishes?"

"No, just one. A belated one."

He clicks his tongue. "Stingy."

"But seriously, the sky is the limit."

"Good, because I have no interest in going to space."

"Pfft. Some billionaire you are."

Linc chuckles. "Billionaire's son."

"I stand corrected."

We pause on the sidewalk and he brushes a strand of hair away from my face, his fingers lingering against my cheek. "What do you get a man who has everything?"

I study his expression, trying to read between the lines.

Searching his eyes, I see spots of vulnerability, a loneliness that expensive suits and a trust fund can't fix. He doesn't want or need material things at all. He wants connection. To be with someone who sees past the Andresen name and the corporate heir facade to everything underneath.

"Just now, I thought you meant stuff. Rich boy problems and all that." My smile softens and I bite my lip. "But that's not what you mean, is it?"

He shakes his head.

"And if that trip to space is off the table and we're not going to be having a tropical resort fling, we're running out of options, leaving just you ... and me ... trespassing."

"You're such a little weirdo," he murmurs, unable to stop himself from smiling. "I think I'm going to keep you, Buttercup."

"What?" My voice goes up an octave.

He winks. "You heard me. That's what I want for my birthday. To keep you."

I stare at him for a long moment, heat flooding past my cheeks and all the way to my toes. Then I laugh, bright and surprised despite the butterflies performing aerial stunts in my stomach. "You can't just say things like that and wink like you're some kind of ... of..."

"Devastatingly handsome corporate executive?"

"I was going to say cocky action film star, Viking, gladiator—"

His hand goes to his chin. "You've never seen me with a beard."

"True, I'm just speculating, given your stature. Film star, Viking, gladiator, professional athlete."

"What did you say?" he asks carefully, almost as if offended or ... something.

I look down at our joined hands, genuinely confused.

"You're strong, like you're used to being physical and your hands—Oly noticed the calluses. They're not desk-job hands. Are you a secret pickleball professional?"

Linc's expression falls into shadow. "What about breaking and entering hands?"

"Maybe breaking hearts," I tease, not really sure where the conversation was going, but wanting us to get back on the laugh track.

As we walk through the empty streets, I find myself studying him from the corner of my eye. There's definitely more to Abraham Lincoln Andresen than expensive suits and quarterly reports. The way he handles himself, the confidence in his movements, even how he boosted himself onto the table at the laundromat earlier—it all suggests he's comfortable with physical space in a way that's different from, say, Nate, who has the same desk-jockey lifestyle.

Linc glances over and catches me staring, and his smile is so warm, so full of the good kind of trouble that I decide some mysteries can wait.

"So," I say as we approach the gallery, "about our little research expedition ..."

"You mean unlawful entry?"

"I prefer unauthorized art history inquiry."

He stops walking and turns to face me fully. "Jules, are you sure about this? If we get caught ..."

"We won't get caught." I inject confidence into my voice because this might be one unknown that I can solve. "I've been thinking about it non-stop." Well, between revisiting our almost-kiss, the way his hand closes around mine, and the song he played for me ...

I add, "If there really is a second piece that accompanies *Echo & Answer*, it might hold the key to everything you're looking for."

His face crimps as if he's not quite convinced. "What makes you so sure?"

"For one, the title is in two parts. Echo *and* Answer."

I pull out my phone and show him the low-quality and semi-blurry photos he took on the fly. "Don't get too excited. We have to stay focused. But look at this corner here. See how the brushwork is slightly different? Like someone painted over the original. And the way Lincoln is positioned —he's clearly looking at something or someone in the next frame."

"Or outside the frame."

"Yes, but see this shadow?" I point.

Linc studies the images and the gradual nodding of his head tells me he's growing more interested despite his reasonable reservations.

"How much do you want to find those letters?" I tip my gaze to his.

He's quiet for a long moment as if thinking about something significant. "More than I probably should."

"Then we do this. I've already scoped out the security situation and mapped out the best entry point ..."

"Entry point?" He looks genuinely alarmed. "Jules, we can't actually break in. That's—"

"We're just photographing for research."

He stares at me like I've suggested we rob a bank. "You're serious."

I bounce on my toes. "I have a plan. We get in, I examine the painting properly, take detailed photos, and we're out. Twenty minutes, tops."

"And if there's an alarm?"

"Did you notice how divided the rooms were in the gallery? There is a section outside the system."

"How did you obtain the security schematics?"

"You don't want to know."

"Probably not."

So I tell him anyway. "Nate was not at all vengeful after being laid off from his job at a data backup and storage company. He may have accidentally let me view some info. Okay, so the motion sensors shift through the various galleries, leaving a time gap."

"Should I be concerned that you seem oddly knowledgeable about this?"

Thinking about my father's untoward dealings, I give him my most innocent smile. "I promise never to use my sleuthing skills against you."

He runs a hand through his hair, and I try not to notice how the gesture makes it stick up in adorable directions. He slides his hand into his pocket and retrieves his penny.

Taking a deep breath, he says, "Heads we proceed. Tails, we abort the mission."

I watch as he tosses the coin into the air and catches it with ease before revealing which side it landed on.

"Let's do this."

I think he's holding his breath until he finally says, "Okay, but we do this smart. No unnecessary risks."

"Obviously. I'm many things, but reckless isn't one of them."

"Says the woman who just proposed breaking into an art gallery."

"*Proposed* is such a formal word. I prefer 'enthusiastically suggested.'"

He laughs despite himself. "You're going to be the death of me."

"Not if I can help it."

The way he looks at me then—like I'm brave instead of

foolish, like my crazy ideas might actually be brilliant—I feel a bit honey-drunk.

"Come on," I say, tugging him toward the back alley. "Let's go before I lose my nerve entirely."

Twenty minutes later, we're standing behind the gallery with a plan. A slow drip of adrenaline courses through my veins. I've felt this once before and understand how my father became addicted. Linc boosts me up to a window that I easily open, hoping he doesn't question my lock-pick skills later. Let's just say I went from being months away from completing my degree to getting an entirely different education.

"I don't think you'll fit through here," I call down.

"You can't go alone."

"Sure, I can. I'm smaller and sneakier. Plus, it's your turn to be the lookout."

Linc's expression tells me he wants to argue, but I'm already slipping through the window before he can stop me.

Inside, the gallery is eerily quiet and emergency lighting splashes the walls red. I slip off my shoes to avoid squeaking on the polished floors and pad toward the south wing on my tiptoes, phone flashlight dimmed to its lowest setting.

I shouldn't be thinking about this right now, but Linc's family history makes my own life seem so boring in comparison. I've had what Oly calls a "greige" life—gray and beige, predictably neutral. Then again, she doesn't know the gory details of the deleted scene when Dad was sick. Maybe that's why I try so hard to be sunny and cheerful. Compensation for a lifetime of ordinary—at least on the surface. I do know the finer points of fraud and forgery, and can read a security system plan with ease. I have my father to thank for that. I can also execute a perfect can-can kick thanks to my mother.

Focus, Jules.

When I find the painting, I realize I've been holding my breath. I take dozens of high-resolution photos from every angle, zooming in on brushstrokes.

From somewhere in the building comes a creak. I tell myself it's old and settling.

In the lower right-hand corner, beside the edge of the frame, there is a slight difference in the paint texture, just as I suspected. My pulse accelerates. It's almost like newer paint sits slightly raised above the original surface.

If there is something hidden underneath, I need to examine this properly, with tools and time. I need to ... borrow it.

The clock is ticking and empty-handed, I hurry back the way I came, coming up with how to handle this. I slip through the window like a cat burglar. Linc closes his big hands around my waist to help me down. However, my feet don't touch the ground. Instead, our bodies zip tight together.

I'm keenly aware of our proximity. How firm his arms are around me. That the space between us could close in less than a breath.

The swoops in my belly.

The rise and fall of his chest.

The heat on my skin.

The way his eyes rake over me.

We're frozen, magnetized together. The authorities will find us like this and we'll be memorialized in bronze, titled, "A Lover's Embrace."

Only we're not that. It's as if we both realize this at the same time and question what's going on. How we got here. Who tricked us?

He lowers me slowly, letting me slide down until my

feet touch the ground. But he doesn't pull his hands away as if he realizes I need an anchor.

I've been a very bad girl. For sneaking around security systems. For having thoughts about my boss that would get me fired.

"What happened?" he rasps.

Does he mean just now, because I'm not sure. All I could think about was the almost-kiss. Which, let's face it, didn't happen. The whole thing could've been a big fantasy thought bubble when really he was trying to figure out how to tell me I had spinach in my teeth.

Reality snaps back. Oh, right. He wants to know what happened in the gallery.

"Let's get away from the scene of the crime."

"Did you commit a crime?" he asks, aghast.

"Not yet."

I hastily draw him away from the gallery, taking an indirect route to where he'd parked his car.

When we're in the clear, I say, "I made an interesting discovery."

Before we pull away, I show him the photos. "See this corner? It looks like someone painted over whatever was there. But I can't tell what it is from photos alone."

"So we have evidence that—"

He's not following, so I interrupt. "I need to borrow it."

He stares at me, speaking slowly. "Borrow. The. Painting."

"Temporarily. Just long enough to examine it properly, maybe do some non-destructive analysis to see what's underneath."

"Jules, that's not borrowing. That's theft."

The reality of being my father's daughter rears its head, feeling like a tattoo that was an impulsive, ill-advised idea—

at some point, someone will see it. “It’s research! I’ll return it as soon as I’m done.”

“How exactly do you propose we ‘borrow’ a painting from a secured gallery?”

“I have an idea. But considering your reaction, you may not like it.”

“Try me.”

I clear my throat. “I could ... make a copy. Replace the original temporarily while I examine it so as not to arouse any suspicion. Then switch them back.”

He looks at me like I’ve suggested we steal the crown jewels. “You want to forge a painting?”

“Not forge. Copy. For research purposes.”

“That’s still forgery!”

“Only if we get caught.”

We stare at each other for a long moment, the weight of what I’m suggesting like a fuse burning between us.

I play my ace. “You said you wanted to find those letters.”

He closes his eyes briefly as if witnessing his internal battle. Finally, he sighs. “For the record, I don’t like this plan.”

“Is that a yes?”

“That’s a ‘I can’t believe I’m even considering this.’”

“I’ll take it.”

The dawning sky fills in the darkness with misty gray, pale purple, and powder blue as Chicago wakes up. I can’t shake the feeling that we’re part of a romantic sunrise painting.

But when I glance at Linc and see the determined set of his jaw, I realize maybe this is exactly what needed to happen to shake us out of our joint stupor of hatred.

He seems slightly upset, but instead of driving to my apartment, he parks outside a doughnut shop.

"What are we doing here?" I ask, imagining this is the first place he could think of to get coffee.

"It's your birthday."

I rub my eyes. "I haven't pulled an all-nighter in—" I interrupt myself. "What?"

"It's your birthday. I may have succeeded at finding a piano in the middle of the night, but I wasn't sure where to find cake at this hour. If you think about it, a doughnut is like fried cake."

I'm touched and my glowy Care Bear heart beams. The softness in his expression tells me he doesn't want this night to end either.

26

LINC

EVERYONE IS familiar with the saying, "It's always darkest before dawn." What they don't mention is that it's always coldest before dawn, too. Yes, even during the summer.

Jules rubs her bare arms as the warmth of the doughnut shop envelops us, along with the smell of freshly fried dough and coffee. We order an assortment of glazed, chocolate, and a "birthday cake doughnut" with colorful sprinkles that she insists I need to try, even though it's her special day.

"We're paying for these, right?" I ask, half joking, but also hoping I didn't accidentally wind up with a dine-and-dasher.

"Obviously."

Jules calls to the woman behind the counter as she hands us our order. "Excuse me, do you happen to have two birthday candles?"

The woman smiles and rummages around, producing two slightly melted candles and a lighter. "Are you celebrating something?"

"That we didn't get arrested," Jules deadpans.

Yet.

The woman looks confused and then breaks into laughter. "You had me there for a second. I'm only on my first cup of coffee."

I feel like the walking dead, yet strangely more alive when with Jules than I have since the Ottawa Outlaws had a real shot at the Stanley a couple of years ago.

We find a small table by the window and she sticks the candles into the birthday cake doughnut.

I light the candles and Jules says, "Make a wish."

"It's your birthday."

"I couldn't very well put a birthday cake with candles in that envelope along with the confetti, now could I? This is your belated birthday—fried-cake substitute—deferred celebration."

"That's a mouthful."

"And isn't that the point? Both of us, on the count of three, make a wish, then we take a big bite." She counts down with her fingers.

I close my eyes, and I find myself wishing for clarity. For the courage to tell Jules the entire truth about who I am, for answers about the letters Mom believed in so desperately, and for this thing between us to work despite all the secrets I'm keeping.

When I open my eyes, Jules is already looking at me.

We blow out the candles together, and as thin trails of smoke rise between us, I realize that maybe what I really want is right here. This. Her. Something real.

"Will you tell me your wish?" I ask.

"No way. You know the rules." She licks the glaze off the bottom of the candles and splits the birthday cake one in half, then takes a chocolate one.

After helping myself to half of an old-fashioned doughnut, I say, "Tell me more about your family. Aside from your triplet brothers, what was it like when you were growing up?" I cannot imagine the lifestyle that spawned this unique woman.

She takes a bite of her doughnut, chewing thoughtfully ... or stalling. "Not much to say. Dad was, um, in the casino business. Mom was a showgirl. She wanted me to live a sensible life."

"Sounds fascinating."

"No, that would be you, a descendant of Abraham Lincoln."

The weight of that legacy settles on my shoulders like it always does. "Is it? Sometimes I feel like I exist in the shadow of one of the greatest men to ever live. Like nothing I do will ever measure up to his legacy."

I instantly wish I could take the comment back. I try to act as if it were offhanded, but that very thought has eaten me up for years.

Jules doesn't seem fazed by my admission. Instead, her expression softens with understanding. "Are we talking about Honest Abe or Frank Andresen?"

I never thought of it that way.

"Maybe the point isn't to measure up. Maybe it's to honor the best parts of that legacy while still being yourself."

The bonds of the past ... and future loosen in my chest. She makes it sound so simple, so possible.

"Besides," she adds, tearing off a piece of a jelly doughnut topped with powdered sugar and possibly trying to lighten the mood, "I bet Abraham Lincoln never wrote anyone a birthday song."

Was that a birthday song or a love song?

I ask, "How do you know? Maybe he was a secret romantic."

"Isn't that what we're trying to find out with those letters?" Her eyebrows crest.

"Is that what you want? A secret romantic?"

The question hovers like the puff of powdery doughnut sugar between us. While I perform an interrogation of my sanity, prepared to blame anything I say or do on lack of sleep, I watch her face carefully, looking for any sign that I've pushed too far.

But Jules doesn't retreat. Instead, she considers my words seriously. I pause before taking another sip of coffee. My pulse is already loaded.

"Do I want a romantic? Yes, I do. A strong, manly romantic. What's your take on it? I sense you have strong opinions or buried emotions."

How can she read me so well? "I used to think romance was phony. Something people did for show, for social media, for status. But I could be convinced otherwise ..." I trail off, meeting her eyes.

"Maybe it's private. Just for the two people in the relationship and not the public."

"I'm starting to wonder if maybe I just hadn't found the right person to be romantic with."

The piece of doughnut between her fingers falls back into the box between us. "And now?"

"Now I'm sitting in a doughnut shop at sunrise with someone who wants to break into art galleries and forge paintings, and I'm pretty sure songs could be written about her every day for the rest of her life." The words come out before I can stop them, more honest than I've been with anyone.

Jules stares at me, birthday doughnuts forgotten, and I immediately worry I've overwhelmed her.

"Linc ..."

"Too much?" I ask, suddenly uncertain.

"No, it's not too much. It's ..." She fidgets with her coffee cup. "I'm not used to people seeing me. Most of the time, I feel like I'm just part of the backdrop."

The sadness in her voice makes my chest ache. I reach across the table and cover her hand with mine. "Jules. You're definitely front and center."

She looks down at our joined hands, and I can see the moment she starts to pull back emotionally. The vulnerability becomes too much, too fast.

"We should probably talk about what happens in," I check my watch, "two hours when we're back at the office."

"Business as usual. We hate each other, remember?" She laughs, meaning it as a joke, but what I despise is the notion of anyone hating her. Most of all me.

I study her face, picking up on the nuances of how her upper lip quirks at one corner in a stubborn way that tells me she's calculating something behind her innocent expression. The fine tension gathering at the outer edges of her eyes like storm clouds on the horizon. "I'm afraid that's hardly the case anymore."

She gives me a small smile that doesn't quite reach her eyes. "Guess we'll have to work on our acting skills."

And I should probably come clean about my actual day job instead of playing the role of a tough executive understudy.

THE NEXT COUPLE of days at Meridian are an exercise in specialized torment. Jules and I exchange polite pleasantries in the hallways, maintain an appropriate distance during meetings, and somehow manage to keep up the pretense that we barely tolerate each other.

It's exhausting.

Every time she walks past my office, I have to resist the urge to call her in just to see her smile. Every time she hands me a report, I'm hyperaware of the brief moment when our fingers brush. And every time Ms. Drecken, our acting COO, makes one of her subtle comments about my "improving relationship with the staff," I wonder how obvious we're being.

Then again, I'm certain she has a pair of flying monkeys reporting our every move.

"Your father mentioned you've been working closely with Miss Lindley on some research projects," Maxine says after a meeting. Her tone is casual, but her eyes are calculating slashes.

I play it cool. "She's thorough. Good attention to detail."

"Indeed. I've noticed she's been quite ... dedicated. Staying late, accessing archived files. Admirable work ethic."

Drecken's gaze, fixed on me, isn't the only thing that makes my skin crawl. Has she been watching Jules, keeping track of her activities? She was at the gallery the night of the Civil War artifact exhibition. Did she notice us sneak off together? I file the questions away and make a mental note to be more careful.

That afternoon, Dad announces he's taking me on a quick, mid-week business trip to woo a foreign investor at a resort in Sand Valley, Wisconsin. It's not far and we'll take the private jet, but the idea of being away makes me want to dig in my heels and stay. I know it's really just an excuse for him to play golf with potential investors while I smile, nod, and pretend I care about quarterly earnings.

He claps me on the back and says, "It'll be good for everyone to meet the future of Meridian Holdings."

The two days drag by in a blur of schmoozing, forced conversations, and sneaking away to check NHL news on my phone ... And to see if Jules texted. When I should be memorizing the names of global hedge fund giants, I find myself thinking about her. Wondering what she's doing, whether she's making progress on her painting copy, what her favorite movie is, book, color ...

The only takeaway, other than that my father must spend a lot of time perfecting his swing, is a comment he made over dinner. We were alone briefly and he noted that I'd been spending some time in the archives. He asked if I've noticed anything of interest. Irregularities. He said to bring them to him, no one else.

Likely, he wants the letters if I find them. But why? It could be to protect his involvement with the fraud, followed by an empty promise to take action against whoever he pins with the wrongdoing. Sounds like a deceptive, if not losing, playbook.

When I finally return to Chicago on Friday morning, Jules appears in my office doorway with two cups of coffee and a knowing smirk. "How was your business trip?" she asks, settling into the chair across from my desk like she's a client.

I roll my eyes. "Learned a lot about ... synergistic market opportunities."

"Uh-huh. Did you have a fling while you were at the resort?"

The question catches me off guard, and I nearly choke

on my coffee before recalling what she said to me in the elevator. "What? No. Definitely not."

"Really? No attractive golf caddy girls throwing themselves at the handsome young executive?"

"It was a sausage fest."

Shaking her head, she laughs. "While you were gone, I kept busy. Our version of *Echo & Answer* is as done as it's going to be. All we have to do is swap it out tonight and we'll have the real McCoy back by Sunday night."

She taps her phone and slides it across my desk. I look at the photos on the screen of the forged copy next to the original, and I'm genuinely impressed. Her version is remarkably detailed, capturing not just the image but the texture and age of the real one.

"This is incredible work. What other hidden talents do you have?"

"I can yodel."

"Is that so?"

"No, but let's count on the fact that during the gallery's opening hours of eleven to two on Saturday, no one inspects the piece too carefully."

"If I recall, the lighting in that wing wasn't bright enough for anyone to notice the subtle differences. I didn't at first."

"The odds are in our favor."

I rub my thumb over the penny I keep in my pocket. "Let's hope so." But my mind immediately starts cataloging all the ways this could go terribly wrong. Security cameras we missed. Unexpected guard rotations. Someone deciding to examine the painting more closely. The copy not being a perfect match.

"We can't overthink this," Jules says, whether to herself or me, I'm not sure.

"If we get caught—"

She lets out a breath. "We won't get caught."

"But if we do, Jules, this isn't just about losing our jobs. This is criminal. We could go to prison."

She leans forward, her eyes serious. "If we do, we can just tell the judge and jury that it was a crime of passion."

Considering that this whole thing is to find Lincoln's lost love letters, I laugh. Then abruptly go quiet. "Jules, why are you helping me, aside from this unique skill set you seem to have?"

I'm about to make a joke about her committing forgery often, like a side hustle, when she looks abruptly away.

"Because maybe I want to believe in true love, too."

Later that afternoon, alone in my office after everyone else has gone home, I find myself digging deeper into the files Jules had flagged earlier. Something about the insurance valuations has been nagging at me, and with Dad's cryptic warnings still echoing in my head, along with feeling like Drecken's eyes are on me, I decide to do some investigating of my own.

The heaviness of dread drops my shoulders because someone has definitely been using company access and resources to make unauthorized decisions about insurance premiums and valuations. The patterns are subtle but consistent—certain pieces appraised significantly higher than market value, insurance payouts processed without proper documentation, and claims approved by someone with executive-level access.

I tilt my head, studying one particular entry. Odd. I didn't realize the Pedrosa piece was in our collection. I recall Dad going on and on about it last Christmas—how it was one of the most significant acquisitions in the company's history.

But according to these records, we've had it for over a year. That doesn't add up.

And the insurance valuation is nearly triple what comparable pieces have sold for at auction.

My stomach sinks as the implications hit me. Either someone is running an elaborate insurance fraud scheme using Meridian Holdings as cover or ... or my father is more involved in this than I want to believe.

The thought makes me feel ill. Dad has always been ruthless in business, sure, but honest. At least, I thought he was honest. However, people change. Mom used to say he was different when they first met, before the company consumed his entire life.

According to her journals, the man she fell in love with wasn't the one she was married to before she passed. I believe it broke her heart.

Maybe we never really knew him at all.

A soft knock on my door interrupts my spiraling thoughts. Jules appears in the doorway, concern pinching her pretty face.

"You're working late," she observes.

"Could say the same about you."

"I was just finishing up some things before tonight." She steps into my office and closes the door behind her. "You look pale. Maybe you ought to go boating with Bear Cub. Get some sun."

"I just spent two days golfing. Also, it's Bīriņš. Anyway, he's back in Latvia before—" I'm about to say before preseason training starts up again, but cut myself off.

"Is anything wrong?" she asks, the picture of innocence, never mind her criminal paintbrush skills.

I stare at her for a long moment, debating how much to tell her. She's already risking everything to help me find those letters. How can I burden her with my suspicions about my own father? About my actual identity?

"Just work stuff. Nothing that can't wait until Monday."

"Good, because we should go get nachos."

"Nachos?"

"Whatever is on your mind is *nacho* problem."

My laugh is delayed. "Jules, that's awful."

"But it's true, and it wiped that troubled look right off your face." Then she slides into the chair across from my desk and fixes me with a penetrating stare, reminding me of when we really thought we hated each other.

"If you don't tell me what's on your mind, I'm going to stare at you until you crack. See that bare bulb above your head? It's the last light you're ever going to see." She imitates a hard-hitting Chicago detective as she puffs on an invisible stogie.

Despite every instinct warning me to protect her from this mess, I find myself wanting to tell her everything. Because if there's one thing I've learned about Jules, it's that she's predictably unpredictable—and exactly the kind of person I want on my side when everything falls apart.

"How much do you know about insurance fraud?" I ask.

Her eyebrows raise. Her complexion is now pale. "More than I probably should. Why?"

I turn my computer screen toward her with the files I've been analyzing on display. "Remember those discrepancies you found?"

"The ones you told me in no uncertain terms to forget about?"

Lips pressed together, I nod with regret. "I followed a few leads and am worried there might be a traitor in our midst."

"Dramatically intriguing." She cranes forward and scans the content on the screen.

"Do you see what I see?"

Never mind a troubled look, her jaw hangs slack.

27

JULES

AFTER LINC SENDS me copies of the files, I spend the rest of Friday afternoon staring at numbers that don't add up and insurance valuations that make my brain hurt. The deeper I dig, the more convinced I become that Linc is right. Someone with executive access has been playing fast and loose with company resources.

My demand for caffeine is high, so after grabbing not one, but three cups of coffee—don't worry, they're not all for me—I visit the Collections Processing Department on the thirty-third floor.

I know I can trust the office girlies. Carmen has been with Meridian for twenty years—she knows where all the bodies are buried, metaphorically speaking. Wendy is newer but sharp, and since she came back from maternity leave, what some people call "mommy brain" has turned into "I'm going to get the job done as efficiently as possible so I can get back to my baby" brain.

"Hi, ladies," I say, sliding into the office like I belong here, because I used to before my abrupt ejection ... upward, to an exec suite.

I'm still undecided whether that's a net gain.

Carmen looks up from her computer. "There's our third Musketeer!"

I've been looking at images of muskets a lot lately, but that's another side project entirely, though I'm quite sure the two must intersect somehow.

We exchange hugs and I inquire about how Carmen's hubby is doing with his physical therapy after shoulder surgery and how many teeth Wendy's baby now has.

"Half a mouthful. He's like a puppy, chewing on everything. Nothing is safe in our house from his gummy exploration anymore."

Carmen chuckles. "Speaking of naughty boys, how are things with your boss these days? You haven't set his office on fire, so I take that as a good sign."

Heat creeps up my neck, but I wave my hand dismissively. "Linc is as impossible as always."

"Linc?" Wendy asks.

"Last month, you referred to him as 'a corporate Ken Doll with a plastic personality.'"

Wendy interjects, "But at the last meeting, she didn't look at him like he was a bowl of lumpy oatmeal."

"Maybe I'm just getting used to his, um, management style."

Carmen gives me a knowing look. "And maybe I'm getting used to my husband leaving his socks on the bedroom floor next to the dirty laundry hamper, but that doesn't mean I like it."

She and Wendy waggle their eyebrows in unison.

Goodness, do I miss them, but I guess my new position isn't the worst.

"It's not like that," I protest, but the lilt in my voice fools no one.

Wendy places her hand on my arm. "There's nothing wrong with warming up to someone. Especially if they're actually decent underneath all those handsome good looks."

"He's still my boss," I mutter.

Wendy asks, "So what's he really like when it's just you two working late? Is there anything sweet or ridiculous that he does?"

The question catches me off guard because it goes past the professional and into the personal. He's funny and vulnerable and surprisingly easy to talk to. He listens when I speak and remembers details about things I've told him. He writes songs and worries about living up to impossible legacies and looks at me like I'm good for more than answering emails.

But I can't say any of that.

I let out a stuck breath. "He's ... different from what I expected."

"Different how?" Carmen presses.

To lighten things up and take the spotlight off me, in my best robot voice, I say, "He's more human, less man-droid."

The two women exchange a look, then burst into laughter.

"I'm not saying she has it bad, but she has it," Wendy stage-whispers.

"Going, going, gone!" Carmen agrees with a flourish.

"I do not have anything," I insist, but my voice comes out squeaky and slightly defensive. Then, clearing my throat, I add, "Except for a favor to ask."

This gets their attention.

I take a sip of coffee, buying time to figure out how to phrase this without sounding suspicious. "I was hoping you two might be able to help me with something. I'm working on a project that requires historical documentation verification, and I need access to previous insurance information."

Because these records are handled by a separate department with different login credentials, the system would show an audit trail of who accessed the files. It would leave digital footprints and throw up a red flag if Linc's assistant did it, whereas it's not out of the realm of possibility for this department to refer to the information.

Carmen raises an eyebrow. "I'm sure Linc would have access."

Without revealing too much, I say, "There may have been a clerical error and because we're the ones who did some of that paperwork, I just want to double check before ..." I trail off.

Carmen nods. "We did help process some of those insurance valuations when we were covering for Leanna."

"Oh yes, I remember those. Some of the numbers seemed off." Wendy pauses, glancing around to make sure we're alone. "Let's just say I questioned my math skills for a while there."

My pulse quickens. "What do you mean?"

"Some of the valuations seemed really high compared to similar pieces we'd processed before. But I figured maybe I was missing something, you know? We never have the full picture."

But the one I have is starting to come into focus.

Carmen says, "I'll email you what I can find by the end of the day and say hi to that big hunk-a-man upstairs."

Wendy giggles and they both wave at me as I leave. But I don't go downstairs. I pay a visit to Suzie in Licensing and Rights Management. A tech guy with a crush on her has access to the equipment I need, so I beg her to ask him in exchange for first pick of our interdepartmental fall activity.

I'm banking on being tasked with organizing it again—Valerie, Mr. Andresen's assistant's PA, passed it off to me last year. I guess all the extra work people have asked me to do is paying off. Time to cash in.

THAT EVENING, I meet Linc behind the gallery at our designated time, my stomach a tangle of nerves and anticipation. The weight of the forged painting wrapped in brown paper in my hands is anything but conspicuous. The longer I hold it, the more it feels like I'm carrying around evidence of every bad decision I've ever made.

"Everything okay?" Linc observes as I approach.

"I'm fine. Just ready to get this over with."

"You're practically feral right now. All jittery energy and round owl eyes."

"I think you like it," I shoot back, surprising myself with the flirtation in my voice.

"Unhinged Jules is definitely growing on me," he admits with a crooked smile.

It was one thing to sneak into the gallery—my original cover story was that I had low blood sugar and passed out in the ladies' room before closing. Now I'm committing a real crime. I fear, like my father, my luck could run out.

"We won't get caught," I say, more to convince myself than Linc.

He runs his thumb over the penny in his hand. "Said every criminal ever."

I release a shaky exhale. "We're just borrowing the painting. It's not like we're keeping it permanently."

"I'm pretty sure that's not how the law works, but okay."

Yet he's aiding and abetting, which somehow makes me think this is legit.

I slip through the same window as before, my heart playing a dirge against my ribs. My guilty conscience makes me feel like I'm about to trip over a live wire and alert authorities about my deviance, but everything is the same as before—long shadows, eerily glowing exit lights, the outline of statues.

However, luck is indeed on my side, and within minutes, I'm carefully removing the original painting from its frame.

The switch goes smoothly, though I'm convinced I've left the replacement slightly crooked. There's no time to adjust it now. I cradle the original in my arms and make my way back to the window, trying not to think about how much prison time art theft carries and whether I'd look better in stripes or garish orange.

Through the window, I spot Linc conferring with two men near the building's corner. My blood turns to ice. I wait, counting down the remaining seconds to pull this off before the security team switches.

One of the guys claps Linc on the shoulder. The other gives him a fist bump. He saunters back to his lookout spot as if this is totally normal and not shady at all to be loitering behind a building in the middle of the night.

"What's going on?" I whisper urgently as I clamber through the window.

He takes the painting first and then extends his arms for me. "Nothing serious. Just some fans."

"Fans?" I blink at him. "You have fans?"

He shrugs like it's no big deal. "Doesn't everyone?" And there's that cocky confidence that used to drive me crazy.

"But seriously, what did they want? Weren't they suspicious about why you were hanging around behind a building at night?"

"I told them I was doing something extremely sketchy."

"You did not!" I hiss.

He grins. "I did. They asked if I wanted help."

"They didn't!"

Arms around my waist, Linc holds me suspended for a pulse-pounding moment. We experience a mid-air blink freeze before he plants me on the ground.

He says, "Actually, I told them I was part of a birthday scavenger hunt."

"And they believed you?"

"People believe what they want to believe. Plus, it's not entirely untrue—this whole thing started with your birthday, didn't it?"

"You're impossible," I mutter, but I'm fighting a smile because this man is becoming harder to resist.

"Now let's get out of here." He holds out his hand for me to take.

And I do.

28

JULES

ALL WEEKEND, while I work on taking ultra-high-resolution photos of every inch of *the Echo & Answer* piece using the tech courtesy of Suzie's crush, I try to ignore the voice in my head that keeps repeating what Linc said on my birthday. *I think I'm going to keep you, Buttercup.*

Keep me like what? Like a trophy? An object? A piece of art in his collection? Like how Westley went into danger and to the ends of the earth for true love?

Then I remember the way Linc looked at me when he said it. I was so focused on his winking eye that I didn't pay attention to the other one. The raw vulnerability there, like he's never let himself truly want something unless he knows for sure he can have it. Despite the cocky comment and the wink, his other eye revealed a possibility that terrifies me.

He knows I'm not a sure thing.

But does that mean he wants me?

People always talk about yearning to be seen, to be wanted. It's a strange sensation when it finally happens. Part of me wants to resist it, doesn't trust it. For so long, keeping my distance has been my protection. If I don't let people in, they can't hurt me. If I don't want things too badly, I can't be disappointed when they don't work out.

But what happens if I let him in? What happens if I stop protecting myself and start living instead?

Maybe I could let myself want him.

Or maybe I'm reading this entire situation wrong and this is how he is with all women—his interactions with Ms. Drecken don't count. Sure, he's been charming toward her during our meeting—and at the doughnut shop, he gave a fifty percent tip. However, I can't help but think the way he treats me is different.

Or maybe I've just been inhaling too many paint fumes and turpentine.

My stomach is queasy, but I think it's from guilt because forging paintings and this kind of behavior was my father's specialty, not mine. I swore I'd never follow in his footsteps.

Yet here I am with a fake diploma, a stolen painting, and a growing pile of lies between my boss and me—someone I'm afraid I'm starting to care about.

Everything is built on deception.

Before I can travel too far down that dead end, I examine the lower corner of the painting and make a discovery that makes me stop and stare ... and stare.

Underneath the surface layer of paint, barely visible but unmistakably present, is what looks like another signature.

SUNDAY EVENING, we meet at Linc's place to return the painting. I'm practically vibrating with excitement as I ride the elevator to the top floor—because of course, he couldn't sink so low as to live closer to ground level like a normal human. At least I don't have to walk up four flights of stairs with this painting.

I note that the building has a concierge service, a gym, and probably a driver on call.

After knocking, I wait outside a dark wooden door in a plush carpeted hallway with gold sconces that make me feel woefully underdressed and out of place. I notice too late that I have paint on my denim shorts—a small smear of brown that could be used as evidence against me in the court of law. Surely, someone like Lincoln Andresen has access to good lawyers.

"Well, that's not incriminating at all," I mutter, trying to rub it off as Linc opens the door.

"What isn't?" Linc's gaze corkscrews down my body and lands on my legs before murmuring, "I'm so grateful for summer. Should buy stock in Daisy Dukes."

"Huh?" I ask, not sure what he means, as I push my way inside. "I have paint on my clothes. This looks bad, but it's too late to change now."

Then I look around, having only set foot in a place like this vicariously through movies—classics with Mom and modern flicks with Oly.

Linc's condo is a luxury high-rise along Lake Shore Drive with floor-to-ceiling windows overlooking Lake Michigan. The view alone would solve most of my financial woes, if not give me a solid dose of tranquility every day. Everything is shiny and clean. Nary a dust bunny in sight. Either his favorite hobby is sweeping floors and polishing surfaces or he has a cleaning service.

Linc must read my expression because he says, "Leave it to my father to pull out all the stops to show me the life I could inherit."

I take that to mean, like the car, this condo is thanks to

Frank. I set the painting on the marble countertop where I glimpse a distorted version of my reflection.

"Hungry?" he asks, pulling out his phone. "I was thinking pizza."

"Pizza works." At least some things remain normal.

"Preferences on toppings?"

"Anything but anchovies."

"What's wrong with anchovies? They're salty little gems from the sea."

I stick out my tongue. "They're fish. On pizza. It's unnatural."

"So is pineapple, but I don't see you vetoing that."

"Because pineapple is delicious. Sweet and tangy. Summer-y."

The corner of his lips teases a grin. "This is important information. I'm learning so much about the real Jules Lindley right now."

"The real Jules has very strong opinions about pizza toppings."

"Among other things."

We settle on half and half—his weird anchovy preference on one side, my civilized combination on the other. While we wait for delivery, I open my laptop and spread out the photos I took and the research materials across his granite kitchen island.

"Okay, prepare to have your mind blown." I arrange the images. "Look at this."

I point to the background. "See this arrangement of trees? And that church with its spire?"

He nods and follows my finger as I lower it toward plumes of smoke from the aforementioned muskets.

"Notice anything unusual?"

Linc leans closer, and I catch a whiff of his cologne

along with that clean minty scent that makes me want to breathe deeper. His lean muscle tells me he could totally lift a car off someone in a dire situation. The crinkle in the corners of his eyes suggests he's plotting something diabolical. The way his full lips hovered over mine that one time in an almost-kiss that definitely left me wanting, highlighted exactly how much he hates me.

At least this is the story I tell myself so I can sleep at night. Otherwise, I might lie awake all night pining.

Linc turns slowly to me as if detecting my sudden sensory overload. "It looks familiar."

"It looks like many small towns during this era of history. I cross-referenced it with historical maps. This depicts a real location. A small Illinois town where Lincoln supposedly stayed overnight during his circuit lawyer days."

His head snaps up. "You're serious."

"Dead serious. But here's the really interesting part—it's floating. There's no foundation."

Much like my head right now, being here in Linc's abode, sitting so close to him might be grounds for me requiring a personal day. Thankfully, I get paid time off.

"Suggesting it's not permanent. Not real?"

I tip my head from side to side. "Now, check this out."

Linc's eyes bulge as he studies the images of the lower left-hand corner, where I discovered another name under the original.

"Most buildings have a base and this artist was no stranger to that, especially considering there are some normally constructed buildings over here." I point behind the image of the former president.

"Good point. So, do you think it could be a map like my mother suggested?"

I enhance the image on my computer. "There's more.

The signature I uncovered doesn't match the attributed artist, Douglas Kennard. This was painted by someone else entirely, someone whose work from this period is extremely rare."

Linc reads the original signature, *Clement Marchand,* that I found under the current signature, *D. Kinnard.*

"Unusual, right? This makes me think more than ever that this is part one of a diptych and whoever made the alterations didn't want anyone to make the association that there was a second painting."

He says, "So they changed the artist's name, meaning we just need to find all artworks by Clement Marchand?"

I tap the air with my pointer finger. "It could be that the two panels will tell a complete story. The composition here suggests there should be a matching piece. See how Lincoln's hand is extended?"

"Almost like he's pointing to something."

"Or reaching out. Also, the way the light falls suggests it's either early morning or late evening—specific transitional moments. Shadows from the other painting form a link between puzzle pieces. I tried to find a connection between the various objects, but I'm thinking the 'map,' as you said, is found more between painting A and painting B."

He swipes through the photos and studies the painting as if willing a connection to be made, to determine if he's seen the match before or any other work by the artist.

Hoping to jog his memory, I say, "It could be a before and after scene. Like maybe Lincoln preparing for a speech versus giving it. Or paired portraits—one of Lincoln, another of Mary Todd, with hidden elements that align when placed side by side. The possibilities are endless, but the point is, this painting isn't a solo piece of art. It came as a pair."

"This is incredible work, Jules. This could be groundbreaking." Admiration and appreciation fill his voice.

It lights a little candle inside that makes me whiskey-warm.

I incline my head for emphasis. "But they were done by an altogether different artist."

His jaw lowers. "Oh. Wow." He repeats the word several more times as realization dawns.

After some quick research into Clement Marchand, we learn that he only painted in pairs, confirming my diptych theory.

Linc says, "That suggests someone wanted these paintings treated as separate works."

"But why?"

We pore over the images until the pizza arrives, and even then, we eat with one hand while pointing at details with the other. The conversation drifts between historical speculation and gentle teasing about toppings, food, and other favorites.

Sometime between analyzing brushstrokes and debating Lincoln's travel routes, we've moved to the couch and have been shifting closer and closer together. Our knees are touching. Every time he reaches for a photo or document, his arm brushes against mine.

My entire body fills with pins and needles, but in a good way.

Facing me, he says, "Thank you. For all of this. I know you're taking huge risks to help me, and I don't take that lightly."

"You're welcome."

At this late hour and in the soft lighting, Linc yawns.

It's contagious and we both, heavy-eyed, smile at each other in a way that makes me forget that I ever hated him.

Full from pizza and the buzz of excitement from our discoveries wearing off, exhaustion rolls over me like a wave softly lapping the shores of the lake below. I let my eyes drift closed, just for a moment. The last thing I remember is my head dropping to the warmth of Linc's shoulder.

29

LINC

I WAKE up to sunlight streaming through the floor-to-ceiling windows. I'm in the habit of sleeping with blackout curtains and experience a peculiar feeling of disorientation, much like when I'm traveling for away games.

The jet lag is the most brutal, but as the room around me takes shape, I realize I'm at home in the condo. Strangely, my left arm feels like it's been replaced by a block of concrete. Numb and prickly concrete.

Blinking away the haze of sleep, I realize Jules is curled against my side on the couch, her head tucked into the hollow between my shoulder and chest.

For a moment, I don't move. Don't breathe. Don't do anything that might disturb this perfect moment.

Her hair smells like cherry blossoms and almonds with a hint of paint thinner—evidence of what brought us here. One of her hands rests on my chest, fingers splayed like she's claiming territory, and I can feel the steady rise and fall of her inhales and exhales through my shirt.

This is not how I planned to wake up this morning.

It's infinitely better.

Then reality crashes back like a bucket of ice water. The stolen painting and all our evidence of wrongdoing are still spread across my kitchen island and now the coffee table in incriminating photographs that can only mean one thing.

We fell asleep.

Together.

On my couch.

After committing what most people would classify as a felony at the gallery.

Jules stirs, making a small sound that's half sigh, half protest against consciousness. Her eyes flutter open, and for exactly three seconds, she looks peaceful and content.

Then awareness hits.

"Oh no, oh no, oh no," she mutters, bolting upright so fast I'm surprised she doesn't give herself whiplash.

"Morning," I manage, my voice rough with sleep.

I instantly regret losing the warmth where she'd been pressed against me.

She stares at me with wide eyes, her blonde hair sticking up at angles that would be hilarious if she didn't look so mortified. "We fell asleep."

"Appears so."

"Together."

"Also accurate."

"On your couch."

"Full marks for observation skills."

She runs both hands through her hair, which only makes the situation worse.

I like abruptly waking up Jules. Sleepy, late-night Jules. All versions of Juliana Lindley.

She asks, "What time is it?"

I check my watch, trying not to focus on how the

morning light makes her skin glow or how her sleep-rumpled appearance makes me want to pull her back into my arms. "Seven-thirty. Plenty of time before work."

Instead of looking relieved, panic flashes across her face. "The painting!" She jumps up and gathers photos from the kitchen island. "We never returned it to the gallery."

Right. The lawbreaking. How did I forget about it so quickly? I was distracted by this amazing woman who happened to fall asleep on the couch with me last night.

She turns in a frantic circle as if trying to get her bearings. "We have to get it back. Today. Right now."

I softly grip her upper arms. "Jules, breathe. We'll figure it out."

"No, you don't understand. This is stolen goods. If we get caught with it—"

"We won't get caught." I shake my head slowly as my mind hatches a hasty plan.

Brow creased, she says, "But we can't leave it here. I'll take it back to my place."

"Absolutely not. I'm not letting you take the fall for this."

"You're an Andresen, high profile. I'm ... nobody." Her voice wavers.

"No one is going to take the fall because no one knows," I insist. "You're being paranoid."

"We're art thieves, Linc. We have reason to be."

"We're conducting an investigation."

"Authorized by what governing authority?"

I can't help but grin at her indignation. "The concerned family of Abraham Lincoln."

She rolls her eyes, but I catch the hint of a smile she's trying to suppress. "Don't joke about this."

"It's better than jumping to worst-case scenarios. Unless

you have a prior criminal history, we have no reason to worry. Should I run a background check on you? Any skeletons in your closet?" I tease.

Jules lets out a strangled laugh. "My closet? You've been to my studio. There is only an armoire."

Taking a risk, I draw her into a hug. "If something goes wrong, I'll make sure everyone knows this was my idea. You were just following orders from your demanding boss."

She tips her head back, but her gaze remains unfocused as if dozens of thoughts collide in her mind, causing a traffic jam. "You're right. No one is taking any fall because no one's going to find out," she repeats, but the tremor in her voice suggests she's not entirely convinced.

I study her face, noting the way she won't quite meet my eyes and the protective set of her shoulders. I suddenly worry there is more to Jules than she's letting on, layers of secrets hidden behind her bright smile and spunky personality. Then again, I'm hardly in a position to judge anyone for keeping things hidden.

"We should probably get ready for work," I say reluctantly. "It's Monday. Your favorite day of the week."

Her eyebrows shoot up. "How did you know that?"

I count on my fingers. "Let's see. Where to start? You're the only person at Meridian who brings leftover weekend energy into the office instead of exhaustion. Last week, you printed out motivational quotes and left them on everyone's keyboards. You often bring a baked good you made over the weekend to share in the lunchroom. You also water the office plants every Monday and hum while you do it. And you always wear something colorful at the start of the week like you're rebelling against the Monday blahs."

A flush spreads across her cheeks. "You pay attention to a lot of unnecessary details."

"Nothing about you is unnecessary." The words slip out before I can stop them.

Jules freezes like I've just confessed to major crimes. Which, technically, I have.

"You like fresh starts," I add, trying to equalize things.

"Hopefully, I don't have one in prison."

My phone buzzes with a text in the team group chat. I glance at it.

> Bīriņš: I'm back in the land of the maple leaf and getting in my morning skate. Coach wants to talk to everyone about conditioning plans. Dun, dun, dun.

He adds the skull and crossbones emoji.

For the first time, possibly ever, my stomach drops at the notion of my beloved pastime and livelihood. Hockey. Training. The life I'm supposed to be preparing for while I'm here playing corporate hack and art thief.

The fans who recognized me the other night outside the gallery flash through my mind—how long before word gets out that I was lurking behind buildings in the middle of the night? Thankfully, they weren't the type to ask for selfies. Maybe they were up to no good, too.

"Everything okay?" Jules asks.

"Just your favorite boating buddy." While that part is true, the next part is a lie. "Nothing important."

It is vitally important. Every day I spend here makes it harder to keep my two lives separate. Every moment with Jules makes me want to tell her the truth, and every text from my teammates makes me regret not doing so sooner. At this point, she'll be upset that I wasn't forthcoming with my real day job.

"I should go and get ready at home," Jules says, moving

toward the door. "We can't show up at the office together looking like this and have people thinking we're ..." She trails off, gesturing vaguely between us.

My lips twitch with a grin. "That we're what?"

"You know. That we're, um, anything other than professional colleagues."

"Right. Professional colleagues who commit crimes together on weekends."

And fall asleep together on the sofa.

DESPITE JULES'S love for Monday, the day passes in a blur of meetings. I can barely concentrate. Every time someone mentions asset protection or insurance procedures, my mind jumps to the painting hidden in my bedroom closet. Every time Jules walks past my office, I remember the weight of her head on my shoulder and the trust she placed in me by falling asleep in my arms.

During an afternoon administrative meeting, I find myself studying faces around the conference table, wondering which of these people might be involved in the insurance fraud we uncovered.

Maxine drones on about protecting company assets and allocating more funds toward loss coverage. I can't tell if her emphasis on the topic is suspicious or just her usual obsession with liability.

Just then, Jules quietly enters and slides a folder onto the table in front of me. Nodding pointedly, I'm not sure if the contents are a hastily scrawled note, alerting me that the authorities are coming and instructing me to make a run for it or if this is the report I requested regarding the discrepancies we've been investigating. If that's the case, she sure is efficient.

"As I was saying," Maxine continues, visibly irritated given the way her eye twitches, "we need to ensure our most valuable acquisitions are properly protected. Our top-tier collections alone represent millions in potential loss, never mind how much individual properties add up on the balance. Right now, it's the Lincoln-related pieces I'm most concerned about."

My head snaps up. Out of the corner of my eye, my father's does too. He probes for clarification, "Are you referring to the pieces we've acquired over the past eighteen months or the original works?"

"There's the Fairfax Collection to be sure," Maxine starts.

The very one Jules and I have been working on.

I suddenly feel as if I'm on a putting green during a thunderstorm ... while on the golf trip last week, one of Dad's friends mentioned a Civil War painting by Clement Marchand. Only, he pronounced it in the French way, *Clegh-men Marsh-an.* Said it was perfect for someone with our "heritage" and made a joke about Lincoln probably spinning in his grave over modern auction prices. I only piece this together now.

"Excuse me," I say, standing abruptly. "I just remembered something urgent I need to handle."

Dad frowns. "The meeting isn't over, Abraham."

"I know. I'll catch up with everyone later."

I practically sprint to my office, my mind racing. If the painting we borrowed is part of a diptych and Dad's friend was right, I think I know where to find it ... tonight.

Jules appears in my doorway with a stack of files, her expression carefully neutral for anyone who might be watching. "You're back fast. In light of the meeting, I thought you might be interested in the insurance documentation inconsistencies," she says formally, but her eyes are bright with discovery.

"I didn't have a chance to look at it. What did you find?"

She closes the door behind her. "I had a little help. The office girlies came through. The insurance valuations for several recent acquisitions are inflated by thirty to forty percent above market value. Someone with executive access has been systematically overvaluing pieces for larger payouts ... going back for at least eighteen months. All Civil War era works. All were authenticated by the same external appraiser and brokered at similar auctions. I can't quite find the connection, but there is one. I'm sure of it." She slides a file across my desk. "Look familiar?"

I scan the documentation, my pulse quickening. "These are all from estates that were liquidated quickly. Sellers who needed fast cash and didn't have time for proper market evaluation."

"Exactly. Someone has been deceiving desperate sellers and inflating values for insurance purposes. It's fraud, Linc. But that's not where it ends." She swallows thickly. "As you see, some of them have then been sold at auction."

I nod in understanding. "Jules, I think I know where the companion piece to our painting is."

Her eyes widen. "Where?"

"There's a charity auction this weekend at the Whitmore Estate outside New York City. High-end collectors, private sales. It's the kind of event where millionaires go to show off their cultural sophistication." I lean forward, excitement building. "One of my father's golf buddies mentioned a Civil War painting from the Fairfax Collection."

"Do you think it could be the other half of the diptych?"

"There's only one way to find out."

"Do you want me to make your travel arrangements?"

I shake my head. "I'll handle that if only not to rouse suspicion." I sit on the edge of my desk. "But none of this answers why someone would go to the trouble of hiding part of a two-piece work."

Jules blinks a few times as if thinking and then snaps her fingers. "If they're selling them separately, they can inflate the values and collect insurance on both pieces individually."

She's sharp.

Letting out a shaky exhale, she drops into the chair across from my desk. "This is huge, Linc. If we can prove the connection between the paintings and link it to the insurance fraud ..."

"We'll have enough evidence to expose whoever's behind this." I pause, studying her face. "But it means we need to attend that auction. Together. As buyers with enough credibility to examine the piece closely."

"I can't afford to bid on a million-dollar artwork."

"You won't be Jules, the research assistant. You'll be my ... consultant. Art expert. Whatever we need you to be ... my plus-one."

Pink creeps up her neck.

An idea sparks. I make a rash decision. "Take the afternoon off."

"What? Why?" She leans forward, concern scrolling across her features.

"Because you're going to need to blend in with wealthy collectors whose wardrobe closet is bigger than your studio apartment. Plus, after everything you've done to help me, you deserve to be spoiled a little."

"Linc, that's not necessary—"

I pull out my phone and start typing. "I'm making you an appointment at the spa on Beaubien. It's not far. Full treatment. Then shopping. Whatever you need to feel confident walking into a room full of Manhattan's art elite."

"I can't let you—"

"You can and you will. This whole thing was my idea, remember? The least I can do is make sure you're prepared."

She stares at me blankly as if the words don't compute. "Why are you doing this?"

Because I'm falling for you.

Because you're refreshingly real.

Because I want everyone else to realize how extraordinary you are.

"Because tonight could change everything." If someone has been stealing from my father ... or even more concerning, he's involved, I need to know. It could affect the jobs of everyone in this company.

Jules looks like she wants to argue.

"The car will be waiting downstairs for you in fifteen minutes."

She opens and closes her mouth. "Okay, but only because this is for the investigation."

"Of course."

"Right."

As she walks toward the door, I catch her smile—small and secret and sweet. And I realize that change is indeed afoot.

But none of that explains how she pulled off the forged copy of the painting so easily.

30

JULES

THE CAR LINC sent to pick me up from the building on Wacker Drive goes all of two blocks before dropping me off in front of a gleaming storefront. I could have just walked. I do not want to contribute to the traffic congestion in this city, people!

Delicate orchids are etched into the glass windows. White marble, with gold accents, frame the entryway of Eau de Calme Spa & Wellness. I've walked by numerous times but never looked twice. It's the kind of place where you have to tip the person you leave your tip with at the front desk.

Taking a deep breath, I push through the heavy glass doors into a world of soft music, breezy lavender scents, and people who seem to glide across the shiny floor rather than plod after a long lifetime of carrying heavy burdens like bills, doctors' appointments, and real-life challenges.

The receptionist greets me like I'm royalty instead of someone wearing department store khakis and a blazer I found at a consignment shop.

"Ms. Lindley? Right this way. Mr. Sullivan has arranged our full rejuvenation package for you."

She doesn't wear a nametag, but tells me her name is Vivant, should I find myself needing anything. Just a pinch on my arm because there are day spas and then there is this place.

I follow her down a hallway lined with flickering candles, feeling like I've stepped into another dimension. In the changing room, I catch sight of myself in the mirror—blonde hair escaping from its half-up, half-down style, stress lines around my eyes from my recent late nights investigating art fraud, and you know, just falling asleep on the couch with my boss.

No big deal or anything.

I have the general appearance of someone who's been running on coffee, chocolate, determination, and now a dash of disbelief for the past month.

After changing into a silk gown, I snap a quick selfie and text it to Oly before I find the nearest exit. It's not that I don't want to have this experience, but will I owe Linc something? Or did he send me here because he felt bad about us dozing off last night? Was he horrified that I had a little drool line coming from the corner of my mouth? I didn't think he noticed, but still. Am I so hideous?

I tell myself to get my head out of the gutters of the Chicago city streets and enjoy the moment. I may never have another experience like this.

Oly and I routinely send each other no-context photos and this is no exception. The fun is in the laughter and the preposterous guesses. Wearing the robe, I take a selfie.

Oly: Spa day or cult initiation?

Me: The first one. This is the before picture. About to get the full Cinderella treatment. Send help.

Oly: Do they have bougie snacks?

Me: Status pending.

Oly: I knew if you ever won the lottery, there'd be signs.

Me: Work thing. Long story.

Oly: Work thing = hot boss?

She sends the peeping eyes emoji.

Vivant leads me into a room where a woman in delicate pink scrubs waits, surrounded by glossy skincare products and shiny instruments. "You're in great hands with Mirabelle."

I want to keep hold of my phone as a lifeline, but Mirabelle gestures with an elegant sweep of her hand that I leave it in a mirrored tray by the door.

"We'll start with the Rivière de Diamantes exfoliating treatment," she says cheerfully, like she's offering me a cup of coffee instead of a procedure I can't pronounce.

For the next three hours, I'm buffed, polished, massaged, and transformed. Between treatments, I sneak peeks at my phone. Like the best friend she is, Oly doesn't abandon me in my luxe time of need.

Oly: Still waiting for details. And the after picture.

Me: I'm currently covered in what the technician called a jade maske—no, that's not a typo. Everything here seems to have the letter E at the end, and not because it's old-tyme like that village we visited on our road trip a few years ago. At present, I'm cuisine.

Oly: Do I need to send the authorities?

Me: Autocorrect. It should say cuisiner.

Oly: If my three years of French serve, that means cooking. I'm not sure that's much better. Don't tell me Linc sent you into a Lion's den of cannibals.

Me: No, that would be tonight.

Oly: You have me worried. NOT joking. I will be down there with a SWAT team in five minutes if necessary.

Me: Sorry, it's possible that I'm high on lavender essential oil. I've never been so relaxed.

Oly: Last I checked, that's not a controlled substance. But your mileage may vary.

Another technician interrupts my texting to have me rinse this mud off before cycling me through a moisturizing process. I send a few more no-context photos so Oly doesn't bust into the building accompanied by men in black and body armor, but otherwise my phone stays in yet another mirrored tray until I get to the manicure and pedicure room.

Me: What I mean is we're going to a fancy party tonight.

Oly: That escalated quickly.

Me: It's not like that. We're investigating something together.

Oly: Investigating or "investigating?" With air quotes and a wink, wink.

Me: The actual kind. Art fraud. Maybe. Keep it on the hush.

Oly: Juliana Grace Lindley!!! Art fraud is serious business. Do you trust this guy?

I pause, my fingers hovering over the keyboard while a technician works magic on my feet. Do I trust Linc? This morning, I woke up on his couch, feeling safer and more content than ... I ever have. But trust is a luxury that I haven't always been able to easily afford.

Me: I'm being careful.

Oly: That's not what I asked.

The hair stylist calls me over before I have a chance to answer, which is probably for the best since I'm not sure what to say. I have no context for how I feel. The photo of me would be a big blank question mark. Maybe with heart eyes.

Two hours later, I stare at my reflection in disbelief. The woman looking back at me has perfectly styled blonde waves that catch the light like spun gold, skin that seems to glow from within, and somehow, they've made my gray eyes look twice their normal size.

Before I leave, a slender woman in a sheath dress leads me to a room with a large poof in the middle and surrounded by geometric mirrors and numerous garment bags.

This woman introduces herself as Jane, a personal shopper. "Mr. Sullivan wanted you to go shopping, but time is of the essence, so he sent me."

She works efficiently, even though this feels very much like a paper doll game show as I change in and out of an assortment of dresses that border on gowns. Offering nothing more than a prim nod, Jane settles on a midnight blue frock.

With a spin of her finger, she instructs me to turn around and take a look in the mirror. The dress skims my curves in all the right places. I hardly recognize myself.

I take another selfie and send it to Oly.

Oly: You look like a movie star!

Me: I was hoping it was more inconspicuous.

Oly: I need details. Times, places, all of it! And take pictures of you two together.

Another text interrupts. This one from Linc. He's waiting. Nerves fire and instead of gliding like the rest of the women here, I suddenly feel like I'm a slug, inching along the gleaming tile. I quickly reply to Oly and hope I don't leave a slime trail.

Me: Sure will, but it's call time. Gotta go. Wish me luck.

When I step out of the spa, Linc leans casually against a sleek black car with his arms lightly crossed. He traded his usual business attire for a perfectly tailored black suit—I didn't get a peek into his bedroom last night, but I bet he has dozens of them lined up in his closet like little soldiers prepared for corporate battle.

When he catches sight of me, his jaw slackens and a smile spreads across his face as if he just spotted a shooting star. Remembering that his mouth doesn't have the night off, he manages to say, "Wow."

Or maybe *now*, as in I'd better hurry up.

Yet, he never takes his eyes off me as I approach. This very much feels like a soft lighting, slow-motion, dreamy romantic sequence moment.

"Jules," he breathes.

I'm already wearing rouge with thanks to the makeover, but my cheeks feel hot to the touch. Could it be a dermal allergy from all those beauty products? I glance down at my garb. "Too much?"

He steps closer, close enough that I can smell his minty fresh scent mixed with his cologne. "You look ..."

I wrinkle my nose. "Like I don't belong in my own skin?"

"Like you belong anywhere you want to be."

Opening the car's door with one hand, he plants his other on my low back, guiding me into the vehicle.

The drive through traffic passes in a blur of me thanking him profusely for the outrageous once-in-a-lifetime spa day.

"Once in a lifetime?" he asks.

"You've been to my apartment. I buy nail polish when it's on sale and only get my hair cut once a year."

As we talk, I keep catching Linc glancing at me, and each time our eyes meet, invisible electric sparks pass between us despite my playing down how pampered and fancy I feel. I know this because I feel it on my skin, my belly, everywhere. However, I know all too well that if I let myself like something too much, I'll be disappointed when I can no longer have it.

Except chocolate. I'll go to battle for the stuff.

After going through a security gate, the car stops at what looks like a big black expanse with some blinking lights in the distance, lining what could be a giant outdoor bowling alley.

But a private jet taxis toward us.

Clutching my phone, I'm suddenly worried and would very much like Oly to call for backup.

Linc jiggles his wrist as he checks his watch. "Right on time."

"Um, where are we going?"

"Did I forget to mention? The Whitmore Estate is just outside Manhattan."

I think he did say that, but it didn't register. "And we're —?" I point to the plane.

"We'll make good time. Be in the air an hour and a half max."

As we board, my brain has to reboot. This is so surreal, I'm certain someone won the lottery—made wise investments or is scamming their insurance company—but it wasn't me.

The jet's interior consists of cream leather seats, polished wood accents, and a flight attendant who offers me champagne before we've even taken off. I accept it because refusing would require admitting that this level of luxury makes me feel like an impostor.

Truth is, I've never tried bubbly and now is not the time to start. I need to remain alert. Anything could happen. Also, let it be known for the record that there is an original Michelangelo painting on the side wall panel of the airplane!

Catching me staring at it, Linc says, "My father once told me that the price of wealth is luxury."

I take that to mean that you have to pay to play. If Frank Andresen showed up at a business meeting in my rust bucket that hardly qualifies as a car, they'd laugh him off the golf course.

"Is this your life?" I ask as we settle into seats that are more comfortable than my bed.

"Part of it." Linc loosens his tie slightly.

"Careful. I might start wanting more of this," I joke with a laugh.

He studies my face. "Would you?"

The airplane's movement distracts me from answering as we take off and the ground falls away below us. I just hope I don't do any falling of my own. Last I checked, I don't have a parachute in my purse.

31

JULES

DURING THE FLIGHT, Linc and I review everything we know so far.

"Let's walk through this again," I say, tapping my chin. "Something is weird with the insurance valuations for the Fairfax Collection."

He runs a hand through his hair. Compared to when we first met, it's less, *I hate it here and you* and more, *I'm thinking*. "My mother was mildly obsessed with finding the Civil War piece."

"Which I believe turned out to be *Echo & Answer*."

"She said it held the key."

"Leading you to the historical society archives," I prompt, grinning because I love when a thread pulls tight.

"Right. And we found the painting."

"Or someone at Meridian did, altered the signature, and then hid it. The Fairfax Collection's insurance valuations have been adjusted four times in the past year. And every time, it's just below the threshold that would trigger an external audit. But it was never a complete collection because of that one missing painting. Until now."

"Maxine, the acting COO, has been managing those."

"She has exclusive access codes to certain files. So do you, as the CEO's son. But ..." I meet his eyes. "When I cross-referenced the access logs with the dates of the adjustments, someone used your credentials twice when you weren't even in the building."

"Are you keeping track of me, Miss Lindley?"

"Don't you wish."

"Maxine, as witchy as she is, wouldn't set me up. The job as VP is all but hers. I don't want it. She knows that."

I let out a breath. "If you say so, but I did overhear a conversation in her office."

He arches an eyebrow as if skeptical, so I give him the verbatim replay. A frown drops his lips. "Interesting. But Maxine is just bitter. I can't fathom her destroying Meridian over it. That would be like cutting off her nose to spite her face."

"Terrible visual, but fair point." Getting us back on track, I add, "This does raise questions about provenance."

Linc's forehead rumples. "If it leads to the letters, I still can't figure out why my father didn't want them found. Unless he's involved."

This is a new piece of info. "Your father doesn't want you finding the letters?"

"He deterred me."

"Maybe so you focus on your exec duties." Or perhaps because he's our fraudster.

"Yeah. Could be." The furrow across his brow deepens.

"I did some digging—probably more than I should have without telling you first, sorry—and I found some really old correspondence. Your grandfather bought the Fairfax Collection at auction, totally legal, but there are hints that Mary Todd Lincoln had specific intentions for some of those pieces. Intentions that maybe weren't ... fully honored."

For a long moment, he's quiet. "My mother spent years trying to find the letters, to prove that romance between—" Linc sighs. "She wanted to believe that even in the hardest moments, even in a war, love could survive."

I know a thing or two about theft and what this could mean for Meridian, but let Linc speak freely.

"If finding these letters means exposing something ugly about how we got the collections or my father's involvement, then that's what we do."

"Or it could be Maxine ... or someone else."

He nods. "I'm not going to let anyone interfere with what my mother spent her last years searching for."

I beam a smile. "Whatever you say, boss."

We turn our attention to the auction gala and Linc gives me a rundown on who's who. Turns out his father won't be in attendance, but Maxine Drecken will.

My stomach grumbles shortly before we're supposed to touch down.

"Hungry?" Linc asks.

"You're not supposed to know I'm human under all this polish and gloss," I joke.

He chuckles. "Jules, this is just our guest pass into the party. I happen to prefer the way you look at about seven thirty a.m."

My cheeks warm and the place between my bones and skin tingles.

"There is food available onboard, but much better than your typical airplane meals. Or, if you can wait about thirty minutes, I'll bring you somewhere that will put our deep-dish pizza to shame." He places his finger in front of his lips.

"Shh. Don't tell anyone I said that, though. I'll lose my Chicago residency card."

My laughter turns nervous because, although I work in a professional environment and I'm as fascinated by the lives of the rich and famous as the next person, I'm more comfortable in my natural habitat. Also, my father taught me some things that saved us a bundle on his health care—even though his other debts eventually caught up to me. However, I never got a lesson on which fork to use first, if it's customary to put your napkin next to your plate when you're finished with a meal or leave it in your lap in case there's a dessert course.

The little things feel really big right now.

Yet another sleek black town car brings us through New York City. I gaze into the fading golden light, caught up in awe as skyscrapers stretch tall and famous landmarks all but wave at me.

"Have you been here before?" Linc asks.

"I've never gone further east than Dallas and that was back when I was seven."

For dinner, he changes the script because instead of going to a five-star restaurant that required a reservation that was made last year, we sit at a table with a checkered cloth in a tiny pizza parlor. I've gathered that we're in Little Italy and this place has been family-owned for four generations. The owner greets us warmly, likely wondering why we're so dressed up.

"This isn't exactly what I expected," I admit, biting into the best slice of pizza I've ever tasted.

"And what was that?"

"Something with far more dollar signs on the menu."

He winks. "That comes next."

Next turns out to be Impresso, a chocolate boutique

that looks like it was designed by someone who thought regular desserts were insufficient. Everything is plated like art, and the menu reads like poetry written in sugar and cream.

"The *noisette* cake," Linc tells the server without consulting the menu. "And two forks."

"And there I was hoping we'd order one of each."

"If you wish."

"I'm kidding."

But was he? A line from one of my favorite movies comes to mind. What Linc said is a variation of Westley's words to Buttercup—the ones loaded with meaning.

But I'm probably reading into things.

The *noisette* is three layers of hazelnut and chocolate perfection, topped with lacy vanilla drizzle, edible gold leaf, and a delicate sprig of mint.

Linc taps his fork against mine. "I noticed your chocolate stash and that the hazelnut chocolates disappear the fastest. I thought you might enjoy this."

My heart springs from my chest at the notion. "I'm addicted just looking at it."

Linc's eyes hover over mine and I can't quite read the smile on his face. Or maybe I'm afraid to.

"*Bon appétit.*"

I take a careful bite, savoring both the incredible flavor and trying not to be reminded of exactly how different our worlds are.

"Good?" Linc asks.

I close my eyes, wanting my thriftiness to take its OSHA-mandated fifteen-minute break, for goodness' sake. "This is life-changing. But I could buy groceries for a week with what this costs."

He frowns. "Jules—"

"I'm not complaining. I just ... to be honest, this is all ever so slightly overwhelming. Not in a bad way, but in a *how I make my chocolate stash last all week* kind of way."

He reaches across the table and folds my hand into his. "You don't have to pretend with me. I know this can be a lot."

"It's ..." I struggle to find the words. "You make it seem effortless. Like you fit everywhere."

"Do I?"

"Size, status, skill—you have the luxury of always feeling like you belong."

He's quiet for a long moment, his thumb tracing circles in the little soft pocket of skin between my thumb and index finger. "I want you to feel like you belong too."

"In your world?"

"With me, Buttercup."

The words send me spinning. He didn't sound possessive or demanding. Just ... him. Like he's offering me a place I didn't know I was looking for ... one I shouldn't let myself want.

I snap a quick photo of us with the dessert before it disappears, remembering Oly's instructions. I make sure I don't have a double chin before I click *send*. In the picture, Linc is looking at me instead of the camera. The context of this particular image makes me feel like I'll never stop smiling.

The car ride to the Whitmore Estate is quiet. I watch the city give way to manicured suburbs, then rolling hills dotted with mansions that could house all the residents of a small village. Linc seems lost in thought, and I find myself studying his profile in the dim light.

The man is a puzzle. Arrogant enough to steal paintings and humble enough to bring me out for pizza while dressed in a gown. Confident in boardrooms but gentle when talking about his mother. Like he operates from an innate, internal knowledge that the world doesn't owe him anything—rather, that the world is lucky to count him among its population. The thing is, he's not wrong. That terrifies me because maybe I want him in my life beyond being his assistant, beyond this summer. But what would that mean?

"What are you really looking for?" My question interrupts the quiet shushing of the tires on the road.

He glances at me, confused. "The painting. The letters."

"But why, really?"

He's silent for so long, I assume he won't answer. Taking a deep inhale, he says, "Because my mother didn't finish looking. Never gave up hope. Because I want to be sure I'm not bound by blood to turn out like my father." He shrugs, suddenly looking younger, vulnerable. "Sorry. That sounds silly."

My heart hiccups. Upon formally meeting Frank Andresen, he's not a horrible man. I don't totally hate him. However, given what Linc said about his mother's journal, he turned away from what's most important in favor of money and power. He hardly sees what remains, his amazing son.

"It doesn't sound silly at all." I twine my fingers between Linc's.

The Whitmore Estate makes every other display of wealth I've seen today seem aspirational, a kindergartner playing dress up with her mom's showgirl clothes. It's a Greek Revival mansion with soaring columns, a fountain in the circular driveway bordered by manicured gardens, landscape lighting, and lots of topiary. Valets in white gloves somehow welcome us like royalty and blend in like wallpaper when we arrive.

This is Linc's world and watching him navigate it with the easy smiles, casual greetings, and the way people gravitate toward him, I realize how carefully he's been managing himself around me. How much effort it must take to make me feel comfortable when this level of opulence is his baseline normal.

Before my phone is put in a locker since there is no photography allowed, I send Oly a quick text, telling her to send help if I'm not at our next brunch date ... or if I fall in love.

32

LINC

THE WHITMORE ESTATE is suitably opulent, but it's modest compared to my father's property outside Chicago—he built what he referred to as my mother's dream house, though she was happiest when we spent summer weekends at the lake cabin. Haven't been there in years.

As we walk through the hallway lined with antiques, I catch Jules taking it all in.

This is my world. Has always been my world. But watching her makes me see it through fresh eyes—how overwhelming it must be, how measured and scripted every interaction is, how much effort people put into appearing effortless.

After schmoozing—as my father says, though he isn't here—we locate our target painting. It's displayed prominently in the preview gallery. Even from across the room, I can tell it's the companion piece we've been searching for.

The brushwork matches the stippling we saw in *Echo & Answer*. The color palette consists of soft pastels against dark undertones. The piece dovetails with the other—where Lincoln was reaching forward in the first painting, a small figure inside a glass structure reaches back toward him in this one.

"Linc," Jules breathes, gripping my arm. "Do you see it?"

In the background—no, not the background, the focal point—is an elaborate glass conservatory. The structure is unlike anything from the battle scene in the first painting. It's geometric with octagonal panels made of intricate iron framework that creates a distinctive star-burst pattern and yet, there's fluidity to it, like flowing water, like a pleasant breeze, even though it appears to be constructed of glass. It somehow conveys a softly flowing gentleness.

"I've seen architectural drawings of this exact design," Jules says quietly.

"Where?"

"I can't remember ..."

"But you've seen the building in real life?"

"One like it ..." She shakes her head as if probing her memory.

I study the painting more carefully. Inside the glass structure, a small figure sits at a writing desk—unmistakably feminine, unmistakably Mary Todd Lincoln.

"If you were to ask me to interpret, I'd say the glass construction was a place where they could be away from political pressure and the ravages of battle."

"A place where he might hide personal correspondence he didn't want in his official papers?" Jules asks, practically vibrating with excitement.

I nod slowly, thoughtfully. "The first painting shows Lincoln at war—his public life. This painting shows Mary in a glass sanctuary—their private life. Together, maybe this is what my mother suggested about the artist showing us where to look for the letters."

"The paintings complement each other ... and most notably, it's signed by C. Marchand." Jules points out. "Two pieces of a whole."

A shrill voice cuts through the muted, genial chatter in the viewing room. "Linc-y baby!"

I freeze. Only one person has ever called me that ridiculous nickname, and I've been hoping never to hear it again, yet somehow Iva keeps appearing like yesterday's bad news.

"None other than Iva and Aiken." I keep my tone neutral as they approach.

Iva has toned down her usual dramatic style for the elegant setting, but she's still cloying eyes, angular figure, and attention-demanding allure. Aiken lurks behind her like a stick figure scribble made by a child.

"Fancy seeing you here," Iva purrs, her gaze sliding over Jules dismissively before returning to me and batting her eyelashes suggestively. "Are you planning to add some special pieces to your collection?"

Every interaction with her is like navigating a minefield. Literally. The woman blew up my life last year.

I glance at Jules. "I have everything I need. We just happened to be in the area."

Aiken grins and pulls Iva closer. "I never leave home without my plus-one."

Iva's smile turns razor sharp as she looks Jules up and down like she's appraising a piece of chain hotel art. "So you're dating again, Linc-y?" She directs the question entirely to me, as if Jules isn't standing right here.

She stiffens beside me, a dainty flush creeping across her cheeks. Before I can respond, a familiar voice joins our conversation.

"Oh no, she's his assistant." Maxine chortles with dry certainty, appearing at Jules's elbow like she materializes from thin air. "Smart to bring someone to handle all the administrative details, Abraham."

My jaw clenches so hard I'm surprised I don't break bones. The casual yet harsh reduction of Jules to nothing more than office furniture while they preen on center stage strikes a match inside. I grip her hand tightly, anchoring her to me and refusing to let her flounder in this pool of fake smiles and manufactured charm.

Jules steadies her voice and lifts her chin. "I'm Linc's art authentication consultant."

Iva's laugh is like crystal breaking. "How interesting, Linc-y baby. You always did like your projects."

Projects. The word carries a suggestion that I throw away relationships when they no longer suit me. I can practically feel Jules withdrawing beside me. The idea that anyone would see her as something disposable, something I picked up to tinker with and discard, makes me want to set the record straight in terms that would definitely violate tonight's expectations for propriety.

Instead, I step closer to Jules. Close enough that she can feel the warmth of my body. Close enough that everyone watching knows exactly where I stand. "She's the tick to my tock," I say with a smile.

Their faces, including hers, cycle through several expressions I can't quite read—surprise, confusion, and maybe a hint of jealousy from Iva.

"The frosting on my chocolate cake." Jules stands taller as she catches on.

I chuckle despite the tension. "The cheese to my pizza."

The auctioneer's voice booms across the room before anyone can respond to our playful banter. "Ladies and gentlemen, if you'll take your seats, we'll begin this evening's auction."

As we move toward the auction room, Jules glances at our target painting again. "That's not good." She gently elbows me.

"What?"

"Seems you and Aiken have a shared interest."

My muscles tense. "Interested in Iva? We most certainly do not."

Her smile fades and I realize how that sounded—too forceful, too defensive.

I lean closer to her, lowering my voice. "Jules, you're the showstopper in this room tonight."

She opens and closes her mouth like she's not sure how to respond. But I follow her gaze back to Aiken, who examines the second half of the *Echo & Answer* painting with an intensity that makes me suspicious. "The Demo King," I mutter under my breath.

Jules nods grimly. "If he gets that painting ..."

"He won't. Whatever it takes." The words come out with determination because the thought of watching that piece of history—and our only lead—be destroyed for internet views makes my vision go red around the edges.

We take our seats as the auctioneer begins the evening's program. Lot after lot of beautiful things pass by, but I barely register them. All my attention is focused on the painting we need and on Aiken's predatory smile as he raises his paddle again and again, like he's warming up for the main event.

Finally, our lot comes up. The auctioneer's description matches what we suspected—a Civil War era piece, recently acquired from a private estate. The bidding starts at fifty thousand.

I raise my paddle immediately. Aiken counters without hesitation. Back and forth we go, the price climbing steadily. Seventy-five thousand. One hundred. One-fifty.

Jules leans closer. "How high can we go?"

"As high as necessary." And I mean it. This isn't just about money, it's about preserving something irreplaceable, about honoring my mother's memory, about proving that some things matter more than fame and fortune.

But the calculation burns in Aiken's eyes as Iva whispers encouragement in his ear. They're not bidding because they want the painting. They're bidding because they know we do, because turning this into a spectacle serves their self-promoting purposes.

The auctioneer calls for two hundred thousand, and both our paddles go up.

Two-fifty.

Three hundred.

I watch our investigation—and possibly our only chance at the truth—slip away one bid at a time. At four hundred thousand, Aiken raises his paddle with a grin that makes me want to cross-check him into next week.

Meanwhile, Maxine glares at me disapprovingly, shaking her head as if to say she's going to report me to my father for spending his money frivolously. She has a point.

When the gavel falls, he's won. Iva looks smugly satisfied, like she orchestrated an elaborate act of revenge. I never told her about Lincoln's lost love letters, but they mean something to me. Jules too.

It must be plain to see and I'm not sorry about that.

As we leave the auction room, I try to memorize every detail of the painting I can recall. The way the light hit the building in the background. The figure seated inside. The positioning of the elements that could be part of a "map," as my mother mentioned in her journal.

"We could steal it," I say quietly as we walk toward the car.

Jules frowns. "We're likely already wanted in at least one state."

"Speaking of which, while you were getting pampered today, I returned the painting."

"You what?" She freezes on the cobblestone path. "How? You can't just walk into a gallery and rearrange the wall art."

"Remember, I told you I have fans. They created a distraction." I wink.

She gapes, dumbstruck.

"True story. But the real question is, how did you create such a great facsimile? I was seriously planning to run a background check on you, but I figured I should ask directly first. That was impressive work," I say with a laugh.

She joins me in the waiting car, but her expression turns guarded. "The secret isn't that I have exceptional art skills. I printed a high-quality version of the original and then painted over it."

"Paint by numbers style?"

"Exactly. It's an old trick ..." She trails off.

"That you learned where exactly?"

"From someone who is no longer with us but wouldn't like me spilling his secrets."

I think about her father, the medical bills, and the way she sometimes gets a distant look in her eyes when family comes up. I can't help but wonder what else she's capable of fabricating. Her interest in me, maybe? Because mine is very real.

"So what next? We didn't get the painting," Jules says as we return the way we came.

Our one lead slipped through my fingers like sand. "I'm

sure that was it. I'll have you back to Chicago before the clock strikes twelve."

"Or else the airplane will turn back into a pumpkin?"

My grin is irrepressible. "You were dazzling in there, Cinderella, and look, you didn't lose a single glass slipper."

"I thought it was Buttercup."

"If you wish."

Cheeks rosy, she turns toward me sharply. "Glass. The glass building in the second panel was made of glass, depicting a future where even buildings made of glass would remain standing. It was a post-war ideal."

I nod, recalling it distinctly and wishing we'd at least been able to get a photograph.

"There was a figure seated inside. Mary," she breathes.

"Mary Todd," I add, accounting for what we already know.

Jules nods vaguely in agreement but seems deep in thought. "I can only assume, but I think I've seen that glass building before. Well, not actually, but an image of one like it."

"You mentioned." I'm already pulling out my phone to search.

Jules practically bounces in her seat as if she now recalls the details. "The World's Fair. Major cities were competing for the honor to host the four hundredth anniversary celebration of Columbus's arrival in the New World. Ultimately, Chicago won."

I do quick math in my head. "But that would've been after Lincoln was gone. 1492 discovery, 1865 assassination, 1892 celebration."

"Right, but at the museum in Chicago, there's a section with all the proposed building plans, well, more like color depictions. The one in Washington, DC, the nation's capital, included a series of glass buildings."

I snap my fingers. "Since the fair was in Chicago, the glass buildings were never constructed."

"The layout was there, where they would've been." She blinks a few times, thinking hard. "Abraham Lincoln would've known about the great Crystal Palace in Hyde Park, London."

I stare at her. "History professor, how do you know all of this?"

"I had to do a project on it in college."

"Cool. So tell me about this Crystal Palace."

"Lincoln and Mary may have visited. It could've been that he considered her his queen, placing her in a glass building, but smaller than the palace. A place just for them. A place they'd be safe in a peaceful post-war world."

Like Mom's beloved cabin by the lake.

The pieces shift around in my mind, but don't quite click into place. "Remember, the diptych was composed by a third party."

"Perhaps Lincoln gave some artistic instruction ... or the world they lived in and the one he wanted for his bride were explored in the love letters."

"Whoa." I let out a long exhale. "I can see your mind is racing a mile a minute, but that still leaves a big unknown. How do the paintings point to the letters?" I say this as much to Jules as to myself.

She shrugs. "That's the extent of my knowledge. I'm a dead end, even if I may have put us on the right track."

My thoughts loop and loop, in an endless circle, and then snap into sharp relief. "The track."

Jules shakes her head. "I'm not interested in going to

any tracks." She trails off, vaguely commenting about her father's interest in horse betting.

"I went to college in Washington, DC, which, in part, is built on a swamp. They had to close the athletic area for a time because of a sinkhole. When they were excavating to shore up the ground, they found some artifacts." I hardly remember the details, but excitement makes my body hum.

"It's a bit of a stretch ..."

I shake my head. "Jules, you haven't given me a dead end. You've given me the key. I happen to have the lock." I pull out my phone and start making calls. "My mother wrote in her journal about her and my father's honeymoon. They spent five days getting lost in the Smithsonian and the National Art Gallery."

"They went to Washington, DC for their honeymoon? That's not especially romantic."

"They both loved history and art." I think about my father now, how he's spent so much time focused on business that he's forgotten what originally drew him to my mother. He's neglected to enjoy the present or prepare for the future, focusing on the things that really matter. "Washington or bust."

Jules gawks at me. "Seriously?"

I grin at her as the car turns toward the airport. "What better thing to do when dressed up like this than to go on a treasure hunt in the nation's capital?"

She tips her head back with laughter as if agreeing to this absurd adventure.

33

JULES

NEVER MIND *Juliana in La La Land*—as Mom used to say to me when I was a kid and she'd catch me daydreaming. I've entered an alternate dimension where I'm apparently the kind of person who jets off to major cities in the middle of the night to hunt for centuries-old love letters with a man who makes me feel like I have a Glowy Care Bear heart.

It's well past midnight when we arrive in Washington, DC, both of us moving like zombies the moment before we realize the couple at the other end of the hall in the mirror are the walking dead. That would be us.

I don't mean as a couple—just the two people who are boss and employee that were once adversaries, and have now settled somewhere north of hating each other.

Not a couple. I repeat, not a couple.

We shuffle through the elegant lobby of a posh establishment Linc booked with a casual phone call from the plane. The suite he's secured could house my entire family—yes, even with room for my bombastic brothers. I'm beginning to think rich people have trademarked marble surfaces, floor-to-ceiling windows, and furniture that you don't have to build yourself using crude instructions and a cheap metal tool. We each have our own bedroom, separated by a spacious living area complete with a fireplace. We're well into August, but the raw D.C. night has me chilled.

"This is ..." I gesture vaguely at the opulence surrounding us.

"Acceptable?" Linc supplies, loosening his tie. Even disheveled from travel with stubble filling in his jaw, he looks like he stepped out of a photo shoot.

"I was going to say extravagant." I fidget with the silky tassel of an upholstered armchair pillow. "My entire apartment could fit in this bathroom."

Linc pauses in the doorway to his room and his brow creases with sudden awareness. "Jules, I don't know what to say. I'm not trying to show off. I have the resources available and—"

"I'm not used to it. I feel like I owe you." My tongue feels clumsy when I speak.

"That's not how this works. I'm dragging you along on this adventure, so I'm footing the bill. If you were searching for something your mother wanted to find, you'd lead the charge." He shrugs, almost apologetic.

"I'm here willingly," I say with a light laugh.

The corner of his mouth tips with a grin. "Good. Get some rest. Tomorrow we'll figure out our next move."

I nod, suddenly too tired to process the weight of everything that's happened. "Good night, Linc."

"Good night, Buttercup."

His pinky links with mine and he squeezes.

Still dressed, I drop immediately into sleep, though my dreams are chaotic—images of Civil War battlefields where every soldier has my face, alternating between the polished version from the spa and my usual self in leggings and an oversized hoodie. Past Jules fights Future Jules in an endless loop of identity crisis confusion.

I wake to creamy sunlight streaming through windows with gauzy curtains and the distant sounds of the city waking up below. My phone shows it's nearly ten—later than I've slept in months. The exhaustion of the last few days must have finally caught up with me.

A soft knock interrupts my mental inventory of everything that's happened. "Jules? Room service will be here soon if you're ready for breakfast," Linc calls.

As if caught with my pants down, I launch myself out of bed and into the bathroom. After taking a hot shower, I wrap a towel around my head, don a soft, cozy robe I find on a hook behind the door, and check my phone.

I almost forgot to submit my monthly payment to my father's debtors. My stomach clenches as it always does, the moment I make the transfer. I remind myself that someday I will be free of this burden. Someday, I won't owe them any more money. I just hope that they never increase the interest owed.

I pad out to the living area where Linc is already dressed casually in jeans and a pullover, looking refreshed and relaxed. The breakfast includes herbed scrambled eggs, hash browns with cheese, and maple bacon, cinnamon apple coffee cake with streusel topping, waffles with blueberry compote and lemon ricotta cream, as well as a variety of pastries with fruit.

"Did you order the entire brunch menu?" I ask, stomach suddenly rumbling.

"I wasn't sure what you liked besides doughnuts." He hands me a steaming mug of coffee with cream. "So I ordered everything."

Linc opens his mouth as if about to say more. I lean closer, anticipating a bombshell. He closes his mouth, then opens it like a guppy.

"Unless you'd like me, your assistant, to prepare a PowerPoint for your presentation, you'll have to share," I tease.

The corner of his lip curls and he lets out a breath. "I've been thinking ... it's like I've been on a waitlist for my whole life, leading up to the year before turning thirty."

"Because of Meridian?"

"My father appointed Drecken as acting, provisional Chief Operating Officer because he's holding out for me."

"I take it that's not the future you see for yourself."

He bunches up his shoulders and then drops them. "My life has been one giant hourglass of expectations and pressure as I near thirty and prepare to step into my father's shoes, taking on more responsibility before taking over the company entirely. That's not the future I want. Not the one I see for myself."

"Some fathers have high expectations for their kids. Some have none."

I'm glad Linc can't read my mind because I'm not proud of the little detour I took from college, which led me to make some questionable decisions to help my father out when he got sick. He was on a job, needed help finishing it. I learned the ropes real quick. The kinds of things not taught in an academic setting. We didn't net enough. The collectors came a-calling.

I'm still on the hook for the money he owed.

Linc nods and adds, "What I'm saying is I want to call a truce between us. Maybe after all this, we can trust each other."

"I'm willing to try ... if you concede."

"About what?"

"That I was right about the chocolate," I say, recalling our very first conversation on the phone during which I suggested Lindt hazelnut truffles are superior to all.

He laughs, nods, and lifts his coffee mug for me to clink as a slow, easy smile rises on his lips. "There was something about you ..."

"That you hated?"

"No, Jules. Quite the opposite."

We settle at the small dining table by the windows, the Washington Monument visible in the distance like an exclamation mark against the vivid morning sky.

I take a bite of a butter croissant infused with hazelnut chocolate spread and nearly moan, it's so good. "Let me make sure I understand our current situation, just in case I hallucinated last night's events. We're in Washington, DC, chasing a theory about glass buildings that may or may not point us toward love letters that may or may not exist, written by your great-great-however-many-greats grandfather to his wife."

"That's an accurate summary, yes." Linc's mouth quirks upward. "Having second thoughts?"

"About the sanity of this whole endeavor? Absolutely. About doing it anyway?" I take a sip of coffee and meet his eyes. "Not a chance."

His smile transforms his entire face, and I have to look away before I do something embarrassing like stare.

I pull out my phone and start researching. "Okay, so about that Crystal Palace connection. The original structure in London was a massive iron and glass building—a revolutionary feat of engineering for its time. If Lincoln and Mary did visit, or even if they just knew about it, the symbolism of placing her in a similar glass structure in the painting has some sweetly romantic connotations."

"A transparent life together," Linc muses. "Nothing hidden."

I swallow a bite of eggs on a wedge of toast. "Exactly. And if the artist included specific architectural details from the proposed DC World's Fair buildings ..." I show him images on my phone. "These were never built, but the plans were widely circulated. Maybe there's something about the location they were meant to occupy."

"But Abraham Lincoln was long gone before those plans came to fruition."

Biting my lip, I think this through. History can sometimes be like a tangled ball of yarn. If you find the right strand and pull, it'll come loose. "Perhaps it was a building he'd originally wanted created during his presidency and the World's Fair proposal architects intended to construct it in his honor."

Linc snaps his fingers and points at me as if I'm onto something. It's a wild hare, but at this point, we're operating on butter, chocolate, and hope.

He pulls out his own phone. "I'm going to call someone at my old college. The athletic department had to deal with the excavation when they found those artifacts I mentioned. I still know someone there."

He heads to the balcony to make his call, and I can't help but wonder about his life here in DC. College years, old friends, old girlfriends. The thought makes me uncomfortable—hot, humid, and prickly. I text Oly instead, giving her an update.

Me: Still alive. In DC. Will explain later.

Oly: As in Washington, DC? Our nation's capital?

Me: The very one.

Oly: Did NYC not meet your jet-setting expectations?

Oly: Did your mysterious billionaire boss kidnap you?

Oly: Should I call the FBI?

Oly: Also, did you wear something fabulous last night?

Oly: Send photographic evidence!

Oly: Also, are you sure he's not secretly married or has a bunch of love children hidden away somewhere?

Oly: Why aren't you responding?

When Linc returns from the balcony, I quickly snap a selfie of us. "It's for Oly. She needed proof of life."

My best friend replies instantly.

Oly: That tells me nothing, Juliana Lindley. NOTHING.

"Is she alright?" Linc asks.

"She's just making sure you haven't spirited me away to commit crimes of the historical art variety."

"Well," he says with mock seriousness, "the day is young."

With another casual display of his resources, Linc arranged for fresh clothing—that must be where his new jeans came from. Shopping bags arrive from stores I've only ever admired from the sidewalk while window shopping. Everything fits perfectly—dark pants, a stylish tank top, and a light blazer for moving in and out of climate-controlled spaces.

"How did you know my sizes?" I ask when I emerge from the bedroom.

Linc rubs his thumb over his penny. "Lucky guess."

We spend the rest of the morning wandering through the Smithsonian as if we're tourists with only twenty-four hours before we move onto our next stop ... or a couple on their honeymoon who don't want to miss a thing.

We're searching for anything by the artists Douglas Kinnard, Clement Marchand, or having to do with Lincoln. In the same way history can be like a ball of yarn, it also leaves breadcrumbs. There have to be clues here somewhere.

Linc repeatedly checks his phone. Tension bunches in his shoulders. No surprise, all things considered, but I prefer the fantasy of us being a couple on ...

Kidding! I'm kidding. I did not just think that.

But my stomach does a disco boogie.

"Tell me more about your parents," I say as we sit on a bench outside the National Gallery of Art, watching families stream past with strollers and camera bags, students with large portfolios, and ordinary museum visitors who're probably as interested in the cafeteria offerings as the history hung on the walls.

"What about them?"

"You said they honeymooned here. That they loved art and history."

His expression softens. "They did, hence my father

becoming a titan in the industry. He's obsessed with preserving it, even more so after we lost Mom. She loved art, paintings especially for the stories they told, the beauty they portrayed, the hope they inspired. She could spend hours in front of a single piece, seeing things that everyone else missed. My father used to tease her about it, but he's snatched up as many of her favorites in the years since. Ironic, I suppose."

"In her memory?"

"It's hard to tell because even before she passed, he was only focused on business and already less interested in the things that used to matter to them both." Linc's voice is soft with sadness.

I reach out and touch his hand, wanting to comfort him.

He gazes out the window. "I think that's part of why finding these letters matters so much to me. It's not just about Lincoln and Mary. It's about seeing what love looks like."

Feeling unsteady with emotion, I say, "My parents weren't like that. Allegedly, my father was charming when he wanted to be, but not reliable. Not the kind of man who wrote love letters. They split when I was too young to remember."

"That must have been hard."

"Mostly on my mother. She kept believing he'd change and then finally had enough. I only saw him a couple of times a year before he got sick." I watch a young couple sharing a pretzel, unconsciously mirroring each other's movements. "Maybe our motives aren't that different."

He squeezes my hand gently. "I'm glad you're here with me."

Me too and somewhere along the way, I've started trusting him without even realizing it. I don't know if I should make a pact with Oly that I not do anything stupid or ... just see where things go. I mean, we've already been to New York and now Washington, DC. What's next? Oz?

We grab a quick lunch at a café filled with young professionals zipping around in tailored suits and confident strides. Watching them makes me think about my real job, the one I should probably be at right now.

"Should I call in sick?" I wonder aloud, then immediately feel guilty. "I've never taken a sick day that wasn't actually for being sick."

With a confident smile, Linc says, "Don't worry about it. I've got you covered."

"What does that mean?"

"It means you're officially on assignment. Research for the company."

"Linc, I can't let you—"

Stealing a chip from my sandwich basket, he says, "Let me handle this part, please."

I nod, agreeing, hoping I don't regret this later.

34

JULES

WE ARRIVE at Linc's old college campus in the late afternoon, and I expect him to want to show me around, point out his old dorm or favorite study spots, and tell me candid stories of all his shenanigans. Instead, he heads directly toward the athletic facilities with a single-minded purpose.

"Not interested in a nostalgic campus tour?" I ask, slightly out of breath from trying to match his long stride.

He lifts and drops a shoulder with a non-committal shrug. "Right now, we need to focus on the excavation site."

The track field stretches out before us, a green bullseye surrounded by black rings in the afternoon sunshine. It's hard to imagine that somewhere beneath our feet there were once artifacts that could unlock a piece of American history.

Linc pulls out his phone. "I'll text Taylor that we're here."

I gather this is the friend who might be able to help us get more information about what was found. But I cannot stop the deluge of questions that have nothing to do with our research. Who is this friend? Are they male? Female? Another ex-girlfriend who'll look at me like I'm punching above my weight? The jealousy that fizzes inside catches me off guard. I have no claim on Linc. No right to feel possessive.

But logic seems to have declined the invitation to enter into this debate.

His phone pings. "Good news. She can meet us in a few minutes."

She. Of course.

"Anyone I should know about?" I try to keep my tone casual.

"Just someone who might have access to the excavation records."

A few minutes later, a woman approaches us from across the field. She's pretty in an effortless, academic way —shoulder-length auburn hair, a timeless outfit, and the kind of warm, welcoming smile that makes it so I can't instantly hate her—not that I would. I only mean she's not Iva.

They embrace, and Linc seems genuinely happy to see her—like they're long-lost lovers. Did they once send each other romantic pieces of correspondence like Abraham Lincoln and Mary Todd?

Her voice carries to me in greeting, startling me from my jealous stupor. "It's nice to meet you, Juliana. Linc has been a stranger for far too long. I can't believe you're back on campus. It's been what, three years?"

"Something like that," he mutters.

I try my best manners. "It's very nice to meet you, too."

"Taylor is a historian," Linc explains.

A *his*-torian, as in do these two have a personal history? The little green monster in me hisses.

Linc says, "Taylor loved it so much here that after graduation, she just couldn't leave."

"I was gone for two years, got my master's, returned for my doctorate, and then, yes, I was compelled to stay." The last part is loaded with meaning.

He holds up his hands. "I had nothing to do with it."

"Oh, no?" Turning to me, she says, "Linc and I dated briefly freshman year—"

Her words turn fuzzy, ones I'm not sure I want to hear, but the greedy part of me needs the truth.

She shakes her head. "This guy was way too much of a goofball for me."

I stare at Linc. "*You're* a goofball?"

"I prefer 'delightfully unpredictable.'" He lengthens his spine and thrusts his shoulders back, dignified.

Taylor snorts with laughter. "Puh-lease. You once got stuck in a revolving door because you were trying to go backwards to impress a girl."

"That was one time," Linc protests.

"It was twice," Taylor corrects. "Different girls, same door."

Despite my earlier jealousy, I find myself warming to Taylor's easy humor. "I'm having trouble reconciling this with the serious businessman I know. The guy that doesn't have so much as a funny bone in his body."

She laughs. "Just wait. When you least expect it, he'll unleash his inner comedian. I would know, lucky for me, Linc introduced me to the man of my dreams."

"You mean 'The Grump.'"

And there I thought that word applied exclusively to him.

"The captain of my heart," Taylor says with affection in her eyes.

"Her husband," Linc adds quickly, and there's something odd about his tone. "They got married last year."

"Two years ago," Taylor corrects, but she's distracted now, pulling out a tablet.

"Time flies," Linc says, gazing into the distance.

Part of me is relieved there isn't anything romantic between these two, but the possessive little green goblin side of me suddenly, desperately wants to know about his love life—past, present, future. All of it.

"Speaking of, you're here for a reason and it's not to rehash our glory days. Those artifacts you asked about ..."

She shows us photos and reports from the excavation. Most of it is routine—broken pottery, old coins, fragments of building materials.

"Unfortunately, most of these are in storage. Otherwise, I'd show them to you. But historians believe this was once a park, and its claim to fame was a unique glass structure."

Linc and I exchange an excited look.

"The glass shards were particularly interesting—thicker than what would've been used in windows at the time. There were also traces of what might have been a foundation for a small building shaped like a gazebo."

"That's very interesting. Do you have any idea who made it or where the blueprints are?" Linc says vaguely.

"I could arrange something, but it would take a few days of paperwork."

"We don't really have a few days, but thank you," Linc says.

"As for the engineers and builders, my best recommendation is to go to the National Library. I have some reference numbers I can text you." She snaps her fingers. "Actually, now that I think of it, I believe the architect was the same person who created the plans for the conversion of the wooden dome of the Capitol building to an iron one. He was familiar with unique structures—metal and glass, mainly, if memory serves. I can't recall his name at the moment, but you'll find more information at the Lincoln Memorial. His grandson was the mastermind behind it."

"This is great. Super helpful," I say, thanking Taylor and feeling like these are some solid leads.

After we say goodbye to her, the car waits for us outside the Sullivan Arts building. I notice this city is filled with sleek black cars and SUVs moving around like apex predators in murky waters.

"Any relation?"

He snorts. "As a matter of fact, yes. My father gave a generous endowment."

"In your mother's memory?"

He nods, and I can't help but think Frank Andresen really did love his wife. However, he just wasn't sure how to show it.

The car Linc seems to have on standby brings us across town. In the fading light of day, the impressive facade of the Lincoln Memorial stands like a monolith of history. I feel like we're somehow part of it, as it's made in real time.

I only hope that I'm not merely part of Linc's footnote.

35

LINC

THE LINCOLN MEMORIAL Museum is a marvel of modern innovation, paying homage to history built into the undercroft of the landmark structure. It includes exhibits, multimedia presentations, and displays, showcasing artifacts along with a timeline that charts every documented moment of Abraham Lincoln's life.

Captivated, Jules traces information placards as if her mind connects dots I can't even see yet, even though I know this history almost as well as my own.

She stops at a display about Lincoln's time serving in the House of Representatives. "Check this out about the places Lincoln frequented while in Washington."

I lean over her shoulder to read, catching the scent of whatever shampoo the hotel provided—spring rain and cherry blossoms.

I remind myself we're here for history, not for me to notice how Jules is golden-hour gorgeous with her vintage-film eyes and warm campfire lips that threaten to turn me to liquid.

"'Between 1847 and 1849, while Lincoln was representing Illinois, he had several places he liked to visit in the nation's capital when he needed to think or write privately,'" she reads aloud. "There was an inn called the Eagle's Nest where he sometimes stayed overnight, and an old private library where scholars say he did some of his most important researching and thinking."

"Do you suppose that includes personal correspondence?"

Jules leans closer to read the placard containing artist renditions of the buildings. I have to step back before I do something stupid like brush a strand of hair behind her ear or whisper something to her that will make us pick up where we left off in front of the Civil War painting at the gallery during our almost-kiss. "Do you think either of these places still exists?"

I pull out my phone, excitement building like the final seconds of a power play. "Let me search ... okay, here we go. A modern office building was built on top of the site of the inn, but the building's basement level apparently contains remnants of the original structure, including what the owners used to call the Lincoln Quarters, preserved in his memory."

"Now we're getting somewhere." Her eyes light up like she's just discovered a chest full of treasure. If you were to ask me, Jules is where X marks the spot.

"What's the building now?" Lifting onto her toes, she peers over at my phone screen.

I continue reading, then groan. "Of course. It's now a security systems company called Checkpoint Secure. We won't be sneaking through the window, that's for sure."

"But we'll need to get inside somehow."

Lowering my voice, I turn to face her fully. "Exactly

how do you propose we break into a security company's building?"

Swishing her mouth from side to side, she considers this. "We don't break in. We act like we belong there."

I arch an eyebrow, already not loving this plan. "Genius, but last I checked, neither one of us has a security systems background unless you have a degree or certificate I don't know about."

Her confident expression falters. "We could go in disguise. Carry clipboards. Wear confidence like an official badge." She grins simply, like she suggested we grab ice cream instead of committing what are probably several more felonies.

This woman is going to be the death of me—either from stress or from falling so hard that I forget to breathe.

"There is also the library to consider," she says.

"And let's not forget about the architect Taylor mentioned."

When my college hockey team captain, Anselm Nerhäuser, met Taylor, it was love at first sight. It took her a while to come around, but they've been happily together for years. Not wanting to sound like a weirdo, I didn't ask Taylor to keep my NHL career under wraps because that would've raised questions that had long answers. Thankfully, she didn't mention anything. However, I was nervous the entire time to the point that I foolishly thought that maybe Jules was jealous at first, thinking Taylor was more than just my bro's bride.

What has gotten into me? If I didn't know better, I'd fear I've been body snatched or agreed to a role in a cringy teen movie. I can't remember the last time I felt this way.

Maybe because I haven't.

We continue to browse the displays outlining the life of

the sixteenth US president. I have to hand it to the museum curators, they did an amazing job highlighting Lincoln's life and achievements, along with celebrating the memorial building itself.

"Here it is. The chief architect for the memorial that Taylor mentioned is featured, too." I point to the exhibit about the construction of the building.

We look up information on the man Taylor said was the mastermind behind this feat of architecture to learn that Amos Price, the architect of this building's grandfather, did indeed replace the wooden Capitol dome with iron. Scrolling through, we also learn he was involved in cutting-edge—for the time—design, including glass structures.

"We need to find out more about him."

"And figure out how we're going to get into the Checkpoint Secure building," I mutter.

When we exit into the evening, the sun is setting, casting distinct columns of shadow off the Memorial. If only my thoughts were so clear, so black and white.

I worry that we're taking the investigation too far ... that we're taking *us* too far.

This isn't only about the letters anymore. Every hour Jules and I spend together, every shared look and inside joke, every moment of seeing her handle unexpected situations with humor and grace, I'm falling a little deeper into something I don't know how to navigate.

And the worst part is, she still doesn't know who I really am. Not the hockey player part, or if my father is involved in a fraud scheme—that could change everything, including her employment status.

I can't let that happen. But what do I do?

I flip my lucky penny and catch it. "In for a penny ..."

"In for a pound of trouble," she finishes, grinning mischievously.

I chuckle. "That's not how the saying goes."

"It's how this saying goes. With us, trouble seems to be the standard unit of measurement."

She has a point.

THE NEXT MORNING, over breakfast—another spread thanks to room service—Jules exits her room looking adorably sleepy. She sniffs the air as if detecting what may as well be her kryptonite: chocolate croissants.

Finding me on the sofa, she narrows her eyes, shakes her head, and abruptly charges my way. "We are getting into a fight today."

I nearly choke on my coffee. "Excuse me?"

"We've been getting along too well."

"Is that a bad thing?"

"Obviously."

Setting down my mug, I ask, "I've been awake for two hours. I took a run, hit the gym, showered, and am fully caffeinated. But no, it's not obvious."

Crossing her arms, she pouts. "Remember how you used to call me Juliette? Or Yulia?"

"I never called you Yulia."

"Ha! You so did. That means the wrong names were on purpose."

Caught. "Well ..."

She shakes her head. "We were engaged in a battle of mutually assured destruction, and now look at us. Sharing a fancy continental breakfast like civilized people."

"The walls came down," I admit.

She drops into a chair and stares at the floor for a moment before peering up at me, gaze pinched and earnest. "Be careful, Linc. I might start to like it."

My upper lip quirks. Ah, so that's what this is about. "I'll admit that at first, you rattled me."

"You were such a meanie!"

"We were instant adversaries."

"Not true. I tried to be friendly Juliana. My mistake. You came in with guns blazing. I could've handled the stiff suit and fake cordiality, but you went full supervillain executive."

"I was very bitter about being at Meridian. I took it out on you. I apologize."

She straightens slightly, chin lifted, and gives me a nod of acknowledgement. "The thing about hating someone is that it gets exhausting over time. It's like being locked in a dark room with a vampire—eventually, you run out of energy to keep fighting. What changed?"

I study her face, memorizing the way the morning light makes her eyes look like crystal, like glass. "I stopped the rude exec act because I realized I was acting like my dad. You were getting caught in my crossfire."

She considers this, nods to accept it, and then quietly says, "You rattled me, too. I kept thinking, 'Obviously this guy thinks he's better than us worker bees, us little debt peons.'"

It's my turn to hang my head in shame. "My father essentially installed me, so I figured if he was going to force me to follow in his footsteps, I'd go all the way."

"I'll admit that from what few interactions I'd had with your father, I hated him, too. Perched up there on the fortieth floor like a vulture."

I chuckle darkly. Or a predator, depending on what's going on with the insurance claims.

She adds, "He's not so bad once you get to know him."

My eyes arc a slow half-circle along the upper lids, weighing the notion as if that's debatable.

She giggles.

It's time to tell her that my father insisted I take the position at Meridian despite the fact that I have a full-time, demanding, and very fulfilling career. "The thing is—"

She waves her hands. "Wait. We're getting too friendly again. We need to bicker."

The moment to confess dissolves. "I prefer to think of it as banter."

"You're such a pest."

I leap to my feet. "Ah ha! That's it. If we're going to pull off our visit to the Checkpoint Secure site, we have to seem like we're coworkers for a pest company. Like method acting."

Her grin turns mischievous. "Something you're all too familiar with. When we first met, I was convinced they sent the villain executive from central casting. You forgot your curly mustache prop."

I tip my head back with laughter, then level her with my gaze. "But that's not what this is anymore, is it?"

Silence slinks between us as if we're both afraid to answer the question and turn back to formulating our plan of infiltrating the building of a security company, which, no doubt, will have a high level of security.

36

LINC

THAT AFTERNOON, we're standing outside Check Point Secure Inc., wearing matching brown polo shirts with name tags—she's Yulia and I'm Dirk. Jules insisted because it rhymes with jerk, to really embrace that we're disgruntled coworkers.

We also had a fake pest control company logo patch produced on short notice. After all, this is a major city and as a billionaire's son, money isn't an issue.

Yulia's hair is slicked back into a tight bun at the nape of her neck and she carries a clipboard. I'm wearing a nondescript baseball hat with my glasses and trying to look like someone who knows the difference between termites and carpenter ants.

As we approach the reception desk in the cold, stone building, Jules says, "Remember, we're here about reports of structurally damaging pests in the basement level. With the earth beneath, once being a swamp, it's a very common problem."

The receptionist barely glances up from her computer.

"Basement access is through the maintenance door. Building management said you'd be coming by."

Sometimes being ridiculously wealthy and having connections pays off in ways that probably violate several laws.

The basement is a maze of modern mechanical rooms and storage areas, but eventually we find a crawl space. In a crouch, we walk through it, leading to a preserved pocket of 1800s architecture, complete with original brick walls and the musty scent of centuries-old wood and stone.

Jules turns in a slow circle, wincing when a cobweb grazes her shoulder.

"It's like stepping back in time," I say, fascinated while she's visibly uneasy.

We find what remains of the inn's foundation—soggy, splintered wood and basically a dug-out basement that's been reinforced but not renovated. Jules hesitantly starts examining every corner with her phone's flashlight while I search for a place where letters may have been hidden.

I find a slim break in the wall, barely wide enough for me to squeeze through. "Check this out. I found a passage that leads to a tunnel."

"Because, of course, there are mysterious underground tunnels beneath Washington, DC. Why wouldn't there be?"

"Stay close," I say as we enter a low, yet cavernous space that seems to go on and on.

Jules's expression squishes up, squeamish. "A tunnel filled with spiders and other creepy crawlies."

"Did you ever watch the Indiana Jones movies?"

"Of course, but that doesn't mean I wanted to star in one."

"Where's your sense of adventure?"

She snorts.

Pointing out the obvious, I say, "You can handle pretending to be part of a pest extermination team, yet you aren't a fan of the dark places where they hide."

"I thought we'd find a vault with the letters in it or something." Her nervous laugh echoes through the hollow space.

"Is safe cracker part of your resume, too?"

"No, actually. But what I imagined was more James Bond. Less Indiana Jones."

"You have some imagination." I laugh.

"What was that?" she asks, going rigid.

I listen and hear what sounded like a door closing, but from far away. I tell her as much, trying to be assuring. "Stay close."

As we go deeper, I do wonder if we'd have been better off calling in professionals ... but for what? Because I'm chasing a lark, some lost love letters, and doing it with the woman who has taken up permanent residence in my brain ... also maybe in my chest where that major organ of mine beats wildly every time she's in my proximity.

The tunnels are narrow, damp, and not recommended for anyone with even the slightest case of claustrophobia. I remind myself to breathe.

Jules remains close at my back, her phone light aloft as I move through the underground maze like I'm following a map when there's nothing of the sort. I think about hockey, the open space of the arena, breathing fresh, chilled air.

"This is insane," Jules mutters.

"This is an adventure," I say, trying to keep morale high even as I scrape my shoulder against another brick wall.

We're making decent progress when this time, I hear a

distant clang and go still. Jules bumps into me, startled. My instinct is to clutch her to me.

"Did you hear that?" I whisper when what I really mean is, *Did you feel that*? The tremor between us? Will there be aftershocks? But no, we're in the underground ruins of early America and may never again see the light of day. If this is the way I go, no regrets.

We listen. It comes again, followed by the faint echo of voices.

"Fellow adventurers?" Jules asks brightly.

"Or Checkpoint Secure discovered that we're not from a pest company."

"It can't be good that someone else is down here. Maybe they're onto us and our fake pest management company," she whispers, grabbing my arm.

Still listening, the voices seem to be getting closer. They're gruff, most definitely not the sound of archaeologists or maintenance workers.

"... Drecken said whatever it takes," one voice says.

"The girl is asking too many questions."

Ice shoots through my veins. I think they're talking about Jules.

"It's not security," I whisper urgently. "We need to run. Now."

"What? Where?" Jules turns, confusion written across her face in the dim phone light.

"They're not after the letters. They're after ...." But I can't say it.

Understanding dawns in her eyes, followed immediately by fear. We turn and scrabble-crouch back the way we came, but the voices are gaining ground. In our panic to escape, we take a wrong turn and hit a dead end. A small piece of dirt, the size of a pebble, drops onto my shoulder.

Then another. Our surroundings judder, dust puffing up, making me think this is the start of a dirty avalanche.

"This way." Jules points to another narrow passage.

We barely squeeze through, emerging into a section where the ceiling is significantly lower and the walls were already slowly crumbling around rough timbers that are ready to quit. Behind us, flashlight beams sweep the tunnels.

"In here," I pull Jules into an alcove as the footsteps get closer.

"Where are they?" one voice demands.

"Must've gone deeper. Come on."

The footsteps recede, but something is wrong. The walls are groaning, and the dirt continues to fall from the ceiling like dusty snow.

"What if they—or we—destabilized things?" Jules asks, gripping my shirt, frantic.

The soft tumble of another clod of dirt follows as if punctuating her statement.

The historical section begins collapsing around us. We hurry toward what I hope is an exit, debris falling behind us as the century-old support beams truly give way.

I will myself to remain calm, clearheaded. I focus on finding an exit, imagining it's the goal and I'm running the puck to it. I spot a narrow passage that leads upward, and once again, we squeeze through as the section we were in completely caves in.

We emerge through what turns out to be a grate in an alley behind the building, gasping, covered in dust, and probably looking like we've been buried alive.

Which, technically, we almost were.

"I knew you hated me," Jules says, trying to catch her breath as she leans against a brick wall.

"Don't say that." The words come out harsher than I intended.

She looks up at me, dirt streaked across her cheek and her hair escaping its bun. She's still the most beautiful person I've ever seen, and she almost got killed because of something connected to me, to my family.

My gaze searches her gray eyes. She's shaken up, but that's understandable. Her hair is mussed, breath shallow. I gently wipe away the smudge of dirt on her cheek.

Overall, she's okay. No injuries. Just dusty from the tunnels. I imagine I'm in need of a shower, too.

Like touching a live wire, a sudden thought jolts me. I can never let anything happen to this woman. I need her to know this, inextricably, but words fail me.

My hands skim her shoulders, neck, and then I frame Jules's face with my palms. A shaky breath escapes. "Jules ..."

Her lips part with a little exhale as her eyes dance from mine to my mouth. "Linc ..."

"Kiss me," I say.

Then our lips meet as if she, too, has the desperate need to be reminded with warmth and oxygen and skin that we're alive.

Our mouths move together in a kiss that sparks and snaps like an electrical current.

My pulse spikes.

She grips my shirt, demanding I move closer.

Our surroundings turn blurry. My thoughts get fuzzy.

There's just Jules. Me. This connection.

I drag my hands along her back, pulling her closer to me. Her heart drums, assuring us both this is real. The kiss deepens, boldly forging its own path forward.

My chest feels wide open, expansive like finally being

able to take a deep breath after a lifetime, never mind the last thirty minutes, of holding it.

The taste of dust disappears, replaced with something sweeter—Jules. My thumb traces the curve of her jaw, and she makes a small sound against my mouth that brings light to a dark part of my interior. A place that hadn't been in fog. But shrouded. Hidden. Alone.

This woman. It's her. No other.

Her fingers thread through my hair, gentle but insistent, and I feel her smile against my lips before the kiss deepens again. Not frantic this time but seeking. Like we're both trying to memorize this moment, seal it away somewhere safe.

I pull back enough to rest my forehead against hers, our breath mingling in the small space between us. Her eyes flutter open, those gray depths now liquid silver in the dim alley.

"I thought—" Her voice catches. "When that wall came down, I thought—"

It was all over.

But we've been given a second chance and I have to seize it.

"I know." I brush my lips across her temple, her cheekbone. "Me too."

She tilts her face up, and I capture her mouth again. My hands map the slope of her spine, the delicate wings of her shoulder blades. Every point of contact feels like a promise I'm making without words.

Does she feel it?

Her palm presses flat against my chest, right over my thundering heart, and I know she can feel exactly what she does to me.

When we break apart, we're both breathing hard, and it has nothing to do with our underground adventure.

"Jules—" My eyebrows pinch together.

She whispers, "Please don't say this was adrenaline or a mistake or—"

I kiss her again, softer this time, trying to pour everything I can't say into the connection between us. Everything about who I really am, everything about how much she means to me, everything about how terrified I am that she's in danger because of me.

37

JULES

STILL SOMEWHERE IN A DC ALLEYWAY, covered in dust, having barely escaped the tunnel with our lives, Linc's gaze hovers over me like he's memorizing every detail of my dirt-streaked face, his eyes heavy-lidded in a way that makes my pulse skip.

When he pulls my face to his again, our lips are poised inches apart. His breath brushes across my cheek, warm yet unsteady.

My pulse counts down. Three, two, one.

Once more, our mouths collide.

Kissing this man is all-consuming—scrambling my head, flooding my heart, turning my knees wobbly.

He shifts the angle of his head and I press closer to the hard wall of his chest. My breath catches, and for a moment it seems like the world holds its breath too.

Want pinwheels through me, sharp and sweet and terrifying.

Delightful shivers cascade down my spine as his mouth moves over mine with an urgency that steals what's left of my thoughts. This is nothing like the decoy, almost-kiss—a distraction for passersby.

This is real.

Every careful boundary we've maintained shatters like glass.

My fingers tangle in his hair, and he makes a low sound in his throat that I feel more than hear. His hands slide from my face to my shoulders, down my arms, leaving trails of heat in their wake. When he pulls me flush against him, I lose track of where I end and he begins.

This kiss consumes me like fire—bright and wild and impossible to contain. My breathing turns ragged, matching his, and I realize I'm trembling.

He breaks away long enough to catch his breath, his forehead pressed to mine again. He lets out a heavy, happy sigh that makes my heart blip.

Then his lips find mine once more, and as if we realize we're no longer escaping the jaws of death, it turns softer. We're not at risk of dying.

Though whatever burns between us could be far more dangerous.

I never knew a kiss could speak so clearly. It's like he's saying, *I see you and I need you and I'm scared of losing you* all without uttering a single word.

The connection between us hums like it's alive, electric, and undeniable. I finally understand what people mean when they talk about falling in love. Because that's exactly what this is—a freefall with no safety net and no guarantees, just an overwhelming certainty that I'd rather crash with Linc than stay safely alone on solid ground.

When we finally break apart, I'm convinced that I've forgotten how to form coherent thoughts.

"We should ..." I start, then stop because I have no idea how to finish that sentence.

Keep kissing!

"Go back ..." he starts, voice rough.

To kissing!

Our eyes meet, his whiskering at the corners with amusement.

We break into laughter. At the absurdity of everything that happened. At us actually getting along as Jules and Linc, not Yulia and Dirk.

Finally, he says, "We need to regroup. Shower."

"Lie low," I add.

And hopefully, I can remember how to act like a normal human being instead of someone whose entire nervous system was rewired by a kiss in an alley.

I somehow manage to remain cool under pressure. Until we get back to the hotel and I shower.

After barely escaping with our lives from the underground tunnel, my hands shake as the hot water washes away the dirt, unlocking the reality of how the crushing weight of tons of concrete could've buried us alive. We could have died. The voices of the people chasing us echo in my ears. Who was it? Why were they looking for me?

Dad. The debt. They were thugs, no doubt. He knew plenty of those.

But in the blur of everything that happened, I could've sworn one of them said the name "Drecken."

I give my head a little shake to dismiss the stomach-clenching anxiety, only for it to be replaced by another kind of nervousness.

Linc and I kissed.

We kissed while covered in tunnel dust and adrenaline,

and it was desperate, like the world was ending yet life-affirming, completely insane, and ... perfect.

After my shower, wrapped up in a cocoon of soft cotton, I curl up on the couch while Linc paces by the windows, both of us maintaining a careful distance—like we're a pair of jumper cables, sparking with electricity. If we close the space, this whole place could combust.

Breaking the silence, I say, "That was some major National Treasure type action."

"Like the movie?"

"Complete with cobwebs."

"I thought you were thinking more like Indiana Jones."

"Does that make me Marion Ravenwood?" I follow with as much of a laugh as I can muster.

Linc saunters over to me, wraps his hands around my waist, drawing me to him. It's a new sensation and I like it. The weight of his arms. The warmth from his body. It's welcome.

He says, "I was always an Indie fan."

"A casual scoundrel, a real maverick."

"He always got the girl." Linc's lips quirk.

"I'll admit, though, that I was also a big fan of Benjamin Gates from National Treasure. He was smart, clever."

"Is that so?"

I tip my head back to get the full view of this massive man. He shaved after showering and from behind his glasses, his eyes sparkle. "As for Indie, I thought he ended up rather lonely in the end."

Linc considers this and with a tip of his head, he says, "Maybe because he wasn't looking for the right treasure." He nuzzles my neck and whispers, "Jules."

I close my eyes and enjoy the trail he kisses along my collarbone like I'm a treasure—a jewel.

His lips brush the hollow of my throat, feather-light and tender. My breath hitches and tingles bubble through me. He pauses there, breathing me in, before pressing one more gentle kiss to the curve where my neck meets my shoulder.

Everything inside me melts, goes liquid and soft.

But then he says, "You're shaking."

I'm unraveling.

"It's been a while since ... well, never like ... I'm—"

He nods, assuring me I don't need to explain. This is new. We're on uncertain ground, thankfully, it's stabler than in the tunnels, which brings to mind our flight to safety.

"Do you think they'll find us here?" I ask, voicing the worry that's been gnawing at me since we surfaced.

He gathers me closer in his arms as if to say anyone who wants to get to me will have to go through him. I certainly don't want him to take unnecessary risks on my behalf, but I feel secure here, together with Linc.

He says, "I signed us into the hotel using a pseudonym."

"Seriously?" I shift uneasily. "Should I be concerned about how good you are at subterfuge?"

His mouth quirks upward. "Let's say I have resources."

Right. Resources. When I'm in his embrace, I forget exactly how wealthy Linc is, how different our worlds are. It's just us. The notion makes me feel small and insignificant, reminding me of when Iva Katz, his ex, with her exclusivity halo, looked me up and down with disregard, dismissing me.

"We need to be more careful," I say to distract myself, whether from the hopelessness I feel about our future or the situation at hand, I'm not sure.

"Yeah."

"That was so sketchy down there. We could have been killed or trapped underground indefinitely."

He squeezes me tight and muffled by my hair, he says, "I won't let anything happen to you."

We order delivery—chicken sandwiches from a nearby place Linc loved when he was a student. The local news airs on the television screen. He reaches for the remote, probably to change the channel, but freezes when the reporter's voice catches our attention.

"... two men were rescued this evening from what appears to be a sinkhole. The men, who have not been identified, were excavated by emergency crews after a section of historical foundation collapsed beneath a commercial building."

Linc and I exchange a look and flop onto the sofa.

The reporter continues, "Allegedly, they were with a pest control company, inspecting the sublevels, when a section gave way. The structure remains sound and the victims are being treated for general injuries at a local hospital."

"Those were the guys chasing us," I whisper.

"Check Point Secure must've thought they were us."

"Good thing we got out when we did." I sink deeper into the sofa, the reality of our situation fully hitting me.

"One of those men said 'Drecken.'" Linc glowers.

So he heard it too. That means these weren't goons sent by my father's loan shark. "Do you think this could have to do with the insurance fraud I discovered?"

He goes very still. "I'm afraid so."

I rub my temples. "But I'm just a low-level worker."

"You're the CEO's son's executive assistant. My father wants me to take over the company. Me, not Maxine Drecken." He looks sharply my way. "If he's involved in the fraud, it could be because he doesn't trust her and thinks I'll keep quiet or ..." But he doesn't finish his thought.

"There's only one way to find out," I say gently.

"That's not a conversation I'm eager to have until I build a stronger case."

"I'll help."

"I can't let you get any deeper into this than you already are. Jules, it's not safe."

"As you said, I'm your assistant. I'm going to do my job ..." I start. Before he can argue, I add, "In for a penny ..."

He lets out an unsteady breath and leans his elbows on his knees. "Jules, there's something you should know—"

Nerves already jangled, if it's about Taylor, after that kiss, I can't hear about his past romances. I interrupt, standing abruptly. "We need to find that private library while we're still here. Then we'll turn our attention back to the discrepancies and insurance."

It's best to stick to the facts, be methodical, and solve this mystery. After that, I can consider the one plaguing my heart.

THE NEXT MORNING, after a night of restless sleep filled with dreams of collapsing tunnels and being chased by human-sized termites, I find Linc already awake. When he sees me, relief relaxes his shoulders as if he's thankful I'm still alive after our brush with death ... or that I didn't steal away in the middle of the night.

We start our research immediately, cataloguing all the libraries that ever stood in this city, making note of the ones that remain. We detail important dates and any historical relevance. It's early afternoon when we finally make a positive match. The private library referenced at the Memorial is still standing and operating as a historic site, open to the public.

As usual, Linc has a car waiting. As we zip through traffic, the events of the last few days trail me, and I cannot help but keep a wary eye out for shady guys lurking around.

Linc remains close to me as we stand at the impressive gates of Tudor Place, a Federalist-style mansion built in 1816 in the heights of Georgetown.

"It doesn't even feel like we're in a city," he says.

"We're definitely not in Kansas anymore," I mutter, approaching the elegantly manicured grounds of a home that was once occupied by notable families and hosted the rich, famous, and influential.

After paying for admission, we enter the vestibule, steeped in US history, the house having been once owned by the granddaughter of Martha Washington.

As we admire the antique décor, I say, "No disguises. No fake identities. This is significantly less likely to get us arrested."

"Let's not speak too soon. Just stay on this side of the velvet ropes." He eyes me like I'm tempted to test out a particularly cushy silk chair in the parlor.

We wander through the elegantly appointed rooms until we reach the "office."

"Do you think the letters could be hidden somewhere in here?" I ask.

Linc shakes his head slowly. "Unlikely. I don't imagine the owner of the home would've let Abraham Lincoln occupy his personal office. Remember, he wasn't even president yet."

"So there must be a library elsewhere."

"Let's hope so."

We continue walking, getting an amazing view of the

Potomac from the second floor, until we filter back to the first floor, using a back set of stairs. Down the hall, Linc goes still.

"Here it is," he whispers as if we're still covert when, as far as anyone is concerned, we're regular tourists, appreciating history.

The library is dimly lit and consists of polished wood and towering bookshelves that contain centuries of knowledge. We poke around until a docent appears and asks if we have any questions.

Only a million.

We try to play it smooth. Do we succeed? That's up for debate.

38

JULES

FOR THE NEXT couple of hours, Linc and I talk to all three volunteers who have a wealth of information about the Washington and Lincoln families.

As a precaution, Linc goes by Dirk again. I'm Yulia and every time someone addresses me, he stifles laughter.

"We're particularly interested in any personal effects or correspondence that might have been housed here during Lincoln's visits," I explain to a helpful woman with a puff of white hair. Her nametag says *Dorothy*.

Should I be surprised?

She quietly taps the tips of her fingers together. "Oh, how fascinating. I really appreciate it when young people are interested in history." She leans into us as if about to confide something. "You know, there are loads of ghost stories about old buildings like this, but I am more intrigued by rumors." She nods meaningfully.

Linc and I exchange a look.

"Some say that Lincoln kept a private study space here, though we've never been able to definitively locate it. The building has been renovated several times over the years and all of the furniture on display is spread between the old garage, the storage shed, and the pigeoneer."

"The what?" I ask.

"The pigeoneer is a small structure to house pigeons," Dorothy explains. "Follow me through the rose arbor and I'll show you."

All the while, she tells us about how supposedly Abraham Lincoln liked the original desk in the library so much, he had it replicated—one for his home back in Illinois, then another for the White House, and had replicas made for each of his four sons.

Dorothy points out the pigeoneer—a large coop-like structure—then looks around surreptitiously and opens the storage shed door. "Call me a romantic, but I'm rather fond of the notion of our former president sitting at his desk, composing his thoughts, recounting his experiences, sending correspondence home, and drafting early versions of what would become historical speeches."

"I couldn't agree more," Linc says.

My body hums with excitement as we enter the shed, only illuminated by the cloudy afternoon light.

Our intrepid tour guide pulls a cloth off of a piece of furniture, apparently looking for a desk that's not too big, not too small, "... but fit Abraham Lincoln, just right," she mutters as she peeks under the protective coverings. Dorothy says, "Sometimes they move things around, especially if they go to auction."

I arch an eyebrow. I would hate for someone like Aiken, the Demo King, to get his destructive little mitts on anything found here.

She adds, "I believe this particular desk used to be in the old conservatory—before it was demolished in 1892. Lincoln was quite fond of it, according to family records."

"The conservatory?" Jules asks.

Dorothy beams. "Oh, yes. The glass house on the south lawn. It was a beautiful octagonal structure with a distinctive star-like framework. It inspired the DC World's Fair proposal, though Chicago won the bid."

"They sure did," Linc says.

"I imagine Mr. Lincoln came here to write or reflect when he needed peace and quiet. The family said he loved sitting in the glass room, surrounded by light." She smiles fondly.

"Romantic, isn't it?" I say.

Dorothy's smile is one of nostalgia.

Linc asks, "The conservatory was demolished?"

"Unfortunately." She pauses and then excitedly says, "Ah! Here it is. Glad we didn't have to venture into the garage."

Abraham Lincoln's desk sits in front of us, a piece of history. The surface is about five feet of smooth, polished oak that glows a deep, amber-brown. The front panel is carved with intricate scrollwork and tiny rosettes. The drawers on either side are solid and symmetrical. The brass handles catch the light, gleaming and winking like they know the secrets of the past. In the center, a panel stirs my curiosity, makes me wonder if there is a small hidden recess. This desk bears the weight of centuries, the echoes of hands that have signed legislation, written speeches, and maybe even dared to peek inside.

"Wow," I breathe.

We ask if we can take photos and examine the desk. As if thrilled by our interest, Dorothy gives us free rein, saying she has to rotate for her hour at the front desk, but that it's okay for us to stick around for a few more minutes if we promise to leave everything as it was and close the door securely.

"It reminds me of the Resolute Desk," Linc says.

"The one in the Oval Office?" I ask, referring to the piece gifted by Queen Victoria to the sitting president, Rutherford B. Hayes, in 1880, out of timbers from a ship that explored the Arctic, called HMS Resolute.

Dorothy nods. "Historians speculate that this desk provided inspiration, but as the Resolute Desk was a gift from overseas and much later, I might add, it remains uncertain."

After giving her our thanks, Dorothy leaves. We look carefully at the desk. Linc also notices something odd about the wood panel running along the side and points it out. "Could be that numerous moves around the house knocked it loose."

The corner of my lip lifts. "Or it could be a secret hiding place."

Pressing gently, we hear a soft click. Behind it is a narrow space, a hidden compartment, but it's empty except for dust and the faint scent of old wood.

"The letters could have been here," I breathe.

"But they're not now," Linc says, disappointment heavy in his voice.

I snap some photos moments before footsteps echo along the nearby pathway. A surge of panic seizes me and I have to take a steadying breath, reminding myself that we're not in a tunnel, no one is chasing us. Probably.

We quickly close the panel, cover the desk, and secure the shed's door.

I glance over my shoulder, but it's only a tour group approaching. Without thinking, Linc and I join hands—a couple strolling on a summer afternoon through the rose garden, admiring the historical architecture.

My mind races like a thoroughbred, thinking about Linc. Too bad no one would put money on me being with him in real life—the possibility of us only exists in this made-for-TV fantasy.

Linc and I spend the rest of the day searching the city, but we find nothing else. No more hidden compartments, no clues about where the letters might have gone, no breadcrumbs to follow.

Thankfully, no more thugs.

"We're at a dead end," I admit as we sit in a quiet room at a public library, surrounded by books that haven't given us any answers.

He says, "We've been gone for days. Maybe we ought to head back to Chicago."

I nod, though the thought of giving up the search makes me feel heavy. "Yeah. I should probably check in at my real job before my boss fires me."

He chuckles. "I don't think you have to worry about that."

Even though traveling by private jet back the way we came is as surreal as when we left, everything between Linc and me is now layered with the memory of our very real adventure, the kiss in the alley, and unanswered questions—and not only about the lost love letters.

Linc seems slightly subdued like thoughts weigh heavily in his mind, too.

Are they about him and me? The men who were chasing us through the tunnels? The fact that he may never find the letters? Something else?

All I find myself doing is staring at his hands, remembering how they framed my face. His mouth on mine. The way we felt together.

By the time we land, I'm a bundle of nervous energy, unsure whether I'm more anxious about returning to work or about what happens next between Linc and me. We share a gentle parting kiss and go home in separate, sleek black cars.

Mine delivers me to Logan Square, and we're halfway down the block to my building when I realize something is very, very wrong.

It isn't there.

Well, the ghost of the building is there, but it's a blackened shell. Police tape flutters in the evening breeze and the smell of smoke hangs in the air. I don't see any firetrucks, but a few official-looking people in hard hats pick through the debris.

The driver leaves, and I stand on the sidewalk, blinking at what used to be my home.

"Excuse me," I call to one of the investigators. "I live here. What happened?"

"Fire started around midnight two days ago. We believe it was an electrical issue. Investigation pending. No casualties or injuries, thank goodness—the building was mostly empty."

Two nights ago. While I was in Washington with Linc. Someone burned down my building.

My phone buzzes with a text.

> Unknown number: Your payment was late.
> Consider this a reminder.

My blood turns to ice. I look around, but no one moves toward me. Nothing seems suspicious or out of place, except for the charred remains of my building, but someone must be watching me.

This is about my father's debt, the debt I've been dutifully paying every month to keep something like this from happening. Dad warned me. Said the guys he owed were bad news. That's why I got involved in his forgeries. They know about me. My father said if we paid them off, they'd leave me alone. It was an impossible position. So I helped him get out of the red. Unfortunately, he had more creditors. But I haven't been late. I've been making every payment on time, even when it meant eating rice for weeks.

Unless the rules changed.

My phone rings, and Linc's name appears on the screen.

"Jules? I just heard about a fire in Logan Square on the news. Are you—?"

"My building burned down," I say numbly. "Everything I own is gone."

"Where are you? I'm coming to get you."

Voice shaking, I say, "Linc, I don't think this was an accident."

"What do you mean?"

I look around the burned ruins of my life, at the police tape and the investigators and the message on my phone that makes my hands shake. "I mean, this got personal."

When Linc's car pulls up twenty minutes later, I'm still standing on the sidewalk in plain sight like a statue. He gets out and wraps his arms around me without saying a word. I let myself lean into him because I hardly have the strength to stand on my own right now.

"Are you okay?" he asks quietly.

"Not really," I whisper against his chest.

Now I know that whatever we've stumbled into—whether it's about Lincoln's letters or insurance fraud or my father's debts—someone is willing to destroy my entire life to stop me.

And I have no idea what to do.

39

LINC

"YOU'RE STAYING AT MY PLACE," I say as we leave behind the burned building in Logan Square. It's not a request.

Jules looks up at me, her face streaked with tears and her eyes pinched with exhaustion. "Linc, I can't impose—"

"You're not imposing. I'll be out of town, anyway. Business." It's not exactly a lie—hockey is my business, even if she doesn't know it yet. "The condo has top security. You'll be safe there."

She doesn't ask questions, which surprises me. Maybe she's too emotionally drained to argue, or maybe she trusts me more than I deserve.

An hour later, we're sitting in my penthouse overlooking the Chicago skyline with takeout containers spread across the coffee table. Jules picks at her pad Thai, moving the noodles around more than eating them.

"I'm ready to confront my father about the insurance discrepancies," I say, trying to fill the silence. "I need to know if he's involved."

"You really think he could be behind it?" Her gaze repeatedly flits toward the windows, toward the city where her life went up in smoke.

"I don't know. But someone with executive access has been using company resources for unauthorized research. The timing with Drecken and those men in the tunnels ..." I run a hand through my hair. "It's very likely connected somehow."

Jules sets down her chopsticks and pulls out her phone. "There's something you should know."

My stomach clenches, making me regret the extra dumpling I ate.

She lets out a shaky breath. "I got this right before you called. When I was standing in front of my burned building."

> Unknown number: Your payments are late.
> Consider this a reminder.

My jaw clenches.

She swallows. "I think the fire has something to do with my father's debts ... not your father or whatever is going on at Meridian." She's quiet for a long moment, staring at the city lights.

"I'm listening," I say softly.

She fidgets with her chopsticks. "I mentioned he struggled with gambling. That he had an accident that left him needing care. What I didn't tell you is that his gambling problem meant he owed some very bad people a lot of money. Instead of inheriting a home like the one we visited in Washington, or anything your father plans to pass on to you, I was bequeathed over fifty thousand dollars in debt to loan sharks."

The number hits me like a body check. Fifty thousand might as well be fifty million to someone on her salary.

"I pay every month," she continues. "Every single month on time. But clearly the terms have changed."

"They took everything from your neighbors, too," I point out. "Burned down an entire building just to send you a message."

"Not everything," she says quietly. "They left me alive. For now."

The casual way she says it makes my blood boil with righteous indignation on her behalf. The men in the tunnels worked for Drecken. But the fire was about her father's debts. Two completely separate threats.

I set down the carton of food and gather her in my arms. "I'm going to keep you safe. Whatever it takes."

She twines her fingers into mine like she's afraid. I kiss the top of her head.

After a beat, I say, "Seems like both our fathers had shady dealings."

"Do you really think it could be your dad?" The question I've been avoiding surfaces again.

"I truly don't know. But it definitely has something to do with Maxine Drecken."

"What do you know about her other than that she used to occupy your office?"

"Not enough. But I'm going to find out." I flip my lucky penny absently. "Let's play it closer to the vest for now."

"Do you have experience with that?" she asks, looking up at me.

"I just mean I don't want to reveal anything until I have solid evidence, then I'll talk to him. If I approach him with any unknowns, he'll dismiss me like—"

Like he dismissed my mother's search for the love letters.

We talk some more about Maxine Drecken and look her up online. Most of what we found is common knowledge and mentions her son working in the arts and entertainment industry. Though I can't find specifics. Having changed the subject slightly, Jules's appetite seems to have returned and she eats some of her pad Thai. When we're done, the night sparkles through the windows like scattered diamonds, and I want to forget about hunting for the past and the danger that's put us in. I want to pause the future and what could happen to Meridian or how she will respond when she finds out I play professional hockey. I want to talk about us. Here. Now.

"Jules, we kissed," I say finally.

Her cheeks flush slightly. "We did."

"I liked it."

She flaps her hands a little as if nervous. "Linc, we kissed like *that*."

I know exactly what she means, but play dumb.

"Huh?"

"You know."

"Like what?" I ask innocently, though the corner of my mouth lifts.

Her lip juts out in the smallest pout. "Like *that*. You know what I mean."

"Do I?" I lean in closer, watching her eyes widen.

She pokes me in the side.

I can't help myself and ask, "Was it the hand-holding kind of kiss?"

"What do you mean?" she asks this time.

I bring her hand to my lips and press a chaste kiss to her knuckles.

She rolls her eyes, but I catch the smile she's fighting. "No."

"A friendly peck on the cheek?" I demonstrate, my lips barely grazing her cheekbone.

"Linc—"

"A polite kiss goodbye?" I brush my lips against her temple, soft and quick.

"You're impossible." She laughs.

"A dramatic movie kiss?" I dip her slightly, hovering above her mouth.

She steadies herself against my shoulders, her fingers curling into my shirt. "Getting warmer."

I straighten us both, studying her face. There is that telltale sweetness in her eyes, telling me she wants this as badly as I do. "Sugar eyes," I murmur.

"Excuse me?"

"You've got sugar eyes, Jules. Sweet and wanting."

Her cheeks blush deeper. "That's not a thing."

"It most certainly is." I smooth a piece of her hair.

She slants her head slightly as if to challenge me, but it's also the perfect angle ... if I just close the space between us.

Instead, I say, "So if when we kissed like *that*, as you said, wasn't one of the kisses I asked about, then what kind was it?"

She tilts her chin up, defiant and playful. "The kind that made me forget my own name."

I arch an eyebrow. "Now we're getting somewhere."

"That made me forget that we'd nearly died."

The air shifts between us.

"It was the kind that made me realize that I want—"

"Oh, you mean like this?" I draw her to me and kiss her again, softer this time but no less intense.

Her breathing turns ragged almost immediately,

matching the drumming of my pulse in my ears. What starts gently quickly deepens, the kiss growing hungry, demanding. My hands tighten around her, pulling her closer, while her arms wrap around my back like she's afraid to let go.

The kiss deepens and everything else falls away except for what she said just before our mouths met.

I want ...

I want Jules and I have a high rate of confidence that the feeling is mutual.

Eventually, we ease up and the kiss turns sweet again. Her fingers roam along the nape of my neck, sending shivers down my spine. My own hand traces the curve of her hips, slow and deliberate, memorizing every dip and plane.

She lets out a heavy sigh when we break apart, and my gaze strays to the way her lips look slightly swollen from my kiss.

"Linc," she whispers, and I'm not sure if it's a warning or an invitation.

"Yes," I say, though I'm not sure what I'm agreeing to, but she can have anything of mine. She can have me.

THE NEXT FEW days pass in a blur of insurance investigation. We try to locate the possible four additional desks, sending the photos Jules took to antiques dealers and Abraham Lincoln estate experts. Meanwhile, I'm staving off the reality that very soon I'll be leaving for hockey prep while playing house with Jules. I gave her my credit card to replace what she needs—clothes, toiletries, and basic necessities when really I want to buy her the world.

She insists on paying me back, while I assure her it's not necessary. She's too stubborn to accept outright charity. I told her not to worry about it. She promises anyway, and I know she means it. This woman, who has every reason to take advantage of my resources, refuses to accept even the smallest gesture without trying to reciprocate.

All I want is to *give* to someone who has such a hard time receiving.

For the first time in my life, I've met someone who doesn't want what I have—money, influence, and fame. Rather, she just wants me.

I check Aiken's social media obsessively, looking for any sign that he's destroyed the painting he won at the auction —*Echo & Answer*. No evidence yet, which gives me hope that we might still have a chance at finding those letters.

When my team captain calls about a mandatory event in Ottawa the following weekend, I almost skip it. The thought of leaving Jules alone, even in my secure building, makes my body flood with adrenaline.

I assure myself she'll be fine here. The place is like Fort Knox. I have the perfect opportunity to tell her about hockey, about my real career, and why I'm going to Canada. Instead, I say it's business and leave it at that.

Why ruin a good thing?

The reasoning is all wrong and I know that, but what else am I going to do—as I rush out the door, call, *Oh, and by the way, I play for the NHL. Byeee?*

She'll find out. But I tell myself we'll deal with it later.

Walking into the training facility feels like exhaling after holding my breath for months. The familiar smell of rubber mats and industrial-strength cleaning solution, the swish of skates on ice, the rhythmic *thunk* of pucks hitting the boards remind me this is where I belong. It's like my nervous system finally remembers how to function properly.

The ice calls to me the second I lace up my skates. I take a few warm-up laps, feeling my muscles remember this language they've spoken since I was five years old. Every stride feels like coming home.

The guys run passing drills, working on conditioning, and I slip into the rotation like I haven't spent the summer playing executive boss. Coach has us do breakaway scenarios next and power play setups. For once, I don't complain when he has us repeat them ad nauseam.

In the locker room afterward, sweat-soaked and breathing hard in the best possible way, I'm adjusting my gear when the teasing starts.

"Not long until preseason begins and you'll be free of your nepo baby summer internship," Johannessen says, tossing a puck my way.

I catch it reflexively, but my mind is elsewhere. In Chicago, with Jules, wondering if she's safe.

"Earth to Linc," Butcher says. "You've been distracted all weekend."

"Just got a lot on my mind."

"Let me guess," Stevens grins. "Girl problems."

"It's not—" I start, then stop. Because it is girl problems, just not the kind they think.

I tell them I met someone, but leave out the parts about our adventures and almost being buried in an underground tunnel.

"Is the problem that you're her boss?" Johannessen asks, holding his hands open for the puck.

I toss it. "Nope. It's an unpaid internship, so I'm not on the payroll."

"Meaning you don't get a weekly check."

I shake my head.

"And yet you flew here on your father's private jet."

I shrug, used to them teasing me about being a billionaire baby.

"Is it the woman I wanted to take boating?" Bīriņš calls in accented English from where he's sprawled on a nearby bench.

"Yes," I say softly, having forgotten about that.

He sits up abruptly, painting a picture. "She's blonde, curvy. Has these gray eyes and is so ..."

I interrupt. "Annoying. Too cheerful. Talks a lot. Way too optimistic for her own good. Drives me crazy." Jules is one of a kind.

"He's smitten," one of them sing-songs before I realize what's happening.

"Yep, drives him crazy. We get it, dude."

Butcher flicks my ear. "It's not fair. This guy has money, good looks, and gets the girls."

Wearing a smug smirk, I toss him the puck.

"So what exactly is the problem?" Stevens asks.

"Don't tell me she's the boss's daughter," Bīriņš asks.

"That would make her his sister since he's the boss's son," Butcher says, flicking his ear this time.

Then, Holden Goudreau, our captain, fixes me with his trademark intense stare. "You haven't told her, have you?"

I clear my throat, admitting guilt.

"Told her about what?" Butcher tosses the puck my way again.

Goudreau snorts. "He hasn't told her about hockey."

I wince. "It got away from me."

"No, it hasn't," my captain says. "You tell her you play hockey. She either cares or she doesn't."

"I just wanted to be a normal guy to her."

"So you're saying, she thought being a billionaire's son

was run of the mill, so you didn't want to pile on that you're also an NHL player?" Bīriņš asks.

"When you put it that way ..."

They all stare at me.

My phone buzzes with a text from Jules.

> Jules: Everything is normal at the office, but I think someone was following me home. Probably just paranoid.

I'm messaging about a flight back to Chicago before I finish reading, while I tell them about the fire.

Bīriņš, whose cousins also live in Chicago, hence the boat, offers to send someone to check on her.

"If your cousins are anything like you—"

He chuckles. "Big, tall, beautiful. Like me, but ladies."

I call Jules and ask if she's okay, prepared to stay on the phone with her until we're face-to-face.

"Oh, hi. Um, I hope it's okay. But I invited Oly over and a couple of friends from work—Wendy and Carmen. She's a grandma, so don't worry, we're not going to have a rager. Mostly cooking and watching movies."

She can do whatever she wants. Invite King Kong and Godzilla for dinner. Relief sweeps through me at hearing her voice. But I need to be there, with her. Now. I tell her as much.

"Where are you going?" Goudreau asks.

"Emergency," I say, already packing up my gear.

"Linc." His voice stops me at the door. "Whatever is going on with this girl, don't lose yourself in it."

I think it might be too late for that.

BY THE TIME I get back to Chicago, I've made a decision. Jules needs to disappear for a while, at least until I can figure out who's targeting her and why.

"Pack a bag," I tell her when I walk through the door. "We're going to my family's cabin."

"Linc, you just got back—" She opens her arms for a hug and I wrap myself around her.

"If you think someone was following you, that's not paranoia, that's a threat." After I picked her up in the rain storm, when she said *If I go missing, people will look for me*, she meant those thugs.

Moving to her room, I start pulling clothes from the closet. "Fox Lake, north of the city. It's quiet, peaceful, serene."

"Like witness protection?" She stops me, eyes pleading for an explanation.

"It was my mother's favorite place. I think you'll like it," I say, tucking her hair behind her shoulder.

Jules studies my face, and I wonder what she sees there. Desperation? Fear? The barely controlled panic that's been eating at me since I got her text?

"For how long?" she asks finally.

"As long as it takes to keep you safe."

She nods slowly. "Okay. But Linc? If there is something you're not telling me—"

This woman, who's lost everything, is trusting me to protect her even though she senses I'm hiding something from her– the one thing I'm proudest of in my life. But I'm afraid once she knows, she'll look at me with the same cool wariness she gave Iva and Aiken—and rightly so.

But I'm not like that. Though I'm afraid because I've kept my hockey-playing status secret for so long now, she'll only see me as one of them.

August is almost over. Summer is ending. Preseason starts soon and I'll have to choose between the life I've always known and whatever this is becoming.

I flip my lucky penny, but every time I ask whether I should tell her, it lands on tails. Not yet.

As we prepare to leave for the lake, my mother's sanctuary, I wonder if *eventually* will be too late.

40

JULES

MOM'S VOICE chirps through my phone. "Juliana! Perfect timing. I was just telling Brad about your new position with a promotion—"

"It's not exactly a promotion, Mom." Though I did get a raise. I've been on autopilot for a while, and when I recently checked my biweekly direct deposit from Meridian, the amount was substantially more than expected. However, the payment to dad's debtors was made, so I don't understand why they had to go and burn my house down.

Oh, right. People like that don't care about people like me.

While Linc packs for the trip to the lake house, I sink deeper into his inordinately comfortable couch. It almost feels like a hug. Cradling my phone against my ear, I cannot bring myself to reveal to my mother that I was chased through underground tunnels in DC or that my apartment building burned down. Never mind that I've never told her about Dad's gambling debts or the monthly payments I make to keep dangerous thugs at bay.

Or so I thought.

"You're working directly with management now! That's wonderful, sweetheart." She's outrageously positive about everything I do. During grade school, I'd bring home what amounted to a scribble with an "Excellent" sticker on it and she'd plaster it on the fridge, telling everyone within earshot that I'm a genius. In middle school, I did a presentation on the water cycle and she was convinced I would someday be president. I have my own personal cheerleading squad named Tina Harris, and while usually I appreciate it, right now I'm feeling defeated all the way down to my bones.

"I suppose."

My banking app shows numbers that would normally make me panic, but the raise helps. I already transferred a second payment to the account number I've memorized. If only I could explain to them that I'm good for the money, that they don't need to resort to arson to make their point. But now they've been paid double this month, so hopefully they'll back off.

A cold fear grips me. What if they decide to make a connection to Mom?

"How are you and Brad?" I ask, desperate to change the subject.

"Oh, peachy. He surprised me with tickets to see an Elvis Presley tribute show for our anniversary next month. Can you believe it? Speaking of, are you going to be at our anniversary party? You still haven't committed. I know it's hard to get time off, but your brothers will miss you if you're not there."

"I doubt that," I say with a laugh.

But Mom's happiness is infectious, even through the phone. After my father ditched us, I never thought she'd find someone again. Brad the Dad might not be my biological father, but he makes her laugh, which is far better than making her cry.

"You sound tired, sweetheart. Everything okay? Any hot dates keeping you out late?"

My mother comes from a time when dating was the ultimate goal. It was the weekend plan that, with any luck, would lead to a lifetime of happiness. While I've diversified my interests somewhat from her generation—meaning my evenings and weekends might include a variety of activities—finding my forever someone is a little hope I keep hidden in my heart.

It's not that it's been broken too badly. More like I just haven't found someone where we click in a way that tells me our primary interest is furthering the relationship, rather than getting a quick fix or pursuing our own separate agendas.

Until now, maybe.

"No hot dates." Technically true. I glance toward Linc's bedroom door. "Just work stuff." Also accurate. However, I did find the Post-it note with my name on it from when he refused to address me by my name stuck to the mirror in his room.

Mom and I chat for a few more minutes about the usual topics—her succulent garden, Brad's attempts at learning to cook, my cousin's engagement—before she has to investigate a burning smell coming from the kitchen.

"Oh, by the way," I say before she hangs up, "if you need to reach me this weekend, I'm staying at a friend's cabin."

"A friend's cabin? Which friend? Is it a male or female friend? How long have you known this friend?"

"Mom—"

"I'm just asking! You've never mentioned friends with cabins."

She's such a mom, skilled at cracking my bad mood and making me smile. "It's only for a few days. I'll call you when I get back."

After we hang up, I sit in the quiet of Linc's penthouse, surrounded by luxury I'll never be able to afford, preparing to run away to a lake house with a man who is out of my league, even if we kissed like *that*. But it's a game. Theater. Our very own World's Fair exposition. A depiction. A showcase. A temporary construction.

How did this become my life?

LINC IS vague about what he was doing on his business trip, but I assume that deciding how best to approach the insurance fraud situation weighs heavily on his mind, which prompted our excursion.

When we leave the tightly stacked buildings of the city, giving way to the open, rolling countryside, I feel like I can breathe again. Apart from the unexpected trip to New York and then DC, I hadn't left my immediate environment in … I count on my fingers, nine months.

"Doing some high-level math?" Linc looks sideways at my fingers as he drives north.

In turn, my attention has been on his hands—how easily he navigated through city traffic, how they're rough on both sides, unlike Nate's. Oly's comment about his calluses has stuck with me. But maybe Linc visits this cabin frequently, chops logs, and does other woodsman tasks.

I wonder what he looks like in a flannel shirt.

Giving my head a shake from the mewling little

thought, I answer his question. "I was thinking about the last time I left Chicago, aside from our adventure."

"Is that what we're calling it?" His laugh is husky.

He asks where my mom lives and I tell him that she and Brad the Dad are still in Las Vegas. That my brothers work for the UFC.

"You mentioned that they worked in sports, but are they fighters?" By the slim line between his eyebrows, I can't tell if this concerns him or brings relief. Both?

"They're brutes and love the barbarism of it," I say, using the comment I often tease them with. "But no, they're not professional fighters, though they all practice mixed martial arts. Since a lot of matches happen in Las Vegas, they work behind the scenes, helping orchestrate the events."

"When was the last time you were home?"

"Christmas, but my mom and Brad the Dad's anniversary is next month. They really want me to come."

"Your boss will make sure you have the time off."

I chuckle because this has become our joke. "I appreciate that—"

Linc yanks his gaze toward me and then back at the road. "You were about to say *but* ..."

I bunch up my lips. He's not wrong.

"I know money is tight after everything that just happened, so if that's the issue ..."

I cannot keep accepting his generosity. I've paid my own way so far and I don't want to become indebted to Linc, too.

Turning up the dial on the radio, I say, "This is a road trip. Let's talk about road trip things."

"Is that a category of conversation?"

"Of course."

"Elaborate."

We talk about traveling, which segues into some funny stories, mostly from him, and then I ask the big, important road trip convo questions like celebrity crush, favorite song, and best movie of all time. You know, the highly controversial things. The things that two people who started out despising each other would fundamentally disagree on.

Time flies by and when we finally pull up a winding driveway shaded by bushy oak and maple trees, the so-called cabin on Fox Lake isn't what any normal resident of planet earth would designate as a cabin. I was expecting a log exterior or, at the very least, some gaps in the timbers, a roof in need of repair, and a single room—I figured we'd navigate sleeping arrangements later.

This is what a realtor would refer to as a lakefront estate. It's three stories of rustic elegance, with a wrap-around porch and windows that reflect the water like mirrors.

"This was your mother's favorite place?" I ask as Linc carries our bags up the front steps.

"She and I would stay here all of August when I was younger. Dad would visit on weekends." His eyes flicker like the turning of a scrapbook full of memories. "She loved the quiet."

Inside, everything is warm wood and soft fabrics, but it's the family photos scattered throughout that catch my attention. Especially one on the mantle—a woman with Linc's eyes and gentle smile, held in a ceramic frame decorated with little acorn embellishments.

"She was beautiful," I say softly.

"Yeah. She was." Linc picks up the frame, studying it for a long moment. "I try to remember her this way. She was very sick when she passed away. Dad was away on business in Hong Kong."

"Were you with her?"

He nods. "She was in hospice care and one day she asked for this photo." His voice catches slightly. "I think she was waiting for him to come home."

The pain in his voice makes my chest ache.

"I had one of dad's drivers bring me all the way here to get it. She held it to her chest as she took her last breath." Linc clears his throat and says, "You can take any of the guest rooms and I insist you make yourself at home."

I squeeze his arm, wanting him to feel like he can talk more about his mom if he wants. "Give me a tour first?"

He shows me his mother's desk by the window overlooking the lake, where she'd write letters and read. The dock through the big windows where she'd swim and paint watercolors of the sunset. The kitchen where she'd bake every weekend. I admire her piano—not at all dusty, which suggests Linc called ahead to have the house readied.

We wander upstairs and I count four guest bedrooms. I take one with a lake view and a balcony. After freshening up from the drive, I go back downstairs.

Linc suggests we go to the local market to get some groceries. I'm about to tease him because I figured he'd have them delivered or already have the pantry stocked, but I have second thoughts.

For one, he drove us here in a slick European sports car, but still. In Chicago, he usually has a driver, food delivery, and everything else seems to appear with a snap of his fingers.

But maybe being up here at the "cabin" gave him and his mom a chance to be "normal," to have a break from the trappings of their wealth and do everyday things like grocery shop.

We take a short jaunt to "The Fox Lake Market," where I stock up on essentials like ice cream and popsicles, and he picks out sensible items like cold cuts and fruit.

As we round a corner past a pink and yellow lemonade display, I discover my new favorite thing is Linc pushing a shopping cart. It's unexpectedly attractive. Criminally handsome. I send Oly another no-context photo. It's of him, taken from behind while in the dairy aisle. She immediately replies with a no-context caption.

Oly: The setting of a rom-com meet-cute.

Oly: Also, where are you?

I risk walking into a pyramid of canned corn, so I hold off on replying. But then my phone pings again.

Oly: Oh, wait. That's Linc. Let me try again.

Oly: This is the start of a legend-dairy love story!

Oly: Solid contender for the Hot Guy Grocery Store Calendar.

Oly: You'd butter believe, he's eye-catching.

Oly: My personal favorite: They need to lower the temperature in those dairy cases, otherwise all the butter is going to melt.

I giggle. Linc looks at me over his shoulder. Although I know Oly is joking about love stories, what if?

He asks, "What's so funny?"

"Oly thinks she's a meme-edian."

"Define that word."

"Like meme plus comedian," I tell him about our no-context photo game and, no surprise, he wants to see what I sent her.

When I resist, he gets suspicious, playfully so, but I can't let him see her texts.

"Come on," he says, stepping closer. "How bad could it be?"

I clutch my phone tighter against my chest. "It's not bad, it's just—"

"Just what?" He's enjoying this, eyes dancing with mischief. "Did you catch me picking my nose or something?"

"No!" I laugh despite myself.

"Then what's the big deal?"

He grabs for my phone and I twist away, nearly stumbling into the sunblock products display.

"It's silly," I mumble, heat creeping up my neck. "You wouldn't get it."

"Try me." His voice goes softer, more curious than teasing now. "I want in on your weird photo game."

I bite my lip, glancing at the screen. There he is, completely unaware, one hand on the cart handle, the other reaching for something on the shelf. His shoulders are broad, strong, and masculine.

"You just looked ..." I start, then catch myself.

"I looked what?"

Like someone I could follow through grocery stores for the rest of my life.

"You looked very focused on the yogurt cups," I finish weakly.

He stares at me for a long moment. "You took a picture of me buying dairy?"

His tone—not mocking, just genuinely surprised—makes it worse somehow. Like he can't imagine why anyone would find him worth photographing in such an ordinary moment.

"Forget it," I say quickly, starting to put my phone away.

But his hand covers mine, gentle but insistent. "Hey. Let me see."

I open the photo so he can't see Oly's texts.

"Is that what I look like from the back?" He tucks his chin.

"That's your takeaway?"

Eyes flirty, he says, "I could not care less about what I look like."

"I find that hard to believe."

"I'm far more interested in what the person taking that photo sees."

His eyes sweep mine and my breath catches, and then he pecks me on the forehead.

I melt right there on the worn linoleum floor. *Clean up needed in the dairy aisle!*

After a brief tour of the town, we return to the cabin, and I make us a snack plate—my specialty.

Linc seems somewhat impressed ... or he was hungry. I can't be sure.

I browse the bookshelves and reach a section with what looks like journals.

He says, "My mother kept a journal for her whole life." He pulls a leather-bound book from a drawer. "This is the most recent. You can read them if you want. She wrote about everything—her thoughts, her dreams, her frustrations."

"That feels intrusive."

"She would have liked you. She would have wanted you to know her." He lets out a small breath. "I want you to know her."

My pulse snags. If I'm not careful, this man is going to break my heart.

Later, while Linc naps on the porch, I curl up in his mother's reading chair and open the journal. Marie's handwriting is elegant and her words paint a picture of a woman deeply in love with a man who was always somewhere else.

Frank missed Linc's birthday again. I know the Borgstrom deal is important, but sometimes I wonder if he's so busy building his empire, he even remembers he has a family. Linc asked why Daddy wasn't here to watch him blow out the candles. I didn't know what to say.

Linc came home from school with a black eye today. He won't tell me what happened, but I suspect it has something to do with Frank's name being in the papers again. I wish we could just be a normal family.

Frank called from London. He'll miss our anniversary dinner, but he's sending flowers. As if roses can take the place of the man I married. Sometimes I feel like I'm raising our son alone.

By the time I close the journal, liquid fills my eyes. This beautiful, loving woman spent years waiting for crumbs of affection from a man too consumed with success to notice what he was losing.

It breaks my heart and a sudden fear strikes me. What if his son is the same? A tear escapes before I can catch it.

41

LINC

I WAKE from my nap to a sniffling sound and find Jules curled up in my mother's reading chair with a pair of tears sliding down her cheeks as she closes the leather-bound journal.

"Jules? Are you okay?" I ask, concerned.

She looks up at me, not attempting to hide her sniffles.

I cross the room and press gentle kisses to her salty cheeks, tasting her sadness on my lips.

She whispers, "Your mom was so sweet, so strong. She loved you and your dad so much, even when it didn't seem like the sentiment was returned."

I smooth my thumb across her jawline, wiping away her sadness. "Sometimes when there's a person in our lives who does the wrong thing, we learn more about the kind of person we want to be." That's something Mom would've said.

The chair barely fits both of us, but I settle beside her anyway, pulling her against my side as we watch the sun begin its descent toward the glassy lake. Jules feels small and warm pressed against me, and I want to shield her from every hurt she's ever experienced.

"Tell me about your past relationships," I say, surprising myself.

"That's a cheerful topic change," she laughs a cute, snorty, watery laugh.

Squeezing her close, I say, "I want to know about your great love story."

She scoffs. "There haven't been any serious ones. My last boyfriend was a lot like my dad—charming when he wanted to be, but unreliable. He'd often miss important events and holidays like my birthday."

"Then we had that in common about our dads."

"He'd show up later with a gift as if that made up for the disappointment."

The casual way she mentions her birthday being forgotten makes me want to give her a celebration she'll never forget, yet all she wanted was a love song. I'll certainly never forget our doughnuts at dawn. "You deserve better than that."

She snuggles against my chest. "What about your love life?"

"A few relationships that never really went anywhere."

The truth is, most of the women I've dated were more interested in my last name or proximity to fame than anything else. Jules doesn't even know my real career exists and aside from paying off the debt she's saddled with, doesn't seem to be concerned about striking it rich. Past girlfriends would insist I take them to fancy events, get us into swanky restaurants, exclusive clubs, buy them clothes, and expect expensive things.

Jules had my credit card for a week and spent a whopping two hundred and eighty dollars after losing all of her worldly possessions.

She turns to face me fully, her eyes searching mine. "Can I ask you something? What happens after? Say we find the letters. We prove there was insurance fraud going on. What then?"

The question makes me feel like I missed a crucial pass, lost a game. I've been so focused on the search, on protecting her, on this growing connection between us, that I haven't thought about what comes next. Hockey season starts in a few weeks. She thinks I'm just some rich kid tolerating my father's insistence that I learn the family business. And somewhere in the mess of insurance fraud and burned buildings and lost love letters, I think we're creating something special.

"I don't know," I admit.

THE NEXT MORNING dawns bright and cheerful, sunlight dancing across the lake like scattered coins. Jules appears in the kitchen wearing one of my old t-shirts that falls to mid-thigh, her hair piled in a messy bun, and I nearly drop the coffee mug I'm holding.

She's gorgeous. All those summer sun freckles dotting the bridge of her nose and spreading across her cheeks like someone flicked a paintbrush. Lips that are way too distracting for someone who talks as much as she does. And her curves make a man forget what he was doing—pouring coffee? The way her hair catches light like spun gold with hints of strawberry. And her laughter ... I'll do desperate things to hear more of it.

When she asked if she could borrow an old shirt for

pajamas back in Chicago, I hoped she didn't notice how many hockey team shirts I owned. But this was also her way of saving money. While I like the looks of her in my t-shirt, I hate the idea of her thinking she can't buy a cute pair of pajamas—or ten—because she doesn't want to take advantage of my generosity or that she'll owe me.

The only thing I want from Jules is ... well, Jules.

"Morning," she says, padding barefoot across the tile floor.

"Morning." I hand her a mug. Our fingers brush in the exchange and send a shiver through me despite the warm late-summer morning. "Sleep well?"

"Better than I have in weeks." She takes a sip of coffee and closes her eyes appreciatively. "I understand why your mother loved this place so much."

I lean against the counter, watching her move around the kitchen. Like a little cartoon thought bubble, the idea that she belongs here pops into my mind. "What do you want to do today?"

She spins to face me and beams a smile. "This is the perfect place to take a whimsy."

"You told me before, 'if you know, you know,' but I still don't know whatsy a whimsy is."

"Then I'll show you." She bounces excitedly on the balls of her feet.

An hour later, we're hiking through the woods behind the cabin. Jules chatters about everything and nothing—the birdsong, the way the light filters through the leaves, a funny story about Oly and Nate's first dating disaster. Side note: it wasn't their last, but now they're married, so they got an HEA, which she explains means a happily ever after.

We wander, stop, look, listen, kiss. This woman has a

way of finding joy in the smallest details that makes me see the world differently.

I have a cooler backpack with lunch supplies, and when we emerge from the loop hike by the lake, I wipe the sweat from my forehead.

Jules points to an old rope hanging from a massive oak tree suspended over the water. "Is that what I think it is?"

"Sure is." I nod, wondering how I stumbled upon such a perfect woman.

"This place just keeps getting better and better." She grins. "It's perfect whimsy material."

I think I'm starting to understand the whimsy—a whimsical wander taken wherever your feet and conversation go. "You want to swing into the lake?"

"We want to swing into the lake," she corrects, already jogging toward the rope and tearing off her clothing to reveal her bathing suit, which is most definitely not a full-coverage burlap sack "swimming costume."

I test the rope's strength, telling her about how pale my mother would turn every time I'd swing on it.

"I bet you were a wild thing as a child," she says.

I chuckle. "Yeah. You too, though." I can imagine her riding her bicycle until dark, climbing trees, and generally causing her mother the same kind of worry I did mine.

She shakes her head. "Nope. I was a super cautious kid." With that, she launches herself over the water with a whoop of pure joy, her laughter echoing across the lake before she splashes down. When she surfaces, hair plastered to her head and grinning like a child, she's the most beautiful woman I've ever seen.

"Your turn!" she calls.

I grab the rope, pausing when I hear the telltale buzz near my ear. A bee hovers by the oak branch, fat and lazy in the summer heat. My hand instinctively goes to the backpack where I stashed an EpiPen, but the bee drifts away toward the wildflowers along the edge of the woods.

"Are you coming or what?" Jules hollers.

Seems as if I survived another close call. This could've ended up with a trip to the ER and a very different kind of afternoon. Perhaps my luck is turning. Maybe Jules is my good luck charm.

"Yeah," I call back, grinning and trying to remember the last time I did something just for fun. Hockey is fun, but it's also work, pressure, and expectations. This is something else. Jules is, too, and I like it, like her. A lot.

The water is shockingly cold, but Jules's laughter warms me from the inside out as she swims over. We tread in place for a moment. Her gray eyes shift like storm clouds, giving way to a sunny day. The way she's looking at me right now makes me feel it shining warmly on me. For me. Us.

Instead of thinking about what's next, I don't want to let go of this. Right now.

Our lips meet in a kiss that I'm certain heats up the lake a few degrees. I never want today to end.

After our picnic lunch, we spend the afternoon taking turns on the rope, floating on our backs, having splash fights that leave us both breathless with laughter.

Later, we return to the blanket we'd spread out on the small, private beach and eat watermelon.

Jules lies on her back, arms resting on her belly, looking up at the clouds. "Thank you," she says quietly.

"For what?"

"For bringing me here. For ..." She turns her head to look at me. "For making me feel safe."

Her sincerity makes me want to give her that and more. I drop a kiss on her smooth shoulder, then lean on my side, propped up on my elbow. "Thank you for showing me what whimsy looks like."

A laugh ripples through her as she draws me to standing. Lifting onto her toes, she presses a kiss on my lips.

It's gentle at first, testing, but then something shifts and we collide—not crashing exactly, but meeting with an urgency that catches us both off guard. The lines we'd drawn further blur and fade until there's nothing between us but want and warmth.

Her fingers run up my arm, leaving goosebumps in their wake despite the late-summer sun. When she reaches my shoulder, she pulls me close and we sink together as the kiss deepens.

Since the moment we met, I was keenly aware of her presence—impossible not to be—but I was afraid to acknowledge the effect she had on me. Tried to pin it down. Trip it up. There's no denying it now. It's an overwhelming pull that I can't deny or ignore anymore.

My hands find her waist and I pull her in, eliminating even the whisper of space between us. Her breath tickles against my cheek as she tilts her head, allowing me to deepen the kiss.

Pulses pound.

Hands explore.

Angles shift.

We pause to catch our breath, faces close together, not willing to part just yet. She kicks her feet off the ground and I hold her suspended. This simple gesture tells me she trusts me, fully, wholly.

On impulse, I spin her around in the pleasant breeze, her hair whirling around us, but we don't separate. If anything, she holds on tighter, her arms wrapping more securely around my neck as the world spins lazily by.

I slant my head and kiss her, and her head falls back as I trail down her neck. Soft, sweet, tasting like fresh water and the summer afternoon. My hand moves to cradle the back of her neck, and she sighs against my lips as we continue to kiss.

When we break apart, she stays close, her forehead resting against mine.

"I could get used to this," she whispers.

"Me too."

WE SPEND the rest of the week wringing every last drop of sunshine out of each day. Jules also reads more of my mother's journals while I catch up on team emails and try not to think about preseason starting soon. We cook together, take long walks around the lake, play board games, do a puzzle, and swim, making the outside world feel very far away.

But reality has a way of intruding.

"Linc ..." Jules's voice cuts into my thoughts.

I look up from my laptop to find her standing by my mother's desk, holding an open journal.

Brows pulled together as she slides her finger along the page, she reads aloud, "'The missing letters might finally complete the story of how our family came to possess the collection that launched Meridian Holdings.'"

My attention perks up. "She wrote that?"

"You didn't know?" Jules studies my face with sharp eyes that miss nothing.

"Reading the journals was an emotional experience," I admit.

Gaze gentle, she carefully adds, "Linc, what if your

father never sought the letters because finding them would expose some kind of dishonesty in how he acquired the original collection that launched his business?"

Hearing her say it, I recognize that the thought had lurked in the back of my mind.

"Do you think that could be why Drecken sent those guys to stop us?" she asks.

I let out a long, shaky breath.

She answers her question, "I think the investigation's outcome could affect a lot of people's livelihoods. Including mine."

Instead of letting her say more, I step toward her and kiss her with a desperation I can't hide. I need to memorize this feeling before everything changes—the way she melts into me, how she responds so hungrily. The sugar sweetness in her eyes when she looks at me.

This pang of longing makes my lungs collapse. Fog clouds my heart and my head until there's nothing but her. Every touch sends me into a trance. Every look. Every time I breathe in her flower blossom scent.

I'm afraid to let go, so I pull Jules closer, wishing I could freeze this moment, keep us in this bubble where the only thing that matters is the way she feels in my arms.

When we break apart, both breathing hard, she brushes her nose against mine and leaves another kiss on my lips as if to say, she feels it too.

42

LINC

WE MAKE DINNER TOGETHER—GRILLED fish and vegetables from the local market—and eat on the porch as the sun sets. Jules tells me stories about her brothers' antics in Las Vegas, and I find myself saying, "I'd love to meet them."

She nearly chokes on her meal. "You sure about that? They're feral and not particularly subtle about it."

I hint, "You mentioned your mom and Brad's anniversary party."

"Yeah, next month."

"Let's go. Together."

She stares at me. "It's in Las Vegas. And you're so busy—"

"Not too busy for family. Besides, I want to see where you grew up."

Her smile is radiant. "Really?"

"Really."

Jules throws me off balance in a refreshing way, though I won't admit it out loud. After years of networking with people who have hidden agendas. How genuine she is, is almost too good to be true. But watching her get excited about introducing me to her family and seeing the way she lights up at the smallest kindnesses makes me want to be the man she thinks I am.

The next afternoon, rain patters against the windows while Jules reads and I doze on the couch. The sound of her sharp intake of breath wakes me from my nap.

"Linc." Her voice is urgent.

I bolt to standing. "I've been staring at that desk all week and just realized something. It's a replica of the one we found at the library."

I'm instantly alert. "What?"

She's already moving toward my mother's desk, running her hands along the wood paneling. "The same dimensions, the same detailing. Different wood stain or finish. Some variations, but what if it's one of the desks Abraham Lincoln had commissioned for his sons?"

I crouch beside her, looking for the secret panel we found on the other desk. The veneer gives and I hold my breath as I peer inside. "It's empty."

"Just some dust and a cobweb."

My thumb rubs my lucky penny.

"If there are others, the letters could be in one of them. I can't believe we didn't think of that before."

"We're not technically sleuths," I joke, feeling the rush of excitement fade. But then I snap my fingers. "Unless there are others."

"Yeah. As I said, the desks made for the other sons—" Jules starts.

"No, I mean other secret compartments. We didn't want to be caught when we were visiting Tudor Place, but we can check to see ..." I'm already running my hands along every inch of the desk, trying to find another loose piece of wood, a crack, anything that would reveal a hiding place.

Easing into my mother's chair, I recall her in this very position countless times. Then I picture my great-great-great-great-great-grandfather. If he were to have something to hide, where would he put it?

I pull out the drawers, one at a time, but don't notice anything unusual. Jules takes my lead and investigates other parts of the desk until we're both back where we started.

"It was a good hunch," Jules says.

I'm not ready to give up. "Abraham Lincoln was tall, so I don't imagine he'd have hidden anything down low."

"He'd have wanted to be discreet if he were hiding something."

"So it has to be right in front of our faces."

Jules puts her hand under the desk's surface and her eyebrow arches.

"Find something?"

She crawls underneath the desk and lets out an excited little sound. "Your instinct that he wouldn't have crouched under here was right, but that's also because he would've known the location of the hidden compartment and could've found the latch by feel. I need something smooth."

"I can go get a screwdriver."

"Or your penny. There's a little mechanism that looks like it needs to be twisted, but I can't do it with my thumbnail."

I pass her the penny and then hear a soft click. My pulse races with excitement as part of the front drawer separates from the wooden seam and a smaller drawer, the perfect size to hide a stack of letters, appears.

I gasp as Jules gets to her feet.

Several envelopes tied with faded blue ribbon sit inside

the narrow space. I can't make my hands move to take them out. What if I'm wrong? What if they're just old receipts or shopping lists? What if my mother spent her last years chasing something ordinary? The biggest question—did she know they were here all along?

Jules doesn't say anything right away. She just rests her hand on my shoulder while I try to compose myself, and somehow that's exactly what I need. "Linc, we found them. I'm sure of it."

My mother spent the last years of her life searching for these. She died believing they existed but never knowing if she was chasing a fantasy. And here they are, real and tangible.

My hands practically shake as I reach for them, half-afraid they'll disintegrate. All at once, relief and vindication crash together in a wave so powerful I have to close my eyes against it.

"She was right," I manage. "All those years, everyone thought she was obsessed with a myth, but she was right—and the letters were with her all along."

Jules moves closer, her hand finding mine. "She was brilliant."

I carefully pull the first letter out of its envelope, the paper surprisingly sturdy despite its age. Lincoln's distinctive handwriting covers the first page—strong, angular strokes. I recognize the script from countless museum exhibits. My ancestor's hand.

"Lincoln's name is right here." Jules points to the signature with a trembling finger.

I imagine my mother's excitement if she could see this. "Jules, we actually found them."

The weight of the moment settles over me. These aren't just historical artifacts. They're proof that my mother's instincts were sound, that her dedication wasn't madness, that she knew what she was doing even when my father dismissed her research.

In the background, I hear the crunch of tires on gravel.

Jules freezes. "Were you expecting someone?"

"No." Cold dread fills my body as I move to the window. A black SUV sits in the driveway, and two men in dark clothing get out.

Jules shrinks into herself, fear replacing the excitement of moments before as she hastily gathers the letters, returning them to the stack and retying the ribbon.

I stride toward the door.

"Who are they?" But she's already moving, tucking the letters inside her shirt and walking toward the front door with determination that looks like courage.

"Jules, what are you doing?"

She doesn't answer. Instead, she opens the front door and steps onto the porch, facing the men who've invaded our sanctuary.

"Are you looking for Albert Lindley?" she calls out, her voice steadier than I feel at the moment.

The larger man looks confused. "Who? No, we work for Drecken."

Jules's eyes go cartoon-round with shock. She walks backward into me as I make a crucial decision.

Whatever this is, it ends now.

43

JULES

"GO INSIDE AND PACK." Linc's tone is low and commanding in a way I've never heard before.

When I don't move because I'm frozen with fright, he adds, "Now."

My legs feel unsteady as I back toward the cabin door, the precious letters still tucked against my chest. Through the screen, I watch Linc stride down the porch steps toward the two men, his posture radiating pure alpha confidence.

I should do what he says. Go inside. Pack.

Checking over my shoulder, I hurry upstairs. After tossing my sparse belongings into my bag, I edge toward the window in the hall. From safely behind the screen, I strain to see and hear what's happening.

The conversation starts calmly enough. Linc's gaze is controlled, even. His hands are loose at his sides. The men stand with their arms crossed. I can't hear a single word because a robin engages in a loud territorial dispute, chirping and calling from the tree outside the window to a squirrel that helps itself to the contents of the birdfeeder.

From the lake-facing side of the house, with its sprawling lawn topped with the Adirondack chairs Linc and I sat in as we watched the sun set over the private beach and dock, you'd never know there is a face-off happening in the driveway.

My body feels coiled with nervous energy. Every muscle tenses as I watch the exchange unfold in frustrating silence. Linc gestures toward the SUV, then pulls out his phone. One of the men shakes his head. More words.

Linc's posture changes, turns menacing. He opens and closes his fist, charged with powerful energy.

The other two men seem to realize who the alpha is. They talk some more.

Every nerve in my body teeters on what feels like the edge of the earth.

One of the men nods as if agreeing to something and then the other follows.

The whole interaction lasts maybe ten minutes, but it feels like hours. Finally, the men get back in their SUV and drive away, leaving only the sound of gravel crunching under their tires and the bird celebrating their retreat or its victory against the enemy squirrel, I'm not sure.

Linc stands in the driveway for a long moment, watching them disappear down the winding road. When he turns back toward the cabin, his face is grim.

He glances up toward the window, likely seeing me. I lift my hand in an awkward wave because it's too late for me to take cover. I don't know why, but I'm hesitant for him to see that I was watching.

When he comes inside, he says, "Be ready to leave in twenty minutes."

"Linc, what—?"

"Twenty minutes, Jules, please." He softens as if he remembers he's talking to me.

Swallowing thickly, I turn toward the stairs as he swiftly moves through the cabin, closing windows and turning off lights. Just like that, our happy little end-of-summer bubble bursts completely.

I help clean up, my hands shaking slightly. The newly found Lincoln love letters are nearly forgotten—a heavy reminder from something as light as paper that our peaceful, intimate week was always temporary.

The drive back to Chicago passes in tense silence. Linc grips the steering wheel like he'll strangle it if necessary, his jaw set in a hard line. Every attempt I make at conversation gets a one-word response or a grunt.

By the time we reach his place, I'm ready to scream from the anxiety building in my chest. The familiar luxury of his condo feels cold now and I no longer feel welcome. But where can I go?

As soon as the door closes, he sets down our bags and marches over to me and wraps me in a warm hug. "You're safe here. I promise you that."

I soften into his embrace and then take the first deep breath since before we left the cabin. I peer up at Linc. "Safe from what? Who were those men? What did you tell them?"

But he's already moving toward his bedroom. "I need to make some calls. We'll talk later."

Later. Unfortunately, I'm all too aware that later is a promise that is often broken.

That night, I lie in the guest bed staring at the ceiling, my mind racing. Every small sound in the building makes me jump. The hum of the air conditioning. The distant sound of traffic. The elevator dinging down the hall.

Around two in the morning, I give up on sleep and pad to the kitchen for water. The blue glow of a computer screen comes from the living room.

Linc sits on the couch in athletic shorts and a t-shirt. He's wearing his glasses and his laptop balances on his knees. In the dim light, he looks older somehow, the playful man from the lake replaced by someone harder.

"Can't sleep either?" I ask softly.

He looks up, and for a moment, his expression softens. "Just taking care of some things."

I settle on the opposite end of the couch, tucking my legs under me. "Can you tell me what happened between you and those men?"

Linc sets his laptop on the table and leans back against the cushions. "I can confirm that they were working for Drecken."

"And …?"

"And I turned the tables."

I tuck my chin. "What do you mean?"

"I told them I'd double whatever they were making if they'd back off, leave you out of it, and tell me everything about their boss." His mouth quirks in a smug smile that doesn't reach his eyes.

My jaw lowers.

"They accepted."

"Whoa. Those are some impressive business negotiating skills."

"Money can't talk, but it has a loud voice," he murmurs.

"Your father would be proud."

He grunts. "Despite not winning the Echo & Answer bid, at the end of the day, Drecken can't outbid me." The certainty in his voice reminds me again of the vast gulf between our worlds.

"Did they tell you anything worthwhile?"

His shoulder bumps up. "Not much."

"But she's after us. Why?"

"They didn't know."

"You believed them?"

"They were just following orders," he says, voice clipped.

"Anything else?"

He points to his laptop. "I also learned that she's been doing some dirty dealings."

"Which are ...?" The anticipation is worse than when I was a kid with a loose tooth that I just couldn't wiggle enough and make it fall out. I'm hanging by a thread.

"It's safer for you not to know."

I study his face in the low light of the computer screen. He's logged into Meridian and was looking at spreadsheets. "And that's it? That's all you're going to tell me?"

"That's it."

The dismissal stings. I thought we were in this together. Linc and Jules against the world. "Well, I guess that's one set of bad guys off my back."

His gaze lands on me. "They're also going to find out who burned down your building."

I should be grateful. But I feel so lost. Almost like a forgery. A fake. Linc is always in command yet perfectly at ease. I hardly know who I am or where I belong. Certainly not in a museum.

I try to cut how dismal I'm starting to feel with comedy. "Thanks. They say it's a small world, even in Thug Town. It's a community, if you will."

"They won't bother you again."

Something in his voice makes me shiver. I've never seen Linc like this—like he's prepared to destroy entire worlds to protect what's his. It should be reassuring. Instead, it makes me feel small and helpless because before we were a team. Now, I feel like I've been left in the dark.

"On the upside," I say, forcing lightness into my voice, "any evidence that I forged the *Echo & Answer* painting went up in smoke."

Along with my fake diploma, though, what's on record in HR should hold up to scrutiny.

Linc remains quiet. Humorless. I can feel him pulling away, retreating behind walls I didn't even know existed. The man who held me in the lake, who kissed me silly—he's disappearing right in front of me.

"I guess I should try to get some sleep," I say finally.

"Yeah. Me too."

As I head back toward the guest room, I remember the letters I wanted to keep safe in case Drecken's men were looking for them. I pull them out of my bag, running my fingers over the faded ribbon.

These belong to Linc. To his family's history.

I leave them outside his bedroom door without reading a single word. Whatever secrets they contain, they're his to discover.

SEPTEMBER ARRIVES with crisp morning air that makes the whole city seem to stand up straighter after months of wilting in the heat.

Back at Meridian, it's business as usual—if you can call investigating insurance fraud and dodging corporate espionage usual. Recalling my very first encounter with Linc—over the phone—and everything since, I leave a chocolate on his desk. It's something of a peace treaty. A love note.

I visit Wendy and Carmen on the thirty-third floor because I miss them and need something normal in my life. I stop by the coffee cart in the lobby and grab three pumpkin spice lattes.

"Jules!" Wendy practically bounces out of her chair when she sees me. "We were just talking about you."

My old office is already decorated for fall, complete with delightfully plump ceramic pumpkins, sprays of silk autumn leaves, corn husks, seasonal flowers, and candy corn overflowing from a glass bowl. It's wonderfully, aggressively cheerful and just what I need.

"How's life working with the boss's son?" Carmen's eyebrows bob as she accepts her latte gratefully.

I let out a long exhale. "It's ..." I pause, trying to find words that won't reveal too much. "Like a corn maze."

Wendy almost chokes on her drink. "A spider's web?"

Carmen adds, "Are you bewitched and bewildered?"

We all dissolve into laughter, which makes me feel alive again.

"So what you mean to say is things are complicated?" Wendy leans forward, eager to hear more.

"We haven't defined *things*," I admit.

Carmen points out, "And there's the whole HR issue since he's technically your boss."

Wendy says, "That's temporary, though, right? I thought he was only supposed to be here for the summer."

The first day of fall is a week away. Soon, kids will be heading back to school, the leaves will start changing, and Linc will go back to whatever his real life is—yachting? Partying? Gallivanting the globe? I have no idea. The thought makes me feel like I'm dropping rapidly to the building's ground floor.

"True," I say, sipping my latte to avoid their knowing looks.

They pepper me with more questions, but I play dodgeball by asking about work gossip and office politics. Still, when I go upstairs, I feel lighter. Ordinary friendships and normal conversations are the things that keep me grounded.

When I get back to the thirty-ninth floor, I find Maxine exiting the side door of Linc's office.

"Can I help you, Ms. Drecken?"

"Just dropping off some files for Abraham."

"You can leave them with me."

She glances over her shoulder. "Oh, he'll find them."

Something about her shifty gaze and the slight tremor in her voice makes me remember that she's after his job—not that he's exactly eager to take it for himself.

In the coming days, Linc is busy with "business," whether that's shady dealings with thugs, uncovering fraud schemes, or regular, straightforward reports, I'm not sure. But a mere week into fall, he and I are on a plane to Las Vegas for Mom and Brad the Dad's anniversary party as if everything between us is ... well, normal.

Linc insisted on flying us first class, which means I spend most of the flight trying not to gawk at the differences between the seating placements, complete with actual legroom. Even so, it's hard not to fidget with the edge of my seatbelt.

"Nervous?" he asks as we start our descent.

"A little. My brothers can be ..." I search for the right word. "Intense."

"I can handle intense."

He's an only child and I was until the triplets came along. He has no idea of the amount of chaos he's walking into. Yes, Bryce, Brody, and Brian are adult-sized, but it's a cover for them still being the naughty, snotty little boys they always were.

Mom practically vibrates with excitement when we pull up to the stucco tract house. She's wearing a new mauve dress and has had her hair done for the occasion.

I rush into her embrace—there's nothing quite like a mom hug.

"Juliana! And this must be Linc!" She pulls him into a hug like he's already family. "I've heard so much about you."

He arches a questioning eyebrow in my direction. Then, with a charming smile that makes everyone love him instantly—and makes thugs side with him rather than their boss—he says, "All good things, I hope."

"Well, now I see why Juliana has been so secretive." Mom winks.

Brad the Dad appears from the back deck, wearing his grilling apron. Within minutes, he and Linc are chummy. The obvious topic of conversation is sports. When Brad mentions Linc's athletic build, he shifts on his feet and asks about the cuts of steak.

The anniversary party is in the backyard, complete with a live band and more flowers than at their wedding—Brad said he got Mom one for every day of their marriage. She's practically floating on a cloud—so happy as friends and coworkers congratulate them upon arrival.

Then the triplets show up.

Bryce, Brian, and Brody are twenty-three now, recent college graduates who still move like they're joined at the hip. They're even bigger than when I last saw them. Gym rats with confident grins.

"Jules!" Bryce scoops me up in a bear hug that lifts me off my feet.

"Easy, caveman," I laugh.

He sets me abruptly down.

Brody squeezes me like a python.

"Gentler!"

Brian starts to toss me over his shoulder, but I play their least favorite game, "Jules has no bones." I make myself a dead weight and drop flat to the floor.

From down there, I point to my rather large and imposing guest, calling, "This is Linc."

He extends his hand and helps me to my feet.

The introductions are a blur of handshakes and back-slapping.

Brian studies Linc's face with a puzzled expression. "You look familiar. Have we met?"

"I don't think so," Linc says smoothly.

"Are you guys getting married?" Brody asks with the subtlety of a freight train blowing its horn.

"What are you, still seven years old?" Heat creeps across my face. "Kids, they say the darndest things."

"Hey, our brainy sister deserves the best," Bryce chimes in, ruffling my hair.

His comment makes me freeze. *Brainy sister*. I still carry the burden of the secret about my educational background —unbeknownst to them, I never completed college. Being home, I'm afraid Linc might ask to see graduation pictures because one of my mother's favorite pastimes is showing off her photo albums.

None of them includes my graduation day because there wasn't one. The truth makes me regret all the deep-fried deviled eggs I've devoured in the last hour. Mom can never find out that I didn't really graduate. Neither can Linc.

After we play a few group games—Mom learned early on that she has to keep the boys occupied and still always plans lots of activities for gatherings—she pulls me aside while Linc is deep in conversation with Brad the Dad about pickleball.

"He's wonderful, sweetheart." She squeezes my hand. "Are things serious?"

"We haven't really defined it," I say, essentially repeating what I told the office girlies.

"He seems like a keeper to me. The way he looks at you ..." She sighs dreamily. "Like you're the center of his world."

If only that were true. If only I could believe that someone like Linc would choose someone like me for more than a temporary summer romance. He dated Iva Katz, for goodness' sake.

Despite my swirling anxieties, we have fun at the party. Linc fits in with my family better than I could have hoped, laughing at Dad's terrible jokes and listening to Mom's stories about her succulent garden.

"I like your family," he tells me as we slow dance to the band's rendition of "The Way You Look Tonight."

"Even my brothers?"

"Even your brothers. I never had siblings." His expression is wistful.

"Do you ever wish you did?"

"Sometimes. Especially watching you with yours. The way you all tease and joke, but would clearly go to bat for each other. It's rare, special."

The song ends, and he spins me once before pulling me back against his chest. For a moment, surrounded by my family's laughter and the warm Las Vegas evening, I can almost believe this is real.

That we're real.

But as the night winds down, I can't shake the feeling

that I'm living on borrowed time. Fall is coming. And men like Linc don't choose women like me for the long haul.

They choose women like me for right now.

And maybe, I think as I watch him laugh at something Brian says, maybe right now is enough.

Ultimately, it's all I have.

44

LINC

MEETING JULES'S family shifted something inside. Watching her with her brothers—the way they teased her but would clearly cage fight anyone who hurt her—made me understand what I want to be for her. Not just a summer romance or a hockey player posing as a businessman. Someone who is there for her. Someone she can rely on ... and make her smile, laugh, and feel loved.

Back home, the lost Lincoln love letters sit on my nightstand, still tied with the faded ribbon. I'm guessing Jules didn't open them. I'm now afraid to read them, afraid of what they might reveal about my family's past, given what Jules read in my mom's diary. But knowing she respected that they were mine to discover gives me the courage I need.

I carefully untie the ribbon and unfold the first letter.

My dearest Mary, These last weeks, the distance between us feels like a chasm, cleaving my heart in two. I know your sister and her husband disapprove of our courtship. It's true we come from different worlds, but we have to ask what's most important? A perfect union or one where we learn and grow and challenge each other? I believe I can provide the security you deserve and the adventures you crave. I want you to know that you are the light that guides me through every dark moment. The hope that sustains me when the weight of the world feels too heavy to bear ...

The words blur as I read. These aren't just love letters, they're a testament to devotion that survived doubt, distance, and disapproval. Abraham Lincoln, who would become one of history's greatest leaders, was once just a man desperately in love, fighting for the woman who believed in him.

Another notes that Lincoln recognized that Mary's family questioned their partnership and he arranged for certain pieces of art and rare books to be gifted to them, like a reverse dowry, indicating that she was his greatest treasure, more valuable than any collection.

Interestingly, they provide a provenance record, which makes me wonder if they're connected to the founding of Meridian.

By the time I finish all three letters, my resolve has crystallized. Jules deserves someone who pursues her the way Lincoln did for Mary. Someone who doesn't let fear or family expectations get in the way of what matters.

First, I need to clean up the mess at Meridian. I have to confront my father. Then tell her about playing for the NHL. Hopefully, she'll forgive me.

On Sunday morning, I wake Jules with a soft kiss on her forehead. She stirs, blinking sleepily up at me.

"Special occasion?" she mumbles, voice thick with sleep.

"Every day with you is," I say, meaning it more than I've meant anything in my life.

Her smile starts small and spreads across her whole face

like a sunrise. I lean down for another kiss, this one lingering, and she sighs against my lips.

"What's the plan today?" she asks when I pull back.

"It's a surprise. Dress for something active, but bring a jacket."

"So mysterious."

I stop by the door to her bedroom, remembering courage. "Actually, Jules, would you go on a date with me this afternoon?"

She presses to sit up fully. "A date?"

"Yeah, like, um, when two people go somewhere together ..."

She tips her head back with laughter. "I know what a date is."

"Will you go on a date with me, Miss Lindley?"

She fiddles with the edge of the quilt on her bed and then looks up at me with a bright smile. "You don't have to ask twice."

After breakfast and church (where she prayed we weren't reenacting an Indiana Jones or National Treasure scene on our date), we stand outside Millennium Park's ice skating ribbon, watching skaters glide across the rink in the still-warm September air.

She asks, "Ice skating? It's like summer and fall are having a turf war over the season."

"Have you ever been?"

"That's like asking if Las Vegas is hot. We spent as much time as possible in air-conditioned venues, the ice skating rink included. My brothers love hockey."

I nearly trip as I step onto the sheer surface. Getting my footing, I glide forward smoothly. It feels like coming home, even if these skates are rentals.

"Wait for me," Jules calls, but she's grinning as she joins me, slightly wobbly.

"You're pretty good at this," I say, skating backward so I can watch her face.

"With the triplets, I had to learn to be athletic fast or get left behind. Mom enrolled us all in everything—skating, swimming, soccer, martial arts."

I continue skating backward. "I had to pick one sport. It was fencing or this."

She laughs. "Show off."

We spend an hour on the ice, racing each other around the rink, playing impromptu games of tag, and stealing kisses when we think no one's looking. Jules's cheeks are pink from exertion, her eyes bright with laughter, and I want to stay here with her, like this, forever.

Afterward, we sit on a bench with Styrofoam cups of hot chocolate. She holds hers with both hands. I wrap my arm around her.

She tips her head to look up at me and says, "Being with you makes me feel melty. Like hot chocolate marshmallow goo."

The simple contentment in her voice makes me feel like a hunting dog lazing in front of a warm fire. I was about to tell her about hockey—about who I really am. But looking at her face, seeing her this happy and relaxed, I lose my nerve. She'll want to know why I didn't mention it before now. I'm afraid she'll think I didn't trust her.

There will be time for truth later. Right now, I just want to be the man who makes her feel like melted marshmallows.

THE NEXT MORNING, I wake her the same way—with a kiss that starts gentle and deepens when she responds. Her arms wind around my neck, fingers threading through my hair as she pulls me closer.

"I could get used to this wake-up service," she murmurs against my mouth.

I nuzzle her neck, breathing in the scent of her skin, trying to memorize the way she feels in my arms. "Good, because I'm not going anywhere."

But even as I say it, doubt creeps in. Preseason starts tomorrow. With that comes training, media obligations, and the demands of a new season. How do I balance that with this—with her?

I push the thoughts away and focus on the present, on the way she sighs when I press kisses along her collarbone, on the trust she shows by letting me hold her like this.

When we part, I say, "See you at the office."

"We're such sneaks. Secret keepers." She laughs, but has no idea how close to the truth she is.

I pause by the door, knowing it's now or never. But I'm already planning to confront my father. Maybe one confession is enough for today. So I make my exit.

An hour later, I walk through Meridian's marble lobby. Security nods at me. They've gotten used to my presence over the summer. But today feels different. I'm not just the boss's son playing the role of a businessman. I'm a man with a purpose to make things right.

My father's office door is closed when I reach the executive floor, but his assistant waves me through. He's standing by the windows overlooking the city, phone pressed to his ear, and doesn't acknowledge my presence for several minutes.

"We'll discuss this later," he says finally, ending the call. "Abraham, to what do I owe the pleasure?"

"We need to talk."

"Sounds serious." He drops into his leather chair. "Could it be about the use of company funds?"

"Ding, ding, ding," I say, though I know he's referring to the New York and DC trip. "It's about some discrepancies in insurance filings, among other things."

His expression doesn't change, but something shifts in his eyes. "I see you've been busy."

Before I can respond, there's a knock on the door. "Come in," my father calls.

Jules enters, carrying a thick folder, but stops short when she sees me. "Oh. I'm sorry, I didn't realize—"

"Perfect timing, actually," my father says. "I asked Miss Lindley to share what you discovered in your investigation."

I do everything not to move like I just experienced whiplash. "Wait. What?"

The corner of his mouth lifts as realization hits me from behind, from a direction I never saw coming. My father has known all along. That means he's involved or—what exactly?

"You knew?"

He levels me with his gaze. "Son, I know everything."

I take a measured breath, wondering what is going on.

Jules looks between us. Clearly sensing the tension, she drops the files and then makes for the door.

"Miss Lindley, please remain. We don't have any secrets here, do we?" my father says smoothly. "We're all on the same team."

She swallows thickly.

"Why don't you kids tell me what you discovered?"

We're both quiet except for the ticking of Abe's old grandfather clock. I came up here fired up, but with a few simple words, my father put out the flames. Now what?

45

LINC

STANDING BEFORE MY FATHER, Jules draws herself up. "Someone has been commissioning high-quality forgeries, having them authenticated by our own experts, insuring them for massive amounts, then claiming tax deductions for 'donating' them or sending them to auction while keeping the originals in private storage."

My father's head inclines in a direction that shows mild surprise. "How long has this been going on?"

Jules looks at me as if for approval. "Based on the patterns we found, at least a year. Someone with executive access has been taking advantage of desperate sellers and increasing values for insurance purposes."

Eyes boring into my father, I add, "It's fraud. Executive fraud."

"Indeed," he says as if this is a novelty.

Jules continues, "But that's not where it ends. These pieces have then been sold at auction."

My father leads, "And you think—?"

Unable to restrain myself as he holds it together as if not at all shaken by this information, I turn to Frank Andresen, the man who loved my mother, broke her heart, and wants me to become him. "Are you involved?"

The accusation hits like a slap as his head snaps in my direction. "What?"

"From the outside, it looks like—"

"Like I'm part of the fraud," he finishes with a derisive snort.

Jules and I have shifted closer together. My father's eyes slide up and down, in between, as if trying to figure out how to play his hand ... or as if he sees something he hasn't in a long, long time. My lifetime, in fact.

I say, "I just want the truth."

"That's a serious accusation, son."

"It's not an accusation," Jules says quickly.

I start, "I'm trying to understand—"

"No, you're right to question it." Then I watch, as if in slow motion, my father turn the tables. "I have a question too. How do I know you two aren't involved and brought this to me to deflect responsibility?"

The three of us are in a standoff, as silence as thick as ice fills the air.

"We both know quite well that I did not want to be here this summer," I say like a gavel dropping.

I don't let myself look to see if Jules flinched.

"Then you have a motive to get the most out of your time at Meridian."

This time, I do look at the stunning woman with bright eyes and stop-traffic, forget-your-own-name beauty. "I already did."

Jules looks at me briefly, storing my comment about her, us, for later. She stands strong. "Sir, I am not running a fraud scheme. I'm risking my job right now."

"Fair point. As for me, I am most certainly not stealing

from my own company." He looks toward the door as it opens again. "Ah, Maxine, how timely."

Jules seems to shrink as every muscle in my body coils with rage.

"Frank, you wanted to see me?" She stops when she spots Jules and me. "Oh. This is unexpected."

"Maxine," my father says with a density behind it I can't place. "We were just discussing—"

"Personnel matters? These two have been quite the pair of firecrackers this summer."

A growl rises in my throat.

"Actually, it's about an audit they ran," Dad says.

My jaw slowly lowers. It's then that I see that my years of learning at his side have paid off. His angle takes shape, suddenly makes sense. He's known about the scheme all along and let Jules and me figure it out. But why? I wonder if he was aware of Drecken's thugs. If so, he could've intervened before now.

The man deals in art, but is an artist himself in the way he crafts business ventures. He's about to let Maxine hang herself.

I'm. In. Awe.

"Speaking of fire, your services are no longer needed, Maxine," he says.

My mistake. He went straight for the jugular.

She stammers.

"If that wasn't clear. You're fired."

"What—why?"

"Before I have security take you into custody, do take this opportunity to defend yourself. I'd like to hear why a promising COO, a person who could've been the next chief executive, deceived me." My father's voice is cool while Maxine tries not to melt under pressure.

She stammers, "I don't know what you're talking about."

"Sure you do. You sent thugs after an employee and my son. You've been working on the side with yours. Robbing from the company that has only treated you well, not to mention the headache it's going to be to correct all the intentional errors you made. Did you really want to make an entire industry's worth of enemies?"

Changing tack, she snorts with derision, stalking toward my father like he's prey—that might be her greatest mistake yet. It's the seasoned hunters you have to watch out for. "I knew you were getting old, Frank. Saw the writing on the wall. Needed to make my stake before you handed over the crown of this castle to someone who'd waste it." She pitches a scathing glance at me and cackles like I'm a big joke.

My father lets the room fall silent before striking. "Are you admitting to wrongdoing?"

"I'm admitting to being smarter than everyone else on this floor, where I belong. Including you, Frank."

His face darkens. "Maxine—"

She tuts. "Oh, don't look so shocked. You've been too focused on your presidential legacy fantasies to notice what's been happening right under your nose. Did you really think I'd just quietly step aside when you decided to hand the company over to your son?"

The words hang in the air like the moments between a grenade's pin being pulled and the explosion.

"The beauty of the scheme was its simplicity. Commission forgeries of minor pieces, get them authenticated through our own people, insure them, then have my son destroy them and collect the insurance. Clean, efficient, profitable."

"But the Marchand diptych was from my collection."

My father's voice is frigid. "Did you really think you could steal from my family's legacy?"

"I was your legacy," Maxine shoots back. "Twenty years of building this company, and you were going to hand it to a boy who doesn't even want it. I earned more than a gold watch and a pat on the back."

"Who was your partner?" my father asks.

"Veronica and Misha?" Jules asks, referring to her assistants.

She caws a laugh. "No, they were just pawns. Useful to keep an eye on you. Remind you of your place. No, my partner was part of the family, though you'd know about that."

Jules lets out a soft gasp at the same time I make the connection.

"Aiken the Demo King," I say, referring to his viral channel that makes the perfect cover.

Jules explains to my father, who would think it's far too pedestrian to be worth a second of his attention. "'Aiken the Demo King' destroys priceless artifacts and costly items, making 'new art.' But in this case, insurance pays out, and according to them, everyone wins."

Maxine smirks. "Well, everyone except the people who thought they were buying authentic pieces."

My father digests this information like a sand worm.

Maxine scoffs. "I wasn't expecting you two to interfere."

My dad says, "I put them on a special assignment."

The pieces are falling into place with devastating clarity. She orchestrated everything—the fraud, the threats, and maybe even the fire lit by Jules's father's debtors.

My father ordered me not to seek the letters because he knew I would disobey.

Jules points her finger at Maxine. "You changed the

Echo & Answer signature from Clement Marchand to D. Kinnard. You wanted to hide that they were a diptych."

So far, I've been following Jules's line of thinking, but she's lost me now.

Maxine's nostrils flare. "Marchand only created matched pairs. If anyone knew one painting was by Marchand, they'd search for the companion piece. Separated, attributed to different artists, I could insure them as two unrelated works and double the payout."

Like the narcissistic villain she is, this woman cannot help but brag about her questionable and diabolical logic.

Now I fully understand what Jules is getting at. "The real Fairfax Collection documentation would have listed both paintings together under Marchand's name, which is why you couldn't let anyone find the start of the list of the gifts to the Todd family, included in the lost love letters. That would have led us to the end of the list—the Marchand paintings donated to them posthumously in Lincoln's memory."

My father snorts as if impressed by the unraveling of the scheme. "Let me see if I understand. You discovered a record of part of the Lincoln diptych in our archives. You realized it was worth more separated than together."

"The insurance possibilities were plain. Almost too good to pass up after the restructuring," Maxine says coldly. "Two paintings by different artists, different time periods, insured separately were worth triple what they'd be as a matched set."

Jules adds, "But you needed to hide the provenance. If anyone traced the Fairfax Collection back to Lincoln's original gifts, they'd find documentation of a Marchand diptych, not two separate paintings."

Maxine huffs. "I was playing a long game. Your mother's obsession with those letters was the catalyst. I thought when she died, the search would die with her. But then you started looking."

"The letters don't just prove Lincoln loved Mary, they prove what pieces Lincoln originally gave to her family, which leads to the full collection. And the paintings, together, tell the complete story." My father folds his hands.

"You're finished, Maxine," I say, surprised by how steady my voice sounds. "We have everything we need to destroy you."

Her smile turns predatory. "Do you? Because from where I'm sitting, you're the one who's been requesting access to forged documents for months. Your little treasure hunt for those love letters made you the perfect patsy."

I go still. My innocent search for the Lincoln letters has created a paper trail that makes me look complicit. Maybe that's why Dad urged me to leave the letters alone. Either way, he counted on Jules and me finding the discrepancies. On us exposing Maxine.

Then Jules steps forward, eyebrow arched. "There is one problem with your theory, Ms. Drecken. We have the letters. You have the painting—or did you and Aiken already destroy it? He won the winning bid at the auction. Looks suspicious."

"I covered my tracks. You won't pin anything on me." Her tone is cold, but uncertainty flickers across her face.

"Lincoln kept meticulous records," Jules continues. "Including records of which documents he gave to which collectors. The letters reference his inventory. Your forgeries are about to be exposed."

It's brilliant and Maxine's confident smirk wavers.

"You'll never prove anything," she says, but she sounds less sure.

"Won't I?" Jules pulls out her phone. "Should I call the FBI now, or would you prefer to explain to them how you've been systematically defrauding insurance companies and auction houses, not to mention attempted murder?"

The room goes so quiet I can hear the traffic below.

Then Maxine clicks her tongue. "This isn't over," she says, but she's already backing toward the door.

"Yes," my father says quietly, "it is."

After she leaves, the three of us exchange baffled looks as if to ask, *Did that really happen*?

My father says, "I'm afraid so. But I have you two to thank."

"So you knew all along? You planted me on the inside, 'undercover boss' style, without my even knowing it?" Wrinkles line my forehead and then a sharp bark of laughter escapes when he doesn't deny it.

My father spins his pointer finger in the general vicinity of the room. "The best part is all of that was caught on the security cams. I use Checkpoint Secure."

Of course he does.

"Did you really find the letters?" he asks with a surprising amount of eagerness in his voice.

"Sure did."

Jules turns to my father and says, "Sir, your wife really loved you. Your son, too. Now I understand why."

Then she excuses herself, leaving Dad and me alone. He comes out from behind his desk and, for the first time in my adult memory, he hugs me and says, "Go after her."

I grip him more tightly, not realizing how much I've needed this hug.

"I'd like to see those letters when you get a chance."

"Absolutely." I start toward the door.

"Oh, one more thing. Jules really is an expert forger.

But I have it on good authority that she truly cares about you."

"What do you mean?"

"She may not have an authentic college diploma."

My brow forms a trench. "Huh?"

He claps me on the shoulder. "Don't worry about it. I'll let the two of you work out the secrets you keep. But don't hold on to them for too long."

With that, his phone rings and he takes the call.

46

JULES

THE ELEVATOR RIDE DOWN to the thirty-ninth floor feels like the slow-motion part of a roller coaster before the drop. Linc and I stand in stunned silence, both staring at the digital floor numbers as if they're a code that might reveal an explanation about what just transpired in his father's office.

When the doors finally open, we walk into the workspace like two people who've just witnessed a magic trick and can't figure out how the rabbit disappeared.

"Did that really happen?" I ask, sinking into my desk chair.

Linc loosens his tie and shakes his head. "Maxine Drecken working with Aiken the Demo King."

"He's her son!"

Linc lets out a long exhale. "Didn't see that coming."

"Not by a long shot."

"I knew she was ambitious, but this ..."

"Is wildly twisted?" I ask, mind reeling.

He nods.

"Insurance fraud on a massive scale?" I add as we exit the elevator one floor down and pause in the reception area.

Linc rubs his hand on his jaw, his stubble like sandpaper.

"That for a second there she was going to try to pin it all on us?"

"Key word being 'try.'" He perches on the edge of my desk and draws me near him.

My heart turns into a little hummingbird at Linc's proximity.

"So what next?" I ask.

He claps his hands together. "Crossing my father is a career death sentence. Maxine is finished. He'll take her for everything she's worth and then some. Probably donate the money to an arts program or something equally philanthropic yet devastating to her ego."

I blink at him. "So Frank Andresen is evil but good?"

"Basically." He grins.

Like I'm sunning myself on the shore by the lake house, I bask in his smile, the first genuine one I've seen from him since we fled.

Linc gestures grandly. "Welcome to the Andresen family. Our philosophy: ruthless justice with a charitable tax write-off."

A laugh bubbles out of me, probably inappropriate given the circumstances, but I can't help it. The absurdity of little old me—from clerical work on the thirty-third floor to executive assistant to exposing insurance fraud, Maxine's dramatic ejection, and Frank somehow knowing about our investigation—hits me like a train coming late into the station.

"Also, it seems like your father knew about it all along."

Linc nods and shakes his head as if he's still working out how.

"We did it. We uncovered a corporate con like spies or whistleblowers." I bounce a little at the glamor of it, knowing full well there will be an investigation, a lawsuit, and likely proper in-office drama if Jeannie and her "tea time" have anything to do with it.

"You did it," Linc corrects, shifting closer to me. "Your instincts, your research skills, your brilliant insight into the Lincoln letters containing references to records related to the missing Fairfax piece, resulting in Maxine's confession."

My shoulders rise in a shy shrug. "All in a day's work."

His eyes sparkle with admiration and something deeper that makes my breath catch. "You were amazing in there."

"You weren't so bad yourself. And we certainly did this together. We make a good team."

The corner of his lip twitches. "Yeah. We do."

Before I can overthink it, he leans down and kisses me. It's quick and sweet, a celebration of victory and relief all wrapped into one perfect package. When our lips part, his forehead rests against mine.

"What's going to happen?" I ask, my voice barely above a whisper.

"An HR filing?" He laughs as we draw apart because this kind of activity between two Meridian employees is frowned upon. "Then again, I don't technically get paid, so I suppose we could have one more ..." He kisses me again.

This one is longer, slower, and I feel suddenly shy about what's happening between us. This isn't just attraction or adrenaline anymore—it's something deeper that terrifies and thrills me in equal measure. I feel like I'm floating.

No, we're falling, and I don't think either of us knows how to stop.

Where we'll land.

If we'll be able to get up.

Then what?

Linc's fingers trace along the curve of my jaw, down my neck, sending a warm shiver through me.

I clasp my hands behind his back, tethering myself to him, to this moment.

He responds by wrapping both arms around me, pulling me flush against him until there's no space left between us.

His breath tickles my ear as he shifts, pressing a kiss just below it, and I can't help the small laugh that escapes—half nervous, half delighted. He smiles against my skin, and I feel it more than see it.

The scratch of his stubble along my neck makes me wriggle in the best of ways, and he chuckles low in his throat, clearly pleased with my reaction. When his mouth finds mine again, he catches my bottom lip gently between his teeth—playful and teasing—before soothing it with a softer kiss.

I could really get used to this.

I want to. I want him.

When we draw apart this time, I ask, "But really, what's next?" I mean this for every possible variation of the question. What's going to happen between us? At the office? For the future?

"I have to travel for a few days—business." He straightens, running a hand through his hair. "When I get back, we'll celebrate."

My pulse skitters, but before I can respond, his phone buzzes. He glances at it and sighs. "Speaking of travel, I need to pack. Flight leaves soon."

Just like that, he's gone, leaving me alone in our shared office with the lingering scent of his cologne and a thousand questions swirling through my mind.

THREE DAYS PASS with a mere few texts from Linc. He's out of the country and busy with business meetings. Likely, his father gave him more responsibility now that Drecken is out of the picture.

In Linc's absence, I have a fierce chocolate craving. I blame the grocery store for putting so much Halloween candy on display. It's entirely their fault that I buy several bags—candy bar miniatures, a fruity assortment, and more snack-size peanut butter cups than should be legal—covering all my bases. Even though Halloween is still weeks away and I doubt trick-or-treaters will visit Linc's condo, I tell myself it's best to be prepared.

Still, doubt plays games in my mind, trying to answer questions that I should just ask the man myself.

What does Linc do when he's not playing summer intern? Jet off to meetings in New York and DC? Go boating with his friend Bear-something? I can never remember his buddy's name. Could he actually have a secret wife and family?

The truth is, even though we've shared so much, I hardly know him outside of the office.

My internal sky clouds over, hiding the sun as I organize files that don't need organizing and respond to emails that can wait. I refresh my phone every few minutes, hoping for some sign that I'm more than a convenient summer distraction. An office fling.

It's all a little pathetic.

Oly and I meet for brunch at our favorite place, even though I'm so far from being able to afford it—what without having massive debt and everything I own wiped out—that I order from the "sides" part of the menu.

"You look like someone stole your favorite Care Bear," Oly says.

"More like someone set it on fire."

She winces, recalling that *all* of my belongings went up in a spectacular blaze that was on the news. "Do you have a stomachache?"

I frown. "No. I just—"

"Are you on a detox or dieting?"

"What? Goodness no."

Oly flags down the waitress. "Excuse me, could you please add to our order? We'd like the pancakes with chocolate chips and spiced whipped cream, pumpkin bread French toast, and one of those fancy crepes from the specials board."

The server's eyes widen at the same time I try to decline, but with a sharp look my way, my best friend isn't having it.

"Once we get some food in you, you'll tell me what's really going on." She talks to me about Nate's new job, keeping up a running monologue of married life until the wagon train of plates arrives, barely fitting on our table.

I'll admit, it all looks delicious, but my heart is back in DC when Linc ordered us room service breakfast.

Oly says the blessing over our meal and then says, "Don't tell me you're just tired. I know this has something to do with your handsome nemesis-turned-real-boyfriend."

There is no use trying to hide anything from her. She'll smoke me out. Also, the pancakes are phenomenal and instantly boost my blood sugar. I cannot help but say, "He's been traveling. Business meetings."

Oly raises an eyebrow. "Ah! So he is your boyfriend."

I gasp and angle my fork at her. "You snuck that in there."

She wears a wicked smile. "So you haven't talked to him in a few days and are now wondering what's going to happen?" As usual, she's spot on.

"He's busy." The words sound hollow even to me.

She blinks a few times and says, "Juliana Lindley, you are obsessing. I can practically see the tornado coming out of your ears."

I stuff a bite of the crepe in my mouth because there's no sense in denying it.

She claps her hands together. "Which is why you need a distraction. Nate got four tickets to the Chicago Breeze hockey game tomorrow night from work. First game of the season. It's against a team from Canada, I think. You, me, Nate, and a cute guy at his office could be your plus-one ... unless you want to save the seat for Linc, you know, if he's actually your boyfriend."

I mumble, "He'll still be out of town."

"Ah, so you would want him in the seat."

But does he want me?

She takes a bite of the pumpkin bread French toast and, after emerging from ecstasy, says, "Come on, it'll be fun. None of us know anything about hockey, but the fans are supposed to be wild—entertaining in their own right."

I consider declining, but the alternative is another night alone in Linc's penthouse, overthinking every moment of our relationship.

"Fine. But I'm warning you, I know absolutely nothing about this sport you call hockey." I intentionally mispronounce it with a little French flair just to show my bestie that I'm not that far gone.

She laughs and I know I'll be okay. I mean, I will. Right?

"Perfect. We can learn together."

Though growing up with three brothers, this is more of

an indulgence than anything, since I do know the rough gist of the game, emphasis on rough. But maybe a bit of rowdy skating with sticks is what I need right now.

47

JULES

THE CHICAGO BREEZE arena buzzes with energy that's infectious even for people who can hardly tell a puck from a pancake—by the way, I wanted to bathe in the spiced whipped cream from brunch the other day. Yes, it was that good.

Oly and I order overpriced nachos and Nate tucks in with a couple of hot dogs.

"Okay, so what do we know so far?" Oly asks, helping herself to a chip slathered in yellow cheese.

"There are three periods," Nate explains.

"That's a good start. But I was talking about Juliana and Linc."

"I thought we were talking about hockey," her husband says.

Glad for a diversion, at least for now, I state the obvious, "It's cold."

Nate's eyes swirl with the kind of frenzied excitement I've seen from my brothers. "And they fight each other."

"Like, actually fight?" Oly asks..

"Sometimes. It's encouraged." He winks.

She grins. "I like this sport already."

The arena fills rapidly, a sea of blue-and-white Breeze jerseys and team merch surrounding us. The energy is electric—music pounding, lights flashing, fans chanting in unison. When the players take the ice for warm-ups, the crowd erupts.

"This is intense," I shout over the noise.

"And we haven't even started yet," Nate shouts back.

Oly leans over during a break in the music. "Want to play red flag, green flag while we watch?"

"Sure, but your potential boyfriends will be the Breeze players and mine will be the Outlaws."

This is but another one of our games we used to play when we were both single. I know she's doing it for my benefit now that she's married and wouldn't so much as dream about another man, But she knows I need to take my mind off Linc—he's all I want to think about.

Speaking of green, I might be pining for the man I once despised.

"We'll just analyze the players based on hockey skills and body language, then decide if they're relationship material. Green flag for good boyfriend potential, red flag for run-away-fast."

I laugh despite myself. "Oly, we can't even see their faces through those helmets."

"That's what makes it fun."

No sooner do we decide that the goalie for the Breeze seems sweet and wholesome, does the game begin with a fury and pace I wasn't expecting. Considering they're wearing skates, the players race across the ice at impossible speeds. My date with Linc sends me spinning in mental circles. He was a really good skater. We held hands. We joked around. I felt so far from hating him … did I ever really?

So much for red flag, green flag. The game zips along with the puck flying between sticks so fast I can barely track it. The crowd roars with every near-miss, every hit, every spectacular save by the goalies.

"Number twelve for Chicago," Oly points out during a brief pause. "Green flag. Look at that hustle."

"How can you tell he has hustle?" I ask.

"The way he skates. Very determined. Probably the type to bring you soup when you're sick."

We're into the early part of the second period when one of the guys is called for a penalty.

Having more fun than I expected, I say, "Definitely red flag."

"For sure," she agrees.

Next, she gives a player a green and red checkered flag when he comes to one of his teammates' defense after the opponent slammed him into the boards.

I'm laughing at her logic when the game resumes and not a minute later, the announcer's voice booms through the arena, "Goal scored by number eighty-three, Linc Andresen!"

My blood turns to ice in my veins.

The crowd explodes around me, jumping to their feet as the player in question celebrates near the goal. I watch in horrified fascination as he raises his stick, skating backward with his arms spread wide, accepting congratulations from his teammates.

Even with the helmet obscuring most of his face, I know that posture, those broad shoulders, the way he moves across the ice with powerful grace.

Linc Andresen. My Linc.

My enemy, my boss, my partner in crime, my adventure trailblazer, er, tunnel-blazer, the best kisser on the planet, Linc, is a professional hockey player?

"Juliana?" Oly's voice sounds like it's coming from underwater.

I can't speak. Can't breathe. The activity in the arena blurs into a watercolor tableau.

The athletic build I admired.

The way he moved on the rink like he'd been doing it all his life.

Why he was so resistant to working at Meridian.

All of it adds up.

I'm so stupid. So foolish.

"Juliana, seriously, what's wrong?" Oly grabs my arm.

"That's him," I whisper.

"Who?" She must not have heard Linc's name broadcast over the raucous noise in the arena.

"Number eighty-three. That's Linc."

Oly's eyes widen as she processes this information. Then her voice rises an octave. "That's your Linc?"

I nod, unable to look away as he lines up for a face-off. He's completely in his element out there, commanding and confident beyond what I've already seen. This is who he really is. Not the reluctant businessman learning his father's trade, but a professional athlete playing in front of thousands of screaming fans.

Oly glares at him from the stands. "Red flag. Red sirens blaring. Alarm bells ringing."

The rest of the game passes in a fog. I watch him score two more goals, assist another, and celebrate with teammates who adore him. The crowd chants his name. A group of women behind us discuss his dating history.

"He dated Iva Katz," one says.

"They broke up last year, but there were photos of them together recently," another adds. "Super cozy at a smoothie shop."

My hands shake as I grip the armrests of my seat. Photos of him with Iva? Recent photos? While he was supposedly falling for me, he was still connected to his actress ex?

Everything we shared—the lake house, the quiet mornings, the way he looked at me like I was someone special—was it all just a convenient distraction while his real life was on hold?

When the final buzzer sounds and Chicago wins five to four, Oly turns to me with eyes full of sympathy. "What are you going to do?"

I watch Linc skate off the ice, accepting congratulations from over the glass. He's in his world, surrounded by his people, living his real life.

And I'm nobody. A temporary assistant with a forged diploma and a burned-down house, sitting in the nosebleed seats while watching the man I thought I knew score hat tricks for a living.

"I'm going home," I say quietly.

"To Linc's place?"

The thought of returning to his penthouse, sleeping in his guest room while he's off playing hockey, and possibly rekindling things with a gorgeous actress makes me want to disappear entirely.

"Actually, can I crash at your place tonight?"

Oly's expression softens. "Of course. You can stay as long as you like. But Juliana, you need to talk to him. There might be an explanation—"

"There's no explanation for lying about who he is." The words come out like daggers. "He let me believe he was a rich kid reluctantly learning the family business. Meanwhile, he's a professional athlete with his name on jerseys and women discussing his love life in the stands. He probably has a hashtag."

As we make our way through the crowded concourse, I try to ignore his presence everywhere—on the lips of fans, on merchandise, on my heart.

My phone buzzes with a text.

> Linc: Hope your day was good. Miss you.
> Be home soon.

I glare at the message, remembering how those same hands that typed it belong to a man who is in this building. A man who just played professional hockey in front of twenty thousand people. How can someone be so close and so distant at the same time?

"You're not going to chase him with a hockey stick?" Oly asks as we wait for Nate to get the car. "Throw pucks through his car windshield? I once super-glued my ex's apartment door shut after he stood me up for my birthday."

I almost smile. "Nope."

"Oh." Her voice drops. "You're icing him out."

The hockey pun isn't lost on me, but I don't laugh. Instead, I feel something cold and protective settle around my heart. This is what I do when people let me down—I go quiet, build walls, vanish before they can disappear on me first.

Dad taught me that lesson well, even if he never meant to.

"Can you bring me to Linc's?" I ask from the backseat of Nate's Jeep. "I need to get my things."

Oly turns around, concern etched on her face. "Are you sure you want to do that tonight? You could wait until—"

"I'll grab a cab to your place." The words come out sharper than I intend.

The city blurs past the window as we drive toward the penthouse. I'm already thinking about Monday morning—about facing Linc at work, pretending I don't know his secret while carrying the weight of mine.

Here's the thing—I never told him I didn't actually graduate from college. I've been deceptive, false. The only difference is that his lie involves fame and fortune, while mine involves desperation and fraud.

Now I have nothing. No home, courtesy of the fire. No job—once HR discovers my educational background. And no Linc, because whatever we had was built on a foundation of half-truths and summer fun that couldn't survive the harsh light of reality.

I let myself feel the dense impossibility of my situation. I'm twenty-seven years old, professionally adrift, emotionally devastated, and more alone than I've been.

But I'm also angry. And sometimes, anger is easier to handle than heartbreak.

48

LINC

THE MOOD in the locker room hangs heavy with the sting of a season opener loss. Hat trick in my first game back—three goals, two assists—but it wasn't enough. Chicago beat us five to four, and the kind of performance that should have been a celebration feels pointless when you're on the losing end.

My teammates sit in various stages of disappointment, some staring at their phones, others removing gear in silence.

I can't shake the feeling that something is off. Maybe it's the adrenaline crash, or perhaps it's because Jules hasn't responded to my text. I told her I missed her, which feels inadequate now that I'm sitting here in my gear, remembering the roar of twenty thousand fans cheering for me, when she's the only one I want saying my name.

My phone buzzes as I'm unlacing my skates.

> Unknown number: Your little assistant isn't exactly what she seems. Check the file I left in your desk drawer. Evidence of fake college transcripts. -M

My blood turns cold. Drecken. Even from whatever hole she's crawled into, she's still trying to cause damage. But what does she mean about Jules not being what she seems? Did she fake her degree? I've always leaned toward my father being wrong about, well, everything. But he did mention she may not have an authentic diploma. Why wouldn't she have told me this? The text plants a seed of doubt that grows with every second I stare at the screen.

"Solid play, Linc," Johannessen calls from across the room, but his usual jokester energy is subdued as he gathers his gear to leave.

I force a smile and nod, but my mind races ahead to getting home to Jules. Whatever Drecken is implying, I need to know the facts or if she's manipulating me.

The drive to my penthouse takes forever in post-game traffic. Every red light and every slow pedestrian crossing is an obstacle keeping me from the conversation I should have had weeks ago. I should have told Jules about hockey. Should have been honest from the beginning instead of playing the ridiculous game of summer intern.

The elevator ride to my floor stretches taut like a rubber band about to snap. When the doors finally open, I hear movement from the guest room—drawers closing, the rustle of fabric.

"Jules?" I call, dropping my keys on the table by the door.

No response.

I find her stuffing clothes into a clean trash bag. Her motions are rigid, tense.

From the doorway, I say, "Hi."

She must not hear me.

"What are you doing?" I ask even though it's obvious.

She doesn't answer.

"Where are you going?" I lean against the door frame, trying again.

She doesn't look up.

Her phone beeps with a text. Oly's name is on the screen. I take that as a reply.

"Why?"

Still nothing. She continues rushing around the room, gathering her things.

The silence stretches between us like a chasm.

"Jules, talk to me."

She doesn't even look my way.

"Look, I know you're upset about something, but leaving isn't the answer." I step into the room, and she freezes. "Stay. Please. We can work through whatever this is."

It's one of two things: Drecken or hockey. Has to be.

She slams a drawer and finally looks at me. Her eyes are red-rimmed but dry, like she's used up all of her tears.

"Here." I pull out my wallet and extract my credit card. "Take this. Whatever you need—"

"I don't want your money, Linc."

The words are clipped, cold. This isn't the woman who whooped as she swung on the rope swing or fed me pieces of watermelon while I counted her freckles popping in the sunlight.

This is someone I don't recognize.

The worst of it is she hardly looks at me.

She moves toward the door, bags in hand, and every instinct tells me to block her path. Instead, I let her pass, following her to the front door like a puppy.

She pauses, hand on the doorknob, but doesn't turn around. "Where were you tonight?"

Like when the buzzer sounds to signal the end of a

period and the puck streaks toward the net, I realize a moment too late what this is about. "I was at work. Playing hockey. For the Ottawa Outlaws. We lost to Chicago five to four. I scored a hat trick, but it wasn't enough. I'm a professional hockey player, Jules. Have been for over six years. The summer internship was me trying to avoid disappointing my father for a few more months before the season started."

She turns around slowly. Recognition flickers across her face. Followed by comprehension. And then, devastatingly, confirmation.

"I know," she says quietly.

"You know?"

"I was there tonight at the arena. I watched you score all three goals."

The words hit me like when Crofton slammed me into the boards. She was there. She saw everything—the crowd chanting my name, the celebration, the version of me that exists in the spotlight.

"Jules—"

"So those 'fans' who were lurking around the gallery building that night weren't random weird people. They recognized you."

I nod, feeling smaller with each word spoken. "Yeah."

"Mistaken identity versus hidden identity," she says, and there's something sharp in her tone that cuts deep. "There is quite a difference."

"I should have told you—"

"When? When you mentioned you weren't officially on the payroll? When we were talking about our hobbies? Interests? College? Surely you played while there. When you just shrugged and said something about your father owning Meridian and wanting to pass it on to you?" Her voice rises with each question. "That's why you didn't need to be paid. You just have oh-so-much money."

"It's not about the money—"

"It is when you're twenty-five thousand dollars in debt because your father was a jerk and the guys he wronged don't want to forget about it, saddling me with his obligations."

She's on fire, but my defenses rise. "As if you haven't done anything wrong," I shoot back.

A heaviness like freshly poured cement settles between us, thick and immobilizing. We're both carrying secrets, both guilty of deception, both standing in the wreckage of whatever trust we built.

"I stole gel highlighters," she sniffs. "And maybe some Post-its from the supply closet at Meridian."

"Is that it?" The text from Drecken burns in my pocket. "I was told that you forged your diploma."

Jules goes very still. Then, she leans against the door as if exhausted from the weight she's had to carry. "In my original application, I added a few little embellishments to my resume. But I'm passionate about art history, and according to my professors, an exceptional student."

"What about graduating?"

She meets my eyes directly. "Yeah, I claimed I have an art history degree. I didn't finish because I had to take care of my ailing father. Alone."

The word *alone* reverberates inside like a tuning fork, leaving silence in its wake. While I was playing division one hockey and complaining about my privileged problems—my roommate ate all my pizza rolls!—she was caring for a dying parent and sacrificing her own dreams.

"And what about Iva?" she asks, crossing her arms in front of her chest.

"Iva?" The name feels foreign in my mouth after months of thinking only about Jules.

"Don't play dumb, Linc-y." Iva's pet name feels like sludge in my ears.

"There's nothing to say. She's ancient history."

"Photos surfaced of you two hugging."

A memory clicks into place. "We ran into each other before the rooftop party. She ambushes people. Plus, that was when you hated me. It meant nothing."

"Right. When I hated you." She hefts her bags.

"Jules, please—"

She snorts. "I was right. You're a chucklechump."

Laughter erupts out of me like a shaken soda can. The sound is completely inappropriate given the circumstances, but I can't help it.

She opens the front door. "Oh, and from now on, I'm Miss Lindley to you. Or Juliana. Actually, you can call me anything but Jules. Julia, Juliette, even Yulia will do."

The hurt and hostility in her tone stop my laughter cold. I know exactly when I chose Jules. Fell in love with her. The name made her mine.

And now she's taking it away. Leaving.

"Jules—"

"Miss Lindley," she corrects sharply, then steps into the hallway.

The door closes with a soft click that sounds like the end of everything.

I DON'T SLEEP. Instead, I sit on my couch staring out at the city lights, my thoughts alternating between static and replaying every moment of my time with Jules. The memory montage plays like a "best of" highlight reel—her laugh, appreciation when I indulged her chocolate addiction, the way she felt in my arms at the lake house, the trust in her eyes when she told me about her father.

She is everything to me. More important than my hockey career, the high of winning a game, and the hope of hitting the Stanley Cup someday.

I screwed it all up. My jewel—because that's what Jules means to me, something rare and precious—and I let everything fall apart.

The next morning, Bīriņš shows up at my door with coffee. He launches into a recap of the game and then goes still, taking in my appearance with a wrinkled brow.

"Do I really look that bad?"

"It's the perfect sunny day for a final ride in the boat before I put it away for the season, but a soggy gray cloud hangs over you."

I let him in and collapse back onto the couch. "I messed up, Bīriņš. Really messed up."

He settles into the chair across from me, his usually animated face solemn. "What's up?"

I tell him about Jules, about the lies, about how I chose fear over honesty and lost the best thing that ever happened to me. He listens without judgment or teasing—a first occasionally nodding or making sounds of understanding.

When I finish, he's quiet for a long moment, then he lets out a laugh.

"Not exactly helpful, bro."

"No, I got it. When I got citizenship here, I learned all about your forefathers. Your great-grandfather or whatever, especially."

The guys will forever be amused that I am indeed related to Abraham Lincoln.

I correct, "He was my great-great-great-great-great-grandfather."

"You know what your boy Abe said about a house divided?" he says with his Eastern European accent.

I raise an eyebrow. Bīriņš quoting American history isn't exactly in his usual playbook.

"It cannot stand," I recite. "But what does that have to do with—?"

He shakes his head. "A heart divided cannot stand either. You divided your heart, kept part of yourself hidden from her. Sounds like she did the same."

He's right. Now Jules and I are standing in the ruins, wondering what happened. We both built walls, both chose protection over vulnerability. And now we're paying the price.

I reach for my lucky penny, the one I've flipped for every major decision I've ever made since I was twelve. But as my fingers close around the worn metal, I realize I don't need luck for this decision.

I know what I want to do. What I have to do.

Setting the penny aside, I get up and find a pen and paper. If my great-great-great-great-great-grandfather Abraham Lincoln could pour his heart onto paper to win the woman he loved, then so can I.

49

JULES

I SHOULD FEEL BETTER about walking away. That's what people do when they've been lied to, right?

They leave.

They protect themselves.

They don't look back.

Lying in Oly and Nate's spare bedroom at three in the morning, staring at the ceiling while they sleep soundly next door, I feel like I've been hollowed out with a rusty spoon.

I wish I had my favorite Care Bear to snuggle—the one with the rainbow on its belly that I've had since I was seven. Or better yet, a large, strong Clark Kent look alike who wouldn't lie about his secret identity for three months.

He was really good at snuggling.

I fit so perfectly in his arms. They were strong, snug, the kind of embrace that I could've spent a lifetime inside.

The argument we had in his foyer replays in my mind like the train that I'll soon have to ride again—looping around the city.

I could've gotten used to being a little bit spoiled, too. I mean, the private jet was a bit over the top, but he did notice the little things. My favorite round truffle chocolates in the crinkly wrapping, for instance.

But the truth is, there was a parade's worth of red flags on both sides. His mystery meetings were probably hockey-related. The gaping hole in his backstory that I should've insisted he fill. The gifts could've been because he felt guilty.

Then again, I had a few flags of my own—like the forged diploma currently burning a hole in my conscience and pointing to the fact that I didn't finish college.

I'm not ashamed of that, but the fact that I hid it isn't a point of pride.

Even when I shut him out, he'd looked unfairly handsome with a hint of stubble along his jaw. Meanwhile, I probably resembled a puffer fish with my tear-streaked face and red-rimmed eyes. I rub my hand across my face, worried that I'm going to break out with acne. Emotional turmoil destroys my skin. The salty tears clog it.

I'm a wreck.

I miss my old studio apartment in Logan Square with its creaky floors and paper-thin walls. I wonder what happened to Screechy and Grumbly—the couple next door whose arguments made me wonder if they were rehearsing for one of the soap operas my mom used to love. Their dramatic fights about whose turn it was to buy milk or whether pineapple belonged on pizza had been oddly comforting background noise to my life—oh, wait. That was a debate Linc and I had.

And was it so bad? We worked out our pizza toppings in the end.

As my tears continue, the scrape of night against the dawn sky begins outside the window, gray bleeding into pale yellow.

Unable to bear being alone, I knock softly on the wall connecting my room to Nate and Oly's.

"Oly?" I say in a voice barely above a whisper.

It's not entirely fair of me to wake them up, but they knew they were welcoming an emotionally unstable train wreck into their home. But I don't plan to be here long. I can't burden them.

I'll figure something out, I always do, even if it means going back to Vegas.

A muffled response comes through the thin drywall. I could probably hear their conversations if I wanted to, just like my old neighbors.

"Guys, could you pretend to be Screechy and Grumbly?" I ask through the wall.

There's movement, then Nate, in a sleepy voice, asks, "What do you want us to do?"

"My old neighbors used to argue about everything through the wall. It felt like home. Could you two have a fake argument?"

There is silence, then Oly, her voice overly loud and dramatic, calls, "I can't believe you did that in my dream last night!"

"It was a dream!" Nate protests, catching on immediately.

Oly whines, "But it was so awful."

"I'm not responsible for dream me!"

"Dream you was very rude! Dream you ate my leftovers!"

"Real me would never eat your leftovers!"

I smile for the first time in twelve hours.

Their footsteps pad to my door, and they slip inside like concerned parents checking on a sick child. They were there for me last night when I arrived on their doorstep looking like a rat drowned in tears and holding trash bags filled with my sparse belongings. They listened patiently while I spilled the whole sob story, brought me tissues, and Nate even did a chocolate run, returning with two grocery bags full of heartbreak supplies—ice cream, tissues, face masks, and enough chocolate to put me into a sugar coma.

"How are you holding up?" Oly asks, perched on the edge of the bed.

"I have to figure out what to do." I pull my knees to my chest. "About Linc, about work, about everything."

Nate settles in the small armchair by the window. "Well, if it were us, we'd fight about it first. A real blowout."

"Then we'd talk like mature adults," Oly adds.

"Communication is key," Nate agrees.

"Apologies to follow."

"Forgiveness next," he concludes.

"Last, but not least, rebuilding trust."

I appreciate their advice, but I'm not there yet. Not even close. The betrayal feels too fresh, too raw. The man I thought I knew doesn't exist. Linc is a hockey player with fans and a famous actress ex-girlfriend. He lives in a world I could never be part of.

Resolved, I announce, "The plan for today is to do my job ... if I still have one."

"Juliana—"

"I have to. If I lose this position, my father's creditors will come after me again." The weight of twenty-five thousand dollars in debt sits on my chest like a boulder-sized piece of fool's gold.

Only, I'm the fool.

BEFORE HEADING to the thirty-ninth floor, I make a detour to my old department. I need to see Wendy and Carmen—a glimpse at my life before Linc Andresen walked all over my heart.

"Juliana!" Wendy practically bounces out of her chair when she sees me. "We were just talking about you!"

The familiar autumn decorations and cheerfulness of the shared office feel like stepping back in time—to a life before corporate espionage and secret identities and feelings too big for my chest to contain.

"Just wanted to say hi," I manage.

Carmen leans forward conspiratorially. "Girl, you have been holding out on us. The rumors on social media are wild."

My stomach drops. "What rumors?"

"About you and that hockey player! People are saying you were at the game last night—that you're dating a guy on the Ottawa Outlaws." Wendy grins. "They're calling you the mystery woman who snagged the guy who used to date Iva Katz."

"Meow," Carmen claws the air.

"But our Juliana is the real catch here."

So they know Linc plays hockey. Did they know all along? Was I the only one in the dark? How did word get out? Do I really want to know?

"It's not a big deal," I lie.

"Not a big deal?" Wendy gapes. "It's official!"

My shoulders sag and then I tell them the story. "He kept it from me."

Understanding passes between them.

"Oh." Wendy's face falls.

"You mean to say ..." Carmen trails off.

"I didn't know Linc, the billionaire's son, my boss, and

the hockey player were all the same person." I leave out the last part about him also being the guy I love.

They're stunned silent.

The only thing to do is share a group hug before I set out for battle.

Upstairs, Linc's office door is closed. Relief and disappointment war in my chest—much like they used to when I was first assigned to be his assistant.

Nothing has changed, yet everything is different.

I'm not ready to see him, but his absence feels like another small abandonment. And if he had told me, what would I think? Would I be okay with him being a hockey player billionaire hybrid? Of course. Honesty is the problem. But I come back to my own secret. If only we'd kept both sides of our street clean.

The big question is, would I forgive him if he apologized? Would he accept my apology?

Thankfully, I don't spot Misha or Veronica, but three envelopes sit on my desk.

The first to *Jules*

The second to *Juliana*

The third to *Miss Lindley*

My fingers shake as I open the first envelope. Inside is a letter written in Linc's familiar blocky letters, the same handwriting I've seen on countless reports and sticky notes over the past three months.

My dearest Jules,

I know I have no right to use that name after what I've put you through, but I can't help myself. You will always be Jules to me—brilliant, fierce, beautiful Jules who challenged me to be better from the moment we met.

I lied to you about who I am, and there's no excuse for that. I was a coward, afraid that if you knew the truth about my career, you'd see me differently. Afraid of how it would change things.

I owe you an explanation. I've been used by people who want something from me, whether it's money, proximity to my father, or fame and my connections. Instead of admitting it hurt, I buried it inside and figured it would be safer to let you like me for me.

But you deserve better than my fears. You deserve honesty, respect, and someone who shows up completely—not hiding behind a summer internship and half-truths.

You asked me once what happens after we find the letters. I didn't have an answer then, but I do now. After this, I want to spend the rest of my life proving that you can trust me. I want to be the man who brings you coffee in the morning and listens to your theories about Renaissance art authentication. I want to spend the holidays with your Mom, Brad, and your brothers, as the man who loves their daughter and sister. I want to give you the birthday celebrations your ex never bothered with and hold your hand through every whimsy you want to take.

I choose you, Buttercup. Not because you're a summer fling or a temporary assistant, but because you're the most remarkable woman I've ever known. If you'll let me, I want to love you exactly as you are—brilliant mind, beautiful, generous heart, forged diploma, and all.

Yours completely, Linc

My vision blurs as I read the last lines again. He knows about the diploma, but he doesn't care. He wants me anyway.

Wiping away tears, I open the second envelope. It contains a check for twenty-five thousand dollars with a Post-it note attached and the following words highlighted in gel *For your father's debt. No strings attached. Think of this as a finder's fee or a donation to a good cause.*

The contents of the third envelope bear Frank Andresen's official letterhead. Inside is a formal letter recommending me for promotion to Senior Research Specialist, citing my *Exceptional investigative skills and unwavering integrity in uncovering fraudulent activity that could have severely damaged the company's reputation and bottom line.*

I stare at the three envelopes, my heart hammering against my ribs. Linc is offering me everything I've been seeking—financial freedom, career advancement, and most importantly, his love.

But even more than all of that, I want him.

The endless loop of my thoughts doubles back. Realization hits me like a freight train. I don't want to be another person in his life who takes his money or his influence. But I'm greedy for him—his attention, his voice, his laugh, and the way he makes me feel like the most interesting person in any room.

I want Linc, but mostly I want to share myself with him. To have a life together.

I knock on his office door. It's quiet. It's too early for him to be napping. I slowly open it, but the room is empty.

Walking to the window, I remember Linc standing in this same spot months ago, like a gargoyle with too much power. I think about how much I claimed to hate him. The irony isn't lost on me now.

Movement below catches my eye. At ground level, a figure in jeans and a plaid shirt holds something colorful against his chest. Not flowers—something soft and plush.

A Care Bear.

It's Linc, and he's looking up at the building like he's searching for something. Someone. For me.

He raises his hand in a small wave. Without thinking, I wave back as my anger blows away like the last of a storm.

My glowy Care Bear heart activated, my feet are already moving toward the elevator. I turn back at the last second, grabbing his executive badge from where it sits on his desk—the same badge he used to bypass the slow elevator.

Maybe we can have a second chance like Abraham and Mary.

50

LINC

STANDING in the plaza under the Meridian office building as the sun glints off the glass windows with a rainbow-bellied Care Bear in my hands makes more than a few people do a double-take.

It's probably not my most dignified moment as a high-profile hockey player—I'm more recognizable as my beard grows in. Not sure whether Jules will approve.—if she takes me back. Big *if* there. But dignity seems less important than the woman I glimpsed in the office window thirty-nine floors above me.

I've been here for nearly an hour, pacing the concrete like a lovesick teenager, getting curious looks from early professionals and the occasional photo from someone who recognizes me. Let them post it on social media. Let the whole world know that Abraham Lincoln Andresen is making a fool of himself for love.

The Care Bear—Cheer Bear, according to the tag—was an internet find of Herculean proportions. It cost me three times the asking price with overnight delivery service.

But if Jules misses her childhood comfort, then she's getting a replacement.

My phone buzzes with a text.

> Bīriņš: You still standing out there like a statue? Girls love grand gestures, but breakfast is getting cold.

I'm typing back when the building's glass doors open. Jules emerges like she's being chased, her hair flying behind her as she scans the plaza. When her eyes find mine, she stops so abruptly that a businessman nearly collides with her.

We stare at each other across twenty feet of autumn-kissed concrete. She's wearing cropped cranberry trousers, a white blouse, and a houndstooth blazer. Even from this distance, I can see she's been crying.

But she came down. She's here.

Neither of us moves for a long moment, as if we're both afraid this is a mirage that will disappear if we so much as breathe.

It's now or never.

I take the first step, then we're walking toward each other, closing the distance. When we meet, just inches apart, I can see the silver streaks in her gray eyes, the slight tremor on her lips.

"Hi," I say, because apparently my vocabulary has been reduced to monosyllables.

"Hi," she repeats.

Her gaze searches mine, looking for something—apology, forgiveness, or proof that this isn't a strange dream.

But maybe this isn't yet a moment for words. Perhaps we need something physical. Without speaking, we reach for each other at the same time. The hug is desperate and fierce, like we were drowning and the other is the life raft. Like we need air and the other is oxygen.

"I don't hate you," she whispers against my shoulder.

"I'll never stop loving you," I say.

"Never say never," she says, voice thick.

"Then I'll say forever." I draw back because I want her to see my face as I speak this truth.

She tips her head to look up at me, tears glassy in her eyes.

"I'm yours, Buttercup."

The Care Bear plush is stuffed under my arm and I hold it out to her.

"Cheer Bear," she says. "For when I need something to snuggle and you're not around."

Does that mean ...?

With shaking hands, she takes the bear and presses the soft rainbow belly against her chest. "You remembered."

"I remember everything about you." I cup her face gently, wiping away tears with my thumbs. "Every ridiculous theory about borrowing and theft, how you like your coffee, and how everything about you makes me want to be better."

Around us, fall leaves drift down like confetti, painting the plaza in shades of gold and amber. Chicago morning rush hour continues with honking horns and squeaking brakes, but we might as well be alone in the world.

"We need to talk things through." Her eyes, heavy, land on my lips. She bites hers and lifts ever so slightly onto her toes, leaning closer.

"We do."

"But first—"

She nods as if she knows what I'm going to say.

I drop my mouth to hers and kiss her, soft and tentative

to start, then deeper as she returns the kiss. She tastes like coffee and hope and the future I want to build with her.

The sweetness of it overwhelms me—not just the kiss itself, but what it represents. Everything we've been through, everything we've survived, led us here. She nuzzles my nose with hers, playful and affectionate, and I can't help but smile against her lips.

So cute. So beautiful. So perfectly Jules.

My chest expands with a sense of fulfillment I've never known, like every jagged piece of my life smoothed over. She invites me in. Smooths out my rough edges. Loves me in far greater measure than she ever hated me.

I can feel it in the press of her lips against mine.

In the hitch in her breath when I kiss the spot behind her ear.

In the way she clings to me, her pulse jangling.

This woman in my arms isn't just my present, she's my future. Every dream I didn't dare to dream, every hope I was afraid to lose, it's all right here.

When we break apart, both breathing hard, she says, "I'm sorry about everything—"

"I am too."

Somehow, that's all that needs to be said about. The sincerity, the surety, supercedes our mistakes. We're equally at fault. Equally remorseful.

"Never again?" she asks.

"You mean we'll never keep secrets again?"

"Never."

"Never," I echo.

"I love you, Linc. All of you. Hockey player, reluctant businessman, descendant of a president, intrepid underground adventurer. I love every part of you."

"I love you too, Jules. Art expert, master forger, Care

Bear enthusiast, woman who makes me want to write love letters like my great-great-great-great-great-grandfather." I grin.

She threads her fingers through mine. "So you and me?"

I nod. "Want to play hooky today?"

She raises an eyebrow. "Hockey?"

I chuckle, relieved not to hear bitterness in her voice. "No, I mean take the day off. I promise your boss won't mind." I gesture toward the building behind her.

"What were you thinking?"

"I have some people I want you to meet."

"Your teammates?"

"They're still in town because of a league meeting. Fair warning—they don't take losses well and they're probably going to want a rematch against Chicago. They might question your loyalty since you were sitting with the Breeze fans," I joke.

Shortly after, we're at a diner near the lake, and Jules holds her own against five professional hockey players who've made it their mission to embarrass me as thoroughly as possible.

"So this is the woman who had our boy moping around training camp like a rejected puppy," Stevens says, cutting his pancakes while his phone goes around the group, showing off video of his twin daughters cheering on the Outlaws to anyone who'll watch.

"I wasn't moping," I protest.

"Were too," Goudreau adds bluntly.

"He'd check his phone every five minutes to see if you texted," Stevens confirms.

Pete Johannessen, never one to miss an opportunity for comedy, leans across the table. "He asked us if we thought sending flowers to the office as an apology was too much. We told him it was too little."

Jules's eyebrows lift.

"Then he asked about chocolates." Stevens shakes his head.

"Then coffee—"

"There's never enough coffee," Bīriņš interrupts, swigging what now must amount to an entire pot.

"Or chocolate," Jules pipes.

"We told him to be honest." Goudreau grunts.

Some descendant of Honest Abe I am. I slope my head in hangdog agreement and mouth *I'm sorry*.

The corner of Jules's mouth bunches with a grin.

"He should have listened to us months ago," Goudreau barks from the end of the table.

"That would've saved everyone trouble," I agree.

Jules laughs, the sound bright and unabashed.

Heat creeps along the tips of my ears. "I may have mentioned you once or twice."

"Once or twice per conversation," Johannessen corrects.

Bīriņš adds, "We were ready to stage an intervention."

"Or lock you in a room together until you figured it out." Butcher's expression is grim.

That's news to me. Then again, these guys are like brothers and can read me like a book.

Jules catches my eyes and her smile is radiant. "I like them."

"They're mostly harmless. Emphasis on mostly." I imagine our dynamic reminds her of the triplets.

After breakfast, Jules and I say goodbye and walk along the lakefront. The sun sparkles on the water like scattered diamonds, and the leaves paint the sky overhead in amber, crimson, and gold. It's a painting my mother would love.

The little acorn of grief in my heart has transformed into a strong oak with roots and branches that reach toward the sun with loving affection for the time I got with her and the mending my father and I are doing to our relationship ... and most importantly, the future with Jules.

"What happens next for us?" she asks, her hand warm in mine.

I tighten my grip, not wanting to lose her because of these circumstances.

"You live in Ottawa during the season. I live here."

It's a question I've been dreading, but also the one we have to discuss instead of ignoring. "I've been thinking about that. You could work remotely for Meridian. Travel with me when you want to. Take online classes to finish your degree. If you want to." I stop walking and turn to face her. "I happen to know a guy who would love for you to have a real diploma, if that is important to you."

She shakes her head. "You can't do that for me."

"I'm not doing it for you. I'm doing it for me because I'm selfish and I want you in my life. Every day. Every night."

I take her hands and she studies them for a long moment, how they fit together, big and small, rough and smooth.

I kiss each of her knuckles. "Also, I have a feeling your father would have wanted you to finish what you started. My father does too. We believe in you."

Her eyes fill with tears again, but she's smiling. "It's a lot to think about."

"It is. But no more secrets between us. No more hiding who we are or what we want." I pull her closer with my arms wrapping her waist. "What do you want, Jules?"

She's quiet for a moment, looking out at the lake where a few brave souls are still sailing despite the October chill.

My inhale remains lodged in my chest, waiting for her answer.

"I want to finish my degree. I want to become the art historian I always dreamed of being. I want to travel with you and see art in museums around the world." She meets my eyes. "I want to cheer you on during hockey games and wake up next to you and argue about whether anchovies belong on pizza and meet your teammates' families and show you all my favorite spots in Las Vegas."

"Anchovies belong on pizza," I say solemnly.

She gasps in mock horror. "Take it back."

"Nope. This is what you're signing up for—a lifetime of controversial pizza opinions."

"A lifetime? I guess I can live with that." She stands on her toes and kisses me, quick and sweet. "What about you? What do you want?"

I don't even need to think about it because the answer is already waiting. "I want to play hockey for as long as my body lets me, and I want to learn the art business from the ground up because it matters to you and because I'm starting to think it might matter to me too." I brush a strand of hair from her face. "I want to take you to Ottawa and introduce you to the city. I want to spend summers at the cabin with you. I want to write you love letters and bring you coffee and never, ever let you doubt how much you mean to me."

"That sounds perfect," she whispers.

"So you're in?"

"I'm in."

I brush a kiss across her mouth. Then we walk back toward downtown as the sun climbs higher, our fingers interlaced, and our future spreading out before us like the lake itself—vast and shimmering with possibility.

. . .

THANK YOU FOR READING! Linc and Jules definitely get their happily ever after and if you want to find out what happens six months later, subscribe to my newsletter for a bonus scene. You'll also get a FREE book called *The Secret Book Boyfriend* (a grumpy sunshine hockey romcom) along with access to my exclusive reader library that includes loads of bonus scenes and epilogues, playlists, coloring pages, recipes, and more!

Please visit elliehall.com/lj

Or scan this code with your device:

Also, if you enjoyed Linc and Julc's story, please consider leaving a review, even just ★★★★★ help other readers find my books.

If you want more hockey hugs in book form, be sure to check out the Nebraska Knights Holiday Hockey romance series. These are shorter in length and focused on the team, true love, and the holidays.

There is also the Love in Hockey Town series—full-length romantic comedies, set in Cobbiton with happily ever afters.

Also, I have two books featuring the Ice Breakers, set in the small town of Maple Falls in a multi-author series.

Get your hockey romcom fix with closed-door content, open hearts, and all the feels!

ACKNOWLEDGMENTS

A sweet thank you to my readers. You are exceptional. Your emails, messages, reviews, and social media love fill my author heart to the brim. The way you champion my stories, share them with friends, and take the time to reach out means more than I could ever put into words (and I write words for a living, so that's saying something). Thank you for being so enthusiastic, loyal, and wonderfully, endlessly thoughtful.

A big, huggy thank you to the dream team who works behind the scenes to bring my books (and this massive one in particular) to life. This includes my editors, ARC readers, content team, and the assorted book elves who keep the magic going and my sanity (mostly) intact. Andrea, Jane, Jane (not a typo—I am lucky to have two Janes), Sue, Jillian, Erica, Jenn, Bernie, May, Chey, Laura, and all my book besties. I adore every single one of you!

A very happy thank you to my family for tolerating my long working hours, the "quick question, hypothetically speaking ..." moments, and my completely reasonable, totally not excessive love of hockey (and chocolate). Also, I appreciate our joint love of the movies referenced in these pages. Goonies next? I owe you all popcorn! You are my real-life HEA, and I am so grateful and blessed.

My husband gets an extra swoony thank you for being my real-life beau who FINALLY "read" one of my books.

Technically, I read it aloud and he listened. But I'm pleased to say he enjoyed it, though that may have been because we were on a very long road trip.

Above all, God, I love you. That's my story and I'm sticking to it.

ABOUT THE AUTHOR

Ellie Hall is a USA Today bestselling author. If only that meant she could wear a tiara and get away with it ;) She loves puppies, books, and the ocean. Writing sweet romance with lots of firsts and fizzy feels brings her joy. Oh, and chocolate chip cookies are her fave.

Ellie believes in dreaming big, working hard, and lazy Sunday afternoons spent with her family and dog in gratitude for God's grace.

Let's Connect

Do you love sweet, swoony romance?
Stories with happy endings?
Falling in love?

Please subscribe to my newsletter to receive updates about my latest books, exclusive extras, deals, and other fun and sparkly things, including a FREE eBook, *The Secret Book Boyfriend*!

Get your free copy here: www.elliehall.com 

ALSO BY ELLIE HALL

All books are clean and wholesome, Christian faith-friendly and without mature content but filled with swoony kisses and happily ever afters. Books are listed under series in recommended reading order.

-select titles available in audiobook, paperback, hardcover, and large print-

The Only Us Sweet Billionaire Series

Only a Date with a Billionaire

Only a Kiss with a Billionaire

Only a Night with a Billionaire

Only Forever with a Billionaire

Only Love with a Billionaire

Only Christmas with a Billionaire

Only New Year with a Billionaire

The Only Us Sweet Billionaire series box set (books 2-5) + a bonus scene!

Hawkins Family Small Town Romance Series

Second Chance in Hawk Ridge Hollow

Finding Forever in Hawk Ridge Hollow

Coming Home to Hawk Ridge Hollow

Falling in Love in Hawk Ridge Hollow

Christmas in Hawk Ridge Hollow

The Hawk Ridge Hollow Series Complete Collection Box Set (books 1-5)

The Blue Bay Beach Reads Romance Series

Summer with a Marine

Summer with a Rock Star

Summer with a Billionaire

Summer with the Cowboy

Summer with the Carpenter

Summer with the Doctor

Books 1-3 Box Set

Books 4-6 Box Set

Ritchie Ranch Clean Cowboy Romance Series

Rustling the Cowboy's Heart (Book 1)

Lassoing the Cowboy's Heart (Book 2)

Trusting the Cowboy's Heart (Book 3)

Kissing the Christmas Cowboy

Loving the Cowboy's Heart

Wrangling the Cowboy's Heart

Charming the Cowboy's Heart

Saving the Cowboy's Heart

Sweet Beginnings at Ritchie Ranch (Books 1-4 Box Set)

Sweet Promises at Ritchie Ranch (Books 5-8 Box Set)

Falling into Happily Ever After Rom Com

An Unwanted Love Story

An Unexpected Love Story

An Unlikely Love Story

An Accidental Love Story

An Impossible Love Story

An Unconventional Christmas Love Story

Forever Marriage Match Romantic Comedy Series

Dare to Love My Grumpy Boss

Dare to Love the Guy Next Door

Dare to Love My Fake Husband

Dare to Love the Guy I Hate

Dare to Love My Best Friend

Home Sweet Home Series

Mr. and Mrs. Fix It Find Love

Designing Happily Ever After

The DIY Kissing Project

The True Romance Renovation: Christmas Edition

Extreme Heart Makeover

Building What's Meant to Be

The Costa Brothers Cozy Christmas Comfort Romance Series

Tommy & Merry and the 12 Days of Christmas

Bruno & Gloria and the 5 Golden Rings

Luca & Ivy and the 4 Calling Birds

Gio & Joy and the 3 French Hens

Paulo & Noella and the 2 Turtle Doves

Nico & Hope and the Partridge in the Pear Tree

The Love List Series

The Swoon List

The Not Love List

The Crush List

The Kiss List

The Naughty or Nice List

Love, Laughs & Mystery in Coco Key

*Clean romantic comedy, family secrets, and treasure *These books should be read in the following order:*

The Romance Situation

The Romance Fiasco

The Romance Game

The Romance Gambit

The Christmas Romance Wish

The Romance Adventure (Books 1-4 Box Set)

The Nebraska Knights Holiday Hockey Romance Series

Stupid Cupid

Redd, Whit & Blue

The Kiss Class

Margo & the Faux Good Luck Beau

The Ex-Puck Bunny

Love at Teamsgiving

New Year's Ever After

A Fool for April

The Pumpkin Spice Proposal Pact

Love at First Skate (Tie-In)

Skating and Fake Dating (Tie-In)

Love in Hockey Town (Ties in to the Nebraska Knights)

His Jersey

My Wife

Her Goal

Our Marry Little Christmas

Happily Ever Hockey (Ties in to the Nebraska Knights)

Worst Best Fake Out

Call Me Up

Right Place Wrong Rink

Crazy, Stupid, Slapshot

Multi-author Hockey Romance (also tie into the Nebraska Knights Hockey world)

Love at First Skate (Love on Thin Ice series)

Skating and Fake Dating (Love in Maple Falls series)

At the Twilight's Last Gleaming (Stars, Stripes & Hockey Nights series)

On the Hunt for Love

Sweet, Small Town & Southern

The Grump & the Girl Next Door

The Bitter Heir & the Beauty

The Secret Son & the Sweetheart

The Ex-Best Friend & the Fake Fiancee

The Best Friend's Brother & the Brain

Don't You Forget About Tea (Tie-In)

SoCal Summer Kisses

Bite sized beach reads

We Go Together

The One I Want

Hopelessly Devoted

Endless Summer Nights

Shore Thing (Box Set)

Love Ablaze

Small town Firefighter Romance

Sparks & Recreation

Friends or Flames

Fire in the Heart

Romance Reignited

Twinkling Fights Aglow

Kindling Kissmass (noel novella)

Stand Alone Titles

This is a Kissing Book (enemies to lovers, grumpy sunshine)

Happily Ever Haunted (a romcom - ghost mashup)

The Secret Book Boyfriend (small town, grumpy sunshine)

Madeleine's Mistletoe Meet Cute (small town, mistaken identity)

Visit www.elliehallauthor.com or your favorite retailer for more.

If you love my books, please leave a review on your favorite retailer's website! Thank you! Ellie

P.S. I have a clean fantasy and paranormal romance pen name: E. Hall that you might enjoy (best read in listed order):

The Court of Crown and Compass Series

Fae of Light and Shadow (prequel)

Fae of the North (book 1)

Fae of the West (book 2)

Fae of the South (book 3)

Fae of the East (book 4)

RIP Magic Academy Reform School Series

Law & Disorder (book 1)

Crime & Curses (book 2)

Mayhem & Magic (book 3)

Shifter Diaries

Life Fated (book 1)

Lies Tamed (book 2)

Loss Hunted (book 3)

Love United (book 4)

❤

www.ingramcontent.com/pod-product-compliance
Lightning Source LLC
La Vergne TN
LVHW100502110826
845146LV00002B/487

* 9 7 9 8 9 9 5 5 9 1 6 0 3 *